ORIGINAL MIX

Sam Carlyle

ISBN: 9781520173702
Imprint: Independently published

1

JOSIE

1984

In the bitter October wind and dwindling light Camden did not look at its best. The pavement was sprinkled with old fag ends and noodle boxes, and a greasy pong of hot oil blew over from the market, where students and tourists milled around, buying pizza, cannabis badges, Peruvian thick-knits, and studded leather. Music floated over to my crowded bus stop – the bouncing tune and gritty lyrics of an Original Mix ska classic. A complicated rush of feelings coursed through me, with a familiar combination of joy and pain.

At last! A red double-decker loomed, condensation dripping down misty windows, passengers staring out, faces as blank as olives. Not mine. I tugged at my lapels, trying to block out the biting chill, as everyone wedged in, the driver hollering, 'Move right down there!' Engine straining, the vehicle lurched off, leaving me hugging my coat, alone and exposed.

A tall, stooped figure in a long coat of battered leather, stumbled down the road, scanning left and right for someone to pester. One of Camden's street drunks. He tripped on some litter and fumblingly detangled a determined plastic bag which hugged at his leg. I tensed, preparing to tell him I'd got no change. If he was insistent, even hauling my shopping, I could probably still out-run a bloke in the grip of five cans of Special Brew. The man staggered closer and I made out a tell-tale neck – red and coarse as corned beef – and the drinkers' uniform of loose, dirt-coloured trousers. His greasy leather coat flapped open, revealing a thin white shirt, and bony, protruding collarbone. In fact, the only thing that marked him out from all the usual drinkers and smack-heads in Camden was his lofty height – and the fact he bellowed 'Josie!' as he lurched in my direction.

He plonked a heavy hand on my shoulder to steady himself. 'Fuckin' great to see ya!' he breathed with relief, as if he'd been searching for me. Slowly, and with great care, he raised his head from the floor on which he was concentrating so hard to stay vertical, and I looked into the once beautiful green-blue eyes of Tom Shepperton.

And only then did I want to cry.

'Wherrar'yer goin'?' he asked.

Tom! It really was *Tom!*

I stared, transfixed with disbelief, chest banging. Over his shoulder, the glowing yellow numbers of my bus approached. He had a cut over one eye and a tooth missing. Oh Christ! 'Hackney.' I dipped from under his hand and quickly stepped onto the bus. Showing the driver my pass, I glanced back, guts filled with guilt. 'Sorry, gotta go.'

Tom wobbled like a skittle and, although his pupils were tiny dots, I detected a desperation – like a part of him was reaching out.

Lurching forwards he slurred, 'May'swell come along.' He stumbled up the step after me, and I watched in dismay as Tom flapped something at the driver, staggered down the aisle and fell in beside me. In the warmth of the interior, a sour smell stung my nostrils, like a mixture of fermenting wine and street garbage. The handful of other passengers stared, waiting for me to barge past and change seats. But I was frozen.

'You live in eas' London then?' he slurred, as the vehicle swung out. Unable to control his body, he was thrown heavily across my lap. 'Sorry, sorry,' he mumbled, as he grappled to sit up.

'Yes, no. Sort of.' I couldn't tell him about my life, especially now.

His presence was unbelievable. Tom was right next to me! Though not the Tom I knew.

'Do you actually want this bus? Where are you based?'

'Here and there.'

Oh god, he had nowhere to stay. I should offer….but no, there was just no way.

'What will you do in Hackney?'

4

'Dunno, check it out…'

I pictured him stumbling around in Marle Street, not knowing which pubs to avoid, or bashing into one of the knife-faced men that hung in shop doorways.

'Isssooo nice to see yer, Josie.' Tom's mouth twitched as he smiled. 'Been a bit down on me luck.' His head rolled around, as if it wasn't part of him. For a moment his chin fell forward onto his chest and he blacked out.

'Shit!' he said, coming round with a jolt. 'Can I nick a fag?'

I dug into my handbag for the old tobacco I carried from habit, and watched his shaking hands fumble with the packet.

'Shall I roll it?' I held out my palm.

'Thanks.' For a second his hand rested on mine, like a lump of cold meat. I offered the finished cigarette, and after several clumsy stabs, he stowed it behind his ear, under a clump of greasy hair.

'Had to sell my guitar,' he said. 'Don't 'spose you could lend me a few quid?'

'Of course!' I unzipped my purse, then remembered spending most of my cash in the toy shop. 'Oh shit! There's only change. You can have it all though.'

'Cheers.'

I emptied a small collection of silver and brass coins into a large bony palm, and he curled his fingers round it, smiling, as though it was precious gems.

The bus started the long descent to where I'd alight. The heartbreak and guilt were so overwhelming I was hardly able to breathe. Tom was there, right beside me needing help, real help. But I couldn't take him home like this. I just couldn't.

I wondered how long I would bear the thumping in my chest.

'I'm getting off soon,' I said, terrified that he'd follow me.

'Where ya live?'

'Not far from here.'

All my instincts screamed that I should bathe and feed him, straighten him out – so he could walk with confidence and vigour again. His head rolled forward once more, and his eyes closed. 'Josie, Josie,' he mumbled.

I thought of my son in his rabbit pyjamas, being read bedtime stories by his Uncle Simon. He'd be waiting for me to whisper, 'Sleep tight, and mind the bedbugs don't BITE!' and nip him with gentle pinches until he squealed with laughter, before tucking him in, with a kiss on his nut brown hair.

It was impossible to bring this huge, smelly, incoherent man to our home.

I slipped the tobacco into Tom's pocket, grabbed my bags and pushed past as gently as I could, pinging the bell on the handrail as I went.

'Wha'? Yer goin'?' He'd regained consciousness for a moment. We were the only passengers left on the bus.

'This is my stop,' I said as the hydraulic brakes hissed.

'Oh. Alright then – see yer.' He sounded so utterly lost.

'Bye Tom.'

I stepped into the freezing cold wind.

'It wass...' he said.

'Yeah, it was,' I replied.

The bus moved off and his head slumped onto the rail in front. And my heart broke all over again, as the doors shut with a shush – like a soft cymbal.

♫

2

TOM

July 1980

'Here we go!' Eddy waved the illicit key at a door, where a huge red sign warned, '*No Entry*'. Then he crunched it round in the lock.

We stepped out onto the roof of Suicide Tower, where a blustering wind started to tug at my hair and suck my jacket.

'Told you – bird's eye view!'

I walked towards the perimeter, and in front was a pattern of grey side roads, small red-tiled roofs, and treetops like broccoli, sprawling up Gosling Street. A few feet from the edge, I halted. One careless stumble and I'd be plummeting right over. Not the idea at all.

'Hey, look at the tiny people going into town!' I shouted, pointing at the ant figures moving along the strips of pavement leading to the city centre.

Eddy came alongside, grinning. 'And diddy cars racing round – over there!' He traced the arc of giant tarmac rollercoaster which was Coventry's ring road. A little van nudging down a feeder road suddenly accelerated like crazy into the stream of traffic, narrowly missing the car exiting across its path. There was an indignant torrent of car horns. 'Fuckin' hell, that was a close one!' I shook my head. Long gone were the days when an odd vehicle might tootle round, avoiding the centre. Time had transformed it into hell's own causeway. You had to be insane or desperate to get away fast. Or both.

Over to the other side, the grey towers of the Polytechnic appeared as toy-sized as they would have done on an architects' model, when concrete was modern and exciting. Now, they were just great, ugly blocks, hunkering over the revamped rubble of the old cathedral, where a couple of tiny blue-anoraked visitors hesitated, possibly wondering what historical wonder to see next. There wasn't much left. Most of new Coventry was thrown up in post-Blitz haste – rows of terraced houses hurriedly spawned, a hard-slabbed shopping centre, laid with the aesthetic allure of a car park, plus the addition of some red brick civic buildings. For beauty, they'd have to go to elsewhere. Our city specialised in utilitarian.

I walked around the square of the big roof, taking the opposite direction to Eddy, peering down to try and see it all with fresh eyes. I spotted Lady Godiva, cold, naked and beatific on her stone horse. And the charmless open air precinct, with its one record shop, where you had to order anything worth listening to. Outside the ring road, past swathes of cramped residential streets, industrial wastelands took over – barren areas of cement chimneys, iron roofs, factories and warehouses, many now derelict.

Our paths met behind the block where the door opened out. 'What d'ya think? Inspired?'

'Lots of people living identical lives, in miniscule boxes!' Eddy gave a snort of derisive laughter.

'There was a hit about that in the sixties,' I said. 'We need another take on it.'

'Let's skin up then.' Eddy gestured at a recess, housing a metal tools hopper. He tried the lid, and shrugged. 'Locked.'

We squatted in the area most sheltered, with our backs to the hopper as I manufactured a generous-sized joint. Then we took turns to crank the lighter, battling with a determined gust which snatched at the flame. Finally the end flared and we were in business.

'Remember doing the Pink Panther on Anarchy Bridge?' Eddy said, after a long draw.

'Course,' I replied. 'The image of you clattering around beside me with that big bucket of paint, is forever etched – your legs were shaking like an old man's.'

'Fuckin' hell, those sheds roofs were steep! Thought I was gonna nosedive to the railway line, and get crisped.' Eddy chuckled and held out the spliff. 'That's not bad stuff,' he added.

'It was harder for me, crawling along with paint pads strapped to my hands and knees,' I said.

Eddy cackled, remembering. 'Fuck! Your face, when you started sliding down and grabbed onto that bit of old gutter – then it came right off, in your hand...' He was laughing like a hyena now, spluttering. 'And you yelling, 'Not too much paint on my paws yer twat! I'm leaving foot prints, not smearing pink shite!''

I started to howl then too, giddy with the idiocy of it all, as the dope kicked in, and I rolled on my side, my ribs vibrating against the asphalt, unable to stop. Finally my laughter was exhumed and I was empty. I sat up and began to roll another spliff.

'Christ, Ed. We got up at 4am, risked our lives to make those ridiculous pink paw prints – and never told a soul. Why did we do it?'

Eddy shrugged. 'Still there though – evidence that the Panther himself walked those roofs. No-one's ever tried to remove it.'

As he took the spliff from me, I pulled a face. ''Cos they can't find anyone stupid enough to get up there.'

'It was all your idea.' Eddy remembered. 'To combat the fact that bridge is covered in shit graffiti and it's the city's spot for muggings. Create something to make people smile, you said.' He gave a long sigh. 'Let's face it, the whole of Coventry's a fuckin' dump.' He passed me back the joint, like we were sealing the fact with smoke.

I shut my eyes and inhaled deeply. 'Ah yes, but it's *our* fuckin' dump,' I said with feeling.

After a few silent minutes, I waved a hand at the vista. 'To be fair, in miniature, it doesn't look so bad.'

'Only 'cos the eternal greyness is broken up by tree tops.' Eddy held out thumb and forefinger to grasp the last of the now-diminished joint. 'But when you're down there...'

'With the little people...' I snickered, as the weed kicked in again.

'...*Being* the little people,' Eddy corrected. 'It's all friggin' concrete and very little else.'

I looked out across the roofs to where my parents lived. They'd been children of the Second World War – after the first one, the 'war to end all wars', had failed to deliver. With the city's aircraft factories targeted, they'd survived continuous air raids and buzz bombs. Years of terror – as everyone in Coventry lost homes, relatives, places of work. And when it ended, they were happy to put it all behind them for lives of safety – steady jobs, veg on the allotment, Sunday roasts and Z-Cars on the telly. But things had changed. Our generation didn't want safety. We wanted jobs alright, but also something else.

'I need to get out soon, Eddy. I've spent all my life here and it's getting worse. I need to *be* something. '

He nodded. Neither of us were strangers to broken dreams and the dole queue. I raised my arms and yelled into the wind, 'Come on music gods – give us a break and get us outta here!'

'You know, not one famous band ever came from Cov,' Eddy said, in his cynical drawl.

'That's why we're going to be the first!' I leapt to my feet and took a few steps forwards. 'See that?' I poked a digit towards the Polytechnic's Student Union building. 'Come Saturday, that's going to host the first of our many mega-gigs! We're gonna put Coventry on the map for something other than a bint in the buff and the friggin' car industry!'

Eddy gave a twisted laugh. 'Alright then, let's write a song about the joys of livin' in Suicide Tower, and the fun of peein' out of a 16th floor window!'

'What about the dog turd someone left in the lift?'

'And the nights in town, getting' your head kicked in.'

'Don't forget the Paki-bashers and the post-match punch-ups,' I said. 'Oh, we've gotta tell the world about Coventry. It's so *very* crap.'

We locked the roof and walked down the many flights to Eddy's flat. The stairwell smelled of cold stone and stale piss.

'That old tramp still sleeping out here?' I asked, as we reached his landing and pushed open the door to the lobby.

Eddy shrugged. 'Not seen him since I offered half a bag of pretty cold chips.'

'What he say?'

'Asked if there was vinegar on 'em.'

'Jeez! Can't imagine becoming that squalid,' I said.

Eddy's place was fairly neat and tasteful for a bloke, with a red, black and silver theme, despite being a City fan. On shelves, a couple of school boxing trophies stood alongside his albums, but otherwise it was all fairly impersonal. He grabbed a bottle of whiskey from the cabinet and fetched two glasses, while I picked up my guitar to noodle round a few chords. 'I've got an idea for a new rhythm,' I said. 'You thought of a title?'

Eddy collapsed onto a beanbag and nodded. 'Wasteland.' He scrunched down into the beans, arranged the whiskey at one side and leafed through his notepad.

'Bleak but jaunty.'

'Oh yeah. We're goin' with the warts an' all approach, ain't we?' He attempted to scrawl loops with a biro, threw it down with an exasperated tut and jumped up to get another.

'Why the fuck not? We're bringing original, total honesty.' I waited for him to collapse back into his seat.

'Agreed then. We'll tell it like it is,' Eddy said. 'Talking of which – you know that turd in the lift?'

I nodded.

'Don't think it came from a dog.'

♪

The downstairs bar at the Student Union was thick with body odour, beer fug and smoke, and heaving with an excited crowd – acne-faced lads in acrylic pullovers, cute young girls in oversized rugby shirts, and an assorted bunch of darkly scowling Goths and multi coloured punks from the art block. The bar was open early, so by the time we walked onstage, the airspace was filled with drunken and competitive yelling. But we had the advantage of microphones.

'Alright! We're Original Mix.' Eddy sounded like a petulant teacher, instilling order on a school trip. 'These are our songs.' Then, in a deadpan voice, 'You can dance if you want to.'

I looked up to Devon, poised over the drums, and we both chuckled. With his back to the band, Eddy clicked his fingers – one-two-three… On the four, I shot an affirmative nod to Charlie on bass, aware of Len in readiness beside me, and we chugged out our first chords.

A clot of pissed-up lads lurched around at the front, spilling pints and stomping on each others' feet. By the third song, the girls round the side were dancing too. Len's guitar twanged in, high and wiry on the chorus, as we sang at same mic. We each took a solo for good measure. The kids below were having fun, wrapped up in the vibe. By the end of the set everyone was bouncing around and overheated, in the low ceilinged bar. We finished with our last number – a jangly, fast beat which took everyone to fever point, then we crashed out our last chord.

'Thank you. We've been Original Mix, and you've been drunk and sweaty,' said Eddy. Then we left the stage.

In the corridor, Charlie pulled at his braces and shouted, 'We doin' an encore?' over the sound of hollering and foot stomping from the bar.

'Let's try Wasteland?' I said to Eddy.

'Alright. Then I want a pint.'

Back on stage, Eddy picked the mic out of the stand and said, 'Yeah, yeah, settle down. We're goin' to sing you a new song, about a city. You might recognise this place.'

Devon gave a couple of stabs into the two-four rhythm, and I watched the kids' faces as Eddy sang about Coventry. Many of them were too out of it to care, but others smiled in recognition and joined in with the chorus on the second time. The punks round the outside, dropped their studied disinterest and I saw a bit of nodding. When Len came in with his vocals, there were a few cries of 'Yeah!' The funky art school girls were listening in admiration too – and after the bridge, when we upped the beat to double time, they began dancing energetically. A brunette smiled at me with direct open eyed invitation, and I grinned back. We finished to a more thoughtful blast of applause and a lot of whistles.

At the bar, the Student Union guy was effusive. 'Fantastic! You can play the main venue next time, 'cos we had to turn people away. Love the new song!'

'Thanks,' I said, though it wasn't quite right. The lyrics and the melody were solid, but something was missing. Before I could find Devon to discuss it, Vinnie slid over and grabbed my elbow.

'Nice one Shepperton. 'Cept your solo was rank.'

'Fuck off.'

'What you need is a steaming soloist.'

'Oh yeah? Who would that be then?'

'Go on – let me try out.'

'We've got two guitars, thanks. We don't need any more.'

Vinnie pouted in disgust, but he hung round like a shadow, until I'd finished my pint. 'You buyin' then?'

'Oh for Christ's sake! What d'ya want?'

'Thanks mate. Pint and a whiskey chaser.'

'Don't push it.'

Eventually he slewed off to go ligging round some Gothy females, and I found the others. As I shared my misgivings about Wasteland, Devon laughed. 'Give yourself a break, man. We did a good gig and everyone's happy. What else you want?'

'What I want –' I took a slurp of my lager. '– is a sound so unique, it takes us right to the top.'

Charlie heard this and raised his glass. 'Oi, I'll drink to that!'

Devon nodded and raised his too. 'Aaright, man. Let's head up there.'

I looked to Eddy and Len. 'Right then – no looking back, it's straight for the top!'

♫

3

TOM

'Oi, Shepperton, wait up!'

I was striding past the art block, where a gaggle of students laughed in the sunshine, when Vinnie's dulcet tones bruised through the air. I turned to watch him jog up, in his usual checked shirt and black leather, fag on and puffing out smoke – the Midlands' own Gene Vincent, minus the charm. He slapped me on the back.

'Long time, Shep mate. Fancy a pint?' He waved his cigarette at The Elm, as if he'd just conjured up the whole pub. 'Was thinking of getting one myself.'

I hesitated. Trust Vinnie. No bloody contact for weeks – since the Union gig, in fact – and now he'd turned up when I least wanted him round. 'Yeah well, I'm heading in there to see Len and Eddy, but... '

'Great! Ages since I saw Len.'

'Thing is Vin, we're having a band meeting.'

But he was already off, calling over his shoulder, 'Come on, yer lofty git! Last one at the bar's buyin'.'

We spotted Eddy and Len at a table, tucked away at the back. Eddy's stool was tipped back against the wall, as he blew out a plume of thoughtful smoke, while Len prodded a beer mat with a forefinger. Discussions were clearly underway.

Soon Vinnie was cherishing a pint like a long lost love, while the rest of us chewed over what sort of new direction we wanted for the band.

I outlined my latest idea, and Len screwed up his face, scratching his short Afro hair in disbelief. 'Ska music? You sure Tom?'

'Devon likes the idea. He thought you'd be well up for playing a Jamaican sound too.'

'Char man! That's old men's music. Me father and mother danced to ska.'

'Thought your mum died when you was a nipper?' Vinnie looked up. 'Weren't you sent 'ere, cos yer old man was on the same gig as mine.'

'What? Sprayin' cars on the assembly line?' said Eddy.

'No, yer twat, workin' nights.'

Len gave a snort of harsh laughter. 'Yeah. Thought he was doin' me a favour. Imagined school in Britain would be genteel or somethin'.'

'Jeesus!' Vinnie and I fell silent, recalling the gritty, teeth on tarmac, bare knuckle brawls of King George Secondary, where the Green Woods kids were more than happy to add a racist element to their imagined grievances.

'You remember your folks dancing though?' I said.

'Nah. But me dad's radio was never turned off, and' sometimes, when a ska song came on he'd say, 'Son, you shoulda seen your mother kick up her heels to this one.'' Len stared for a moment into his empty pint glass, then pushed it roughly at Vinnie. 'Your turn next, rude boy.'

Vinnie frowned. 'Nah mate. Pretty sure it's yours.'

We were interrupted by a roar of laughter. At the front of the lounge, a clot of students sat round, discussing their finals shows in loud voices. One girl stood out because of her spiky blond hair, and the fact she was protesting, laughing and waving her arms around. Her style was a bit wacky for my taste – though she had big, bright eyes and a great smile. She was in some heated debate with a guy from Liverpool, who lounged back with a superior smirk.

'I fuckin' hate that bloke,' muttered Vinnie. 'Thinks he's God's gift to the birds.' This was rich coming from him, but he was too engrossed to see the rest of us swap incredulous looks. 'Look at him,' Vinnie continued, '– in his paint-spattered overalls. Fuckin' hell, he's even got a soddin' paintbrush over his ear!'

'What're they arguing about?' said Len.

'The future of art, or some bollocks like that,' said Eddy, and we both grinned. While I'd stared into trays of darkroom chemicals at Coventry Poly, Eddy had been painting at Wolverhampton, so we were both versed in the occupation of talking arty bollocks.

'Jeesus!' Vinnie's general stance was that he hated students – though half his mates had completed some sort of art degree. The rest were in the building trade like him. And some of us – through dire necessity – had stuck our fingers in both pies. But none of that bothered Vinnie. Inconsistency was part of his rough portfolio of charms.

There was a scrape of furniture, and the punky-looking blond bounced up, banging the table with her fist. The scouse guy said, 'Don't worry about it larr – in ten years you'll be walking the high street with a buggy and a trail of snotty kids.' The others all hooted, as if he'd said she'd be leader of the National Front.

'Fuckin' hell, he's fer it now,' said Vinnie with delight. The girl drew herself up, pale with fury, and carpet-bombed him with words, without, it seemed, needing to breathe. He was a lazy, self-obsessed, working class snob, incapable of having a reasoned argument with a woman, she yelled – by which point the whole pub had turned to enjoy the show – he only used chauvinistic stereotypes to reduce women's productivity to breeding and fucking, because he was threatened by the creativity of thinking feminists and the idea that the world might just manage without male artists, their phallocentric misogyny and their tired, lame images of women as mere sperm receptacles who reflected the glory of the male ego and perpetuated the myth of man as mighty stud. And so it went on – for several minutes. When she sat down there was a round of applause from the rest of the pub. She stood again slightly and bowed.

Vinnie shook his head, 'Ha! She's a fuckin' wildcat that Josie.'

'Go tell her,' I said. 'I'd like to watch.'

Before we turned back to our conversation, I stole a look at her face. A flush of colour was returning but she actually did look quite upset. I'd always avoided all that aggro, the photography department being less explosive than the fine art crowd. But there was something exciting about that level of passion and conviction.

That weekend, I went to the Cat and Bugle. Trevor was trying to bag a regular DJ slot, and I'd promised to mosey along. He played some good stuff – northern soul, old R&B, bit of Motown and reggae of course, and a few current tracks, though there wasn't much in the charts worth listening to. I spotted the same girl – Josie – dancing with her dark-haired friend. She wore tight black trousers, and a top with a big bow across the back – like she was someone's birthday present – and for a moment I couldn't help wondering what it'd be like to unwrap that gift. I had a couple of beers, waved hi to Trevor, and was about to leave, when he put on Nina Simone's, 'My Baby Just Cares for Me'. Most people abandoned the dance floor – probably because of that awkward swing rhythm – like ol' Nina's pushing a bike with a kink in the wheel. But Josie was still dancing in time, making slow figures of eight with her hips, eyes were closed, arms in the air. Her hands twisted round each other, like a flame flickering.

After that, she seemed to pop up everywhere. And each time I saw her, laughing with a shopkeeper, or stomping through town with her mates in some crazy outfit, my spirits were lifted and I found myself smiling. It wasn't like I fancied her or anything – she had a great figure, but she was platinum and outrageous. Not my type at all.

A few months later, I popped into the bar side of The Elm again, looking for Vinnie. Against my better judgement, I'd finally let him join the band. I spotted him in the lounge, standing talking to some students, wearing his rakish lad expression, and my chest tightened in surprise. Sitting opposite that dark-haired girl, was Josie. She wore a tight red jumper – way too snug to ignore the shape of her breasts – and on her other side a Swedish-looking bloke had his arm around her. For some reason I felt a kind of dismay. I'd never seen her with a boyfriend.

The blond guy said something and gave a pouty look. Josie laughed and kissed his cheek. 'Simon, you're such a big baby. Don't be so bloody daft.' She punched his arm.

Ha! I emitted a soft snort of laughter to myself – nowadays gay blokes seemed to get all the best girls. Then Vinnie bent down and squeezed her shoulder. She smiled warmly, face turned up to him. Christ almighty. Surely she wouldn't fall for that? Vinnie's moves were as bloody obvious as they were legend. Finally he turned and spotted me, then sauntered round to the bar side with his drink. I met him by the door.

'What're you doin' with that lot?' I asked.

'Great birds, Josie an' her mate Franki. Just got me a pint.' Access to the student grant was his main rationale for hanging out in The Elm. He took a long contented slug.

My voice came out surprisingly cold and angry. 'Don't forget, we're rehearsing in half an hour,' I said. 'Wanna lift?'

'Nah, I'll hang on here, get the bus up.' He craned his neck, checking over the bar to see Josie's table. 'You not havin' a drink?'

'No and don't be late.' I turned and stalked out. At the van, I dropped the keys twice, swore, slid in and slammed the door. Fucking Vinnie! Why had I even let him join the band?

I drove off, and as my burst of fury subsided, I was baffled. There'd been plenty of time for a swift half, so my irritation with Vinnie made no sense. It was only as I pulled in to the kerb, I realised what had really bugged me. It was that girl Josie. I just couldn't bear watching him put a hand on her again.

4

JOSIE

Bloody hell, it can't be! I was strolling in the Saturday shoppers, wondering how to create a weekend's fun with only two pound notes and some change, when I saw a tall, wide shouldered man in the throng. Brown leather jacket, black cap and flash of high cheekbones – I was almost sure it was *him*. At least, I thought so. The idea was as thrilling, as if I'd just spotted a budgie in my dad's allotment. So, as he disappeared into the supermarket, I skirted the dawdlers to follow.

At the store's entrance, warm air oozed out, tickling my nose. I stood on tip toes. He was ahead, just leaving the cigarette stand, where a mumsy-looking assistant beamed at something he'd said. A sighting of that coppery brown hair would seal it, but hidden by his cap and turned up collar, I couldn't tell. If he'd just turn round! I elbowed through the shoppers.

This was Coventry's new *super*market, a refrigerated, highly lit warehouse. At the other end of town there was a fresh produce market, where you'd find everything much cheaper given time. And god knows, the one thing most of us had was time. But the sense of privilege here was seductive.

Passing the cigarette kiosk, *bloody hell - sixty pence for a pack of fags!* I turned right at the bakery, inhaling sweet, yeasty aromas. No time to linger. The tall guy was now at the end of *'Pasta and Rice'*, placing a packet into his basket. I caught a tantalising flash of chin and neck as he looked down. Then he took a couple of long strides, face obscured by a rack of herbs, and vanished down the next aisle. I hung back. He didn't know me, of course. But with my bleached hair and wearing last night's party clothes, I was now drawing disapproving glances from several shoppers.

When I rounded the corner, he was a few feet away, back to me. I dropped to my haunches and grabbed a couple of tins, pretending to be fascinated by soup. When I glanced up he was gone.

Damn! I still hadn't seen his face. I slammed one of the tins back and, clutching the other like a hand grenade, I stalked along the wall of dairy fridges – screwing my eyes down each aisle. But by the time I got to booze at the far end, I'd lost him. He must have doubled back, and gone.

I was now at the quieter part of the shop, populated by one shabby old bloke, weighing a four-pint tin of beer in both his hands, as if deciding whether he could lug it across town by himself. I felt in my pocket, and the pound notes rustled in tight conspiracy. Ah well, since I was here…

By the time I joined the end of a long checkout line, ten minutes had passed. I shuffled along, staring out of the plate glass window, where a kite-shaped patch of clear sky peeped from between two tall buildings. Brain ticking over, I started to select imaginary paints to mix that colour of blue – it would need a touch of cadmium red, the tiniest amount on the tip of a brush. A light tap on my shoulder brought me back to earth. I looked around to find a tall guy with high cheekbones and amazing eyes. He was dressed in black jeans and a tan leather jacket. A fringe of coppery brown hair flopped down from under the peak of his cap.

'Hi. It's Josie, isn't it?'

'Yes.' I croaked, in surprise.

He smiled warmly. 'I've seen you round.' He laid a palm on his chest. 'Tom Shepperton,' he said.

'I know,' I said, then added a shrug. 'Small city.'

I knew exactly where I'd first seen him. Before Christmas, Franki had cadged an invite to a party at a huge house in Brownshill. We'd hung round the edges, sipping wine and feeling like imposters, when I'd noticed him on the other side of the room, leaning with one foot back up against a doorframe, listening to a stylish woman with sharp black hair and scarlet lipstick. There was something so sensuous about the curve of his neck as he bent down to hear her, that I couldn't peel my eyes away.

'Ah, the beautiful Tom Shepperton. He's a musician.' Franki had followed my gaze.

'Of course he is.' I rolled my eyes. Coventry was chock full with ex-students-now-aspiring-musos, whose meagre earnings were immediately re-invested in alcohol.

'They say he's actually very talented,' Franki said. 'Word is, he's on the way up and out.'

'Best of luck getting out of Coventry!' I said, and we both chuckled.

As I watched, Tom Shepperton ran a hand through his hair. His brow creased, as if slightly pained about whatever the chic woman was saying.

'He's gorgeous,' I said.

Franki pulled a face. 'You wouldn't want to get involved there, Jose. Heard he's a bit of a shag monster.'

I sighed. 'The beautiful ones always are.'

Finally, he put a hand on the woman's shoulder to give it a squeeze, then wandered off. I looked round the party. Everyone was older than us, better dressed, less awkward. I'd surely never felt more out of place.

'What're you doing in here?' I waved a hand at the supermarket. It wasn't as if I was chatting him up. We were just fellow shoppers.

He shrugged. 'Getting some stuff to cook later.' There were fish, vegetables, and rice in his basket. 'How about you?' His voice was light and friendly.

We both looked at the rubber belt and I blushed. There was no hiding two bottles of cheap red wine and family-sized tin of tomato soup, that were now in slow procession along the conveyor.

'I'm trying the Red Diet.'

'Nice.' He grinned. His eyes were a complicated bluey-green. Difficult colour to mix. I thought about what Franki had said. He needn't think that I'd fall at his feet.

We moved forward and I tried to think of something else to say, handing my change to the checkout girl. She was issuing Tom with an air hostess smile, ignoring me entirely. But when she looked in her hand, she frowned. 'Yer ten pence short.'

'Oh shit!' Now I'd have the added humiliation of putting something back. I rummaged inside my jacket pockets. 'Hang on. I've probably got more change somewhere – it could be in the lining.' *Oh for fuck's sake!* I pulled out a fistful of tissues and old library tickets.

'Here you go.' Tom dropped a coin into her palm.

'Hey, thanks,' I said, mortified. 'It was the soup that tipped it over.' I emitted a dry laugh to disguise my embarrassment, and the checkout girl shot me a peevish glare.

Stepping away to let him pay for his stuff, I willed my flushed face to calm down. Outside, we stood on the pavement for a moment. I stared at the white chest of his T-shirt and swallowed.

'Are you playing tonight?' I sounded about ten.

He shook his head and smiled. 'Rare Friday night in. What're you up to?'

'Not much.' I let my eyes follow a passing bus. 'Telly and a few drinks with Franki.'

'She's the dark haired girl from London?'

'That's right…' How the hell did he know that?

'Which way're you going?' he said.

'Up through town,' I said, trying to keep the hope out of my voice.

'Oh.' Some thought flickered across his face. 'I'm headed the opposite way.' But he didn't move.

I had an overwhelming urge to keep him there talking, so I studied the gum-splattered paving slabs for inspiration. But the sensation of awe had poked a finger into my brain and effected a lobotomy.

'Well…see you round I guess.' He gave a little lop-sided grin. 'Good luck with that special diet.'

He touched my upper arm lightly, and goose bumps zinged over the surface of my whole body. Then he lifted his hand in a quick wave and strode off.

♪

At home, Franki was on all fours on the floor, cutting fabric. I clattered in and she sat back on her heels. 'Wassup? You look like a relative just died.' She clapped a hand over her mouth. 'Oh gawd, sorry Jose, that was a bit tactless.'

I shook my head. 'Forget it. I'm the bigger pillock, by a long mile.' I sunk onto the sofa and sighed. 'A little diamond of opportunity dropped right in front of me, and I didn't know how to pick it up.'

'Oh right.' Franki stood up. 'I'll get some glasses.'

In our dingy back room, warm light from the old standard lamp transformed our wine into bowls of ruby light. I hugged my knees up on the sofa, listening to Franki, a veteran of urban survival. Curled up in her silk robe on the sagging armchair, with her ruffled black hair, red lips, and coal-dark eyes, she dispensed wisdom in a soft Essex drawl, like some seaside fortune teller.

'Can't blame you for getting steamed up over Tom Shepperton,' she said thoughtfully. 'Lovely guy, amazing musician – and 'course dead sexy too.' She gave a raw, throaty laugh, and I covered my face with my hands in despair.

'Franki, he's so cool and I was a *complete arse!*'

She chuckled and patted my knee. 'Hey, it's not like it matters Jose. The lookers are always shits to women. He's probably bad news. An' I mean, it's not like you'll ever see him again, is it?'

She was right of course. So we drank our wine and invented inappropriate lines to say to famous people we'd catch shopping. And, as usual, my feeling of failure began to slip away with our laughter.

5

TOM

'Fuckin' hell Eddy, you're so bloody negative!'

Vinnie's voice was the first thing I heard as I climbed the creaky stairs to the recording studio, and felt the now-familiar tightening in my chest. The room was cluttered with drums, mic stands and electrical gear. Cables trailed across the floor and the ambient aroma was a mixture of ashtrays, rubber and burnt dust. For several weeks a Roland keyboard had leant against the wall, Len's taped note pointing out, *'Bottom G don't work'*. In fact nothing had improved since we'd been working on our new set – especially our band dynamics. And now Eddy was sitting on a bass amp, one foot resting on his other knee, pinching at the sharp crease in his suit trousers and wearing a sour expression, while Vinnie paced about on the burn-marked carpet. Between his flat-top haircut and the collar of his checked shirt, his face looked like red thunder.

'I'm just saying, we need better songs for an EP,' said Eddy. ''Tinseltown' is okay for the A side and 'Stompin' Skank' works for the B – but we need at least two extras, and good ones!'

He held out his palms to elicit my support, but I wasn't in the mood to start the day refereeing. I tried for a neutral tone. 'Course. We want to give the best value to anyone shelling out for our record.'

'So we need *three or four more songs*.' Eddy's voice changed to a whine.

'Well, I think 'A Lesson in Manners' would work.' Vinnie stuck his chin out to defend his song. His aimed a glare at me, then Eddy.

Eddy shook his head. 'Nah, the sound's all wrong – too wishy washy.'

I should have sorted out exactly what we were recording before now but, in truth, I was playing it pretty much by ear. Luckily, nobody in the band had worked this out yet. Vinnie clenched his teeth and I put my guitar case down, ready to separate them.

'Where's Pete?' I asked, suddenly struck by the lack of the studio's sound engineer.

'Coming back at three, when we know what we're doin',' said Vinnie with a scowl.

'And Leonard, Devon, Charlie?'

'How the hell do I know?' said Vinnie. 'You're such a bleedin' mother hen, you find 'em.'

I knew I should stay and cool down the situation. But I was sick of catching shrapnel between Vin and Eddy. 'I'll go down and look in The Cobbler's,' I said, and slid out.

I found Devon and Charlie huddled in the pub's corner we'd now adopted as our own. As always, the gloomy interior of The Cobbler's Arms looked like somewhere you'd enter only when all other options had been snuffed out. Streaks of daylight fought in through greasy windows, hitting a haze of cigarette smoke, which perpetually lurked under the dark ceiling. The carpet, which may once have been red, was peppered with ill-assorted tables and chairs. At its far end, the bar offered various draughts of wife-beater, and industrially-sized bottles of spirits hung like church pipes, along the back wall. In front of these, the landlord's ancient and despondent face was propped on his hands, as though he'd just watched his last fiver limp in, on the fuzzy screens at the bookies next door.

A couple of elderly white-bearded men in turbans sat side by side at two separate tables, behind amber pints which looked as flat as tea. They smiled at everyone who passed, as though they were on some cool veranda being graciously saluted, and both waved at me as I loped to the bar. 'Whatcha,' I said. On the other side, a couple of young white guys in oily overalls, rapidly poked change into a fruit machine, which jangled its happy tune, but remained fruitless. Pints and glazed meat pies on a nearby table denoted a dinner break in progress. There were a few other people dotted about, mainly Asian blokes in twos and threes. Nobody seemed in a hurry, and there was more smoking than drinking in evidence. But it was only twelve o'clock. There was the whole long day to go.

I carried my drink over to the others. 'Big poof,' said Charlie, grinning. 'What're ya drinking girly halves for?'

I pulled at one of his red braces, letting it twang onto his bony shoulders. 'Ow!' From the dark patches under his pale eyes, I guessed his pint was medicinal. Devon just laughed his deep laugh and sipped an orange juice. He didn't often drink, but he made up with other vices. At thirty, and the oldest and wisest of the band, he was exempt from the piss-taking, and generally found our antics mildly amusing – though I guessed there were probably limits to this indulgence. Raymond, Len's nervous young cousin sat next to Devon, drinking a cola. He'd come along to the last few sessions as we needed a keyboard player. Len said his ambitions were to study at college, so God only knew what he thought of the musical chaos we created.

'What's happenin' upstairs Tom?' Devon indicated the studio with a jerk of his head, making his thick dreadlocks bounce like ships' ropes.

'Usual story – what songs to do and which sound to go for,' I said. 'No blood spilt yet – but we ought to go and pull them apart sometime soon.' I noticed a Guinness left on the table. 'Where's Len?'

'Getting' stuffed, over there,' said Charlie. I walked in the direction he'd pointed, and found Len gripped in a fast and furious game of dominoes with three other West Indian guys, old regulars. Judging by the teeth sucking, the high-pitched cackles and the look on Len's face, he was getting both stuffed and mounted. Each player slammed down his piece like lightning, to a hail of comments, and Len's head darted round as he tried to keep up. I stood back and watched, keeping out of the way. When the victor scraped his winnings across the metal board, I caught Len's eye and raised an eyebrow to our table, by way of question.

'You wanna try your luck young man?' said the old fella nearest me. His white teeth gleamed like a pirate's pearls. 'No thanks,' I laughed. 'I'd like to keep my shirt on.' Len stood and we crossed the floor to a rattly percussion of, 'Fool! You never know till you try,' and, 'We give you a head start!'

Len slumped onto the bench next to Devon with such a childish scowl that we all exploded into laughter. I waited for him to take a long draft of his pint and recover.

'What do you think?' I said. 'What song should we put down next?' The glumness fell from his face and his big, dark eyes narrowed. Len kept out of the endless rows between Eddy and Vinnie, so I wasn't sure what was coming next. He sat forward, hands cupped round his pint, chewing the inside of his mouth.

'After Tinsel and Stompin'?' he said, appraising our circle of expectant faces. 'Aarright then. I think we should cover Dance Hall Skaman.' He set down his pint down with a clonk.

'No way, man! It's too well known.' Devon shook his head firmly, and Charlie grimaced in agreement.

They were right to be cautious. You wouldn't cover a Jamaican classic like that, unless you could do it justice. Unless...

'We'd have to *really* change it,' I said.

'How?' Charlie pulled a disbelieving face.

'Keep the lyrics, but maybe increase the tempo and jazz up the rhythm.' I thought out loud. 'Make it more rattly and edgy. Give it a contemporary feel.'

Len nodded fast. 'That's what I mean!'

Charlie considered this, then his face stretched into surprised agreement. Devon nodded slowly, and said, 'Yeah. A faster beat, with a more choppin' feel mebee?'

'Like this?' Charlie tapped out a rhythm on the table with his forefingers and chanted 'Jah, jah – jah,jah, jah,jah, jah,jah'

'Yeah, but harder – on the rim – like gun shots.' Devon, produced two pencils from his top pocket to use as sticks.

Len nodded with enthusiasm. 'Man, we could make that tune steam!'

Raymond followed all this, in a state of shy bewilderment.

We sat trying out rhythms and singing guitar riffs, and Len pattered out the lyrics, until finally Eddy and Vinnie appeared, looking flat and defeated.

When they'd got their drinks we huddled round the table and went through the idea. Vinnie nodded. 'Okay by me.' He shot a glance at Eddy. 'But who'll do the vocals?'

Everyone looked to Len, including Eddy.

'What, me?' he said.

'You know the words,' said Eddy, folding his arms. 'An' I ain't murdering it – it needs a Jamaican voice.'

'You wan' me to sing?' Len stared at me with raised eyebrows. Len's talents were ever flexible – guitarist, engineer, and recently the band's impromptu toaster – spouting lyrics over the music like incantations. He'd never sung for us yet, but I could see from the secret curl on his lip, he was made up.

We piled up the studio steps, excited as hell to get going.

Len tapped me on the shoulder before we followed everyone else in. 'Wait up Tom.' I stopped and turned to him. 'Listen – you need to take some control, man. Make sure Vinnie an' his nonsense don't hijack this thing.'

I nodded.

'I mean it Tom. This is a good band. We could go somewhere, if we all pull together.'

I pushed open the doors and clapped my hands. 'Listen, we've got a couple of hours till Petulant Pete gets back,' I said. 'Let's try and nail the bastard.'

By the time Pete arrived we had the whole arrangement. Charlie and I swung into a twangy bass and guitar intro, and Len called, *'Dance Hall Ska Man!'* in a voice that made the hairs on my neck spring up. Then the band erupted into a fast ska/reggae rhythm, Raymond chunking out piano chords, while Len half sang, half toasted the lyrics. He had a rounded, melodic voice – clear, but kind of throaty. Eddy, Vinnie and myself clustered round a mic and tried out backing vocals until we got something we all liked – tuneful, with a hint of the football terraces. I jumped into the technician's booth and got Pete to crank up the reverb and add a bit of tinny echo on the mixing desk, which gave our voices a weird distant feel. He frowned a bit, but nodded, to agree we'd go with it. And instead of recording the instruments and vocals separately, I plumped for recording the whole song live – for an edgy, raw feel. At this point Pete was truly not a happy man, muttering about 'leakage' in a way that made Charlie and Vinnie snicker like lewd schoolboys.

When we'd done our first take, Pete's face was animated and he tweaked knobs on the mixing desk as if he was on the Star Ship Enterprise.

'Okay!' he said, coming round to our side of the glass. 'We need another vocal mic, 'cos you're dropping out Vinnie. And I want a thicker mat under Devon's drums, 'cos something's rattling that's got no business to. But don't nobody move – we need to get this down while I'm mad enough to think it's possible.'

By eight o'clock we were all done. We listened back to the track with open mouths. The faster rhythm and eerie backing vocals made Len's voice more present and poignant, and Vinnie's solo was just stinging. Such a mixture of disparate sounds just shouldn't have worked. But it did.

Pete shook his head in disbelief.

'You fuckers are somethin' else,' he said. 'You'll go far – if yer don't kill each other first.' Vinnie and Eddy grinned. 'Now all piss off outta me space. I wanna play around with the mix and I don't need your interference.'

This time no-one argued, and I stayed out of the sound booth. Pete was a grumpy old sod, but he knew his stuff when it came to mixing.

So we sat in the studio smoking.

'What's happenin' tomorrow?' said Charlie, looking at me.

'Same process all over again ainit?' said Vinnie, lighting a fag.

The comment brought a torrent of groans and cursing, but there was still an optimistic gleam in everyone's eyes when Rick arrived.

Rick was our manager in the sense that it was his studio, he organised most of our gigs, and he kept some sort of account of the cash we took on the night, all through his company, 'Paradise Sounds' – an off shoot of 'Paradise Plumbing', whose regular work kept me off the dole. We were one of a small handful of bands that Rick managed – the others being stalwart punk groups, whose fees usually balanced out their venue damages. With his sloping shoulders, long 70's style hair and old fashioned jeans, Rick's lack of cool was profound. But he read all the muso press, bought tons of records and he could also play a passable bass if you were desperate. Besides, he had as many qualifications to be a manager as I had to be a plumber – so neither of us could point a finger.

When he heard the extra track, his face lit up. 'Yeah, we need to release an EP of this stuff soon and we should think of a bigger tour – or maybe several….yeah, that might be it, lots of mini tours!' You had to love his optimism. We hadn't even worked out how to finance the record yet.

'How the hell we gonna set that up?'

'Nothin' to it. You concentrate on getting the songs right and leave the rest to me.' He thumped me on the back, and went off to plan his campaign, smoking his fag between thumb and forefinger, like it was Churchill's cigar.

It was shame he hadn't worked with a map, as he had us bouncing up and down the motorways like a kid on a Spacehopper, pinging back home for a cluster of non-gig dates. We'd be going back and forth from Coventry for weeks.

A few days later we huddled together, studying the tour schedule, alongside my RAC road map. Vinnie looked at me pointedly. 'Yvonne will be fuckin' livid you'll be away so long.'

'Not my problem,' I said with a shrug.

'Yeah, right.' His grin was a mix of sarcasm and pleasure.

Charlie's finger was on Sunderland. 'Where's bloody Norwich?' he said.

'Down on the lumpy bit,' I replied.

'Shit!' Devon gave an unhappy sigh. 'I get car sick so bad. What were you thinking of man?'

Rick's cornered expression swiftly transformed into his hypnotic enthusiasm.

'Look, it took a lot of fancy talking with venues, at this short notice. I booked you in where they found gaps.' His eyes shone with achievement. 'Anyway.' He played his trump card. 'Ragged Moth Records might be interested in you, if the tour goes well.'

So that was that. Rick had alerted a hip, independent record company. I was pretty angry he hadn't spoken to me first, but the others were elated, so it was like I'd stepped onto a moving walkway. Whether I liked it or not, we were now heading off.

♪

'You've got to be kidding!' I said as a rusty old minibus puttered to a halt, near the kerb where our equipment was piled. On the side panels, ill-matched paint had been sprayed over the words, 'Saint Luke's Grammar School' with its fancy crest, and 'Original Mix' was inexpertly stencilled on top.

'It's just for the first few gigs, till I can sort out something better,' he said, with a wave of his hand. But he didn't look me in the eye.

The door opened, and a familiar form swung out of the driving seat.

'Welcome aboard! Your pilot today is DJ Trevor Lyons and we will be cruising up the M6 at seventy miles an hour, listening to some mega sounds!'

There was much laughing and hand slapping between Trev and the band, and we introduced him to young Raymond, taking it all in with a sort of shell-shocked enthusiasm. Trust Rick to supply a crap vehicle with a great driver. As the rest of the guys started loading up through the back doors, I turned to him.

'Listen Rick, we're yo-yoing between two dozen gigs in various godforsaken parts of the country. Seriously, how many of them do you think this…Tonka Toy will make?'

He issued his signature brushing off movement. 'Don't be such a worrier Tom,' he said. 'This van's been running for years. The school only sold it 'cos some rich old boy bought them a new one.'

'And the MOT's probably due.' Vinnie muttered from one side of his mouth, as the other clamped on a fag. He was lugging a bass amp past us. 'Oi, Shepperton, you gonna giz a hand or stand there moanin'?'

The gear refused to leave enough room for the people, so we had to unload, remove some of the back seats and load it all back up again – this time with more success, though it was tight. We were all in great form, heaving and cussing at each other good naturedly. Eddy and Vinnie baited each other with something definitely approaching friendliness, as we joked about who we'd leave behind if we couldn't make it work.

'You two would leave most room,' Vinnie said to Eddy and me. 'Think of the space taken up by all those fuckin' changes of suit.' He poked a mic stand through a small hole between two amps, as skilfully as a dentist exploring between molars.

'Or we could leave out that twattin' big guitar, and your ego.' Eddy sucked in cigarette smoke, putting a finger to his mouth in mock contemplation. 'Creating the space for at least four more proper musicians.'

Devon shook his head and laughed. 'Glad we're all settin' out on good terms.'

'Shit! I'd hate to know what bad terms sounds like.' Charlie hefted in the last few coils of cable in, which landed with a rubbery thwack.

I was glad everyone was so upbeat. We needed to start out with a positive vibe. We'd played some great gigs in the Midlands, but we'd never done a real tour, and there were so many dates. If we were going to take the UK by storm, impress Ragged Moth, and release our EP, we needed to pull together and stay focussed, no distractions.

But it seemed we were a united force – for now anyway.

♫♪

6
JOSIE

'Franki! Guess what?' I screamed upstairs, waving a letter. It was two weeks since my encounter with Tom Shepperton. I'd spent days sketching, signing on, and being 'persuaded' to enrol in a Touch Typing course. But nothing new or exciting had happened – until now.

'I've got that Youth Training Scheme job! I'm going to be teaching art and cookery to kids who've been in trouble.'

Franki appeared from her bedroom, goggling like a fish. 'You're kiddin'. When do you start?'

'Going in Monday, to discuss details. They're sending me on a trainers' course first.'

Franki bounded down, and as she stepped into the living room, I grabbed her elbows and danced her round. 'Five thousand pounds a year – *five thousand quid!* No more bloody typing and we'll be rich!'

We'd both scraped by since college, taking bits of work on badly paid community arts projects, barely worth signing off the dole for. This was my first real job, and I'd hit the jackpot.

'Let's invite Simon and buy fab things for tea.' Franki clapped her hands. 'Like fresh prawns and whole trout.'

'Tinned strawberries too!' I jumped up on the sofa and started trampolining. 'And rosé wine!'

The Pink Diet, I thought with a note of regret.

We walked across town to drop a scribbled note through Simon's door, as he'd never forgive us if we left him out of a celebration. Then we bought our feast.

It was a good day for bargains at the market, and our arms were stretched with carrier bags.

'Let's take the bus back,' I said, thinking of the long walk home.

'You sure?' Franki frowned. We never wasted money on bus fares.

'Yes! I'll be getting paid soon,' I said grinning.

The bus was packed, so I made for the stairs. 'I wouldn't go up there duck.' An old lady with a helmet of purple-tinged curls clung to a pole as the bus swung out.

'Wassup?' asked Franki, squeezing through behind me.

We heard a deep throb of thuds across the ceiling as someone ran along the upper deck. This was followed by swearing, shouting and another cascade of fierce banging. Everyone looked up at the ceiling. It seemed a miracle that a foot wasn't dangling through it. The pounding continued, sometimes muffled, as if someone was jumping from seat to seat. In amongst the shouting and laughing, I thought heard the word 'Adolf'.

'We'd better stay down here.' I grabbed a strap with my free hand. The bus halted abruptly, and everyone shot forward then fell back against each other, grimacing and muttering 'sorry, sorry' to fellow passengers. At the stop outside, two young gum-chewers in denim miniskirts looked up to the top deck. The whole bus vibrated with feet stamps, banging on the windows and woof whistles. The girls pulled disgusted faces, and flicked up vigorous double Vs of fingers. Those above us went wild with delighted cries and foul language.

As the bus toiled up our hill, the laughter and shouting upstairs continued. I looked at the turbaned head of the driver. His wary eyes darted to the periscope device which allowed him to see the top deck but, from his anxious frown, he clearly wasn't going to try and evict these particular trouble makers by himself.

By the park we stopped again. There was an avalanche of boots as a lanky skinhead fell, feet first down the stairs, obviously propelled from behind. 'Fuck off Adolf!' he shouted, lunging for the centre door, and banging my shoulder hard as he jumped out. 'Oi!' I said, rubbing my arm. Three more green bomber jackets whizzed past, and the last kid stomped on my toe as he passed.

'Hey! Mind where you're going!' I yelled, without thinking.

The skinhead paused on the step and turned back. He was a meaty lad with a scarred head, whose braces strained down over a rounded stomach. Our faces were even. *Oh Christ!* I recoiled, waiting to feel the punch of a fist. But his expression was mild. 'Sorry 'bout them lot,' he said. 'An' I didn't mean to step on yer foot.'

His mates on the pavement jeered. 'Caam'on Adolf, put the fuckin' birds down!' The skinhead jumped off the bus, landing with a thud on the tarmac. We gaped after them as they disappeared into the park, still aiming kicks at the back of each other's legs.

When they'd gone, the passengers tutted amongst themselves, puffing out their cheeks and shaking their heads, in obvious relief.

'I hope the kids you're teaching aren't like that,' said Franki with a gallows laugh, as we sat down on two vacated seats.

'Oh crikey, what if,' I said, laughing.

♪

Monday came round far too fast, and as Franki saw me off, I was filled with apprehension. She leant against the pea green of the door, in a black kimono splashed with red flowers. And, with her dark hair and pale morning face, Franki was all blocks of colour – a Matisse painting waiting to happen.

'Good luck doll!' The kiss she blew me exhaled with a plume of smoke. I walked away, insides wriggling with nerves and shut my eyes for a second, longing to change places.

My new workplace was inside an industrial unit. I stepped over the ledge of a metal door and gingerly wound my way through the parked vehicles, holding my skirt away from the grease and oil of exhaust pipes. Big doors to various businesses were dotted around the sides of the low car park. I could hear the hum of machines, and a rhythmical punching sound like a huge stapler. When I got to the Youth Training Scheme's entrance, trickles of sweat crawled down the inside of my shirt from my armpit and I fought a rising nausea. The sound of coarse laughter came from inside and I heard a couple of thumps, as if furniture was being knocked over. My chest began to hurt from its own pounding. I hesitated and took a couple of deep breaths, trying to recall my older brother Ally's voice: *'Josie, you can do whatever you set your mind to.'* I tilted my chin higher, pushed open the heavy door, and stepped into an area which looked like an indoor prison yard.

In front of me, was a terrifying mass of maleness – a silent frieze of staring faces, muscled limbs, bright orange-lined bomber jackets, and skulls sporting skinheads, buzz cuts, afros. One lad held a leg mid air to jump up on a bench, one hovered over someone's shoulder, a couple were passing something illicit, and a defeated-looking lad was handing over a cigarette. A black lad was standing over a small Asian kid, his fist drawn back. In panic, I dropped my eyes and saw a forest of denim turn ups, white socks, and oxblood calf-length laced Doc Marten boots. When I looked up again, faces had craned round each other to see me better. The black lad hauled the little kid up like a rag doll, and pushed him away.

'It's the new cooking woman!' someone said from the rear of the mob. A thought popped up from the only bit of my brain not concentrating on resisting flight. *That's weird - they said I'd be mainly teaching art.* A stocky boy pushed his way to the front and his mouth slowly curled, like the smile of a gingerbread man.

'Hey! You was on the bus on Saturday!'

And for the second time, I looked directly into the eyes of the kid whose nickname, I now knew, was Adolf.

♪

When I arrived home, Franki was sitting at her sewing machine. In the past few weeks, she'd turned our front room into a sweat shop, filled with berets and hats, in velvet, brocade, felt and fake fur. They perched jauntily on the arms of the chairs, hung from the mantelpiece, and sat in piles on all the shelves in both alcoves.

'Hilary wrote today. She says I can get a stall in Camden,' Franki said, as we stood slurping tea and surveying the hat colony. Our old art college mate Hilary sold garments with bizarre pockets and functionless zips.

'Great idea,' I said. 'Would it be expensive?' I tried on a purple beret and appraised myself in the mirror.

'She says I can share hers.'

A cold sensation slivered through my stomach. 'How would you do that?'

'I'll need to move back to London….stay with Hilary,' said Franki slowly. '…save up a deposit to rent my own place.' She was trying to read my face as if I was a juror. 'I'm really sorry Jose – but there's nothing here for me in Coventry now.'

As half my world fell away, I removed the beret. Then I plonked a green dayglo tri-corn hat on my head, and curled my mouth into a reassuring smile. 'These are really great, you'll easily sell them.'

Franki came up behind and we looked at my reflection in the mirror. 'Apart from that one – that's blaady 'orrible,' she said. We both grinned.

I struck a pose and pointed to the door. 'It's time to go forth!' I said. 'Make your fortune in the world of hat couture.'

'Thanks doll.' Franki wrapped her arms round my waist and we gave each other a hug. 'You know I'd stay if I could.'

'And you know, if I had a choice, I'd leave too,' I said.

Franki raised a questioning eyebrow.

I shook my head. 'Not yet. I can't give up on the first real job I've ever had. And the boss says when I've established a cookery programme I can have complete artistic freedom with the arts side. Plus, don't forget, I've still got to pay off my bloody overdraft.'

'Then we'll write to each other,' she said. 'And when I get a place, you'll visit.'

But I couldn't think of a future without her yet, so I focussed on the present. 'Hey! You know what this means?'

'What?' Franki frowned in puzzlement, until I leapt on the armchair, shimmying like a belly dancer and called. 'Farewell party!'

7
JOSIE

It was the day of Franki's party. I hurried home from shopping, eager to transform our shabby, rented terrace house into a magical grotto, with the help of fairy lights and fabrics. A mad spring heatwave had burst through the gloomy winter, so we were relocating our furniture into the garden – to make room for dancing and the masses of people we'd invited. But first I needed to grab more beer from the corner shop, before Raj barricaded his premises against the out-flowing football fans. Everyone in Coventry knew how to avoid the weekly mêlée of kicking and casual violence that followed Saturday's match. But I was still terrified of being caught up in it.

Seeing that most shopkeepers had already rolled down their heavy-duty shutters, I sped up. The main road was empty and there was an eerie hush, apart from a small Ford van coming down the hill. The little van suddenly swerved across the wide lane, pulled up just in front of me and its door opened across the pavement. A Doc Marten boot emerged with purpose, and a tall figure started to unfold from the driver's seat. I was about to break into a run when he caught my arm.

'Hey, Josie – stop!'

I registered black jeans, a slim physique with muscled arms, a white T-shirt. And I looked up into the face of Tom Shepperton.

'You didn't recognise me,' he teased.

I blushed. My god, he was *so* gorgeous!

'You've got a van.' I knew very few people with cars.

'Been working with my mate Rick. We kind of own it together,' he said.

I read out the logo, *'Paradise Plumbing'*.

'My trade alongside music.' Tom smiled broadly. 'Gotta make a living to live.'

I made a bad joke about how plumbers should play tubas, to which he gave a good natured chuckle and we chatted for a bit. He was leaning with one hand on the roof of his van, the other hooked in his front jeans pocket. The T-shirt stretched tight across his broad chest, and his eyes hadn't left my face. Were they bluey-green or greeny-blue? By the time we started talking about bands we liked I was babbling, almost overwhelmed by how much I was attracted to him.

A roar of triumph rolled down the empty street from the football ground.

'Shit! I need to get home before they finish.'

He nodded. 'Yeah, course. See yer round then.'

A thought hit me. 'Hey, we're having a party tonight,' I said. 'Why don't you come?'

'Okay.' He nodded with enthusiasm. 'What's your address?' As I rattled it off, he bent and scrabbled around in the sheaves of paper, cassettes and debris that littered the van. Then he stood up with outstretched palms. 'I can't believe it. Haven't got a bloody pen!'

It was the perfect alibi, of course. He was nothing if not a gentlemen. Another cheer mushroomed up, the official sound of a score – minutes before the unofficial one got settled. I looked at my watch in panic. 'Sorry, better get a move on.'

'Okay, then.' He smiled and lightly touched my arm, as he'd done outside the supermarket. A charge of excitement shot through me again. '30 Richmond Road, right?' He tapped his temple, as if logging it. 'See you later!' he called.

I waved back, knowing that this wasn't even a possibility.

Back at the house and laden with extra beer, I unlocked our door as the final whistle rose from the stadium. I emerged from kitchen to living room, and Franki padded downstairs bearing strings of fairy lights.

'Raj gave us a couple of doughnuts.' I plonked one on a plate and handed it over. 'They don't last and Dipti won't eat them. She's still trying to get her figure back.'

'Yum,' she said. 'Any more good news?'

Then I remembered. 'Oh god, yeah! I saw Tom Shepperton on the way up from town.'

'Wow!' She pulled wicked face. 'You manage to speak this time?'

'Actually, we had quite a chat.' I gave a dry laugh. 'I even invited him to the party.'

'Blaady hell, Jose! Reckon he'll come?'

'No chance. Didn't even write down the address.' I wiped the crumbs from my mouth and sighed.

'Hey, nothing wrong with dreamin' gal.' Franki stood to take the plates out. 'Let's face it, he's way out of our league – not like our Vinnie.'

We both snickered. Vinnie was one of many casual pub-and-nightclub mates – musician, dreamer, heavy drinker and party animal. He was a chancer and always on the cadge, but he always made us laugh.

♫

By eleven o'clock, the pubs had shut and our house was packed. Franki, ever the party belle, was resplendent in black lace and long purple gloves. She'd invited all her old boyfriends – not an insignificant number – and two of them stood at opposite sides of the room scowling at each other. Several DJs had taken over the sounds, and we'd hit a 60s R&B groove. People continued arriving – some I knew and many I didn't – and I'd been busy pointing out the loo, finding extra ashtrays, and keeping everyone happy.

'Josie, come and dance!' Franki shouted over the music.

I was squeezing back from the kitchen to join her, when over everyone's heads, Vinnie beckoned me to the front room. 'Oi, Josie! It's the pigs. They wanna speak to you.'

Oh great. Our first warning. After a third call they'd make everyone leave. I pushed through to the front door, where someone was arguing drunkenly with a police officer.

'Oh, it's you!' he said.

He'd once escorted me down the stairs from a squat party in a dodgy warehouse, when some skinheads had started a fight with a black DJ.

'Hey, we've got the same shoes,' I'd said, as our Doc Martens thumped on the treads.

He gave a short laugh. 'Wanna sign up? You've got half the uniform.'

'Same uniform, different sides,' I'd replied with firmness.

Two other police had stumbled out after us, restraining a tall muscly skin, with *'Gob'* tattoed on his upper arm. My evictor turned to assist in handcuffing the still-struggling bloke. As the music re-started, I'd given him a flash of smile, a swirl of skirt and slipped back inside. When I passed by, he'd shaken his head and wagged a finger, tutting.

And here he was again. But this time not so friendly.

'Strange smelling smoke.' He narrowed his eyes, trying to scan over my shoulder.

I stood against the jamb, my arm barring the doorway. 'Josh sticks,' I replied.

'If you say so,' he said. 'If we're called back, we'll have to check for ourselves.'

I shut the door, annoyed. I'd have to stop any more gate crashers coming in, or Franki's final party would be ruined.

By the time I'd admitted one person I knew vaguely and turned away five others, I was thoroughly pissed off. We hadn't exactly kept the event a secret, so the whole of Coventry was turning up. Vinnie had gone off to locate a beer for me. But he was dependably undependable. So I was stuck in the role of bouncer, unable to dance with Franki, and desperate for a drink.

Another knock at the door. At the bottom of the steps, I made out the silhouette of a bloke, wearing a woolly hat and carrying a cardboard box.

'For Christ's sake, don't even start to bullshit! I don't know you, and this is *my* party.'

'It's Tom!' As he tilted his head, his cheekbones caught the street light, then his hair sprung up when he pulled off his hat. 'You didn't recognise me?'

A hot flush of embarrassment surged through me, and I thumped my forehead with the heel of my hand.

'Twice in one day!' He laughed, stepping up next to me. 'And I brought booze in case you were running low.' He opened the box lid revealing cans, wine, even spirits – he'd spent a fortune.

'Wow thanks! You are most welcome kind sir.' Still red-faced, I waved him into the house.

'Catch you later.' He grinned back at me and, as he entered the crush of the living room, where everyone was drinking and dancing, he was greeted with cries of welcome.

Vinnie stood behind me, holding out a beer. 'Can't believe old Shepperton's turned up,' he said raising an eyebrow. 'Friend of yours?'

I was elated that Tom had arrived, but it didn't change the fact that I was stuck at the door and still thirsty.

'Where you find this then?' I said spritzing the can open with a scowl. 'On the moon?'

'One great step for womankind,' he said with a shrug.

After an hour, it seemed safe to leave the door unguarded. Tom was deep in conversation with another musician. As I squeezed by, he gave me a sidelong grin. A tall black guy grabbed his sleeve, requiring an answer to something important. Tom mugged at me and I gave him an encouraging smile, hoping he'd come to find me.

I wedged myself against the cooker, alongside Simon and his man of the moment. They were talking about the clubs and pubs they frequented in Birmingham, Coventry's more worldly cousin. Tom's face appeared at the top of the kitchen steps. 'Any beer left?'

At last – our chance to talk. But as I opened the fridge to extract a tin, a purple glove flapped over Simon's head, and I heard Franki's frantic voice.

'Fuck! Someone's been sick on the bathroom floor! Where's the blaady mop?'

I passed the can into Tom's outstretched hand. 'Outside!' I called, then grimacing at her elaborate attire, added, 'Don't worry, I'll sort it.'

Pulling a rueful face at Tom, I grabbed a bottle of disinfectant from the window sill, and fought my way through people congregating between the back door and the bathroom.

Franki patted my arm gratefully. 'Then you *have* to come and dance with me.' She pulled a sad face. 'We haven't had a bop together and it's our last chance.'

Much later, I stood at the back door smoking. We'd had a great time dancing, and now the music had turned nostalgic. Through the window I saw Franki, arms round an old flame, swaying. The thought of life without her ran through my head, but I stopped it dead. That kind of reflection only led to dark thoughts about other people I'd loved and lost.

In the darkness outside, there was a whispered voice I recognised. My old college mate Kevin was propositioning a woman, who was murmuring her consent. When I kicked the metal dustbin she staggered out adjusting her skirt, and disappeared into the party.

'Kev, what the hell are you doing?' Usually I'd mind my own business, but his girlfriend was a good sort and deserved better.

'Jeezus Josie, I dunno – what am I doing?' His eyes were glazed and he was having difficulty standing. I led him to the outdoor parlour and dropped him onto a settee, where he promptly burst into tears. After half an hour of confessional drunken sobbing, he sank into unconsciousness.

When I returned to the party everything was winding down. The alcohol and dancing had both run out, and people were slumped round the sides of the darkened room, as if they'd been thrown there and slid down the walls.

'Your Kev's comatose outside,' I told his girlfriend, who was chatting to the girl from the garden. She rolled her eyes. 'Lightweight – just can't take his drink.' I managed a smile.

Franki was in the front room, bidding farewell to people. 'Where've you been?' she asked. 'Tom was looking for you, before he went.'

'Shit! He's gone already?' The last time I'd seen, he was in deep, music conference with Trevor Lyons and a beautiful Jamaican woman, wearing long amber earrings. They'd made a trio far too cool for me to interrupt.

'Yeah, he had to get up early – said to tell you *'great party'*. I think he wanted to talk to you.'

Shit, shit, shit! Once again, possibility had rolled away, like a coin down a drain.

When the last person had left, I found Vinnie alone outside. He was lying in an old armchair, picking out a riff on my cheap acoustic guitar. It was a bluesy number, haunting and beautiful.

'Hey,' he said. 'Wanna hear my new song?'

'Course I do.' I slumped into the chair opposite. 'Don't suppose you've got any booze?'

He looked at me as if insulted, and pulled a bottle of whiskey out from behind him. 'Courtesy of Mr Shepperton,' he said. And we both grinned.

8

TOM

We had a couple of weeks break from touring, and I hadn't seen Vinnie since our last rehearsal when I'd become so strung out, from trying to pull everyone together. I'd begun to regret involving Vinnie, despite – or maybe because of – our long history. After the session, I'd been in The Cobblers winding down with a lone pint, where he'd found me and started ranting about my giving too much credibility to Eddy's ideas. Then I'd just snapped.

'Face it Vinnie, you're just knobbed off cos Eddy's the front man, so he gets all the attention!'

It was a stupid truth to voice out loud, as I realised – the moment I saw the look on his face.

'Fuck you!' he said, and turned tail. I'd gone to his house the following day, but he wouldn't answer. For Chrissakes, it was like we were still nine years old. So I left him to it. Experience said he'd be back when he'd stopped sulking. The band was happy to rehearse without him, but I was annoyed, as we'd begun to rely on his particular solo guitar sound, as an important part of the mix.

The next Saturday, driving down Gosling Street I spotted Josie – swinging up the hill in some kind of military jacket and beret, with great big boots under her skirt. For once she was alone, so I swerved the van over to say hello. I can't remember what we talked about – but it was great to be near her. And it made me pretty horny too, if I'm honest. At one point her skirt started to peel away at the side – it was one of those wrap things. She tucked it back, joking about being left standing in her knickers, boots and beret, like the paramilitary branch of M&S. I laughed, but it was a picture I had to suppress very quickly. She talked fast, changing from outrageous to shy, like an indecisive sun on a cloudy day. I was pretty hypnotised.

Then she invited me to a party at her house. Normally I avoided those sorts of things. They were always full of drunks throwing up, bad music, and everyone talking crap – followed by the inevitable risky stagger through town in the early hours. But her eyes were shining like Christmas so I thought why not?

When I arrived, I was surprised who was there. I spoke to Lee from Style Set, several of People Squad and the three punk girls from Dog Spytt. Vinnie was slouching around too, which caught me off side. He didn't look that happy to see me either.

'You done much last week?' he asked. His eyes had that filmy look our school goldfish got before they pegged it. He was pissed and just within pre-fighting mode.

'Not much,' I said, 'We're somewhat short of a fuckin' vital guitarist.'

He waivered on the spot, as though resisting a gale force wind. 'Had shtuff to do,' he said. 'Be 'round Monday though.'

'You better,' I said. 'We're recording at Rick's.'

We'd decided to record enough material for a potential album, but that news could wait. I'd no urge to be further involved with Vinnie wearing his lager head.

Otherwise it turned out to be quite a good night. Barbara Williams asked if I'd put down a track with Beat Generation at Cloud Nine studios for their new EP. She wanted an open, acoustic feel on second guitar and Jackson suggested me, which was big of him because he could definitely have done it himself. I pointed that out, when I spotted him in the kitchen later on. 'Nah man, I stick to me own sound,' he said, from the business end of a large joint, which was being passed round. 'Ya want some?' I shook my head as I'd promised Rick to spend Sunday working on the next leg of the tour.

I liked Jackson. At Poly, he'd made carvings in soft sandstone – curved shapes with an arm, or a leg appearing out of the grainy lumps. In our final year, I took some great photos of him. My favourite was Jackson leaning over a great dinosaur egg of stone, goggles pushed up. The halogens overhead reflected in the beads of sweat on his dark forehead, and the shaft of light coming through the big open roller door hit all the dust motes around him. He was working on a foot that pushed out of the soft-textured stone, and his profile was intense and concentrated, as he used a small chisel to sculpt an emerging toe.

We all thought we were bound for success, until we left college and reality slapped us in the mush. It was funny how so many of us turned efforts to our music. Or maybe it wasn't. Since becoming a teenager, all I'd wanted, was to shake off the stranglehold of Coventry, make my mark on the world and start really living. It was a matter of finding the right format – and now I had it.

By the time I'd chatted to everyone I knew, it was getting late, so I looked for Josie. She'd flitted round sorting out various crises, before joining in when everyone went bonkers to a Motown set. The party had thinned out, and I discovered her in the garden with some bloke who was in a real mess, explaining how sorry he was for something, and actually blubbing. I stood in the shadows by the side door and listened. Her voice was soft and patient as she placated him – another drunk who'd have forgotten everything in the morning.

Fairly soon he crashed out along the sofa with his head in her lap, and Josie looked down to pat his arm in a distracted way. Then she leaned back and just stared ahead. Her face was orangey from the fairy lights on the fence and the candles on the low table in front, and her expression was serious, focussed inwards, like someone who's absorbing sad news. It had been several years since I'd used it, but I thought of my camera. Then I had a sudden, mad urge to scoop her to me and hold her close – tell her everything was alright. It was crazy thinking, and I hadn't drunk more than a couple of lagers. I took a couple of deep breaths of night air. I must have inhaled too much of the dope buzzing round in that small kitchen.

I could have gone over and spoken to her then. But somehow it didn't feel right, so I wandered back into the house. At the front door, I thanked Franki before I left.

'Have you seen Josie?' she said. I shook my head. 'She'll be so disappointed, she *really* wanted to talk to you.' Her dark gaze tunnelled into mine and I hesitated, wondering if I should go back to the garden and interrupt Josie's thoughts.

'Come round sometime,' she said. 'I shouldn't say this, but Josie likes you a lot.' She clapped a hand to her mouth, and staggered a bit. 'Oh Christ, I've drunk far too much!'

Franki was still giggling when she opened the door to let me out. As I walked towards the van, she called, 'Hey Tom, I might be pissed, but that's still completely true!' And she blew me a kiss.

It was her drunken honesty, and the image of Josie's unguarded face in the glowing light, hanging behind my eyelids before I fell asleep, which gave me the final push to act. But I never imagined what might happen next, or that I'd spend the following days and weeks trying to suppress a stupid grin whenever I thought about her.

9

JOSIE

The next day, out in the keen sunlight, our furniture and fairy lights looked tatty and forlorn, and the house inside was littered with fag ends and beer cans. But it wasn't just the smell of stale beer and tobacco making me feel sad and queasy. My best mate and ally-in-fun was leaving town. We were no longer bowling along taking life as we found it. It was time to face the adult world.

When we'd returned the house to some sort of order, Franki disappeared into the bathroom and emerged in a cloud of steam, towel-wrapped, her face and neck a blotchy pink.

'Sure you won't come to the pub? Hair of the dog?'

'Nah. Head like a sack of wet cement.' In reality, Vinnie had hogged the booze before passing out on the sofa. But I couldn't face anyone else asking how I'd cope without Franki, when I had no idea. 'I'll have a long bath and watch some telly. It's a school night for me, remember.'

'Poor babe.' Franki rubbed my shoulder as she passed by. 'It's great you're sticking it out.'

'Don't.' I fought to swallow a big lump in my throat. 'It's my first proper job. I've got to stick at it.'

'Good for you. Don't let the bastards grind you down.'

Franki left in a hum of perfume and dark glasses, and I was knotting the last bag of rubbish, when there was a tentative knock at the door. I shuffled over, clanking the sack behind me.

Tom Shepperton stood on the path, fresh as a soap powder advert in a white T-shirt and jeans. He must have left something and come to retrieve it.

'Oh god – hi!' I touched my hair, self conscious. 'I'm still tidying up from last night.'

'Yeah, good party.' He grinned. 'Lots of people I hadn't seen for ages.'

'Like Vinnie?' I'd asked Vinnie about about Tom, but he'd been tight-lipped and evasive.

'Yeah…like Vinnie,' Tom said slowly. A little crease appeared on his forehead as though he had a question, but was reluctant to ask.

'Come on in. I was about to make a cuppa.'

'Shall I take that out for you?' he gestured at the bin bag.

'Cheers, chuck it on top of the others.'

I walked to the kitchen, beaming insanely. I couldn't wait to tell Franki that Tom Shepperton dropped by, and helped put out the rubbish!

Tom wandered into the lounge. 'Furniture in the living room, novel concept,'

'We thought we'd try it, but I'm not convinced,' I called. My hand shook slightly as I filled the kettle to set on the gas hob. *Tom here, in my house!* I took a couple of deep breaths to try and calm down, then returned to the back room and perched on the arm of a comfy chair, trying to appear casual.

'So this is where you and Franki live?' Tom sat on the couch, long legs stretched out under the coffee table.

'Just me from Wednesday,' I said. 'Unless I relent and let Howard move in.'

His smile dropped for a second. 'Who's Howard?'

'One of Franki's exs. Not ideal, to be honest, so I've said no. We probably wouldn't get on…' I paused, aware I was babbling again.

'What's he like, this…ex?'

I pondered a moment. 'Lugubrious. It would be like living with a depressed Eyore.'

Tom leant back and chuckled.

'Besides, I don't have to find anyone else 'cos I've struck a deal with Raj, my landlord.'

I explained that Raj managed several properties for his family, and was always moaning about late rent and moonlight flits. Tom smiled and in the thin afternoon light, his eyes seemed clear jade green. I found him so attractive, it must surely be lit in neon words across my forehead. I dropped my gaze and fiddled with a loose thread on the sofa arm.

'Sorry I didn't really talk to you last night,' I said. 'I'd forgotten you don't get to enjoy your own parties.'

'I came to find you in the garden,' said Tom. 'But you had your hands full.'

I frowned, puzzling about what he meant. 'Oh god, you mean Kev?'

'I heard you talking to him – you were kind.' Tom was looking at me thoughtfully. I was becoming mesmerized. My face went hot again.

'Ah, 'twas the demon drink that called him!' I said quickly, in a cod-Irish accent. And the kettle whistled bang on cue, making us both laugh. I went to the kitchen and returned with two mugs and a packet.

'Fancy one of the world's worst biscuits?' I asked. 'We think they could be Russian. Might taste like hamster bedding – but it's all I've got.'

'Sound great, bring 'em on,' Tom said.

I coiled myself into the armchair opposite, suddenly aware of my bizarre appearance –
leggings, stripy knee socks, hair tied round by a scarf, and still sporting my favourite sleeping T-shirt – a faded black one, with 'Dennis the Menace' raising a triumphant fist on the front.

Tom was on the edge of the sofa, nibbling a biscuit. His face creased into puzzled distaste as he swallowed. 'What exactly are these?' he said.

'Sorry, I warned you they might be awful,' I said.

He looked a bit uncomfortable and I suddenly wondered if my armpits smelt bad. A wave of shame swept over me and I clamped my arms to my body, sinking further back in my chair with a sheepish smile. Tom looked up and his face coloured slightly.

'Actually, I came round to see if you fancied coming for a drink – if you're not busy,' he said.

Not busy? I'll just clear the rest of my life!

'That would be fab! Though I'll have to change.' I waved at my attire in apology.

'You look great to me,' he relaxed back into the sofa, still holding the biscuit. 'But I can come back about six, if you like.'

'Okay, great!'

We both grinned at each other, not knowing what to say next.

'You don't have to eat that,' I pointed to his hand. 'I won't be offended.'

'No, it's all good.'

And grinning, he popped the remainder into his mouth.

♫

When I'd bathed, I raced upstairs. For a date with Tom Shepperton, I needed to achieve the glamour of that woman I'd first seen him with. Dismayed by my wardrobe, I went to plunder Franki's collection. Eventually I settled on tight ski pants, a slash-necked top, and a beautiful mohair cardigan that shed fur like a cat. I dried my hair and tied a black silk scarf round it, leaving the ends to hang loosely down the back of my neck. Then, ignoring the row of clumpy Doc Martens, I slipped on pointy-toed ankle boots with little heels and looked in the mirror. Would I do?

By the time Tom arrived I was sick with nerves and regretting the whole outfit. He stood in the doorway.

'Wow!' he said, narrowing his eyes. 'Great look – kind of late 50's beat era.'

I began to squirm under his scrutiny. 'Well, I'm a retro girl at heart,' I shrugged. 'The 80's have no real soul.'

Tom gestured to his van. 'Fancy a pub in the countryside?' he said.

Images of lush trees and rolling hills rose up in my imagination, bittersweet reminders of my childhood.

'What? And leave all this gorgeous concrete behind?' I walked over to the vehicle, which promised *'Paradise'* with its *'Plumbing'*, before he could change his mind.

As he drove, Tom pointed out his parents' home on the outskirts of town, down one of the rows of endless terraced houses. His mum was a school cook and his dad an engineer at the big car factory. He had two much older sisters. One was married in Canada, and the other lived in Birmingham.

'I think I was a bit of a late mistake,' he said, grinning.

'Nice mistake to make,' I said.

'Thanks.' I noticed the tips of his ears had reddened.

Tom spent his childhood running round with other kids on the streets, fields and railway embankments, or in the local park playing footie. I was surprised to hear he'd gone to school with Vinnie – and Vinnie's sister, of whose existence I hadn't known. He admitted they'd got into plenty of scrapes – but nothing too delinquent.

'Anyway, that's me – just a typical Coventry kid,' said Tom. I thought of the typical city lads that I was to work with. There was no comparison.

'How did you get into music?' I asked.

'We used to go to a youth club which was crap – but they had a set of old drums and the local priest bought a couple of guitars. I think he thought we'd play at church.'

'And did you?'

'Not likely! He was a bit of a perv and anyway when he heard the punk racket we made, he gave up on the idea. Then I got my own guitar and started playing old blues and R&B songs – and messing round with reggae. I wasn't much of a punk anyway.'

'How come?'

He laughed. 'Wrong kind of hair. Couldn't get on with the whole Mohican thing.'

His thick russety hair was cut short at the back and sides and heavy at the top. I imagined running my fingers up the nape of his long neck and into his crown. Tom glanced at me sideways, and I looked down at my lap.

'I'm more interested in other music really – stuff that digs into your bones.' He narrowed his eyes and gave me a quick look. 'D'you know what I mean?'

I nodded, and he smiled. 'Thought you might.'

We drove into a small car park. The pub was an old brick building with ivy round the door and hanging baskets, cascading with blousy pink geraniums and frothy white 'baby's breath'. We sat outside, our table overlooking fields in the distance, and a little pond in front, where a couple of ducks puttered round, as if trying to look busy. The sky was pale blue with a rosy glow on the horizon. It felt we were a million miles from the city.

'How about you?' Tom said. 'What are you up to at the moment?'

I sketched out what my job would be, when I'd completed my City and Guilds trainers' course, finished drafting my cookery programme, and started actually teaching the ex-offenders who I'd been getting to know. I omitted the fact I was becoming so nervous, that I woke each morning with stomach cramps.

'Sounds like it'll be tough,' he said. 'I've seen those skinhead twins you mention in town, with a much older bloke.'

'That's Gob – he's the bloke they aspire to be,' I said. 'They say him and a mate marched into an office once and stole a photocopier so they could reproduce fascist material. They carried it right through town without being stopped.'

'You're kidding?'

'He's been on remand a few times,' I continued. 'So they all look up to him. He's scary – a real National Front nut. Came into the unit last week, and told me how much he liked prison, because of the discipline. He's up again soon for GBH. They all reckon he'll go down again.'

'Sounds like a good thing.'

I sighed. 'Yeah, but the others will just admire him more. I think they just hang round with whoever'll have them.'

Tom was gazing at the ducks thoughtfully. 'They just want a sense of belonging,' he said. 'We get a lot of young lads at our gigs. It's like they need something to believe in – a cause or movement. It's shit being unemployed. You begin to feel like you're worth nothing.'

At the thought of going in again on Monday and facing the endless rough banter and name calling of the trainees my stomach contracted, so I shook my head, like a dog surfacing from a cold lake. 'Hey, let's not talk about work.'

Tom gave me an appraising look. 'Fair enough. Another drink?'

When he returned, we sipped our drinks in silence. The sun had sunk below the horizon now, sending a last burst of cocktail colours seeping up into the pale sky.

'It's lovely here.' I stretched my arms above my head, taking a big lungful of air. 'Hmmm! So good to get away from the grungy ol' city for a while.' And Tom smiled at me, making my heart flip as lightly as a pancake. We talked about our time at art college, albums we loved, old music from the 50s and 60s, what artworks we'd buy for Coventry art gallery given free rein and endless cash. Then conversation turned to favourite books, and foods we liked to cook. It was amazing our tastes were so similar, and also the amount of things that made us both laugh.

An hour or so later, as we walked back towards the van I gave an involuntary shiver. I'd left the hairy cardigan in the van.

'Cold?' said Tom, and before I had time to answer, he'd slipped his jacket round my shoulders. The tan leather was soft and warm.

'It suits you,' he said. 'Put it on properly if you want.'

I slid my arms down the sleeves and my fingers peeped out of the cuffs. He stepped round to the front of me. 'Here, let's get this right.' He gently untucked the collar, then he let his hands rest on my neck and leaned down to kiss me. His lips tasted sweet and malty from the beer.

'Is this alright?' he said, looking down at me.

I put my arms over his shoulders and moved closer. 'Dunno. Do it again and I'll tell you.'

His mouth was warm and the tips of our tongues touched as we kissed. I shut my eyes and ran my forefinger and thumb from the nape of his neck to his crown.

'Mmmm, that's nice,' he said. He pulled me towards him and wrapped me in a hug. I could feel both of our chests hammering.

'How am I supposed to drive now?' he said into my hair. I inhaled the fresh laundry scent of his T-shirt and felt his hands clasped together in the small of my back. My body was humming. When I looked up I saw his eyes were closed.

Finally he took my hand and we walked back to the van.

We were strangely shy on the drive back. As Tom drove through the winding lanes in the dusky half light, past straggly hedges and overhanging trees, there didn't seem to be anything to say, so for once I kept quiet. The sky was now dark, smoky blue, with a deep red band on the horizon, where a single cloud hung, lit golden from below.

'Sometimes I miss the countryside,' I said.

'Would you live anywhere rural again?' Tom asked.

'What?' I chortled. 'One bus an hour, and nowhere to go – you must be joking! I'm an urban convert,' I said.

'Let's get you back to civilisation then.' And the little van revved up a note, as he stuck his foot down.

♫♪

Back at Richmond Road, Tom sat hugging a mug of coffee on the sofa.

'Franki must still be out,' I called from the kitchen, opening and shutting cupboards. 'She's drinking with Simon, saying her goodbyes. Probably stay over at his.'

It felt strange being home, as if we'd been away for ages. I was nervous again, and shameful about the poor state of our house. I let the door slam shut with a despairing sigh.

'What are you looking for?' Tom craned round the sofa to see.

I stepped back into the living room sighing, 'I thought we had bag of sugar somewhere,' I said. 'Can you drink it without?'

'Come here.' He rested his cup on the table and patted the seat beside him. I sat down and he moved over to kiss me. There was the sound of crunching metal from amongst the cushions. Tom reached under me and dug out an empty beer can.

'Let's go upstairs,' I heard myself say.

He put a hand over mine. 'Are you sure?'

Before my brain could catch up with my heart, I curled my fingers round his, and stood to lead the way.

My bedroom was small, but I'd decorated the white walls with prints and little pieces of art. 'Nice room,' said Tom as I turned, then he cupped my face in his palms and kissed me again. I bent down to unzip my boots and kicked them off. Once I was shoeless he was even taller. I draped my arms round his neck. 'How's the weather up there?'

Tom put a hand to his forehead and groaned. 'Altitude sickness – may have to lie down.'

With his hands round my waist, he manoeuvred me round, backed back and sat on the bed, pulling me gently towards him. I stepped forward, tripped on my boots and he caught me as I tipped on top of him. 'Sorry, sorry,' I said, laughter and nerves bubbling into mild hysteria. 'I'd join a circus, but they wouldn't take the risk.'

'I'd better pin you down for your own protection.' He rolled us both over so we were lying along the bed. Our legs entwined and I wrapped my ankles around his. I heard a thud on the carpet as he prised off each of his shoes. 'What a gentlem…,' I murmured, as he kissed me again. Then his mouth left mine and I felt a trail of kisses butterfly across my collar bone to my shoulder.

'There are laws about that,' I groaned, as he kissed the delicate skin in the bend of my elbow.

'Let's break them all,' he said.

I wriggled out of my ski pants, like a snake shedding skin, giggling as he knelt at the bottom of the bed and tugged at the ankles. When I was free, I sat up and pulled his T-shirt over his head. The money in his jeans jangled, as they hit the floor. I buried my head in his chest and inhaled a faintly seaside aroma of sun-baked skin and salt. He pushed me gently down and kissed my belly. I ran both of my hands up through the back of his hair and then down his spine. He shivered and moved away. We were lying on our sides.

'You're lovely.' He stroked his hand slowly down my side, dipping into my waist and over my hip, '– and shaped like a guitar.' He raised an eyebrow and grinned.

'Thank god. If I was shaped like a piccolo it could be a whole different story,' I said.

'Come here.' He pulled me towards him and we kissed me again. Then our remaining restraint was swept away, along with our underwear.

'Oh god, you better stop doing that,' he said after a while. We lay on our backs, panting. I wanted him with every cell in my body.

'Are you sure?' I said.

He rolled his eyes to the ceiling, grinning. 'No.' And he placed his hands on my cheeks and brought my mouth towards his. I gasped as he entered me. There was a strength and tenderness between us which was beyond words. We moved together, eyes interlocked, until I could no longer keep mine open. The dark, warm space in my head, was pulsing with orange, violet and red. I heard my voice cry out and there was a new kind of urgency in Tom. He reached out, briefly touching my face with his fingertips. I pressed my nails into the firm flesh of his buttocks. 'Oh Jesus!' His face creased and relaxed, then he collapsed on top of me and breathed into the pillow.

We lay still for a long time, bodies slick with sweat and hearts thumping. Eventually, he raised himself on one elbow and lay stroking my hair. We gazed at each other, as if we'd just discovered something unexpected.

'Hello you,' he said and smiled.

I frowned. 'Sorry, have we met?' I said.

There was a second's uncertainty in his eyes, followed by a huge guffaw and a well-deserved poke in the ribs. I squealed and socked him with a cushion. And when we'd finally had our fill of fooling around with soft furnishings, we started to kiss and did it all again.

And for once I had no thoughts of the past, the future – or even about work the next day.

10

JOSIE

Amazingly, Tom returned the next evening – and then the next.

'You're not sick of the sight of me?' he asked in the third week.

'I'll let you know if that happens,' I replied, pulling him in to the living room. 'Right now I just want you for your body.'

He gave a saucy laugh. 'Sounds great.'

'No, I mean I want to draw you – clothed, that is.'

Tom mugged disappointment. But then he agreed to lie along the couch, one leg straight and the other knee raised, reading the paper, so I could sketch him while we chatted.

He was so easy to talk to, and interested in everything I was – art, social issues, and music of course. I wasn't sure what sort of 'thing' we were getting into. But I knew that whether we were lounging around looking at art books, talking about films, or listening to Ally's R&B records on my old Dansette player, it felt easy and natural.

Tom told me how he'd started photography. In the school holidays, aged sixteen, he'd made a series about workers, starting at the car factory where his dad worked – men sharing a joke after hours of repetitive work on the car line, his dad out cold in an armchair after a week of night shifts, shiny-faced canteen women dressed in tabards, brandishing ladles at a queue of blokes, all licking their lips in anticipation of hot pot and sponge pudding. Since then he'd chronicled the city's gradual changes – shame-faced men lined up outside the dole office, winos in the park clutching bottles of 'Thunderbird', clashes of football fans in the middle of the road, the cheap shops which shot up like weeds with their 'Everything Must Go!' signs.

He'd made a series about Asian businesses too – waiters polishing glasses for pristine white-clothed tables, and later on, lager-heads falling out of the doors to be sick on the pavement. He'd taken pictures of shy smiling women in saris at sewing machines making jeans, and the sweet shops on Formishill Road. In one photo, the shop owner held out sweets on a silver tray to the camera with a broad smile – mouth-watering cubes of sugar-and-milk confectionary, piled in a pastel-coloured pyramid, flavoured with pistachios, cardamom and rose.

And I saw the images as clearly as if they were in front of us.

One evening Tom taught me how to jive – like his sisters had taught him as a kid. 'Stop trying to lead!' he said, as I flunked another turn and collapsed laughing on the sofa. He pulled me up.

'Come here. You don't have to be in control. Don't think – just let go.'

So I shut my eyes, and let him guide me by the arms and waist, moving as easily as a fish in the tide. When I opened them, he was looking down at me with amusement and something else that made me want to feel his skin on mine again.

'You're a natural,' he said. 'Pity we can't go back thirty years and find a dancehall.'

He spun me round and round on my shiny-soled shoes with his long arm, while he puffed on a cigarette, until I begged for mercy and fell panting on the couch. Then I felt his warm mouth over mine and his hair brushing my forehead and neck and moving down my body. Our clothes peeled away with our sense of time and self until we melted into one, with overpowering joy and relish. That I could become so abandoned and open was both exhilarating and scary.

There were times when his band had gigs out of town. But as soon as they returned he came round. I felt closer to Tom than I'd felt in any other relationship, and I couldn't contemplate a time when I wouldn't see him. Though I knew it was there, just out of vision.

One night he was sitting on my bed, with his head bowed over my old Spanish guitar, tightening the strings to try and tune it. He looked over to where I was sitting cross legged on the floor.

'I've written you a song?' he'd said. 'Wanna hear it?'

It wasn't some soppy love song. The chords were soft, but in a chunky ska rhythm.

A flash of light, a splash of colour
An art school deb, a dancefloor mover
If it's alright, I'm just a fool for
The urban kinda girl

She's kinda bright, not melancholy
Put up a fight and you'll be sorry
If it's alright, I'll hang around
The urban kinda girl

She knows the streets, but she's still classy
You soon find out, she's quick and sassy
If it's alright, I'll stick around
The urban kinda girl

He broke off with a shy smile. 'There's more, but… what do you think?'

'Nobody wrote me a song before.' I grinned like the Cheshire Cat. 'Will you record it?'

His face clouded over. 'We don't really do this kind of thing,' he said.

I got up and ruffled the back of his hair. 'Not for public consumption, you wally,' I said. 'Just for me.'

He smiled again. 'You like it then?'

The next evening, he knocked at my door and handed me a cassette. Written on the case was, *'For Josie, from Tom x'*.

'It's not properly mixed or anything,' he said. 'I did it at home. Just me and my acoustic guitar.'

'Exactly what I wanted,' I said. We stood on the doorstep, looking at each other.

His face was suddenly serious and he took a long breath. 'Listen, I won't be around as much for a few weeks,' he said. 'We've got a big run of tour dates – still trying for our big break.'

'Oh,' I said, adding. 'Hey, that's great!'

Tom was staring at the carpet. 'It's our last rehearsal tonight, then we're off early tomorrow – so I can't even stick around now.' His eyes moved round the floor as if he was searching for something. 'Shit! I wish you had a phone.'

He stepped forward and kissed me lightly on the cheek, then held me tight for a couple of seconds, before pulling away and walking to his van, parked on the opposite side of the street. At the car door he hesitated, then strode across to me again.

'Listen Josie, let me take you to a restaurant when I get back.'

I was surprised. Nobody I knew ate out, and it wasn't just the cost. 'Oo-kay,' I said, trying to sound enthusiastic.

There were only a handful of places to eat in the city – mostly curry houses, frequented by gangs of boorish drunks who treated the waiters with contempt and casual racism. It wasn't a great experience.

'I mean somewhere nice,' he said. 'I'll think about it and stick a note in the post.'

He folded his long body into the driver's seat, shut the door and rolled down the window. 'See ya kid!' he said, raising his hand.

And I made a little return wave, like some sort of army wife.

11

JOSIE

Finally, I'd finished my course, and was to start teaching. The boss, Stan, had asked me to start everyone cooking first. As Barry said, 'Most of them can't recognise food unless someone plonks it on newspaper and asks if they want vinegar.' I was disappointed of course, having planned all sorts of exciting arts activities. But I could see the priorities, and art came second.

I stocked the kitchen, pored through recipe books, and pieced together a programme, based on flour-covered memories of school baking, recollections of solid Northern meat-and-two-veg dinners, and a large dollop of common sense. By now I'd been at the unit long enough to know everyone's names and I'd overheard a lot about how they lived their lives. But at the week's end I was still nervous when Barry, one of the painting and decorating tutors, trooped his group in to me for the official introductions.

First in were skinheads, Darren and Mark – lanky twins with greyish-white complexions and, from what I'd overheard, little imagination – and behind them a tiny Asian boy called Tash. Then there was 'Adolf', the pot-bellied skinhead I'd met on the bus, wearing a shiny green jacket, embellished with swastikas in black felt pen. And finally there was a serious, black lad called Michael, who seemed weighed down by sadness. He surveyed me with heavy, bleak eyes.

They were sixteen, only five years younger than me. And after six months together, they seemed to have reached a grudging recognition that they were lumped together for the duration. But that didn't mean they liked each other – or make them any less daunting. I said a few words of encouragement, but they stared at me without expression.

As their boots tramped out of the kitchen, Barry put out a hand to stop Michael.

'Stan says not to fret about your court case,' he said. 'Go up tomorrow morning and he'll talk you through it.'

The lad nodded.

'Michael – try not to worry lad,' Barry added. The boy nodded again, but his expression hadn't changed as he left.

'They're supposed to have solicitors for all that – but some are bloody useless,' Barry shook his head. Then he clapped his hands together with a full round echo. 'Look, they're not such bad lads, Josie. Just keep 'em busy and don't let arguments develop.'

He picked up his coat from a chair, but a slight frown creased his forehead and he paused. 'Oh yeah, you might get Gob as well. He really only comes in Fridays for Sports. But Stan's not thrown him off the scheme yet, so officially he still exists. He's a bit of a hard nut – too old for us really – but don't take any of his nonsense neither.'

♪

By Monday morning, I was as anxious as a bomb diffuser facing their first ticking device, but determined not to let it show. The awkwardness of being shut in a room with five, testosterone-fuelled, ill at ease youths was palpable. How the hell would I get these big sullen lads to comply? All the other tutors had the advantage of being men. I was a woman with only one initial plan. If it failed, I'd have to resign.

I started right in, while I still had the nerve. After finding out what they could already cook ('Nothin''), why they thought they might need to cook ('In case the chippy burns down?') and countering the reasons against it ('But when I leave home, me bird'll cook fer me, ainit?'), I issued each trainee with an apron, a large frying pan from the rack, a cutting board and knife, two rashers of bacon, one sausage, an egg, some mushrooms, a large tomato, slices of bread and a small dish of baked beans.

'Whose gonna eat it all, Miss?' Tash cradled an egg in both small hands, as though he'd just laid it. His apron was rolled round at the waist several times, but still hung down to his trainers.

'You are – if it's edible.'

Five pairs of eyes stared at me in disbelief.

'I ain't paying for it!' said Darren with disgust.

'It's part of your training – the scheme pays.'

'What's the catch ?' Michael frowned at his food with suspicion.

'The only catch is – if you don't cook it nicely, it won't be good to eat.'

Michael turned to give the items on his board fresh appraisal. He sneaked a couple of sideways glances at my deadpan face.

'You can ask me anything you need to – so think it through carefully before you start.'

I crossed my arms and watched as they each contemplated the raw food spread in front of them. I'd been awake since six that morning and my guts were tight and crampy. I leant back on the tall fridge, so its coolness could seep through my shirt. Nobody moved. I noticed Darren was an inch taller than Mark, and he had the small white worm of a scar behind one ear. Their shaved heads bent over their boards in conspiratorial closeness. Adolf nudged Darren and pointed at his board, where he had arranged his sausage and mushrooms to represent male genitalia. Tash stood biting his lip. Michael stood back, arms folded, and stared at the raw food as if waiting for it to be snatched away.

Mark broke the silence. He spoke in a low voice, as if I couldn't hear from six paces away. 'Nan made scrambled eggs once, I wanna do that,' he said decisively to his brother.

'S'that allowed?' Darren hissed, glancing over his shoulder at me.

'It's my fuckin' egg – she said so.' He turned to address me normally. 'Ain't it Miss?'

'It's your egg,' I agreed. 'Do you know how to do it? You'll need a splash of milk to whisk with it, and some butter to stop it sticking to the pan. They're in that fridge.' I pointed. Mark crossed the floor with uncertainty, watched by the others.

'How about everyone else – are you going to fry or grill your bacon and sausage? Will you fry, boil or poach your egg?' I said conversationally.

'What's poach mean?' said someone. And my heartbeat dropped to a bearable rate, as the session started for real.

After an eventful hour, each trainee carried his plate of burnt and blasted ingredients to the big table with care and ate.

'That's the best grub I eva 'ad,' said Adolf, rubbing his chubby stomach.

'It were a proper 'builder's breakfast' weren't it, Miss?' said Tash.

As I nodded the tense muscles in my neck crunched. The salty smells of seared butter, oil and bacon were making me nauseous.

'When we was workin' in Spool End, sometimes Barry took us to the caff for chip butties, an' he had this. It's the 'Full English', aint it?' Adolf leant back on his chair, brimming with national pride.

'Cost him a packet though,' muttered Michael.

'How much do you think it would cost to make for yourself though?' I said. 'Clear the table and fetch your logbooks, so we can work it out. And please could someone unbolt that hatchway, for some fresh air.'

'I'll do it,' said Adolf, jumping up. If you could ignore the shaven head and felt pen swastikas, he seemed like quite a pleasant lad.

And when they were all engrossed in writing, I looked over at the five trainees hunched at the table, with their books and calculators. Maybe teaching here wouldn't be so hard after all.

♪

12

JOSIE

However, teaching cookery to opposing factions proved more difficult than I'd imagined, and the sessions were peppered with personal questions, which I fought off as best I could.

'Where you get your clothes, Miss? The charity shop?'

'Does your boyfriend dress like a boat person too?'

'How come you stand up for Tash Miss – you goin' with a Paki?'

But I refused to budge. 'You don't need to know about my private life to learn how to cook. And stop being racist.'

I kept to this line of resistance, but they remained united in their curiosity, particularly about my attitudes. And when I failed to react to direct questions, they had to fall back on the familiar.

So, in the second week, both my bicycle lights and my tobacco were stolen. The lights were finally returned to my cycle anonymously, when I pointed out to the air around me, nobody else needed bike lamps and they were too ancient to sell. However, the tobacco remained missing in action, presumably through arson. I'd left it on the table when a timer buzzed and I ran to rescue some jam tarts. I vowed not to drop my guard again.

'You *never* said they wouldn't cook proper, if I turned it up high!' yelled Mark one day, angrily slamming down a dish full of charred lumps – the roast potatoes he couldn't wait to taste. He rounded on me, brandishing the wooden spoon he was using to try and dig them out. 'You *never* said!'

I took a step back. Even wearing a clean apron and acting like a toddler, a big, furious skinhead was still intimidating. 'You're right Mark. I'm sorry, I did forget to say.'

I changed my voice to lecture-mode. 'Okay, everyone listen, timings are absolutely vital. To cook food through to the inside, we need more time and less heat. More heat only crisps the outside.'

'An' these are well crispy, ain't they Miss?' said Tash, prodding at the coal-like mass with a digit.

'I'll fuckin' crisp you, yer little shite!' Mark raised an oven-gloved fist.

'You finished that pie topping yet Tash?' I stepped between them, and pointed Tash back to his chore. 'Right now Mark, we're going to part-boil some potatoes, before roasting them. Let's see how the cooking time is reduced when they start off half cooked.'

These daily incidents tested my patience and ingenuity. Every morning I woke before six, and lay in a sweat, as anxiety danced like snakes in my guts. I tried to keep the peace and stop arguments between the lads before they ignited, but it was like skipping along a minefield.

Tash was my secret favourite, although he drove everyone mad, buzzing round the kitchen like a mosquito, tampering with food and changing the readings on weighing scales. His pranks amused nobody and seemed designed to attract a beating. One Friday morning, I pulled first Darren, and then Mark, off Tash for the umpteenth time, and I finally sent him out of the kitchen for his own protection. When I turned to deal with the others, Darren put his hand on my shoulder and his sad eyes looked at me earnestly.

'Let me take the little Paki outside Miss, and give him a proper lesson,' he said.

'Thank you for that kind offer Darren,' I said. 'But, as you well know, violence doesn't resolve conflict.'

'He *is* an annoying little Pa... I mean bastard, Miss,' said Michael, in a reasonable voice.

'Look, I've asked you all to cut the racist language,' I added, ' And *please* stop calling me Miss.'

Michael sucked his teeth, and said quietly, 'Char! How can I be racist? I t'ought you been to University Miss.' He shook his head before turning to carefully spread jam on his sandwich sponge.

The three skinheads gave me a long look, as I tried to summon up some sort of United Nations address in my head.

I sighed and opened the door. The casual racism by everyone towards Tash was offensive, but often seemed just another way to insult him. The most important thing seemed to be to identify one person they could look down on, then trample on them hard. The skinhead twins took great care to avoid all direct contact with Michael, and vice versa, but in their dislike of Tash the three of them were united.

'Come back in Tash, you better work over there.' I directed him to an empty worktop. 'Pancake batter please, page forty eight.'

'I know about makin' pancakes already,' he said, swaggering over.

'Well now you can practice doing it without annoying anyone,' I said.

Half an hour later, everyone sat eating plates of Tash's fluffy pancakes and waiting for the sponges and scones to bake.

'These are alright, as it goes,' said Adolf, helping himself to a squeeze more lemon.

Tash's smile was smug. 'Me Mum showed me, ainit?' he said. 'I can do chapattis and parathas too.'

The skinheads automatically pulled faces and made vomiting sounds.

'What we doin' this afternoon Miss?' said Michael. 'Cos I got a 'lickle bizzniss' to take care of in the dinner break.'

'We got Sports Afternoon, Miss?' said Mark.

By now I hated sports, even more than I had at school

'We're going roller skating with Barry's group,' I said with a sinking heart.

The pancakes bounced, as several fists thumped the table.

'Fuckin' ace!'

I should have been glad that they all agreed on something.

♪

At the roller rink, ten lads piled out of our minibus and rushed in, shoving and jumping up on each other's backs. As Barry locked the van, Gob, the lanky skinhead who was supposed to be in my group, sloped round the corner, a set of skates slung over his back.

'Oirrght Bazza. Oiiright Miss Josie.' He leered at me. 'Thought I'd come an' do a little skatin', seein' as I'm the best in Coventraay.'

'Hello Gob. You coming back on the scheme then?' said Barry.

The lad spat on the pavement, then cracked his knuckles one by one. 'You kiddin' man. Cooking's for birds, ainnit?' He turned to me. 'You gonna show us how to skate, Miss?'

I gave a nervous laugh. 'I don't think so.'

Gob walked to the entrance, shaking his head in disappointment.

'You'll have to do it,' said Barry in a low voice, as we watched him disappear. 'Or they won't respect you.'

'They don't anyway, I said. 'And do I really want the respect of a load of kids who only live to beat the shit out of each other?'

'Now, now,' said Barry laughing. 'I thought you were a big, lefty liberal.'

'That was before I worked with this lot.' I pulled a face. 'My liberal soul curled up and died in week three.'

The cavernous skating rink smelt of mould and sweaty socks. Pop music boomed out from huge speakers, which hung from the corrugated iron roof. The trainees were pulling on their boots, and trying to elbow each other off the benches. I spotted Tash sitting on his own, delicately tying knots in his laces. Barry passed me a set of heavy skates with scuffed blue wheels. I took my time putting them on, lashing them as solidly as possible, the plastic hard and unforgiving on my ankle bones. On the rink, the lads started zooming round, still pushing and jumping each other. We had exclusive use of the rink for our session, which was just as well.

'Come on Josie – showtime.' Barry helped me up by the elbow, and guided me to the barrier.

'Barry, I can't,' I said with wide eyes. 'I've absolutely no sense of balance on skates.'

'Don't worry, I'll help you round,' he said.

Barry wasn't much faster than me, but his stocky form seemed at one with gravity in a way my taller body wasn't. At every movement, I buckled forwards and backwards in the middle and my skates threatened to roll out from under me. Barry kept a firm grasp on my arm and I held my back straight. We progressed round the edge of the rink like two pensioners. After a while, the tension in my abdomen began to relax, and I even pushed out a few extra strides to keep pace. I glanced at the middle of the rink. Three of the bigger lads circled Tash, and were pushing him roughly from one to another like a toy on wheels. He suddenly crouched down and made a breakthrough in the gap between them. Then he skated off backwards, giving them the finger. They all gave chase with a roar.

'He's on a suicide mission that one,' said Barry, then yelled, 'Oi lads! No fighting or I'll send you all off.'

'You'll have to come and get us first, granddad!' shouted Mark, and everyone laughed. But they seemed to have been distracted from their mission.

Darren and Gob loomed up behind us. 'How ya doin', Miss? You're gettin' quite good.'

'Thanks Darren.' I stared ahead, using all my concentration to keep my body vertical.

'Why don't we take you round?' said Gob. And, before either of us could object, they squeezed in either side, seized me under the arms, and I was snatched away like a field mouse in the claws of an owl.

'Byeee!' Gob called to Barry and we accelerated into the centre of the rink at an alarming rate. The music changed to high energy disco. I was aware of a whir of wheels and blur of legs pumping past. We were flashing round the circuit, right in the thick of it. I was so terrified I couldn't breathe. *Stop, stop!* I willed. But their hands were firmly fastened round my upper arms and I could see their denim thighs moving like pistons on either side.

'Don' worry, Miss, we got you now.' Gob's voice was full of nasty laughter. We banked round and, against all odds, they increased speed even more. Then as we headed towards the far end, I was abruptly released and found the barrier flying towards me.

I heard Barry's voice somewhere crying, 'Brake, brake!' And I thought, *I know I will!'* Seconds later I rammed into the side barrier and everything went black.

♪

Back at home, holding an ice pack to my head, I prepared to face another exhausted and lonely night in with the telly. Tom had been away for almost two weeks, and I'd begun to wonder if I would ever see him again. After all, we'd made no promises of any sort, and surely he was on the point of leaving town altogether.

The doorbell rang, but I lay still. The day's bruising to body and pride, left me in no state to deal with some poverty-pleading scally selling dusters. But a second knock followed the first.

'Alright, *I'm coming!'* With a melodramatic tut I hauled myself up from the couch and opened the door. 'Tom, you're back!' I dropped the hand holding my ice bag, in surprise.

'What's up?' He stepped in and kissed me lightly on the forehead. 'Ew, cold!'

I grinned. It was fantastic and amazing that he'd come round again.'Bit of headache after a crap day at work.'

'Need someone to sort out the big boys?' he said with a teasing grin.

I sighed. 'Just lock them up and throw away the key.'

'Hey, it's not like you to be glum. Come here.' He wrapped me in his arms and I felt as safe as if he was a bullet proof vest, until a little voice inside said, *Careful Josie, don't get used to this.*

'Cuppa?' I said.

He gave my upper arms a last squeeze before dropping his hold. Then he gazed at me with his head on one side, smiling.

'What's wrong?' I said. 'Something disgusting on my face?'

'No way,' he said. Then his eyes flickered as he remembered. 'Sorry, can't stop. Just dropped by to say we've got a gig at the Students Union on Saturday – tomorrow.'

'You're playing *here*? Wow, that's great!' My gloomy mood washed away with excitement.

'D'you think you'll come?' Tom asked, and I saw a hint of shyness in his face.

'Of course!' I said. 'I'll bring Simon.'

'I'll put you both on the guest list then.' He looked at his watch. 'Oh shit, sorry, really gotta go – we've a long rehearsal, which will be tough enough without me being late.' He put his hand up to my cheek, suddenly serious. 'Josie I want you to know something…'

'What?' I knew this moment would come. I tensed, readying myself for the worst.

Tom looked awkward. 'It's just that…' His eyes searched mine, as though deciding something. Finally he smiled. 'Look, you better take some aspirin for that poorly head, and I'll see you soon.'

I shut the door and stood for several moments, my hand resting lightly on my cheek where his had been. I closed my eyes to reconstruct the image of his face, and wondered what he was about to tell me. Then I realised what he'd said. I was finally going to see Tom play live!

13

JOSIE

'Down't know why I let yow talk me into this.' As we walked down to the Polytechnic buildings, Simon's Brummy drawl was at its most doleful.

'You owe me,' I said. 'You promised me that film wasn't scary, but I spent the whole time with my hands over my eyes.'

'Honestly! Yer such a big poof.' He punched me lightly on the arm.

'Takes one to know one,' I retorted, and we bickered playfully until we got to the Poly.

'Blimin' eck, wharra crowd,' said Simon. Outside the Union building, a sizeable, and mostly male, mob had congregated – students, townies and regular Coventry gig-goers, including quite a few black lads, which surprised me. There were also quite a lot of skinheads, kitted out in the usual fashion – tight, half mast jeans, Doc Marten boots, smart, well-pressed polo shirts and braces. In amongst the jaunty pork pie hats, and tousled student hair, their white shaved heads shone like lightbulbs.

'We'll be eaten alive,' said Simon, then added, 'Often an attractive opportunity, but that's one ugly-looking bunch.'

'Come on yer big jessie,' I said with false bravado. 'We'll stand at the back away from all the moshing.'

Simon stopped and raised an accusing eyebrow. 'What the flippin' eck's that?'

'You know,' I said airily. 'Barging around with elbows, jumping up and down and stuff.'

'Oh Christ!' His tone was testy. 'You forgot to mention we were going to spend the evening being rammed by skinheads.'

'Not us. We're going to find some little nook at the back from where we can observe the band and their most ardent fans.'

'Who'll all be moshing?' Simon was firmly stuck to the spot.

'Who may –,' I took his arm to coax him on. '– in a moment of high excitement, break into an occasional mosh.'

Simon laughed. 'You're so full of shit,' he said. 'I warn you, the minute one of those pseudo-Nazis touches my arse I'm leaving. Call it what yer like, but I know man-on-man action when I see it.'

We eased our way into the noisy crowd. There were groans and complaints all around.

'Oi! We all wanna fuckin' get in,' said one pock-faced lad.

Alarmed that Simon would bottle out, I edged between another two angry big lugs and shouted, 'Scuse me, staff here – let us through!' I clamped one hand onto the bottom of Simon's denim jacket and yanked him behind me, like a toddler dragging a teddy bear.

'Hey! Who you pushin'?' said one big guy.

'We're Union staff,' I said. 'If you want to get this queue moving, let us through.'

'Oh bloodaayell!' muttered Simon in despair, behind me.

'Orright then.' The big lug turned round and shoved a passageway alongside him. 'Let the two blond tarts in, they're staff!' He pushed a smaller guy aside, with meaty hands. I wasn't sure if he was being funny or just assumed anyone with hair was female.

'Charming,' Simon muttered, as I hauled him onwards.

'Just keep up!' I yelled back.

There was further resistance at the front. Those who could see into the venue were straining like greyhounds. A couple of thin-limbed students at a desk were nervously taking money and admitting people one by one. Beside them was planted a solid-looking professional bouncer who, judging from the welt in his eyebrow and long scar down his temple, appeared to face trouble head on.

'We're on the guest list.' I stared imploringly into flat black eyes.

He looked unimpressed. 'Names.' He repeated these in a grunt to the students, who fished out a crumpled paper from under their cash box. They studied the list and shook their heads.

'You said he promised!' hissed Simon, glancing at those shoving behind.

'We're Tom Shepperton's guests,' I said to the fresh-faced youth on the desk. 'We're on the band's list.'

'Oh right,' he turned the paper over. 'Josie and Simon – any ID?'

'You're joking!' I felt someone's boot catch me in back of the leg, and sensed people were realising we'd got through on false pretences.

Through the chink under the bouncer's elbow, I saw a familiar figure in a sharp suit strolling downstairs with a brimming pint. Vinnie only dressed that smartly if playing. He must be in Tom's band.

'Vinnie!' I hollered as loudly as possible.

'Hiya!' He waved and turned to go down a corridor.

'Vinnie, get us in!' I yelled before he could disappear.

He sauntered over. 'What's up?' he said to the students. A couple of shouts came from the crowd, prompting Vinnie to offer a lob-sided grin and give the thumbs up to a few people he recognised.

'Just need to ID these two,' said the student with an aura of self importance. He pointed at our names and Vinnie grinned at me, chewing his gum. For a moment I thought he was going to pretend not to know us, for a laugh.

'Yeah, that's them,' he said finally. 'Better let them in before they get mashed.'

We squeezed past the big bouncer, who immediately re-filled the door frame with his bulk. Vinnie stepped back into the hallway, away from the those filing in. He looked pleased. 'You've come to see me play then?'

'Wouldn't miss it,' I said quickly. 'You remember Simon?'

'Orright.' Vinnie nodded to Simon. 'Better get backstage or Shepperton will give me more grief. See ya later.'

As we started up the stairs, he called, 'Hey Josie! Stay away from the front. Gets a bit lively, if you know what I mean.' And he was gone.

I turned to Simon who was planted on the stairs, arms folded, as people pushed past. 'I don't believe you,' he said. 'You knew it was going to be this rough?'

'C'mon, he's just being cautious.' I strode up the steps, aware that Simon had witnessed Vinnie borrowing money he couldn't repay, chatting up women with big, jealous boyfriends standing feet away, and staggering around town after a skinful of beer.

'Oh yeah, I forgot, he's big on caution!' Simon called after me.

But he followed me up to the bar queue. 'You're buying,' he said factually, as our pints were pulled.

We threaded our way back down, through people streaming upstairs for drinks. As the main hall doors swung open, we were assaulted by the noise from a four piece band on stage – a crude mix of punk and rock. A fat, pink-faced bloke was bawling out lyrics and wiping sweat from his brow, the drummer bashed away like a kid on pots and pans, and the lead guitarist was twanging his instrument and lurching round the stage. In front, a small jam of ardent supporters were dancing wildly. Occasionally someone writhed up in a pogo, like an electrocuted eel, and the crowd wobbled and barged each other as his body crash-landed.

I steered Simon to a space at the back. 'Fuckin' awful!' he mouthed, as he found a piece of wall to lean against and nurse his pint. It was going to cost in beer money to keep him happy.

Worried-looking stewards, dotted around the big hall, were relaying a message from person to person, through energetic yelling. Despite their black T-shirts announcing 'SU STAFF' in white capitals, they did not exude collective control. Something was going down.

I looked over at Simon, watching the support band with disinterest. Wedged in his left ear, I spotted one of the yellow earplugs issued by the Poly's sculpture department. The band finally issued their final shattering chords and the lardy singer raised a balled fist. This triumphant finish was undermined by a plastic pint which curled towards the stage, and bounced off his belly so dregs of beer spattered his shirt. He responded by giving the finger to the whole audience, and was cheered. Several more items rained down as the band trouped off, still gesturing. SU staff scuttled onto the stage and cleared the debris.

People were pouring in. Blokes outnumbered girls by about twenty to one, and the air was heavy with smoke and male energy.

The PA system was offering punk and reggae in turn, with the crowds baying and jeering their allegiances as each track started. Every so often a ripple of disturbance could be seen in the welling bodies and shouting was heard from a core where the scuffle had broken out. The room felt as if it was just one accidentally spilt pint away from a riot.

I stood on tiptoes to try and see the stage, gradually being blocked from view by a forest of shaved heads, hats and large, leather-clad or square-suited shoulders. When the place was full, I wouldn't be able to see Tom from our position at all.

'Let's go nearer,' I mouthed to Simon, standing with his arms folded. He pulled a face and shook his head. So I moved foreward alone, squeezing into a knot of rockabillies in checked shirts and shiny black bomber jackets.

'Stand 'ere love.' A big bloke with sideburns and hair sprouting from the neck of his shirt, pointed to a gap in front of him. His sleeves were rolled up, displaying the image of a be-quiffed cartoon cat on his forearm.

'Vagabond Kats,' he said when he saw me staring.

'Cool,' I replied, though strictly speaking tattoos were for sailors, ex-cons, old and skinheads. I was aware of being a sole female surrounded by much machismo. And, for the hundredth time, Franki's absence felt as sore as a newly missing tooth.

The PA music faded and a student compère arrived on stage. Despite his Che Guevara T-shirt and green army trousers, he looked quite effete, so was greeted with an outburst of wolf whistles.

'And now for the moment you've all been waiting for!' He shouted over the catcalls. 'Masters of ska – Original Mix!' He stalked off, giving a rather camp salute.

The noise from the floor was ear-numbing, as the band strolled from a door at the side of the room and onto stage. The drummer came first, waving his sticks at the crowd – a heavy set black guy, who tossed long dreadlocks over his shoulders as he settled down behind the kit. Behind him was a pallid skinhead with a cheeky smile, dressed in jeans and red braces, carrying a bass guitar which he plugged into a big amplifier. He was followed by a cute black kid, who wore a jacket over jeans. He took up position behind the keyboards, flexing his fingers and eyeing the crowd nervously. Vinnie sauntered on then, guitar slung over his shoulder like a rifle. Tom was behind him, also wearing a sharp suit, but cradling his instrument in an arm. He seemed to melt into the background – blocked from view by Vinnie. And finally the two last musicians arrived – a tall, skinny black guy in a pork pie hat, grinning widely as he leant down to slap hands with the people in front of the stage, and an attractive white guy with a disdainful look, who stood behind the front man's mic.

I recognised the lead singer as Eddy Knowles, formerly of 'Eddy and the Know-alls', who'd had a brief period of local fame in my first year. He took hold of the microphone and gave the crowd in front of him a derisive sneer. The noise subsided into an expectant hush. 'Yo Eddaaay!' yelled a voice. Ignoring the cry, Eddy held up a commanding hand and gave a single click with his fingers to the band behind him. The keyboards flew into a four bar riff and the three guitarists punched in on cue, followed by the drums and bass, which picked up a chunky, fast ska/reggae beat.

Eddy took a step forward and began to sing, glowering at the audience, his voice a mixture of plaintive harmony and angry incantation,

> *'We've got to live in this crap city*
> *Think of your neighbours, black and white*
> *It's not their fault it ain't that pretty*
> *It takes a tough man not to fight.'*

The rest of the band and all the audience, joined in with the last line,

Put down the knife man!

The crowd surged forward, pulling me along, like I was part of a cluster of magnetised iron filings. In the middle of the song, the guitarist with the pork pie hat, swung his instrument round his back, and ran to the front of the stage. Sweat poured down his dark forehead from under his jaunty brim as he chanted,

'Goin' to try some lovin'
Spread the joy around
Now we're all together
Need to make some sound!'

He held his microphone up to the audience and there was a roar – then he began careening round the stage in a half running/half dancing style, chanting out more lyrics as he went. I realised this must be what Tom meant by 'toasting'. The band cranked up the pace, and I was lifted up and down by the crazed knee-pumping dancing going on all around me. Vinnie started a fast guitar solo, striding backwards and forwards as he played, throwing out riffs, which he ended with a flourish, one knee bent and shaking the stem of his guitar at the audience. He was trying to look serious and cool, but I detected a pleased grin playing round his pursed lips.

And, behind him, Tom finally came into view, stepping forward and glancing at Vinnie to see what he was doing. One hand ran up and down the frets of his guitar and the other picked at the strings like a harpist's, filling melodic notes between Vinnie's lightning flourishes. The stage was filled with organised pandemonium – Vinnie's manic showcasing, the crazy dancing, Eddy's snarling posture, the drummer's dreadlock's spraying out as he pounded out rhythms, the young keyboard player, absorbed in a never-ending series of fast chords, and the thin guy in skinhead gear, who thumped a big Doc Marten boot in time with his bass line. It was as if the stage was perched on the edge of anarchy – the real punk thing – a sense that anything might happen.

To the left, Tom was like a pool of calm. His head was bowed over his guitar, slightly on one side as though listening to the whole band, whilst his fingers ran up and down the strings. He seemed removed from the room, from the sweat and smoke and pounding feet – as though he was inside the music looking out. When he looked over at the rest of the band, his face was thoughtful, eyes screwed slightly against the spotlights. A lick of hair fell down as his attention returned to his hands. A surge of emotion and longing rose in my chest. A thought popped up and repeated like a mantra, beating in time to the music, '*I could be falling in love.*' And as the thought took shape, the room seemed to close in on me.

♪

I'd begun having my recurring nightmare again. Though more than a decade old, it still seemed every bit as real as the yellowing news clippings, or the memorial printed for the church service. Its images were now as familiar as the faces of my brother Ally's ashen-faced school friends, when they'd given their evidence at the inquest.

In my dream it is always dark. Ally and his friends come running over the top of the mountain in their crunchy cagoules, backpacks bobbing. I watch them from the clouds, where my disembodied self floats in dread. Ally's favourite teacher, is bringing up the rear. 'Careful on this scree!' he shouts. But the boys are whooping, sliding sideways down the steep side of stone chips, as if their walking boots were roller skates. Ally is at the front. He's looking back and raising his hand, palm flat against the wind, keeping perfect balance as he gains momentum, sliding and scraping downwards. 'Look round Ally!' I try to scream. But I make no sound. I see the laughter and life in his eyes one last time. Then I am floating by the ledge below the cliff on which he lies, head thrown back at an impossible angle. The other boys are craning over the top and calling. I am pleading with him, 'Wake up Ally, open your eyes, wake up!' His arm is stretched back hanging over the long drop down the mountainside, his hand grey and lifeless. Beneath the craggy cliff, the moors are carpeted in soft dark heather, and dotted with grazing sheep. Now there is only the two of us. 'Wake up Ally!' I can't bear the searing pain inside me. I look down and where my stomach should be is a deep red bowl – empty and shiny as liver. I cradle my empty belly and start to howl. How can I live with no guts? 'Ally, Ally!' Hot tears fall from onto his neck, which is twisted so awkwardly.

Last week, I'd woken up before the part where my parents walk away down the long black road, their arms round each others sunken shoulders, unaware of me struggling to run after them, laden – as I always am – with Ally's huge backpack. And I'd gazed at Tom's head on the pillow over at the other side of the bed, his cheek eerily pale in the darkness of the room and his right arm was stretched out towards me. I put my hand out to touch him, but he was just out of reach. I looked down between us, to see the sharp fall of cliffs and the sheep, heads down in the heather. My heart raced. I grabbed Tom's cheek and pulled his face towards me. His eyes were empty sockets. *No!* I tried to put his arms around me, but they were unresponsive, dead weight. Looking down at my stomach I saw it was now a mass of red and white innards – tubes of unnamed swirling offal. 'Oh god, how am I going to keep this in?' I thought.

'Josie, Josie! Wake up.' Tom's soft breath on my face had been tobaccoey and human. His arm pushed under my back and he pulled me towards him. 'You okay? Sounded like you were hyperventilating?' I burrowed my head in his chest. 'Weird dreams,' I mumbled. 'Scary'

'C'mere.' He wrapped me in both arms. 'I'll keep the monsters away.'

And I'd drifted back to sleep with the sound of his heart's rhythm pumping in my ear, my wet face sticking to his smooth skin, and the realisation I was becoming dangerously attached to him.

♪

At the Students' Union, as I crumpled in the crush of pounding bodies, someone's hands heaved me up from under the armpits. 'Steady on love!' The bloke with the sideburns was laughing as he righted me. The audience surged forward, dragging me sideways in the flailing mass.

The air was sticky with beer fumes and sweat and my gelatinous legs were sucked up off the floor. Around me pork pie hats and 'suedehead' cuts bobbed, and the floor vibrated under the stomping of boots. The heat and movement were starting to make me feel sick now. The band cranked up the tempo once more, and I caught sight of the toaster bloke pacing round the stage like a caged panther and Eddy leaning over the audience, eyes like dark hollows in his smooth oval face as he sang,

'We're tomorrow's generation
If tomorrow ever comes
We can face the day together
If we put away our guns'

Someone's knee knocked into my thigh as I was pummelled by several elbows and knocked further forward. From the side, more people poured in – streaming through a fire exit door which a couple of SU staff were trying to push shut, their shouting pointless against the jubilant cries of the gatecrashers – skinheads and 'townies', shoving and jumping their way in. In the wedge of bodies, I couldn't breathe. I had to get out. The band crashed into the opening chords of a song called, 'Wasteland'. Everyone sang along with the words. Tom was striking chunky reggae-like chords, keeping eye contact with the drummer, whose hands which were now pattering out conga beats. Eddy's deadpan voice sent more doom-laden lyrics over the top of the joyous melodies, like thunder clouds rolling over a summer's day. It was the perfect blend of dark and light, pessimism and hope. And suddenly I understood what had brought all these disparate groups here. This band knew what it was to be pissed off, poor, angry, and trapped in a small forgotten city, with no aspirations for the future. They knew that the only joy now was music.

I looked at all the bouncing faces turned upwards to the stage – lit with excitement, singing out in ecstasy and, as the energy round me seeped in, my panic lifted. I stopped trying to resist the movement of the crowd, and let myself be carried with it, bobbing up and down, grinning like everyone else. Gradually I was shoved to the front of the stage. Above me I saw Eddy's slim cut trousers and the toaster guy's dog tooth jacket as he romped past, his deep voice rolling patois into the microphone. Vinnie went down on one knee to produce a waterfall of notes in a bluesy cry. He looked over and winked at me, shaking the neck of his guitar as if wringing out the last few drops from a bottle. I found myself laughing out loud. The music had tapped into a seam of something sad and bleak inside me, and now it bubbled up like larva. I looked for Tom. He was interspersing chords with delicious runs of notes. I was glad he hadn't noticed me, so I could soak up the sight of him – his lean frame, the mop of hair he was too busy to brush back, his curve of his long neck, his high cheekbones, and the slight pulse of his hips as he played.

Towards the end of the gig, a couple of blokes grabbed the opportunity to jump up on stage and start dancing. Tom looked up to the drummer, giving a wide smile, which he returned with affirmative nods. I felt several hands on my shoulders, as people levered themselves forward and up. Two stewards at one side of the stage screamed at their counterpoint opposite, but he held hands out helplessly, palms up. The toaster bloke wore a big kid's grin and even Eddy Knowles looked as though he was hiding a smile underneath his mask of indifference. The room was now packed and the stage was full – white and black kids, students and skinheads, all alive with energy and music. As Vinnie moved forwards he swung the neck of his guitar over the heads of several gangly youths and Tom bent down to extricate a lead from round someone's boots. From my vantage point at the front, I saw the stage bending under the beating of feet.

As the space around me opened up, I squeezed out to the back where I found Simon, smoking and jiggling round to the music, no sign of earplugs.

'Not goin' on stage?' He yelled with mock surprise.

'This is their last song. Let's go, before we're crushed trying to get out,' I said. 'The heat's made me feel a bit sick.'

Outside we gulped in lungfuls of cool night air and I flung my arms out to embrace the space around me. Simon took my arm. 'Chips,' he said in a decisive tone. And we set off up the hill.

Despite our early departure, a sizeable queue was stretching out of the chippy. The woman we called 'Beehive Brenda' was shovelling and wrapping chips as fast as she could, as her bulldog husband dangled two pieces of battered fish over the fryer like wet flannels. He stood back as they hit the oil, spitting and hissing. 'Four minutes for fish!' he yelled, turning back for more.

'Anyone just want chips?' said Brenda. And she rolled her eyes, when about twenty people shouted, 'ME!'

Simon and I waited our turn just inside the doorway, making our own entertainment by nudging and poking each other in the sides. I got him in such a ticklish spot that he squealed and jumped backwards.

'Oi! Fuckin' well watch it!'

'Oops, sorry.' Simon had backed into two tall skinheads trying to exit. Laughter fell off his face like a skipper dumping concrete, and he quickly retreated out to the pavement.

'Oiright darling?' The first bloke gave me a leery gap-toothed smile and I saw it was Gob.

After the skating incident, Stan had said he'd kick Gob off the scheme. I wondered if he knew this. We were both crammed in the doorway, his neck about a hand stretch from mine, the tattoo of a spider creeping out from under his T-shirt collar. I pressed myself against the doorframe. He moved his face closer. 'Say hi to the kids for me,' he said and a flicker of defiance shot across his cold eyes. 'I'm in Court next week. Mightn't see them for a while.'

I didn't move.

Gob peered at me, then shook his head slowly, as if I was ultimately a disappointing spectacle.

'You better keep 'im away from Green Woods.' He jerked his chin towards Simon, who looked ready to run. 'We don't like queers up there. But yerrin luck tonight, 'cos I've got me chips.' His voice was factual, as if he was relating the bus times.

With a last hard look, he brushed past me, and his mate followed. We watched their tight half mast jeans plod brazenly down the hill, and people straggling up the pavement dipped into the gutter to avoid them.

'Shall I shout *'nice arse'*?' said Simon when they were truly out of ear shot. 'It's lovely you're making such nice new friends by the way.'

'He'll be back in prison soon,' I said.

'Oh goody – does that mean I'll be able to visit Green Woods – wherever the fuck that is?'

We could be as witty as we liked now we weren't so scared.

A while later we lay along my bed, propped up by pillows, listening to reggae and swigging cans of lager.

'There's something weirdly sexual about all that skinhead gear.' Simon popped another chip in his mouth, and ruminated. 'It's like army uniform.'

'You mean you respond to the one hundred and fifty percent of testosterone that's squeezed inside the clothes?' I said.

'Maybe,' he said. 'You know I once dated a squaddie in Birmingham?'

'You told me,' I said. 'Mr. Six Times A Night, then Fifty Pushups Before Breakfast,'

'Very happy days,' said Simon. 'Except he was terrified someone would find out he was gay, so he called it off, in case he got court martialled or something. Talking of secrets, what's going on with mister Smooth Guitar?'

'Nothing really – he just comes round and we hang out together.'

'Horizontally.'

'No, not all the time. We listen to music and talk a lot.'

'About what?'

'You know, films, music, art, what we want to be when we grow up – the usual shit. It's hard to explain.' I grinned to myself. It was just as well depressive Howard had never moved in, to burst the bubble. I was paying more rent – but as long as I had a job, Simon nearby, and Tom there whenever he could be, living alone was okay.

'Don't you ever go out together?' said Simon.

'Not really – but I prefer it like this. None of that annoying girlfriend-boyfriend stuff.' I wondered if this was really true.

'Well as long as it's fun and he doesn't break your heart.'

'Like how?'

'He's a musician duck – it's in the small print. Besides aren't Original Mix getting quite well known? Someone at the gig said 'Wasteland' might even chart.'

I breathed out a surprisingly big sigh. Simon turned.

'Flippin' 'eck, look at your face. Didn't you know you might be sleeping with a pop star?'

'It's hardly fucking pop!' I said.

'Hey, grumpy cow – is it that time of the month again?'

A little thought tugged at the hem of my consciousness. 'No it bloody isn't. As a matter of fact, my periods stopped,' I said. 'The doctor says it's the stress of my job.'

'All I'm saying is don't get too attached.' He peered at me for a while and then wriggled his arm under my neck, pulling me into a cuddle. 'Oh deary me, it's already too late isn't it?' he said and gave me a squeeze. 'Don't worry, Uncle Simon will be here if it all gets complicated.'

I sat up and hugged my knees, considering if it already was.

'Want the last chips? You didn't have many.'

I shook my head. 'Not got much appetite nowadays.'

'Yes, you do look pretty scrawny,' Simon said. 'I thought cooks were supposed to be fat and jolly.'

'I'm not a friggin' cook!' I said.

'Ooh, sorry. What are you then?' Simon pouted at me.

I stared at him, thinking, and hugged my legs even tighter.

'Christ Simon, I just don't know any more.'

♫♪

14

JOSIE

We were making iced fruit cakes – this being the group's last week with me. It was the zenith of my self-devised cookery programme, which I'd decided to call, 'From boiled egg to Christmas cake in six weeks' if anyone asked. They never had. All the other lads were out on site and, without the usual backdrop of whirring lathes, calls, laughs and curses, there was an unaccustomed silence.

In our domain, however, the two rooms were hot and heavy with cakey smells and spices, and with Tash at court for his hearing, the kitchen had settled into a rare and companionable peace. Adolf and Darren were wiping flour and cake dough from the surfaces, while Mark washed up bowls, wearing big yellow rubber gloves, which protected the grime in his fingernails from being dislodged.

'Nah man, you missed a bit,' said Michael, who was drying mixing bowls with a towel. He pointed a long brown digit at the stubborn food and plopped it back into the washing up water.

''S'not my fault, I can't see proper – you need a better light over the sink Miss.' Mark scrubbed at the bowl, rinsed it with piping hot water and handed it back.

'That's better,' Michael said, sucking his teeth. 'Jus' watch what you're doing. Don't wan' no food poisoning thank you.'

From the counter, I looked up from a Royal Icing recipe, surprised at the comparative civility of this exchange, and wondered if they'd actually learned something after all. The main door outside creaked open and there was the sound of cautious footfalls on the concrete floor.

'Hello?' a voice called. The feet came in through our anteroom and appeared at the open door of the kitchen. ''Ere you are – where is everyone?'

Gob took in the kitchen set up at one glance.

'Orright!' Mark and Darren looked up in bashful awe, as though minor royalty had appeared, and Adolf grinned. I removed a cake out from the oven and placed it on a mesh rack to cool.

'I'm alright, as it goes,' Gob said, chewing lazily on some gum. I peeled the greaseproof paper from the sides of the cake, keeping watch from the corner of my eye. The body movements were casual, but his eyes darted round the room like a lizard's.

'So – yer miss me at Sports? Stan don't want me goin' no more.' He sneered as he chewed. 'Don't give a fuck what that old git says, it's a free country. I'll be there when I fancy it.' He looked over my shoulder at the cakes. 'These lot make *them*?'

I gave a slow nod, 'Uh hmmm.'

Against all my rules, Darren swung up onto the freezer and sat rotating his feet. I felt the other three watching to see what I would do.

'Darren, could you please take out the last cake?' I asked, still fiddling with the paper on the other one. He flashed a glance at Gob, who was lounging against the door frame.

'Whose is it?' he said, adding. 'I ain't touching anythin' that little Paki made.'

We all knew Tash baked his cake the day before and this comment was just for show.

'It's yours.' I looked into the oven's window, adding, 'The biggest.'

Darren swung down with a leering grin and swiped an oven glove from off the counter. I moved over, aware of Gob's presence just a few strides away.

'So you got them all trained, then?' The hinges of Gob's jaw pulsed through his cheeks, as he chewed.

'Everyone's done very well,' I said with a sideways glance. I was itching for him to leave and strongly aware of the empty, echoing silence of the unit. The upstairs offices suddenly seemed a long way off.

'Nobody else here then?' he said, as if he'd read my mind. The three skinheads still gazed in awe and, at the sink, Michael had dried each bowl at least twice.

'Stan and Barry are upstairs if you want to see them,' I said.

'Nah, yer alright.' Gob took a step towards me. 'Stan's a tosser and Barry's a little poofdah.'

Darren gave a raw laugh and dumped his cake on a cooling wire. Leaving the cake in the tin, he discarded the oven gloves and resumed his former seat. Gob leaned across the counter and flicked through the pages of my recipe book with one hand.

'You make all this shit?' he said to Darren, his finger jabbing a photo of a curry dish.

'That? Nah, not me. Don't touch that Paki food.'

Adolf shot me a look.

'Everyone gets to choose their own recipes,' I said evenly. Gob took another step forward to stand by my side. On the short wall behind him was a magnetic strip, which held all the knives, ranging in size from small paring knife to meat cleaver. Unintentionally, my eyes darted up to it and back again. Gob turned his head. When he turned back he was chewing with exaggerated slowness, as if in a spaghetti western.

'You got some nice blades here.' He reached up for a big cutting knife, then weighed it in his hand, staring at me and still chewing.

'Please put it back,' I feigned boredom but my heart was now thumping. The clock above the knife strip said that nobody else would be here for at least another hour.

'Yeah, very useful these,' he continued.

Adolf's grin had dropped. He checked my face with a look of concern. 'Aw Gob, those knives ain't even that sharp,' he said.

Gob ran the point of the blade inside a fingernail to flick an imaginary bit of dirt onto the floor. He weighed it again, contemplating and then took a few swipes at the air between us. I stood stock still, my fear mixed with rising anger.

'How come they let you have big knives like this, anyway?' he said, not taking his eyes off mine for a moment, his mouth curled into a false smile at one side.

'There's no problem with knives when they're handled properly,' I said in a tight voice. I could feel my chest contracting.

Right then I hated Gob as much as I feared him, and I knew he was enjoying both.

Gob leaned towards me. 'But what if some bovver boy came in?' His body tensed, almost imperceptively. 'Someone could come in and grab you – like this!' In a split second he was behind me, holding the knife to my neck, his forearm like a rod under the hand I'd automatically shot up to protect my throat.

'Fuck!' said Mark and Adolf simultaneously. Darren jumped down from the freezer.

'If someone got you like this then,' continued Gob conversationally.' What would you do?'

As the steel pressed against my throat, pure anger rose, blocking out my disbelief and panic. *Get that knife away from my neck!*

'Stan's coming!' Adolf's voice piped like a seasoned lookout.

Gob's arm relaxed for a second and there was a flurry of white – which could have been the kitchen tiles as we whirled round, or it could have been my fury. Then a flash of silver and a clatter, as the knife hit the floor. Somehow Gob was bent over with his arm twisted up his back.

'Arrgh!' he cried. I looked down, surprised to see my hand clamped round his wrist, with his arm bent behind right up to his neck. I was leaning over him, breathing heavily, and every muscle in my arm jammed like a trapped piston, as if it wasn't even part of me.

'Ahh, ahhh!' Gob's voice sounded choked. How had I even got into this position? I stared down and noticed his finger nails were actually very clean, with clear crescents and perfectly trimmed tips. His hand looked greyish white and oddly dead. The muscles on his forearm were bunched and I realised it was only a matter of physics that he was now in my grasp. This was what Ally had called a half-Nelson, when he was showed me and Joshy his wrestling holds.

'Lemme go! I was just jokin' with you,' gasped Gob.

The heat returned to the tissues of my arm as I released his hand and stood back. Gob straightened, rubbing his wrist.

'Shit! I was only messin' round,' he said.

'We don't mess with knives here.' My voice was steely, but my head started to spin. 'And we've got to finish cleaning up.'

'Yeah well, I got things to do too.' Gob gave his wrist a final rub, and shrugged his shoulders, adjusting everything back into place. He made a couple of little steps towards Mark, eyes flicking in fury to the spot where I was planted. 'You boys better be there tonight,' he hissed through tight lips. 'There's some things we gotta take care of.' He winced slightly as he straightened his denim jacket.

'We'll be there,' Mark and Darren chorused, as Gob sauntered to the lobby with exaggeration. Reaching the door he turned, and unwrapped a piece of chewing gum to lob in his mouth. He screwed the foil wrapper, letting it fall to the floor.

'You wanna be a bit less rough Miss, I might have been forced to hurt yer.' He gave a barren laugh. I managed to hold his gaze. We all stood, frozen, listening to his footsteps as they echoed across the concrete floor outside and through the main unit door. Then four pairs of eyes turned to me.

'You alright Miss? He was well out of order,' said Michael.

I forced my lips into a little smile. 'Fine, thanks. Can you start making your icing? I need to pop upstairs.' They nodded.

My legs started to fold as I reached the stairs, and at the top I almost collapsed. In the staff loo I sat heavily on the lid and put my head in my hands. My heart was still pounding. At the back of my nose and eyes, hot tears welled up, stoked by self pity and anger. 'I *can* do this,' I whispered to myself, through clenched teeth. 'I can *fucking well do it!*' I sat there for an age - until my blood had stopped racing. Then I checked my mascara and unlocked the door.

'There you are! I was looking downstairs.' Maureen was the ancient frizzy-haired secretary, with a face like Pekinese dog. 'You need to sign some timesheets, and I'll have a letter ready for Michael Greyson's mother, before he goes.' She spoke with briskness, then eyed me. 'Everything alright?'

'I'm fine,' I lied.

'It's just that those lads were down there on their own.' A lipstick, the shade of pink blancmange, creased with disapproval on her pursed lips.

'Just came up for a pee. Why, what's up?' I took the forms and propped my still-shaking elbow on the desk to sign.

'They said nobody could go in the kitchen.' She was obviously put out. 'I told them I'd fetch Stan if they didn't open up.'

'What were they doing?'

'They seemed to be frosting a fruit cake.' Maureen spoke with some disbelief. 'It looked quite professional. That tall black boy said the secret to glossy icing is lemon juice.'

Downstairs I found the kitchen door locked. 'Hey, open up – it's me!' I called.

Michael peered round the door. 'We didn't want anyone wandering in and messin' stuff up.'

'No, you're probably right.'

'We done one Miss,' said Adolf. 'The one that was made yesterday. We used it for practice.' I went over and saw that Tash's fruit cake had been blanketed in white. I pinched a tiny bit of icing from the bottom then turned to the four waiting figures.

'Yes, you've got a good stiff consistency.' I noticed there were none of the usual snickers at the word 'stiff'. 'Like I said yesterday, if it's too liquidy, it never sets. And it's very shiny. It's quite hard working icing – did you beat it by hand?'

'It's well tough on yer wrists, but we took it in turns, and added the lemon, just in drops – like what you said,' said Darren.

'Adolf was best – cos he's such a big wanker,' said Mark. And we all laughed.

'Well, we can't do the other cakes till they're cold,' I said. 'So you may as well knock off early.' Nobody moved.

'You sure?' said Adolf.

'Yes, go – before I find some more cleaning to do,' I said.

As Darren and Mark filed out, and Michael ran upstairs to collect his letter, Adolf hesitated, hand on door, as if trying to say something.

'Listen, thanks for earlier.' I gazed at him steadily.

His eyes dropped to the floor and he chewed his lip. 'Don't know what you mean.'

I stared at his stubbly head, until he was forced to look up. 'Your quick thinking diffused that situation.'

Adolf shrugged with awkwardness.

'You're a bright lad,' I said. 'And you learn fast. You could get on well in life, if you wanted.'

He shook his head and plucked his jacket off the hook with a bashful smile. 'Nah Miss, I ain't nuthin' special.'

'You could be,' I said. 'If you avoid knocking round with those less clever than you.'

He eyed me with doubt, wriggling his arm into a sleeve. Seeing those felt pen swastikas once more I wondered how he'd ever manage to extricate himself from the others. 'You've got a good brain.' I said, as he left. 'Just use it wisely.'

Exhausted, I sat down at the table jotting notes for the following day, until I became aware of Michael hovering at my elbow.

'See ya tomorra Miss.'

'Yeah, see you.' I glanced up briefly.

'Don't forget to keep the door locked,' he said.

'Okay.' I pretended to be absorbed in writing, not wishing to think about the day's events a minute longer.

'I mean it, Miss.' I looked up to find his stern face staring pointedly at me.

'Okay, okay,' I smiled. 'Go on now – you're crowding me.'

'Me, Miss? I'm crowdin' *you*?' And for the first time I heard Michael give a long, melodic laugh of joy. Then his feet tramped across the Area, until the entrance door closed with a decisive bang.

15

TOM

It was mid morning as the van blasted down the motorway, with the Spring sun shining down and cows grazing in undulating fields on either side. We were somewhere in Lancashire – Josie's countryside.

I was daydreaming about how sensual she was in the morning – the way her legs curved round mine and her sweet sexy smell – remembering when we'd eaten toast in bed and I'd licked the melting honey away as it dribbled down her throat. We'd been seeing each other every possible moment and even though it was only a few months, I knew this was the real deal. Whatever possibilities the future held, Josie surely had to be part of it. I thought of the letter I posted last week – scribbled in a locked bathroom for some privacy – saying I wanted much more than a casual fling, and asking if she'd move to London with me. As I'd written, I'd been full of nervous excitement. What if she said no?

I was interrupted by Charlie banging on the door. 'Oi Tom! I need a piss. What you doin' in there – knockin' one off?'

So I'd given up my perch on the edge of the bath, quickly sealed the envelope and scribbled *13 Richmond Road, Coventry* on the front, before Charlie broke the door down.

Everyone was knackered and looking forward to the next short breather at home. There was a lot of snoring and dribbling in the rear, where most of the band were catching up from the previous night's excesses, despite music blaring from the speakers.

On the front seat Len and I were next to Trevor, listening to an old Burton Watts gig on the tape player. The funky drop bass dominated, partly due to the competing noise of the van engine and the poor quality of the recording, so it was difficult to catch all the lyrics. But the raw, excited sound of Watts' voice cut through – along with calls of support from the Jamaican dancehall. It was easy to imagine slick two tone suits, cheeky short-brimmed hats and crisp white shirts of the 60's 'rude bwoys', to which Watts' referred – and to see a choppy ocean of sweaty brown arms and bobbing heads, skanking along to the music.

'I love this vibe, we've gotta capture it,' I said.

Len laughed. 'You wanna give them even more of this ol' man's music?' He raised his voice to be heard. 'Orright. But if we cover this one, we gotta mek it even sharper.'

'Yeah, sure – but you think it'll work?'

'Why not? It worked with Skaman,' said Len. 'But let Eddy sing this one – make his own sound with the lyric.'

'You okay, with us doing a more ska covers?' I asked, trying to scrutinise his face.

Len frowned. 'Noone owns most o' these island songs. They got passed round 'nough times in the sixties. We'll make our own steamin' versions and jus' see if kids like it.' He gave a shrug. 'We're just bringin' it up to date. We're not pretendin' we don't its roots.' Len grinned widely. 'How else they hear they gonna hear ska? Anyway we're a mixed band – the Original Mix!'

'That's what I think!' I laughed. 'How many other racially mixed bands do we know?'

'You gotta hear Papa Delight next!' Trev shouted over the roaring engine, which seemed to be getting louder. He pointed to a box of cassettes at my feet. 'It's the green one.'

I leaned down to rummage, my head by the glove compartment.

'The van sounds kinda clunky from under here,' I yelled to Trevor. As I came back up, he swung out into the middle lane to overtake a Mini that was struggling to hit 60 mph.

'I'm losing umph on the accelerator too,' he said. 'Oh shit!'

Brown smoke was seeping out from round the bonnet.

'Go on yer fucker!' bawled Trev at the nervous bloke in specs driving the Mini. Spotting our smoking van, his owlish eyes widened, and the little car strained to accelerate.

'Put yer soddin' foot down!' I gesticulated at him. A huge truck was tanking along behind us and another hemmed us in on the fast lane, with a third up the Mini's backside.

'Jeeoisus Christ!' Trev shouted, as the wagon in the fast lane indicated to pull across us. 'We'll be juggernaut sandwich!'

He honked madly at the Mini and the lad suddenly managed to pull away, leaving just enough room for us to swerve across to the hard shoulder and sink down into the grass verge. The truck behind blared his horn, and the gap between the other two lorries closed with alarming speed. Trev stuck his arm out of the window to motion a fisted 'wanker' salute. The three of us piled out, then Trev drew the sleeve of his leather jacket over his hand, and wrenched open the hood. A foul, oily burning smell poured out with the smoke, but no actual flames.

'Shit! Is either of you a good mechanic?'

Len and I both shrugged. 'Nah, not really.'

My dad would have stuck his head inside and immediately known what was up of course. But somehow, with college, then plumbing and music, I hadn't got round to it.

The others disembarked, stretching their limbs.

'Fuckin' hell, we killed the van!' said Charlie.

'Suicide more like.' Vinnie lit a fag and looked around him. 'Who knows about engines then?'

We all stared at each other – from face to face, as if someone had the vital knowledge but wasn't letting on, like players in a game of mechanics poker. And I felt laughter boiling up inside me.

It was probably tiredness, the endless cheap hotels and stupidity of the tour, and the fact that I didn't have a clue about anything anymore – where we were going, how we were going to get there, and why the urge for us to be a huge, roaring success had grown and mutated like a virus inside me. I looked around me. We were so fucking hopeless – Charlie with his braces hanging down and his deathly white face, Devon scratching his dreads with crumpled shirt tails poking out of his flies, Vinnie with his scuffed American jacket and a fag lolling on his lips, Eddy blinking and puffy eyed, and sleep-creased Raymond. We were from a city of giant engineering miracles which once made it great – but none of us knew a fucking thing about the basic combustion engine.

I felt my stomach muscles contract as the laughter growled out of me. Vinnie looked up and started to smirk too – then Devon shook his head and his tongue vibrated in his open mouth as he began to silently chortle. Len and Charlie both saw Devon and doubled up with laughter at the same time. Even Eddy couldn't stop his indifference cracking, as our mirth licked at him like a bush fire. He snorted, sending a spew of snot from his nose across the hard shoulder, which seemed so funny I thought my stomach would burst. Hearing the gale of uncontrolled laughter, Trevor took his head out of the engine. Smoke sooted his high, round, cheekbones black, so he looked like a miner emerging from the pit. 'What?' he said – and with that I staggered onto the grassy bank, roaring and clutching my belly. Vinnie fell back next and then Eddy, followed by the others – until we were all rolling on the grass howling. Trevor looked perplexed.

'So nobody can sort this?' he said, and the sight of his standing with a hand on one hip, clueless and smutty faced, sent us all off again.

When we'd recovered, we sat in a row on the grass, smoking and deciding what to do. Rick's transportation plan hadn't stretched to breakdown recovery – so we were looking at paying a fortune to a local garage. We were counting out what cash we had between us, when a police car pulled up.

Charlie quickly stuffed the joint he'd been smoking into the soil beside him.

'Oh great,' said Eddy, his voice heavy with sarcasm. 'It's the pig cavalry.'

After some debate with the police, it was agreed that I'd wait with Trevor and Raymond for a tow truck, while the others piled into a Black Maria van – the only vehicle available to take five people. But Vinnie became a bit touchy at the idea of being locked in the back and a few choice words were passed on the subject, resulting in him being cautioned. Charlie objected to this and was cautioned too.

Later, Devon related how he and Len managed to calm everyone down, but when they arrived at the local police station, the desk sergeant took one look and assumed they were being booked.

'Man, he was just itchin' to throw me and Len in a cell.' Devon shook his head. We were sitting in a pub working out what to do next. 'That tall one had to tell him four times that we were only waitin' for you three to arrive. He jus' couldn't imagine why two black men had stepped in the station, if we weren't being arrested.'

I went back to the payphone to try getting hold of Rick again. But I returned with bad news.

'Rick's gone for a hire van, but it's gonna take him at least three hours to drive up here,' I said, to a hail of groans. 'And it's much smaller – so two of us will have to hitch back.'

'Uh-huh, not me an' Raymond.' Len folded his arms. 'We ain't gettin' almost arrested a second time, for jus' tryin' to get home.' Devon nodded his head. Trevor had gone to find a B&B as he waited for the van to be fixed – so he'd taken the briefcase containing all our cash takings from gigs. I realised – too late – I should have got Rick to bring some money with him for train fares. I looked round at Charlie, Eddy and Vinnie.

'Only one way to decide this,' I nodded to the opposite wall. Everyone followed my gaze.

'Darts!' they said in unison.

The darts competition brought our spirits back. So much that by the time Charlie and Eddy had effectively whooped our arses, Vinnie had forgotten what the actual point was, and he insisted on another pint for the road. So it was gone four o'clock when we arrived back at the motorway, having cadged a ride from a local at the bar.

'Can't wait to sleep in me own bed,' said Vinnie, as we waved the bloke off and stuck out our thumbs. We had two nights in Coventry, then another string of tour dates.

'Don't count yer chickens,' I said as another truck swept past, hydraulics snorting as it changed gear to speed down the slip road. A little white van shot past, nearly taking my hand off, but before I had time to gesticulate, it screeched to a halt on the hard shoulder and reversed back at speed.

'Gerrin' before the police see ya!' the driver yelled. Vinnie yanked the handle and scrambled over the seat to the back. I threw myself onto the passenger seat and slammed the door.

'Thanks mate. It was looking like a long wait,' I said. The van smelled of fish and the driver was a young bloke, with a round, sunburnt face, sporting a woolly hat and green waterproofs.

'Youse are lucky not to get knabbed. They don't like hitchers round 'ere,' he said, in an unmistakeable Brummy voice.

Brian was returning from a sea-fishing competition in Wales, where he'd landed, 'Nothin' burra ugly big dogfish and a load of bait and fry.' He shook his head in regret. 'Sometimes they just down't like yer rod.'

Vinnie and I used to try our luck in the canal as kids, so we talked about fishing a bit, then moved on to discussing Birmingham, music, and why we were hitching in the first place.

'I've seen a few good reggae bands recently,' said Brian. 'Me girlfriend's half Jamaican and there's a couple of West Indian clubs we go to. I get an easier time in those places, than she does at The Plaza with me.' At the mention of girlfriend I suddenly froze.

'Shit! What time is it?' Brian looked at the dashboard clock. 'Ten past five, why?'

'How long's it gonna take to get to Birmingham?'

'Be there by seven thirty or eight, if there's no holdups,' he said.

Shit! My heart dropped like a sandbag. Even if Brian dropped us at the station and we jumped on a departing train, we wouldn't hit Coventry centre till gone nine. I remembered the quick postcard I'd sent from Durham the first night we were away. *'Hey Josie – meet me in the Bombay Rose at 7pm on Thursday 10th. I've booked a table. Tom x'.* I'd chosen a postcard of Durham jail, and added, *'p.s. Oh yeah – we're staying in all the best hotels.'* It had been strange and fantastical spelling her name out for the very first time – like writing to the Tooth Fairy. I'd been instinctively guarding whatever you'd call the thing that Josie and I shared – especially from Vinnie. This meal out was the first time we would exist in the real world as a couple. And the letter I'd posted last week would be the real tester of how she felt about me.

'Wassup Shepperton? Surely yer not on a promise?' As Vinnie thumped me on the back, a big alarm bell rang in my head, and memories of all the things of mine he'd trashed over the years – a new bicycle bent as he crashed down a plank pretending to be Evil Kineville, the transistor radio he'd somehow prised the knob off while looking for pirate stations – a trail of accidents to hide from my parents, including the mysterious disappearance of the crook from a china shepherdess, which was my mum's pride and joy.

'Promised to phone my folks early tonight,' I answered Vinnie as neutrally as possible. 'You thinking of stopping off anywhere Brian?'

'Probably call at the services after Stafford for petrol. Be about 7pm though'.

I shut my eyes and tried not to think of Josie getting ready to meet me, putting on some clingy outfit and doing her hair.

Vinnie leant over my shoulder and started talking to Brian about the band.

'Original Mix are pretty well known in the Midlands now,' said Brian. 'I saw youse play ages ago, in a small pub in Coventry. But the skinhead following you're getting is a bit hardcore for some people.'

'They're not our only fans,' said Vinnie. 'We get a mix – West Indian kids, townies, casuals, waaay too many fuckin' students, and some punks and Rastas. Depends where we're playin' whether there's a big skinshead presence or not – and what kind of skins they are.'

'You'll have to come to a gig,' I said. 'We're on in Leicester next week – if we get another van that is.'

Vinnie blew a stream of smoke with a sneering laugh. '*Another* van? Rick'll get down and give that fucker mouth to mouth to get it back on the road. He's a crap manager and a cheapskate. Twenty bloody gigs we've done – all over the bloody country – and how many has he come to? Big soddin' zero!'

'Well,' I said cautiously. 'He's been trying to get us a record deal.'

'Bollocks! We should never have bought that idea. We should just publish ourselves – like you said in the beginning Tom.'

I twisted my neck round to look at him. Vinnie rarely called me by anything as civil as my first name, and despite all our shared history, his loyalty was questionable.

'You takin' the piss?'

'No, straight up. You're educated – you could work out all the angles.' He was stubbing his fag out on the underside of his boot, but the vindictive grin was nowhere to be seen and when he looked up his eyes were even and steady. 'Len might know some people too.'

I slouched down in the small seat, and stretched my feet up on the dashboard. There was silence apart from the purr of the van's engine and the heavy sound of passing trucks.

'Distributing a record would be tricky,' I said slowly, scratching the back of my head to help me think. 'But maybe we could flog it to record shops in big cities somehow – or do mail order through one of the fanzines.'

'One of me mates writes 'Pump City',' said Brian in a bright voice.

'Wow, that's a great little paper,' I said, sitting up. 'Get him to come to a gig!'

Pump City started out as a Birmingham fanzine, but now it covered gigs northwards and right down to London. In almost every pub, some guy in a Parka wandered round flogging the mags. Unlike a lot of the music papers, it was smart, acerbic and witty – people were even prepared to pay for their own copy, rather than wait til one was passed round.

Suddenly the world was full of opportunities again. For the next fifty miles the lights of Brian's little van devoured cat's eyes in the black road and our ideas raced ahead, until we hit a major tailback, and crawled along at ten miles an hour, in a solid caterpillar of traffic.

'Very sorry sir, the lady has left,' an Indian man said down the crackly line. Vinnie and Brian had disappeared into the services for a piss and I stood in the cold phone box shovelling money into the slot.

'Did she leave a message?' I heard the desperation in my own voice. Down the receiver, the clank of cutlery and hubbub of voices, told me I may as well be a million miles away. I thought of Josie sitting in the restaurant on her own, feeling more and more let down, and I wanted to kick myself.

'The lady was here for quite a while,' he replied slowly. He hesitated – there was something he wasn't saying. 'I offered to phone a taxi sir, but she declined.'

'A taxi?'

'Our manager thought she should not walk through town alone. But…he could not persuade her.'

I imagined Josie, upset, confused, and a bit drunk, weaving her way through the city centre, negotiating gangs of leery lads on their way from pub to pub, and I thumped my head with my fist.

The man continued, 'We didn't know how long you'd be detained, so the lady said we could give the table to another party.'

'Yes, thank you, I'm sorry for the inconvenience,' I said.

'It was no trouble,' he replied. 'You'll make a reservation another time?'

'Maybe.' I plonked the receiver into the cradle with a 'kerchunk', leant my forehead onto the cold glass pane of the telephone box and shut my eyes. Josie had sat there for over an hour, conspicuous and alone. No wonder she'd had a few drinks. I'd stood her up, like a real shit.

Vinnie thumped on the glass, making me jump.

'Oi Shepperton – c'mon! Traffic's moving, and Brian says he'll take us to meet his writer mate, Fozz.'

'What – *now*?' I hauled the heavy door open.

'You got something better planned?' With his back to Brian, Vinnie pulled his, 'don't be a loser' expression. 'This could be great for us man. If Pump City gets behind us, we're sorted.'

I looked over. Brian munched on a burger, beaming like a new convert.

'That'd be fantastic mate,' I said, nodding vigorously.

I'd have to make it up to Josie big time, but that needed to wait. Opportunities like this didn't pop up often. When they did you had to grab them with both hands and reel them in.

16

TOM

We met Fozz in 'The Lord Admiral', an old city boozer which squatted on a corner, its leaded windows glowing red and green, like jewels. Inside we were assailed by smoke, beer, a barrage of loud voices and, deep inside, live music. Vinnie headed for the bar's enamelled pump handles and brass plates, single-minded as a whippet, while Brian scanned the room. I looked around at the folk crushed together, laughing and jostling in a goodnatured way, as people struggled by with drinks. There were quite a few girls there – some pretty ones too. My chest tightened as I remembered Josie – oh Christ! I needed to explain myself to Josie. I reached into my jacket for cigarettes.

'There he is!' Brian pointed to a place at the back by the stage. We pushed our way through to a knot of people squeezed round a table, arriving just as the band issued their final chord, and the whole pub clattered, clapped and whistled. A nerdy-looking bloke – presumably Fozz – sat against the high backrest facing the musicians, arms crossed with a pile of mags in front of him.

Brian greeted everyone in turn with a handshake or a dust of knuckles and, while everyone budged up and extra stools were passed over heads, I studied Fozz. He wore thick black-rimmed spectacles – the type that got kids called Buddy Holly at school – and the sort of buff-coloured mackintosh a reporter in an old film might sport. He looked like a real square, but there was something unusual and obsessed in his gawky manner and in the twitchy bird-like eyes behind those TV screen glasses. As I sat on a stool next to him, he gave two jerks of his head and rubbed his chin.

'Original Mix, yeah, we know you. Touring fuckin' hell holes. Missed your last Birmingham gig. Heard you're good though. Punk-reggae mix, that it?' His sentences rattled out with the clatter of a typewriter.

'Not quite.' Brian mimed drinking a pretend pint and I gave the thumbs up. 'We're developing a whole new sound, with the emphasis on great dance music.'

Fozz was nodding, like his head was on a spring – but at the last phrase his shoulders tightened and he gave me a deadpan stare. 'Dance, as in disco?' He shuddered at the notion of mirrorballs and blokes in tight satin trousers doing choreographed moves. I rolled my eyes.

'Fuck no! Dance as in skanking – music as in ska!''

A sly grin slid across his face. 'Just checkin'. Gotta have some quality control.'

A hand came over my shoulder, gripping a pint of lager.

'Cheers Brian.' I turned round. Vinnie was there too, with one arm slung loosely round the shoulder of an attractive dark-haired girl in heavy makeup, a miniskirt and red tights. 'This is Cherry,' he said.

'Cheryl,' she corrected.

'Thought you was a Cherry.' He leered down her top.

She blushed and sniggered. 'Not really.' And she looked down at me with big eyes. 'I saw your band at The Plaza last year – you're really cool.'

Vinnie's face tightened. 'I've joined since then,' he said.

'Thanks,' I said to Cheryl. 'You'll have to hear the new line up.' I raised an eyebrow at Vinnie. 'We're even better now.'

Two guys opposite moved out from their seats, and Fozz caught the cuff of one of them as he passed. 'Tell Screamer he's covering 'Aching Skulls' in Leicester next week – cos Lofty's going to Stoke.'

The bloke's eyes saucered. 'Shit! Lofty's reviewing 'Dad's Dog's Dead'?'

Fozz grimaced. 'Dirty job – but gotta be done, mate. The people need to know.'

The two lads moved away, laughing. Seeing my confusion, Fozz said, 'Metal meets prog rock. Keyboards with fucking string effects. Totally regressive.' He shook his head sadly. 'Rather stuff leeches in my ears.'

♪

A couple of hours later we were at Pump City HQ – aka the terrace house Fozz had inherited from his grandparents. Fozz and I sat on the floor drinking whiskey, discussing logistics and distribution, while Vinnie and Cheryl tucked into cans of strong lager and fooled around on the sofa. Brian kept himself entertained by playing Fozz's vast collection of albums, housed on a wall of ceiling to floor shelving.

There was a lull in our dialogue, and the music continued to pipe out in tinny monotone, through a small unimpressive record player, though there were two large unused speakers in the room. Fozz looked up from rolling a cigarette and saw my puzzled face.

'Got a much better player in the other room.' He gave a series of nervous fast nods. 'But I review with this. Best to hear stuff on same crap system as every other fucker in the country. Brian, mate!' he called to the kitchen where Brian had gone to get another beer. '– use the other deck. Comes through to the big system in here,' he explained to me.

Brian removed the record from the turntable, and moments later the reedy voices were replaced by clear, warm, deep tones – setting off a raw edge in the lead vocals. The band sounded vivid and energetic now. The tune was a punching folksy sound with heavy percussion and strings, and one of those hand drums you saw at Irish sessions.

'You trod with yer boots on her camomile lawn
You never thought twice you were doin' her harm
You talk like a poet when you've had twenty pints
But the thrust of yer fist is her poem tonight.'

'Nice track. Who's the band?' I asked Fozz, as the volume receded.

'Gilding the Lily – Birmingham outfit. Three blokes, two women,' said Fozz, head bobbing. 'Fantastic cello bassline on some tracks.'

'Sounds like Irish folk with punk.'

'That's about the size of it,' said Fozz. 'Lots of bands are mixing it up now. Taking stuff from other musical cultures – like you're doin' I spose.'

'It's the way ahead.'

Fozz sat, knees up, leant against a big comfy chair. Under their big frames, his eyelids closed, but one of his hands tapped against his thigh – as though one bit of him had to be on alert at all times. On the sofa opposite, Vinnie and Cheryl giggled and drank in equal measure. Ignoring the fact she was wrestling Vinnie's hand from under her skirt and, relaxed by whiskey, I described my utopian dream – where musicians of all nationalities shared skills, instruments and sounds, inventing whole new types of music, to bring different people together, especially the youngsters.

'A lot of working class lads are becoming like lost sheep,' I said. 'It's unemployment which kills off their humanity. We can't let the National Front and BNP keep recruiting them.'

'The NF's gaining support round here too. Why the fuck would you want to join up with those dickheads?' said Fozz.

I blew a series of smoke rings up at the swirls on the ceiling and pondered.

'Weell…suppose you've got some kid sitting round his estate, puffing weed, with nothing to do 'cept harbour bitterness and anger – then someone invites him to help plot race hate campaigns, against the people they say have stolen his opportunities. I reckon it gives his life a purpose again.'

I paused and we both sighed at the same time. Then, I raised my glass in a toast, and gave a sarcastic laugh. 'It's our job to take all that pent up anger and turn it into music instead!'

Fozz gave me a long look. 'Yer a bit of an evangelist when you get goin'. Your old man a minister?'

'Oh yeah, he's Leader of the Armchair Militants wing orright,' said Vinnie. We both looked up, surprised he'd been listening. 'All fuckin' mouth and no march.'

His words were a bit slurred, but the tone of his voice was unmistakeable. My old man was keeping his head down at work nowadays, staying clear of union strongmen like Vinnie's dad. But Vinnie had never been so vindictive about him before and it rankled, especially as my parents had practically brought Vinnie and Yvonne up, when their mum died.

'Well look where the hard left's getting us,' I said. 'All the bloody strikes and workers still crushed like maggots. My dad's getting on and needs to keep his job – so he's stopped making waves.'

'Unlike ush – who make such a fuckin' big political stance.' Vinnie pointed a wavering finger at me. His eyes had become small slits in his drink-sodden face, but he had a point. I had a sudden thought.

'Hey! We should hook up with the 'Rock Against Racism' people,' I said. 'They're arranging festivals all over now. We can join a bigger voice.'

'More gigsh playing for fuck all – great! Go for it Shepperton!'

Vinnie's comment coincided with his torso slowly sliding down the sofa cushions. We all watched as his head thudded softly onto the chair arm, and after a few minutes, a familiar rhythmical wheezing clarified that he was out for the night.

'There's a couple of spare rooms upstairs,' Fozz said as he stood up. 'Help yourselves. I'm gonna crash.' There were creaks and thuds as his unsteady feet propelled him up to bed.

Brian's cheerful moon face appeared at the living room door. 'That's yer DJ done fer.'

I waved at him from my cross-legged position.

'Stay in touch Tom.' He gave a fisted salute. As the front door thudded shut, I surveyed Vinnie snoring on the sofa and met Cheryl's charcoaled eyes. Her half smile told me she was also quite pissed, and I wasn't entirely sober myself.

'You've got lovely hair, Tom.'

She reached out and wiggled her fingers, as if to touch my head. Despite the booze, the sensation in the crotch of my jeans reminded me that it was usually about now when these situations got complicated, so I stood like a shaky giraffe with a hard on. 'See you in the morning,' I blurted out. 'Need to get my head down.' Then I fumbled my way up the stairs, before everything I said sounded like some sort of lewd gag.

♪

I was dreaming of Josie, standing on the hard shoulder of the motorway, staring at me with sad eyes. I sensed that Len was beside me too, trying to tell me something very important. I couldn't make out what, as he was hissing in my ear, his voice soft and low.

'Tom move over, let me get in with you,' the whispering was urgent now. I opened my eyes. In the half light, in front of my vision, was pair of white legs under a black T-shirt. The legs shifted, revealing a flash of red knickers underneath. My brain kicked into semi-consciousness.

Cheryl crouched down so her face was near mine. 'It's too cold in the other room.' She was shivering. 'There's a sleeping bag, but it's really thin.'

Too drugged with sleep to put up much of a fight, I moved to face the wall as she slid under the bedclothes. Her hard nipples brushed against my back. 'Let's get some shut eye,' I mumbled. The longing in my groin threatened to take over. It would be so easy to fuck her and disappear in the morning. It wasn't like I had the past of a choirboy. But she was pretty drunk, so when her warm hand came snaking round my waist and travelled groin-ward, I gently moved it back behind me and shifted to make a bit of clear space between us. Christ, it was going to be a long night.

A few moments later she shot up, and I heard a terrible retching down the toilet. I padded into the bathroom and handed her a dressing gown I'd found on the door. She took my hand to stumble up.

'Better now?' I asked. I wasn't feeling that clever myself. 'I've found an extra blanket. I'll take the other room, so you can hog the bed.' I smiled.

She looked teary. 'I don't usually drink so much.' She sniffed and wiped a mascara-etched face. 'Oh god, I really need to lie down.'

I pulled the gown round her shoulders, led her back to the room, and tucked her in like she was a kid. 'Call me if you think you're dying.' But she was already asleep.

As I slid into the other bed, I suddenly thought of my dad's 'sex talk' when I was a cocky seventeen year old and we were piling up bricks by the garage, for a new greenhouse. 'Sleeping around is like being an alcoholic, lad,' he'd said. 'You don't care about the quality or what company you keep as long as you get some.' I'd hoped he was finished, but he'd gone on. 'I sowed me oats during National Service, like everyone else. But when I met your mum at The Roxy and we started stepping out, that was different. When you find a good 'un, hang on tight and don't blow it.' And with that, he'd picked up the handles of the barrow and pushed it round to the front yard.

In the whiskey-fug of my head, I thought how dad had disapproved when I'd married Yvonne. But he'd like Josie, I knew he would. Just the idea of taking her to meet my folks, gave me a little thrill of pride.

♬

I woke to the smell of frying bacon. Downstairs, Vinnie, Fozz and Cheryl sat at a back room table, cluttered with the breakfast remnants, record sleeves, magazines and two ashtrays. 'Help yourself to whatever's left.' Fozz looked up from a fanzine and nodded towards the small kitchen.

'Shall I cook you something?' said Cheryl, with a bright smile.

'S'alright, I'll sort it – thanks.'

It took me a couple of minutes to fry some eggs and throw them between slices of bread. When I returned to the back room, Cheryl gave me a sly look of intimacy that caught me offside. My head felt thick and stupid from the whiskey, so I didn't respond. I wasn't much of a spirits drinker.

I sat down by Vinnie. One of his hands was stirring extra sugar into his coffee and the other was repeatedly tapping his cigarette end on the side of the ashtray. Underneath the table I could feel the vibration of his foot. This was behaviour I understood. Vinnie harboured a myriad of bitter injustices, pressurised into a small nuclear nugget, which any perceived offence or irritation could ignite. It was best to let him blow and hope the fallout wasn't too toxic. I ate my sandwich in four big bites and threw lava hot tea down to follow it. Fozz's help was going to be invaluable and I didn't want him offended.

'Listen thanks for everything Fozz,' I said. 'We need to get back to Cov. But I'll call you, to sort something out.'

'Cool man,' he said, still reading. Then he looked up, eyes squinting in those huge black spectacles, like some Open University lecturer on late night telly. 'D'ya think *'cyber-punk with necromancer undertones,'* nails The Spider Sistas sound?'

'Dunno mate, never heard them.' I grabbed my jacket. It was probably this sort of question which had yanked the detonator from the inner grenade that was Vinnie's patience.

'C'mon Vin, let's go. See ya Cheryl.'

'When?' She looked like a puppy who knew it wasn't going on a walk. Maybe Cheryl had annoyed Vinnie.

I shrugged. 'Come and see us, next time we play somewhere local,' I said.

Vinnie stood by me, wearing his unreadable silent look, which was as good as a four minute warning. I propelled him out of the door, then set off at a lick down the road. He caught up and stomped along, hands dug into his jeans pockets. I waited for him to say something, but he remained silent.

Finally I stopped and faced him. 'Alright – I get it. You think Fozz is a tosser. But his fanzine's support would be like a bloody ticket printer.' I strode away, pumped up and primed for a full show down.

'I know that!' Vinnie had caught up. 'He's a fucking geek – but he's straight up.'

I was baffled. But our feet were thumping out a regular speed on the paving slabs now, and my head started to fill up with the plans I'd hatched with Fozz last night.

'Reckon Cheryl will come to a gig then?' Vinnie booted an empty fag packet into the grass verge.

I looked sideways at him and frowned. 'Dunno. Didn't you get her phone number?'

'I'm not the one that fucked her!' he spat at me. His face had transformed into a red ball of fury. As I digested this, I thought of the number of times Vinnie had whisked a girl away from me – and later, she'd be crying with her mates, Vinnie having moved to new pastures, or gone to get rat-arsed.

I quashed my smile and sniffed. 'We shared a bed for warmth, mate. What can I say? Damsel in distress? You'd have done the same.'

Vinnie's jaw was clenched so hard, a vein in his neck was pulsing. I turned away, so he couldn't see me laughing. I didn't often get chance for the upper hand. After a few minutes I turned back. 'Nah, I'm kiddin'. She puked her guts up and I slept in the other room.'

'You're a soddin' liar!'

'No, really.' I narrowed my eyes at him. 'Anyway, what do you care?'

'I don't.' He shrugged. 'Don't give a shit.' But he looked too pleased for someone with no particular interest.

I heard a familiar rumble behind and turned. 'Bus!' I yelled, and we set off running, exploding into the vehicle, coughing and laughing, our differences forgotten.

At the train station, I tried to marshal my thoughts, to plan some sort of band strategy, while Vinnie asked a young woman for a light. She offered her cigarette, and he gave one of his snake charmer's smiles, settling into easy chat up mode. I looked around at the platforms of Birmingham New Street – each busy island full of passengers, bags, suitcases, everyone anxious to board the right train before the guard whistled and doors slammed shut. Over the sound of engines, the announcement boards clacked as they changed, and there were streams of tinny, almost undecipherable announcements. Dirty neon lights hanging from the roof gave the station a nasty urine-coloured light and, much of the station was covered with a patina of thick black grease. But the air was vibrant with excitement, and I heard accents from all round Britain – Scottish, Welsh, Liverpudlian, Mancunian, West Country – and from overseas – Indian, Caribbean, even African. People were on the move. They knew where they were going and the next step of their adventures. And what did I know? Nothing – except I was going to run round Coventry like an idiot for a day, preparing to spend more weeks on tour. Ahead of me were hundreds of hours in a clapped out minibus which stank of petrol, vomit and unnameable body odours. I issued a long sigh as I felt in my jacket for cigarettes.

Vinnie extricated himself from conversation with the young woman, just as her face suggested she'd been hooked. He shrugged down into his leather jacket, gave a parting nod and she watched him saunter away wearing a puzzled and slightly hurt look, unaware she'd escaped pretty lightly.

A long heavy goods train came speeding through the station on the opposite track – a flatbed, transporting shipping containers, some round like oil tankers, some huge box-like structures. The line seemed to go on forever. As it disappeared the sound it made was still throbbing through my head: 'daddleeadah, da-da, da-da DAH-dah, DAHdah…. daddleeadah, da-da, da-da DAH-dah, DAHdah,' a syncopated rhythm, made by different weights of cargo on the tracks.

My fingers twitched on the outside leg of my jeans, pattering it out. Like everyone, I'd hadn't heard a lot of music from outside Europe and America, but that rhythm sounded similar to some African beats. I kept it going in my head, tapping it out with my palms and my feet. And when we boarded our train, it was ingrained in my whole body. Vinnie didn't ask. He was engrossed in the sports pages from a discarded tabloid. Words were piling into my head with this imagined drum configuration. I took out my notebook. This was one to work on with Devon, our beatmaster extraordinaire.

Back in Coventry centre, it felt like I'd been away for ages. I threw coins into a payphone, trying to find someone at home, until

Eddy told me they'd dropped all our sweat-stained suits at the dry cleaners before piling our equipment into the studio.

Half an hour later, I was walking through town, holding several cellophane shrouds over an arm, when I spotted a familiar sight. Tight skirt, stilettos, straight dark bob with a severe fringe and brooding eyes. Yvonne was coming my way. I looked round for a shop to dive into, but she'd seen me.

'Tom! I thought you were on tour!' She launched at me, all sickly perfume and eager eyes, planting a big red, lipsticky kiss on my cheek. I rubbed away the greasy patch, peeled her arms from round my neck, and glanced round the crowded shopping precinct.

'Yvonne, stop that!'

'Why babe? Aren't you pleased to see your wife?'

'Ex-wife.' I said with firmness.

'Oh yeah.' Her face tightened with that furious look. I stared over her head, hoping for some kind of deliverance. In amongst the milling shoppers, I thought I saw a shot of blond.

'You're looking good Tom. Success suits you.' She gazed up at me with flirtatious eyes.

'Yvonne, I've gotta go,' I turned on my heels. 'Give me regards to your fella, wassisname....'

'He's asked me to marry him, you know,' she called, and I reeled round. She was standing with hands on her hips, her face defiant.

I stepped over and touched her arm. 'You should marry him, he's a good bloke and he loves you.'

'You used to love me.' Her eyes welled with tears. We'd played this out many times, but it still filled me with a mixture of pity and guilt.

'We can't keep going through this Yvonne,' I said gently. 'We're not kids any more. Besides you don't want to be back with me – you're just scared or something.' It was always so hard. Every response made me sound like a cruel bastard.

'I can't believe you let me go,' she said in a quiet voice.

'Just be happy Yvonne. We separated for a lot of reasons, and you know we were right.' Her face studied mine, and then her eyes widened.

'You've found someone else!' Her tone was incredulous.

I stared at the plastic wrap on my arm, saying nothing, and she took a pace back. 'I don't believe it! Even Vinnie didn't say. You two sticking together – just like in school!'

I was incensed. 'I don't have to tell you and your brother everything about my fuckin' life!'

'How serious is it?' Yvonne clutched her handbag to her, as if she imagined I'd snatch it, or was preparing to wallop me with it.

I shook my head. 'That's enough now.'

As I moved off she grabbed my jacket by the zip. 'If you marry again before I do, I'll never speak to you again in my life!' she spat out.

The prospect of her eternal silence was attractive, though highly unlikely. I pulled my lapel out of her grasp. 'Bye Yvonne.'

As I strode through town, Yvonne's idea started to take root. I'd even consider getting married again, if it was to Josie. I swerved round a lad pushing a double buggy with tiny twins inside.

'Mind out! You're not pushin'a bloody shopping cart!' said the girlfriend behind him.

The lad rolled his eyes at me as he tried to control the pram, so I mugged back, then turned to watch them go.

Yvonne and I hadn't been nearly adult enough to have children, but with Josie? Yes, we might even have a kid at some point.

I smiled. It was all possible. I just needed to get myself in the right place with music first.

17

JOSIE

'Christ! You look like a moggie everyone forgot to feed.'

Simon ruffled my unkempt hair and sauntered past me, as I held the front door ajar. He was carrying a large bag. 'How's it going with lover boy?' he called back.

I couldn't bring myself to tell him about my shameful evening in the restaurant, sitting opposite an empty chair. Or say how bereft I felt when Tom was on tour. And after spotting him in town the day before, in a clinch with a stylish dark-haired female, I definitely wouldn't admit to my jealous suspicion that he had another woman.

It didn't matter. I could see by the gleam in Simon's eyes, he wanted to talk about himself.

'I've got news.'

He passed through the living room like a guided missile, jumped down the two steps into the galley kitchen, and there were clunking sounds as he dug around in the cutlery drawer. When I joined him, he'd brought out plates and popped the kettle on the hob.

I leant on the doorframe rubbing sleep out of my eyes, as he removed a white box carefully from his shopping bag. I peeped inside, to see a circle of sparkling butter icing.

'Oh god! What the hell's that?' I said. 'Why're you harassing me with hideous confectionary on a Saturday morning, when I've woken up feeling like shit?'

'It's after twelve yer lazy moo, and we're celebrating.' Simon lifted the cake out with both hands and placed it onto a dinner plate. When his blue eyes met mine, they shone.

'I've got a job in Birmingham. I'm moving back.'

I turned towards the living room to hide the shock on my face.

'Oh come 'ere yer big softay,' he said in his lilting Brummy accent.

He rotated me by the shoulders and gave me a hug. 'It's only forty minutes on the train from town centre. Anyways, you've got that terrible job and yer secret lover to occupy you.'

'I'm sorry, Simon,' I said. 'But first Franki and now you – everyone's leaving!'

'Per'aps you should think about it too.' Simon gave me a final squeeze, before guiding me across to the sofa and pressing me down to sit. 'You've been in Coventry for five years. If it was a jail sentence, you'd be out for good behaviour by now.'

He handed me a tissue from his jeans pocket. 'Blow,' he said firmly. You're not getting snot on me fancy cake.'

Simon returned bearing a tray, with china teacups and linen napkins I'd bought from a junk shop. As he cut out two enormous triangular slabs, I eyed him sheepishly, ashamed that I hadn't immediately shared his jubilation. 'What's the job?'

'City Art Gallery.' He pushed one wedge onto a plate and handed it to me. 'Glorified art bouncer really. But I get to take guided tours when I've been trained and know my Botticellis from my Bacons.'

'You're kidding?' The idea of him retraining in art history was ludicrous. Simon knew the exact date of hundreds of paintings, plus the type of paint and brushes used.

'I know.' He rolled his eyes. 'Apparently they have to tell you what to say – in case you have Unsuitable Opinions.' He made a little moue with his lips. 'I don't care, as long as I get a uniform and a key on a chain – and I can wag my finger at anyone going within five foot of the pictures.'

We'd spent many a long giggly hour dodging reprimands from ushers at our local art gallery and museum, so I could see how the 'poacher turned gatekeeper' role would appeal to him – but only to an extent.

'Won't you get bored though?' I eased more cake into my mouth, though the sugar in the first bite had made my teeth ache.

'Probably,' he replied, with his mouth full. 'But the Director's about a hundred and four – so can't last forever. I shall crawl up the greasy pole, with the agility of a greasy polecat.'

I nodded slowly. He'd got it all worked out. I'd been absorbed in my job and my love life, while the people I really cared for were moving on. I felt a sad yearning for those lazy unemployed hours we'd spent having laughs and killing time in the cheapest ways possible. I hadn't appreciated the flawed perfection of it at all.

'You'll be fine.' Simon looked at me steadily. 'We'll write to each other, and who knows? One day per'aps we'll both afford phone lines, so you can tell me what I'm missing out on, here in beautiful Coventry.'

I pulled a revolted face and he guffawed.

'At least there's a proper gay scene in Brum,' he added. 'And it's fairly safe – not like 'ere.'

'Fancy spending your last night at The Weasel then – for old times sake?' I laughed.

Coventry's one 'gay friendly' pub was a place for all misfits – Goths, punks, art students – and a natural target for people who wanted to attack anyone different, a desire which ran high in much of the city's population.

'Yeah! Why not?' Simon was full of bravado now his route from the city was lit up like a fairytale path out of the scary forest. 'I'll be moving at the end of next month. We'll go then.'

'Christ, I was only joking.' But by his eager face, I could see he'd got a grip on the idea.

'No, let's do it – let's dress up and celebrate my leaving in style. I know exactly what we'll wear!'

After my poor reaction earlier, I couldn't really object.

'Okay, if you insist on spending your last night in jeopardy – The Weasel it is.'

♫

Later, as I peeled my clothes off for bed, I caught sight of my reflection in the long mirror in the wardrobe door. I ran a palm over my belly and felt a tightening in my guts. I hadn't been eating much recently. The thought of work caused such a revolt in my system that I'd lost time of the times I'd been sick. Not proper food poisoning vomiting, just the regurgitation of disgusting, half chewed lumps, which floated like pieces of upholstery in the toilet pan. I couln't eat at work, so I told the trainees I ate a healthy evening meal. Though in reality, biscuits and cigarettes often took the place of protein and two veg.

My situation with Tom was unreal. I knew that. But the last few months with him had been pure joy and brought up feelings I couldn't even name. When I'd seen him in the shopping precinct, talking to that black-haired female, I was delighted, about to go over. Then she'd kissed him and they stood very close – clearly not just a friend. The salty taste of confusion rose up in my mouth again. Christ, I hoped I wasn't going to be sick.

It was no good. I needed to end it, before I got hurt, although I couldn't bear to think about what happened after that. Simon was right – I was drifting, in a city I hated and a job I loathed. And soon I'd be all on my own.

18

JOSIE

'Hi stranger! Long time, no see. How's the tour going?' My voice sounded as high and shallow as a TV presenter's. Tom gave me a long look, then put his hands on my cheeks, kissing me like someone who means it. A longing expanded in my chest. But I'd made a decision.

'Josie, I'm *so* sorry,' he said.

I could see he was, but I wasn't sure what for – standing me up in a curry house, or for having another woman.

'The thing is, I couldn't get to the restaurant in time. Our van broke down, so we had to hitch to Birmingham.'

I stared into his worried green eyes, and my earlier resolve started to melt.

'It doesn't matter,' I said waving a hand. 'Forget it.'

'Are you sure?'

'Of course. I'm making coffee. Want one?' I dodged out from under his arms, and stepped down into the kitchen.

'Yeah, okay, coffee would be good.' He sat down on the sofa, and then called, 'Hey, you've been drawing!'

I was glad for some conversation, while I worked out how to tell him. 'Just quick sketches to remind me I was once a creative being.'

'Can I look?'

'See the yellow book. It's mainly people and places.'

The kettle whistled so I poured hot water on instant brown granules, and groped around in the fridge. When I crouched down to peer inside it purred with an electrical emptiness.

'Bugger!' I still wasn't used to Franki not being there, tending to life's basic necessities. 'I'll have to pop over the road for milk.' From behind the sofa, I put a light hand on Tom's shoulder to steady myself as I struggled into my plimsolls. I couldn't resist ruffling his head. 'Back in a min.' I'd forgotten how smooth and strong his hair felt, and how good it felt to touch him.

It was making what I had to say much harder.

Raj was leaning across the counter of his tiny, stock-crowded shop reading the paper. 'Hey Josie. Yer tall feller is back, then?'

'Not for long.' I pulled a face. 'He's a musician on tour, so he'll be off again soon.'

Raj frowned. 'I thought he was Exotic Plumbing?'

I laughed. 'Paradise Plumbing. That's a former incarnation.'

Raj nodded thoughtfully. 'Maybe he'll get sick of travelling and settle down to his trade again.' His face brightened. 'Then you might have a family.'

'You're kidding! Anyway, he wants to head for the big time.'

'Oh.' Raj looked crestfallen. 'Where does that leave you?'

'Hey, I'm a big girl who looks after herself. No bloke's gonna have that much control over my future.'

Raj shook his head. 'You're independent, like my wife.'

'What d'you mean?'

'She's studying for her degree with Open University, watching lectures on television at 3 a.m. while she feeds the baby. Says it stops her brain from turning to dahl.'

'Well women need projects too.' I prodded the paper. 'After all, you've got your footie.'

Raj scowled. 'Don't bloody well get me started on that.' He pointed accusingly at the vast blue football stadium doors, which overlooked the end of our road. 'Did you see the fighting last Saturday? A group of fans shouted *'Get lost Paki!'* at me and my cousin, and threw cans at us.'

'Shit! Whatcha do?'

'We ran to his car and got the hell out. We'll watch it on TV from now. What a place! I can't even support my own team, and my shop is twenty yards from the bloody pitch!'

Inside the lounge, Tom's head was bent over my sketchbook.

'You've got a great eye for line and texture,' he said. 'I love the one of the big, sad woman on the bench, with the hundreds of little flowers on her dress. Must have taken hours.' He patted the seat beside him. 'What else you been up to?'

'Went to The Cat and Bugle with Simon last weekend, but the DJ was crap. Don't know where Trevor Lyons is.'

Tom grinned. 'We've got him. He's driving the van and acting as roadie.'

'Wow! Why?'

Tom laughed. 'Good question. Can't be the money, so must be the adventure of the road. Difficult to sum up the allure of the A40.'

He put an arm round me and pulled me towards him, suddenly serious. 'I meant what I said you know.'

'About the A40?'

'No! In my letter.'

'You mean the postcard of Durham jail?'

He frowned. 'Not that. The letter I sent last week.' His frowned deepened. 'Didn't you get it?'

I shook my head.

Even as I was conjuring up a good way to break it all off, the idea of Tom writing to me created a warm feeling, which curled up inside.

'Shit!' He stood up. 'You didn't get a letter from me?'

I couldn't understand his difficulty in grasping this fact. 'No,' I repeated. 'Tell me what you said.' But he was walking out.

'Hey! Where you going?'

I heard the front door open and Tom said, 'Oh bollocks!' The door clicked shut. For a second I thought he'd left, but he walked back in slowly.

'I lost the bit of paper with your address on. Thought it was number 13. But you're at 30.' He looked devastated.

I considered this. 'Thirteen, thirty – I spose it sounds the same out loud.'

A thought occurred. Whatever he'd written must be bad news. That's why he was being so serious, and looking at me with such concern. Of course! He'd told me about the other woman. He was probably with her the night before, while I sat like an idiot in the Bombay Rose, surrounded by helpful waiters. Can I get you a drink madam? Shall I fetch you some poppadums? Would you like to use the phone to call your friend, madam? I'd pinballed between the tables to the loo, with diners staring up at me in disapproval, and stared at myself in the mirror, anger seeping through prickling tears. What was I even doing there? He'd probably forgotten the whole thing. I wasn't the sort of girl who got wined and dined. Bloody hell, I never even asked for it! Why hadn't I told him not to bother? Despite all my convictions about women's rights, I'd been stood up in the most traditional way. And as I'd wiped my face, I'd vowed never to put myself in that position again.

Remembering this, and looking into his dismayed green eyes, filled me with sudden decisiveness. I wasn't going to ask him what was in the letter, or who that other woman was. And I wasn't going to stop seeing him. He had his life and I had mine. This was the 80's for Christ's sake. We didn't need to own each other like chattel anymore. It was probably only a matter of weeks before he left Coventry for good. So I'd enjoy my time with Tom for what it was. No promises, no demands, and definitely no bloody dinner dates.

Tom still hovered by the living room door. He seemed in a quandry.

'Listen Josie, I'm just so sorry about the restaurant. But I've got plans, let me explain...'

'Shush, it doesn't matter, honestly.' I jumped up and put my fingers over his lips. 'You're here now. Stuff coffee. I've got a bottle of wine, or there's some vodka – or let's have both!'

I swept all the books onto the floor, kicked them under the chair and gave a wicked leer. 'You ever played strip poker?'

He blinked at me several times, as though he'd lost something. Then a grin slowly spread across his face.

'No, but I'm open to learning.'

19

TOM

When we hit Essex our tour took a serious turn. Looking out from the stage side curtains, I saw the venue was filled with skinheads. Cliques of shaven-headed lads hung over the balconies, laughing, spitting and pouring beer on the people below. And in the front of the stage, a mass of lads with pale heads, wearing white shirts and braces, pushed and shoved. I raised an eyebrow at Charlie standing beside me, with his red braces and close-cropped cranium.

'It appears your people await you.'

'Bloody hell!' he said. 'These are hardcore.'

When he bounced up on stage, he was greeted with an almighty cheer. But Eddy's sharp-suited appearance received a less appreciative reception.

'Farckin' queer!' yelled a voice, as he touched the back of his hair nervously.

Len grabbed a mic, 'You rude boys all wanna do some skankin'?' His voice was magisterial.

I could taste trouble, so I decided we better face it head on. Without letting a beat in, I played the opening line to 'Race Unite' over the roar of the audience. Devon and Charlie picked up the rhythm and, without looking up, Vinnie took over the melody. Eddy clutched his microphone like a broken bottle as he started in on the verse. *Come on Raymond* I thought. The skinheads in front of him were jeering as he stared at his set list, in frozen incomprehension. I waved at Len and he stabbed a finger at the set list taped to the top of the keyboard. Raymond's face reanimated. His hands jumped to life, and the whole rhythm line became thicker and more confident. I smiled over at him and we both bobbed our heads in time. The audience was now a pumping mass of dancing arms and legs. Len was leaping round with his usual jauntiness and crashing out chords on his guitar. In the bridge section of the song, he chanted,

Black and white, race unite
We all get together for the bigger fight
White an' black, stick to the fact
We all gotta watch each others back

There were some punches in the air by way of agreement but, half way through the second verse, an unmistakeable dull two-note chant started, from somewhere in the middle of the floor. *'Sieg Heil, Seig Heil!'* Vinnie looked at me. 'Fuck, no!' I mouthed at him. Several boneheads in front started making 'Heil Hitler' type salutes. I looked over at the chief bouncer on my right. He was standing with his arms crossed, chewing gum, as if this was all in a day's work. Len repeated his chant and we went round the chords again. It wasn't supposed to be done twice, but it seemed like the way to go. *'Seig Heil, Seig Heil!'*

Charlie ran to the front of the stage to remonstrate with the skins, bass guitar swinging uselessly as he pleaded them to stop, his palms upturned. Len was shouting something in Eddy's ear. To keep the tune going I picked out a basic bass line on my guitar, and in front of me Vinnie swapped to my rhythm. I squinted out beyond the spotlights. There were two main blokes – unsmiling, older, harder faced – agitating the lads around them with organised determination. I strode to the stage front and held both my hands up at the chief bouncer, who finally looked my way. His face was impassive.

'Seig Heil, Seig Heil!'

'I'm not fuckin' having this!' I shouted to Vinnie.

But before we could act, Eddy and Len jumped off stage, charged at the two hard nuts, grabbed their collars, and propelled them to the side door. It happened so quickly that none of the crowd intervened. The music ran to a dribble as we watched in amazement. A shocked-looking manager threw open the side door and the NF skins were shoved out – with some belated assistance from the bouncers, recalling why they were there.

When Eddy and Len turned round there was a cheer of appreciation from the audience – including those that had been Sieg

Heiling a moment before. They both jumped back onto stage and Eddy shouted down the mic,

'We play to black and whites, to rude boys and skinheads – but we won't play to fascist bastards. We're Original Mix!'

There was another big cheer and I looked up at Devon, who was shaking his head.

The rest of the gig went well. The audience had undergone a metamorphosis, turning into a bunch of cheery working class mothers' boys, and we did an encore of Race Unite at the end with everyone joining in.

In the dressing room afterwards it was another story.

'What the fuck was that?' Vinnie flung his guitar on a sofa and rounded on me.

'How the hell should I know?' I shouted back.

'What's Rick playing at?' he yelled. 'How many more pits of National Front arseholes is he sending us to?'

Len came in smiling. He'd been trading slaps on the back with people who'd been up on stage dancing at the end. 'Chill man,' he said to Vinnie. 'It was only them two – the rest was good as gold.'

Behind Len, Devon was frowning. 'Nah, I don' like it Tom. That situation could have gone either way.'

'Well done for evicting them,' I said to Eddy.

He pulled a face. 'What a shithole.' Then he went out.

'You okay Ray?' His expression was so serious, that I gave him a can from one of the four packs on the table, and took a tin myself.

Vinnie was still railing. 'Rick should be here to sort out this kind of mess, the useless bastard!'

'He's probably got his head in some bloody washing machine,' said Charlie with a dry laugh.

'We're giving it bollocks out there every night – and we've got a part-time bloody manager.' yelled Vinnie. 'It's shite!' He thumped the wall with his fist for emphasis. We all winced.

'Arses in gear! Trev's round at the back exit!' Eddy shouted in at the door.

'Vinnie's got a good point,' Devon said to me, as he picked up empty drum cases, and made for the corridor. 'We all took time out from our life to make this thing work.' He was missing his wife and their beautiful little daughter.

'I'll call Rick from the hotel,' I said to Devon's retreating figure.

In the venue, Trevor and Charlie were packing gear and moving it towards the door.

'Here, gimme those.' I grabbed the keyboards from Raymond, holding out the other hand to relieve Charlie of his bass amp. 'Jeeesuz! This bastard gets heavier each gig.' Hauling gear had built up my muscles, but it was still a chore.

'S'alright for you, yer lanky git.' Vinnie had his guitar slung across his back. He was dragging a laundry bag containing stage clothes, spare cables looped across his shoulders, bandit style. A four pack of beer dangled from his hand. 'At this rate my knuckles will be scraping the floor.'

'Like they aren't already.' I dodged his Doc Marten boot which was aimed at my shin. His outburst had acted like a pressure valve, but he'd blow up at me again soon if I didn't do something to improve things. I had no idea what though.

I shoved the exit door with my shoulder, trying to avoid banging my ankles with the amp, and it only took a moment to absorb the scene in front. Len and Eddy were pressed against the back doors of the van by the two skinheads who'd been ejected from the gig. One of them had a piece of iron bar in his hand. Another was holding a knife in the direction of Eddy's cheek. Two other lads were firmly planted on the tarmac behind them, waiting on their mates for direction.

I shot my arm out, winging Vinnie with the keyboard, to bar his exit.

'What the f...'

'Shurrup!' I hissed, and he saw what I meant.

We both lowered our gear soundlessly.

I pointed to the two skins at the rear. 'After three?' I whispered and Vinnie nodded.

'Why don't you fuck off back to your own country?' The skinhead with the metal cosh pushed a sneering face in at Len.

'Coventry's not a fuckin' country,' said Eddy with a sneer, and there was a moment's incomprehension in which I heard myself say, 'Three!'

Lunging forward, I grabbed the taller bloke round the throat, pulling his left arm backwards with mine, before he had time to react. As we grappled, Len swung at the guy in front producing a grisly thud, and the iron bar hit the floor with a clang. Len winced, clenched one of his fists with the other and brought them both back into the abdomen of the bloke as if he was pitching a ball. As I struggled with the lanky guy I thought, *Christ! I've never been in a fight before*, but for a fraction of a section I'd got him wrapped up like a python. The metal of his wrist watch dug into the flesh between my thumb and finger and I could see the chicken flesh of his white neck, dark spots of blood where he'd picked at his pimples. Then I felt a terrible scraping down my shin and a crunching weight in my right foot. The white hot pain which followed his boot made me momentarily loosen my grip and he tried to twist up into the arm lock. As his fist hurled towards my face, a dark shape grabbed the wrist, and another secured the arm which had escaped my grasp. The lanky skinhead was no match for Devon's substantial drummer's arms.

'You gonna take off now?' Devon held the bloke's arms above his head, like drumsticks.

'Yerra faakin' black bastard!!' said the kid.

'And yer a likkle pink bastard, wriggling like a worm,' said Devon.

At his feet, his mate was rolling on the ground coughing and choking, clutching his stomach. Eddy and Vinnie had the knife guy up against the van doors, and I saw Vinnie delivering a swift knee in the balls. The shorter bloke who Vinnie had jumped was already stumbling off down the road.

'Shit!' Charlie tripped over the gear we'd dropped, as Trevor and Raymond dominoed up behind him.

'What's goin' on out here?' boomed the big bouncer over their shoulders. Suddenly the alleyway was floodlit. The three remaining skinheads were released and, like magic, disappeared into the darkness beyond the glare.

My shin throbbed but I wasn't damaged.

'You alright mate?' I asked Eddy. A line of blood trailed from the corner of his mouth and he wiped it away with his sleeve.

'Let's just get out of here,' he said, opening the van doors. His bleak tone reached new depths.

♪♫

20

TOM

The following morning, in the hotel's breakfast room, I was still trying to quell my fury.

'Fucking stupid racist bastards! How do you put up with it?'

I was talking to Len and Devon. They both looked steadily at me and said nothing. Then Devon leant forward. 'You can't let idiot people like that put a cloud in your sky,' he said slowly. 'You allow that ignorance to infect you, an' you start letting them win.'

With an exasperated sigh, I stared up at the nicotined swirls on the ceiling. 'We've gotta do something about our fan base. We can't be associated with the politics of those fuckin'.... dickheads, or let them hijack our gigs.' I couldn't even find the right words for my dismay.

'We just about got away with it, that the truth,' said Len. 'If word gets out, it could escalate, man.'

'I don't understand. How can you love the music, and not respect the people who created it? How the fuck can you be racist and love Jamaican ska?' I studied the ceiling, as though its dirty patterns might form some answers.

Devon's sarcastic laugh rolled over me: a big bass rumble which came from inside his chest.

'That's the beauty of being so ignorant. Them National Front boys don't clutter their mind with that kind o' consistency, Tom. That's you thinking, not them.'

Len nodded in agreement, sucking his teeth.

'Well, we've gotta change things,' I said. 'We need to do something that says categorically, if you like Original Mix you can't be a neo-fascist.'

A long stare passed between them, as though I was finally getting something.

I leant forward. 'I spoke to Jackson about getting us on the billing at one of those free Rock Against Racism gigs,' I said. 'What d'you think? It'd be a start.'

'Free as in unpaid?' Len frowned.

'Come on man, we gotta do it,' said Devon.

Len rolled his eyes and sighed, but then he slowly nodded, 'Yeah, I spose you're right.'

'Yo! Guess who we found in the caff down the road?' Vinnie's voice from the door interrupted our conversation. From behind him stepped Fozz, with his mac, leather satchel and dark rimmed glasses, looking, in the bright seaside daylight, like some tax inspector from the 1960's.

'Hey, Fozz man!' I strode over, smiling. 'Great to see ya. What brings you to the UK's swingin' south east coast? It can't be the happenin' nightlife.'

He gave a few birdlike bobs of the head. 'Actually I'm following a very interestin' band. I may even have a go at getting' them national coverage.' He gave me a twitchy smile.

'You're kiddin'! Not us?'

'Thought I'd keep in the background for a few gigs and interview you later. But somehow Vinnie spotted me.'

Vinnie rolled his eyes. 'Wasn't exactly hard mate. You was the only one in that punk caff without a pierced face or a red Mohican.'

'Come and meet the others,' I said to Fozz. 'How come you were in that cafe?' I asked Vinnie as we walked over.

'Got talkin' to some girl. Leggy blond in fishnets. Had to be done.' At the word blond I thought how he used to pally up to Josie, and my chest tightened in automatic possessiveness.

Fozz was already shaking hands with Len and Devon, who both looked bemused until he passed them a copy of Pump City.

'Arright now! I seen this paper,' said Devon. 'You only write about punk bands though?'

'Not at all.' Fozz budged up, to let Vinnie shove in beside him. 'We've been waiting for the next big movement.' He blinked, pushing his specs up with a thumb. 'There's talk that you could be it.'

There was silence as I exchanged glances with Len and Devon. It was like the first time we three met up with Eddy in the

Cobblers, and talked about the music we wanted to create, then went to the room upstairs and played a bit of stuff – just arsing around, trying stuff out, sussing out each other's styles. And we were all hoping, and waiting, checking that internal buzzmeter – the zing that starts from your stomach and sherbets up through your chest and throat and makes a great big stupid grin appear on your face as you think – yes, this is it, the thing that's goin' to make the kids go wild. This is great fuckin' music!

'Says who?' I spoke first.

'Well….ehum,' Fozz's eyes darted round the table as he cleared his throat. 'Mainly me at the moment. But I spoke to the editor of New Sonic Waves, and if I produce an article he likes, he'll consider printing it. I'm gonna base the piece around how Original Mix are going down in the places most hit by the recession.'

'You're in luck then,' said Vinnie with a sneer. 'We're only playin' in godforsaken shitholes like this.'

'Our manager has an uncanny eye for choosing apocalyptic towns,' I explained.

'See! You *know* he's a fuckin' waster.' Vinnie wagged his cigarette at me.

So we agreed Fozz could travel with us when he wanted to, squeezed in with his little suitcase – which, when opened, revealed a few neatly folded T-shirts and underwear, notebooks, clean sheet paper and a small portable typewriter.

'He's a bit of a weirdo Tom,' said Charlie in the alleyway, as we loaded the van up after that night's gig. 'An' it's goin' to make travelling even more cosy.'

Devon was struggling out with the bass drum and several other cases pinned under his big arms. 'How we gonna get away, with you chattin' like old wimmin.'

'You not comin' to this nightclub then?'

'Nah, man. Calling the wife, then I want me beauty sleep.'

Vinnie stuck his head round the exit door. 'Come on lads. Let's see if we can sort young Raymondo a bunk up. Pillock says he's startin' to pine for Coventry.'

Trevor put his hands on his hips and started to grind his pelvis. '*You jus' gotta wine and pine,*' he sang.

'You lot definitely need a night of beer and babes,' I said, then turned. 'Not tempted Devon?' But he just laughed.

'See yer there!' Trevor called, as he and Devon drove away.

Charlie and I set off up the road. The others were ahead, marching with drinkers' determination – Len in his pork pie hat, long hands sticking out of sleeves that were always too short, Vinnie's flat top haircut and jug ears hunched down into his leather jacket, and Raymond's slight laddish form, recently padded out in a new flight jacket.

'Where's Eddy?' I asked Charlie.

'He's got off with some bird.'

'Yer kiddin!'

'Said he was goin' back to her hotel.'

I looked away so he couldn't catch my expression. Eddy's business was his own.

'He's a lucky bastard,' Charlie's voice was bitter. 'One snooty look and they fall at his feet.'

I laughed. 'How long is it since you got some Charlie?'

I'd known Charlie since he used to deliver milk with his dad – a ten year old daredevil, who jumped on the back of a moving milk float to sit whistling, swinging his legs.

'Bloody long time, since you ask. I'm too fuckin' amiable. They only go for that sullen shit.'

He was right. Even with his skinhead look – red braces, half mast jeans and dazzling white shirt – he was still more like the housewife's favourite than a dodgy bad boy.

'How about you Tom? You ever see Yvonne?'

'She's getting married again.'

'No shit. Whose the lucky fella?'

'Some guy from the Council. Won her over with a proper job and regular hours.'

'You bothered?'

'Nah. We were finished a couple of years back.'

'You miss the guaranteed legovers though?'

We passed a couple of boarded up cafes and I stared into a locked arcade, its shove-penny and slot machines sitting heavy and dark inside the shadows. Charlie looked sideways at me. Then he punched my arm.

'You old fox. You got another thing going?'

'Look – don't let on Charlie.' I said quickly. 'I don't want anyone knowing yet.'

He shrugged. 'Oiright. Secret's safe with me mate. That mean it's serious?'

We turned the corner. In an unruly queue, under a flickering blue neon spelling out 'Ramsey's', Vinnie and Len were already entertaining a group of giggling girls, while Raymond had his hands in his pockets, trying to look cool.

'Yeah, pretty serious…' I slowed pace. 'Actually, I'm nuts about her, Charlie. When this tour's ended, I'll make it public. But I don't want to muddy the waters now, so keep it to yourself.'

'Vinnie know?'

'No. An' don't tell him, cos…'

'He'll fuck it up, I know.' Charlie mugged at my surprise. 'Well, *that's* hardly a state secret.'

♫

The nightclub was surprisingly swanky, with concealed blue lights shining eerily under glass bar shelves and round the edges of seating.

'Eighty pence a pint!' Vinnie mouthed across the bar, and pointed at me. 'You better be getting them in Shepperton.'

'It'll be the best part of a fiver for a whole round!' I said, appalled.

'You're the only one with that kind of money,' said Len. We jus' paid eighty pence to get into this place too – more than people paid to see us play tonight.'

The money Rick and I had allocated for hotels, food and other expenses was disappearing like smoke. But Len put a hand on my shoulder. 'Come on man, you need to keep the band sweet. Buy the first one, then we're all on our own resources.'

As I turned to the bar, I heard Vinnie say, 'Bloody hell, look who's 'ere!' Then in a leery voice, 'Hello darlin'.'

For a milli-second my heart jumped in my throat – *Josie!*

I spun round to find a couple of charcoaled eyes looking up at me expectantly. But she was much shorter than Josie, with shoulder-length dark hair. I was still surprised.

'Cheryl! What the hell are you doing here?'

She grinned back at me. 'Came to see youse play – an' brought me mate.' Behind her was another girl, pretty, blond and very young. 'Thought we'd have a weekend by the seaside.'

Christ! We'd done so many gigs, I didn't even know it was the weekend. As I handed pints over to the lads, and ordered two Bacardi and cokes, I watched a tenner disappear.

Vinnie squeezed past to grab drinks. 'Here you go girls.' He shot me a challenging look.

'Thanks Tom,' Cheryl said sweetly over her shoulder, and Vinnie guided them over to one of the banquettes.

Trevor arrived. He nodded over the floor. 'Those two were at the gig. They're well into the music.'

'Them girls better not lead me lickle cousin astray. Me aunty's set her heart on him becoming a doctor,' said Len.

'Looks like he's starting on the practicals.' Charlie pointed to the dance floor where Cheryl's friend was leading Raymond out for a smoochy slow number. We watched as he wrapped his arms round her waist.

Fozz appeared as if by magic, eyes scurrying around behind his frames. He waved to Cheryl, then said, 'Good going, Tom. With a Birmingham following, you'll have great home support.'

'Didn't plan it mate. They just turned up.'

'Brian's been playing your demo at The Lord Admiral – so some of them will come to gigs too. And my piece will help.'

'What piece?'

He shuffled in his satchel and pulled out a copy of Pump City. We crowded round to read it.

'*Dare to go where musical politics never went before,*' read Trevor.

'*Fighting recession depression with lightning bolts of Jamaican-inspired sunshine.*' Len grinned. 'Yeah man, I like it,' he said.

'*A finger up to this Thatcherite state's 'stop and search' mentality*'. There's not much about the actual music Fozz.' I said.

Fozz rubbed his chin, head bobbing, lips pursed. 'Thought we'd go in by a different door. That's what interested New Sonic Waves.'

'Well I 'spose you know what you're doing,' I said. 'As long as it brings people to gigs.' The idea of having a solid fan base sent a shiver of excitement through me. It was going to happen for us after all. Even though I wasn't sure what 'it' was – each gig I wanted it more. I slapped Fozz on the back.

'Bring it on mate – do whatever you need to!'

His beady eyes had a little sparkle of pride in them.

'Hey, let's all have another drink!' I said. Len and Trevor both raised their eyebrows, and pushed empty pints at me. I was about to blow the weekends' expenses but, what the hell?

The rest of the night was a bit of a blur. Odd images returned the following day – Raymond necking with Cheryl's mate, Trevor and Charlie dancing like mad boys to a northern soul number. Vinnie and Len arguing over something to do with Eddy's singing. I didn't care. I was on a high. Fozz introduced me to two students from Sunderland who raved about the sound, and asked if we were going to the north east. Len passed me a whiskey chaser and I recalled talking to Cheryl about Midlands bands. More pints. My thirst was immoveable. By the time the house lights flared and we were ushered out, I was very drunk. We were going to make it. I knew it now. There were forces at work bigger than us.

♪♫

Amazingly, I didn't have a hangover. At nine I blundered into the bathroom bursting for a piss, and knocked over my guitar case.

'Tom, I swear, you wake me one more time…' Devon sounded like he might be about to break his pacifist ideals. I looked round at the beds. From under a mess of covers I heard Charlie's steady snores, and I smirked to see that young Raymond's bed was unslept in. A memory surfaced of working up some new song with Charlie – both twanging our strings softly, excited by some weird chord changes.

I pulled on my jeans, shoes and a fresh T-shirt, grabbed my guitar, and closed the door gently behind me. The neighbouring room looked like the aftermath of an explosion. Clothes, bedding and bottles lay on every surface, and the bodies of Vinnie, Len and Fozz were splayed across the beds as if they'd been thrown in unconscious from the door. Eddy appeared from the bathroom, looking pinkly shaved and scrubbing his teeth. For once he looked like the healthiest specimen among us. He gave me an uncharacteristic smile.

'Watcha Ed. Good night?' I said.

His face shut down like an electric gate, and that sad, defensive expression flooded back into his dark pupils. For the thousandth time I wanted to tell him I knew. But I didn't.

'Wanna come and work on a new song?' I said instead.

♪

21

TOM

'Hey Josie! Open the door, it's me!' I called a second time.

Each time we were in Coventry I tried to see her as much as possible. Just thinking of being with her kept me bouyant when the mood on tour became grim, and it helped me keep something like good humour going on in the band. I hadn't managed to ask her about moving to London yet. But there was plenty of time for that.

I prised open the letterbox, and peered through to the living room, where her bare feet rested on the arm of the sofa. Ten scarlet painted toes wriggled into life, then disappeared, as she padded to the door.

'Sorry, fell asleep,' she said. Her eyes looked a bit puffy and the halo of her hair was squashed on one side, like a half blown dandelion. I ruffled her head. 'You're all flat.'

'I know' she muttered.

'Come through.' As she walked into the lounge, she stretched her back and arms upwards, like a cat. From behind, I wrapped my arms round her waist and she turned. As we kissed, her body relaxed against mine.

And I realised how much I missed this – the soft but solid Josie-ness of her, and the knowledge of her normal world, where people went to proper jobs, uncluttered by constant arguments and unvictimised by neo-Nazis. Her place was beginning to feel like an oasis. She never asked much about the past or future, seeming to live in the here and now. These moments kept me anchored, in the stupid frantic whirlwind of the tour. Her breasts were warm and firm against my chest and her pelvis brushed mine. Christ, I was only just in the door and I wanted her already.

'Hey,' she pulled away from me and smiled. 'I made some lentil soup. Want some?'

'Okay,' I said uncertainly. I wasn't really a lentils man.

When she carried it in steaming away it smelled good though. She passed me half a lemon. 'Try a squeeze of this. Brings out the flavour.'

I tasted it with caution, then grinned. 'This is great. What's in it?'

'Just lots of veg and herbs with lentils,' she said. 'Plus a bit of cumin and tumeric.'

I laughed. 'Simple recipe then?'

'Oh, I never use recipes at home,' she said, surprised. 'Just throw stuff in till it feels right.'

We decided to go out for a stroll. Even though it was past dusk, I was glad to get some fresh air. We were back at Rick's again for a few days, trying to record the last track for our EP. The atmosphere in the studio was choking, with Vinnie and Eddy throwing tantrums. And we still hadn't got our fourth song down.

Len had urged me to get a grip, when the two of us went to The Cobblers for a break. 'I know Vinnie's your mate man, but he's gonna split us all up,' said Len. 'If we'd stayed in that room, I'd have had to show him me fist.'

At the previous night's gig in Birmingham, we'd seen Len sock a bouncer who was manhandling a kid scrabbling up on stage to dance. In the mash of bodies, the guy didn't see who'd hit him and Len leant down quickly to give him a hand back up, with a big crocodile smile. Eddy had to turn his back to the audience, so he could laugh without ruining his trademark scowl, and the sight of him trying to hide his amusement cracked us all up. Vinnie missed his solo and we went round the chorus several more times, and by then we were laughing like idiots on a train who'd missed their stop. Eventually Vinnie jumped up, legs scissoring the air, and twanged down on his guitar, emitting a screaming chord to get us all back in the song. Devon was still wiping tears from his eyes at the end of the gig.

'If I ever feel the urge to form a heavy metal band, I give you a call man,' he said.

Vinnie responded with an appropriate pose and rapid tongue flicking. Maybe it was those moments that kept us all together. But

Len was right. With the tensions between Eddy and Vinnie, it was getting harder to find the right glue.

Outside the locked park gates, Josie stopped. She put her hands on the side of my head and drew little circles on my temples with her fingertips. Her big brown eyes were full of concern.

'What *exactly* is going on in here?'

'Not much.' I looked up at the inky violet sky, glowing orange from the city lights below. A warm spring breeze rustled through the tall blackness of trees inside the railings, and a slight smell of grass cuttings and flowers wafted out.

'Come on,' she said. 'There's a gap along here.' We squeezed through a place behind the bus shelter, where a railing was missing.

'Oh shit!' She giggled as we struggled in through the wide thatch of bushes. 'I've lost a shoe.' We both knelt down and groped around in the old leaves and twigs for it, blind as moles. Our hands met, and I twisted my fingers inside hers.

'I love you,' I thought – and the realisation that I'd spoken out loud sent a missile of shock down my throat – but at that exact same moment she yelled, 'Got it!' chewing up my words as if they'd been eaten by Packman.

I stood shakily and pulled her up with our interlocking hands. We were in a kind of natural cavern in the bushes, totally hidden from the outside world. She felt around in the darkness, bending down, to slip the shoe back on. As she leaned against me I breathed into her hair. It smelled of some flowery hair stuff, with a tinge of tobacco. I burrowed my nose into the back of her neck and kissed it. She emitted a little sound of pleasure. Her skin was sweet and salty, like toasted nuts. I wanted her very badly. I gathered her towards me and kissed her mouth firmly. The tip of her tongue found mine. All my confused thoughts about the band, about the future, about what I wanted, flooded together into one force, and I only wanted one thing. I pulled her down and we fell onto the bark and crunchy leaves. The only sound was her short breaths in the darkness. Her hand touched my shoulder, tugging me back towards her. 'Tom,' she whispered. 'Tom.'

'Hang on,' I mumbled, ready to explode.

I felt her fingertips tracing my face and cheek in the dark and I could see her eyes shining up at me, reflected from a distant light somewhere. Her other hand was unbuttoned my jeans. The satiny softness of her hand on me made my brain fizz like sherbet. Soon we were lost in each other, thrown together like small flames, building into one fiery torch. I was aware of a pulsing sensation around me. And for a moment and nothing else mattered except my body in hers and the way we moved together. I soared. Then I fell down, down into darkness the other side.

We must have both fallen asleep because the next thing I knew there was a snuffling sound in the leaves nearby.

'Josie,' I whispered.

'Hmm?' She'd been out cold too. I put my mouth to her forehead, and her soft lips ran up my neck and cheek up to find mine.

'We've got company,' I said. We both looked out. The hulking clouds had withdrawn to reveal a sliver of moon which lit the flat stretch of the park. The fox I'd heard was now sniffing the ground, following some invisible scent across the gleaming grass.

'I hope he finds his lady fox,' she said, as we sat up and dressed. She knelt with her knees between mine and we looked into each others' eyes, now visible in the moonlight. She leaned forward to kiss me and I stroked the small of her back. 'Do you still want to walk a bit?' she said, and then giggled. 'That's supposed to be why we're here.'

Surprisingly I found I did.

The park wasn't huge. We strolled round the tree-lined edges, brushing against lower branches and looking across the silver grass. The frail stalks in the middle beds were studded with the black silhouettes of heavy roses. Josie wound her fingers round mine and we smiled at each other. It was the simplest relationship I'd ever had and somehow also the most complicated. Luckily I'd never had to explain it to anyone. The fact that I was still keeping it such a secret was a mystery, even to me.

22

TOM

As the van motored down the M1, I sat in the front with Devon, with the others huddled in their adopted spaces, our bodies automatically moulding into the shapes required by the metal and plastic of the sparsely upholstered seats. After months of touring, we'd finally finished all our gigs, except for London.

'Can't believe we're playin' The Triangle,' said Charlie. He spoke to Len beside him . 'Hey Len, remember us three bunking off work to see Leroy Johnson in that all-dayer?'

'First time you and Tom heard live Jamaican ska. Not like that punk mess supportin' him.'

I laughed at the memory, and turned round. 'There were over a dozen bands on that bill. I think the ones that gobbed at us were called Head Mash.'

Len grimaced. 'I should have mashed their heads alright. That filth went all down me new jacket.'

'Leroy J was the dog's bollocks though,' said Charlie. 'And we're playing on the same stage!'

In the seats behind us, there wasn't a face without an excited smile.

♬

Backstage at The Triangle, I lit my millionth cigarette.

'Will you stop pacing around Tom?' said Charlie. 'It's like having a bloody great giraffe passing by. I'm trying to re-tune here.' Charlie had been serious instrument shopping, blowing weeks of wages on a fancy new bass, which he was cradling with the care of a new father.

'Why you wanna spend that much cash, man?' Len could take whatever guitar you thrust at him and play like it was his own.

'Dunno how you had money left.' Vinnie eyed the bass with obvious envy.

142

Charlie grinned. 'Some of us don't blow all our dosh on loose liquor and hard wimmin.'

'Stuff off!' Vinnie gave the edge of Charlie's chair a light kick. 'I ain't never had to pay for sex.'

'Yeah, but how long you gonna hold out for Cheryl to let you get jiggy?' said Eddy. I twirled round, just in time to see Eddy thump Vinnie playfully on the arm and Vinnie leap up to thwack Eddy, not so playfully, on the jaw. Charlie snatched his bass and jumped across the room, as a table upended. Eddy reeled back in surprise, then threw a punch at Vinnie without so much as dropping a beat, and Vinnie went down with Eddy on top of him, fighting like a tiger.

'Jesus!' Len and I ran over to haul Eddy up by the arms, still kicking and cursing.

'Yer fuckin' bastard, I'll nail yer bollocks to the wall!' Vinnie rushed at Eddy as he struggled between us.

'Stop it Vinnie, STOP IT!' We're on fuckin' stage in half an hour!' Devon and Trev rushed in from the corridor and lunged at Vinnie from behind. Devon threw a powerful arm round his chest.

'Yer don't wanna do more damage, Vinnie man,' he said.

Eddy twisted free and shoved his face at the mirror. 'Oh shite!' He had a cut lip and the corner of his eye was starting to swell. I cast my eyes frantically round the dressing room, then upended a litter bin and thrust it at a stunned Raymond, who stood against the wall.

'Get a load of ice from the bar.' He gave a nod and scarpered.

How had the atmosphere turned toxic so quickly? 'I don't believe you two! We're close to getting signed and you're behaving like prize twats!'

When Eddy and Vinnie sat at other sides of the room, with bags of ice on their wounds, Devon pulled me out into the corridor with Len in tow. 'Who started all that business?' he said.

I slapped the wall in exasperation. 'I can't believe Eddy could fight like that! He was a bloody maniac. And I could punch Vinnie's lights out. What's his fucking problem?' I was still trembling with fury.

'Them Ragged Moth people, they here tonight?' said Devon.

'One of them, but he's a senior guy.'

Devon stomped back into the dressing room. 'Listen now! I ain't just spent months away from me family for you two to mash this band's future.'

Everyone was silent. From the venue, clapping and cheering signalled that the final support act had gone back out for their encore.

Devon picked up a drum stick and pointed at Vinnie then Eddy. 'You two go out and play like the best of friends. We need to let these London people know what we're made of in Coventry. Char!' he sucked his teeth.

'Original Mix – yer on in two minutes!' someone shouted at the doorway.

'Come on, this is it!' I yelled. There was a flurry of activity as people grabbed jackets and instruments.

'Oi, Tom.' I turned. 'You'll need this.' Vinnie held out my guitar strap. I snatched it from him. 'Don't fuckin' speak to me!' I hissed.

As we approached the wings, there was the loudest drumming of feet I'd ever heard. The air was unbreathably hot, and the smell of bodies and spotlight-seared smoke hit my face like a mask. The Triangle was the biggest and most famous venue we'd played and, as we ran on, the thunderous roar of the audience vibrated through my chest.

'We're Original Mix from Coventraay,' drawled Eddy. 'And we're here to show you what real dance music is.'

'Do it Eddaaay!' Cheryl's unmistakeable voice peeled up to the stage. I pulled my guitar into my hips and I saw Vinnie hitch up his own, like it was a loaded rifle. Then we gave it to them.

♫

We ran back into the dressing room, punching the air, and Devon grabbed my fist giving it a big affirmative crunch, then lobbed me a towel. 'We did it, man! We played The Triangle!'

My smile stretched so wide it ached. I wiped the sweat from my face and neck. 'I heard some fuckin' fancy flourishes from our drummer too!'

'I was inspired, man. That vibe was good!'

Everyone herded in, all shouting at once.

'Whoa Shepperton!' Vinnie clapped me on the back. 'They fuckin' loved us!' I bristled, still furious with him about earlier, but he didn't even notice.

'Spot that Moth guy, standin' by the back bar, Tom?' said Charlie.

'Them London kids were straight onto the rude boy sound alright!' said Len, as he stretched over for a coathanger.

'Hey Tom, yer jammy sod – looks like my work is done!' Trevor was slapping his palms off each other, as if wiping them clean.'Rick's talking about you all stayin' down here. So I reckon I'll get back to Cov after tomorrow's gig.'

I felt a pang of regret. The whole band respected Trevor without reservation. He'd become our rock, and it would be very strange without him.

'Right then Trev.' I pushed him towards the door. 'To the bar, for your send off!'

As we reached end of the corridor I realised something. 'Shit, left my fags behind! Be right back.'

I was turning the dressing room key, when I heard a light secretive cough from the next room. Fearful for the security of our gear, I kicked the door open, shot a hand out to stop it swinging back in my face, then stared in surprise.

'Fozz! What you doing in here?'

He was hunched over a work table, with the club's techie, the guy we called 'Ska-mad Steve', and in front of them, reflected in the beam of an angle-poised lamp, was a flat mirror. Fozz blinked up at me and from behind his specs, his eyes shone like oiled raisins. 'Blimey, you made me jump. Shut the door Tom.'

Steve was straightening a line of white powder along the mirror with a razor blade.

I stepped in. 'Cocaine? You must be kidding!'

'It's fantastic!' Fozz gave a couple of excited dips of the head. He pointed. 'Try some. Make those touring heebie-jeebies go away.'

I bent down to look at the powder on the glass, fascinated. I'd never seen real coke before.

'Go on, you deserve it after that gig.' Steve passed me a rolled up tenner. 'Hold it just above and inhale.'

I leant over, for closer inspection. In the mirror, my cheeks stuck high and pale, and my eyes stared back, green and watery – the face of an exhausted fish.

'Christ, I look like shit!' I said, and my breath scattered the powder across the silver surface.

'Yo, back off!' Fozz pushed me away. 'That's valuable wares you're blowin' round. Make like a hoover not a hairdryer.'

I straightened up, then patted his back. 'You know mate, what I fancy being is an alcohol pump. I'm gonna suck up a big, cold pint. Chased down by several more pints.'

'Why not do both?' Steve was carefully scraping the stuff back into an even line with the blade.

I rolled the wrapped note between my thumb and finger, thinking. Then I placed it on the edge of the table. 'Nah, not tonight. Gotta talk to the record guy. Oughta stick to known poison.'

'Another time,' said Fozz. 'When you need a really nice buzz.'

Steve inhaled the last line, and his eyes closed as he held his breath. When he opened them he looked more alert. 'Don't know what you're missing.'

He beamed at me, eyes sparkling, as further down the corridor I heard Trevor shouting my name.

♪

23

TOM

November, 1984

Hoping to score enough to get me through the night, I lurked at the back door of The Orb in Kentish Town. I didn't mind what I scored, as long as it was strong and enduring.

'Wanna make some quick moolah, mate?' A gaunt, lanky punk, with piercings in his cheeks, ears and nose, stood beside a pile of music equipment, rolling a joint.

I nodded.

He pointed to a clapped out transit, parked nearby. 'Help get this gear in the van then.'

While I lugged amps, speakers and stands to the vehicle and loaded them in, his two mates emerged, arguing about their gig.

'An ahm tellin' yaa, it's got six friggin' verses!' The short, fat punk's face turned pink, as he protested.

'No-one faakin' cares, yer cunt!'

'I wrote it, I faackin' care!' At this, Six Verses kicked a nearby binbag, then applied himself to repeated booting, until chicken bones and take away boxes were strewn across the road, and the black plastic a tattered memory. Sated, he wandered to the van and stood watching me, as I eased a speaker stand into a space just under the roof. He strolled to the side door and, seeing I'd left the bench behind the driver free, he muttered. 'Faack me.' Then he shouted to his mate 'Oi! Where's the rest?'

His mate bounded over. 'You finished? Faackin' 'ell. How you keep that seat empty?'

I shrugged and held out my hand. 'Fiver,' I said flatly. I'd be lucky if they didn't spit in my face and drive off laughing. It had happened before.

Their other two members drifted over and were taking in the spare seat situation. 'We can all fit in there easy,' said Piercings. 'I ain't catchin' no night bus.'

He shoved a hand in his back pocket, to pull out a small wadge of notes and ripped off a bluey. I took it with a nod, and stood back as they squashed in and gunned the engine. A few yards away, the van screeched to a halt. There was some discussion going on inside and then Six Verses leaned out.

'Oi, mate! Wanna do that again?'

The fiver crinkled in my hand, thick and substantial. It meant for a few days I'd have chips and a four packs of strong lager – the minimum required to get some sleep. I might even be able to buy some grass from Spanner, the ex-squaddie who'd taken residence upstairs in the squat, and grew his own.

'When?' I said.

'Know The Barbarian, Ferris Lane?'

'Yeah, I know it.' The fights there were legendary.

'Tomorrow night, six o'clock. Fiver to unload, and a tenner to stay an' load up after.'

It was the best offer I'd had in weeks. 'I'll be there at five thirty,' I said. 'Don't give it to anyone else.'

Six Verses stared back at me hard, then nodded. 'Here mate – catch!' He lobbed out a small silver packet, which I caught mid-air. The transit spluttered into high revs and with a crunch of gears they were off, leaving me in a petrol-infused cloud of exhaust fumes. I sat on a low wall and opened the crumpled tin foil in my hand. A small block of Morrocan and a couple of blue capsules. It was a start. At my feet a photo snarled up at me – it was Piercings' ugly mug on a flyer. I picked it up to find out their band's name and read 'Reknaw'. Wanker spelled backwards. Very funny.

The back door behind me opened and a scruffy figure emerged and lit up.

'Oiright.' He sat beside me. 'Seen the singer from that band what was just on? Reknaw.'

'Wanker,' I said.

He shrugged. 'Probably. But he wanted to buy somethin' offa me.'

I turned. 'Oh, yeah?' I felt the edge of the fiver digging into my hip, through the ripped pocket of my jeans.

'What you sellin'?'

24

JOSIE

I was sanitizing the work surfaces when the boss appeared. Stan had an inexhaustible supply of sombre suits and maroon V-neck pullovers, always worn over a shirt and tie. With his white-streaked black hair, and bushy beard, Stan was like a kind old badger with the lads, and seemed to have a vast supply of patience.

'Guess who's back?' he said.

One of his hand's rummaged in his jacket pocket, no doubt searching for keys, as a familiar brown face appeared in the crook of his elbow.

'Tash!' I said. 'What happened to your placement?'

Stan pulled Tash out from behind, like a bear pawing out a cub. 'Don't ask. Let's just say there was a mis-match. Anyway, he's all yours – until we find something else.'

There was a taller person behind him too. 'Scuse Stan, can I get past?'

Stan moved aside to let Michael in. As he passed, Stan put a hand on the boy's shoulder. 'Come up after lunch and we'll go through your Hearing again.'

Michael nodded, his face impassive.

Then Stan extended a fist and gave Tash two soft thumps on the top of his head, as if signalling him to drive off. 'Be good for Josie,' he said.

'I'm always good, ain'it?' said Tash to me, unblinking.

'Lord give me strength!' I heard Stan mutter as he left.

I watched Michael's preparations. As usual he hung up his jacket with care, peeled off his jumper, and straightened his T-shirt, adjusting the collars and smoothing down every last pucker. Then he wound an apron around his middle, before he came into the main room.

'You back on cooking small ting?' he said to Tash without much interest.

Tash had picked up the potato peeler, and was trying to peel the plastic edge of the cutting board. He gave Michael an impish grin. 'My placement weren't suitable, so Stan's findin' me a better one.'

'If you say so.' Michael shrugged.

'Looks like it's just us three today. What do you both fancy making?' I leant over and gently removed the peeler from Tash's hands. 'How about chicken pie and apple crumble? We could try making real custard.'

'Itchy fingers can do crumble,' said Michael. 'That nasty stuff sticks under your nails. I'll make pie. Can I add mushrooms?'

'Of course you can.' I plonked four big cooking apples on the board in front of Tash, moving the peeler just out of his reach. 'Okay, what's the first thing you do?'

'Get an apron and wash me hands, ain'it?' His face tilted up at me with a know-it-all expression.

'Bloody hell!'

'Miss, you swore!' said Michael. The ghost of a smile flickered briefly on his face.

'Yes well, it was the shock,' I said.

Half an hour later, Tash was dicing apples and Michael was browning onions in a large frying pan, so I retreated to the table to catch up on my trainee logs. Their peaceful industry was such a rare pleasure, that I sat back for a moment, taking the chance for some downtime.

'You had your Hearing?' Michael asked Tash. He was stirring the spoon in a slow figure of eight.

'Had it last month,' said Tash.

'Mine's next month,' said Michael in a quiet voice. 'How did your's go then?'

Tash's eyes were wide. 'The magistrate was well fierce. He asked me if I was a delinquent.'

'What d'you say?'

'Told him I was a British Asian, like the woman at the police station said. The judge man told me not to get clever.'

'What they give you?'

151

'Ten months suspended sentence, an' I got bound over.'

'You gotta stay out of trouble for ten whole months?' Michael gave a wry smile.

'Me uncle wishes they'd locked me up. On the weekends, I have to work for his family.'

'What's he do?'

'He drives a bus, an' me Aunty runs his sari shop on Fortishill Road.' Tash pulled a face. 'It's full of ladies changin' their minds. An' them big rolls of material are heavy, man.' He flapped a hand over his head as though brushing off an imaginary pest. 'The women laugh at me and mess at my hair.'

'Don't sound too bad though.'

'If I don't get a real job, uncle says he'll send me somewhere they'll really straighten me out.'

'What, Pakistan?'

'No, Leicester.'

'Shit! You better behave then small fry.'

After lunch Tash left with Stan to visit a possible new placement, and I turned to Michael.

'Right Michael – we're going to do a full stock take,' I said. 'We'll empty the fridges and cupboards and I'll call out the items as I put them back and you can write them down.'

'Wan' me to make a list of what's missing too?' His dark eyes filled with a solemn purpose.

'Great idea! Then we'll have a shopping list.'

After a couple of industrious hours, we stopped for a tea break.

'You've got a lot of common sense Michael.'

I set our mugs down on the table, then went back for a wet cloth to clean up some spilled pepper. 'Do you know what placement Stan's got in mind for you?' I said as I wiped.

Michael shuffled the papers in front of him and looked at his feet. 'I've got me court case soon,' he said. 'He's probably waiting to see what happens.'

152

Although he seemed burdened by some heavy knowledge, Michael was an intelligent lad, much less impulsive than Tash, and not half as bitter as the others. And I never pried about how how the trainees had got into trouble with the law. If they told me that was fine, but otherwise I stuck to cooking.

'Once that's over though – what would you like to do?' I dried the table with a teatowel.

Michael's hands were gripped round his mug. His face was deadly serious. 'It's Crown Court,' he said. 'I think I'll be going down.'

I lowered myself onto a chair, and viewed him. His pupils were deep and black as dungeons.

'Are you sure?' I said gently.

He nodded and I decided to break my own rule. 'What are you charged with Michael?'

'Rape.' He stared into his tea.

Surely it wasn't possible. 'Did you do it?'

Michael watched a bubble moving round the edge of his mug. 'I don't know,' he said flatly and looked up. 'There was four of us and this white girl. I knew one of the lads, but only 'cos I'd seen him round. We were on the railway embankment, drinking tinnies and someone said 'let's do some glue'. One moment I was laughing and it was daylight. Then I woke up and it was dark. I don't remember what happened in the middle.'

'What does your solicitor think?'

'They found that girl down the embankment and she was all battered. I had some scratches too – and we were the only ones there. My solicitor says it's don't look good.'

'And they didn't search for the other lads?'

'They didn't have to. It's her word against mine. My solicitor says she was out cold when they found her, an' she doesn't know what happened. But it'll be hard to prove it wasn't me – and the judge wants the case closed now.'

'When did it happen?'

'Nine months ago. They keep deferring my Hearing.' By the ease of Michael's delivery, he was well-versed in the language of legal jargon.

'I'm really sorry Michael,' I said.

'It's alright,' he said. 'I just wanna finish the cooking bit. Decorating's okay, but I like cookin' better.' He gave a weak smile and I felt my eyes prick with tears.

I went into the kitchen, and busied myself collecting dirty tea towels.

'You won't say nothing Miss?'

'Course not,' I said. 'It's your own business,'

'Thanks.' Then he added, 'You know them Christmas cakes we made? Can I ice mine up sometime and take it home?'

'Of course,' I said. 'Why?'

'My mum never had the money for a Christmas cake,' he said.

'Well, we'll make sure she gets one this year,' I replied.

25

TOM

Over a café breakfast in Camden, a forlorn-looking Rick admitted that his usual 'no job too big' attitude had been thoroughly tested by the guys at Ragged Moth and their big brother company, United Associated Artists – or UAA as they were known.

'They were dead keen at first, saying they'd go to your gigs. But they kept pullin' out.'

'What reason they give?'

'Too far to travel, no one available, that kind of shit. Been down four times and met a different guy each time. Each one wanted to see the tour schedule, look at press cuttings and hear the bloody demo tape all over again.' He speared a sausage with his fork and stared at it mid-air. 'Sometimes I can't remember why we wanted them.'

I grabbed his arm. 'Cos you said we needed the distribution a big label could offer. And the exposure in the press,' I said. 'C'mon Rick, yer big yetty. You got us recorded and touring – and with Fozz's help we've shifted loads of records. Plus that guy from Ragged Moth was at The Triangle last night.'

'I s'pose.' Rick munched on his sausage in sulky agreement.

'An we've played our arses off,' I continued. 'Some of those venues were rockin'. The kids are wild for the ska sound, and we've got a real fan base. They were there last night – just for us.'

'You mean those girls from Birmingham?'

'Not just them, some lads. We met them in Sheffield or Leicester – Jesus, I don't know, we've seen so many desperately poor towns, the UK's one big fuckin' closing down sign to me now – the point is they travelled right down the country, 'cause they think that we're it.'

'Oh yeah? An' what's that?' Rick had really lost his mojo.

'I dunno, the right buzz, the dog's bollock's. The sound that gets blokes on the dance floor again, after years of watching disco girls twirl under mirror balls, to songs by castrated dicks in satin pants.'

Rick raised an eyebrow. 'The metal heads dance,' he said.

'No they don't Rick. They shake their fuckin' hair, doing the grebo – like they're trying to de-louse themselves. No offence meant.'

He shook his head, at my clear lack of understanding. But, as the last piece of bacon disappeared into his mouth, he looked thoughtful. 'It's true, the gigs have packed 'em in, and your EPs have been flying out.' He gave a short nod to himself. 'An' I've had to get another load of copies cut, plus take on some kids from an unemployment scheme to help pack 'em. So at last we've recouped our losses on the van.'

I lit a fag. 'That mean we're not stoney broke?'

'Not now. But we could do with a bit more bung to keep the sump from leaking more oil.'

It always came down to plumbing with Rick.

♪

Later, at the record company's Camden office, one of Ragged Moth's young executives lounged in a big swivel chair, still bearing puppy fat under his pristine Lacoste T-shirt, one denim-clad leg resting on his knee. 'Look, to be honest, we like your sound and the vibe's great. But you're still a hell of a risk for us.'

He tapped his fingers on one of his leather boots – expensive-looking pull ons, the colour of shiny new conkers. 'How many EP's you sold?'

Rick told him.

'All promoted through this little Birmingham fanzine?'

We nodded.

'So you're looking for a cash injection, as well?' The executive's expression showed more amusement than derision, as if his day had just got more entertaining.

'Actually,' I leant forward to prop my elbows on my knees. 'What we want is a publishing deal and a distribution deal. We'll carry on putting out our own records.'

The executive was incredulous. 'You know what that means?' he said.

'We get the record sales and you get the percentage for the distribution and publishing,' I answered.

'It usually works that we're the ones giving the percentages.'

'We like to break the mould.' I kept my expression blank and my voice even.

'And why should we do this?'

'Because that way we take all the risks. You put a set amount to recording, promotion and distribution and give us a loan. We'll all sign up to a guaranteed number of singles and albums per year. And if we bomb, your losses are limited and you'll still get your money back.'

He frowned. 'How?'

'We'll put Rick's business against the loan.' Rick eyes nearly shot out of his head, but the bloke was still fixated on me, like I was a talking dog.

'Fuck! Never heard anything like it. And what if we say no?'

'We'll go elsewhere. There've been other approaches.'

The guy's eyeballs flickered round, as he calculated the competition. He smiled lazily. 'Not Amoeba Records?'

'Can't say mate. But they know the terms and there's still interest.'

He ran a hand over his forehead. 'It's bloody mad you know. Nobody gets that sort of deal.'

I didn't blink. Beside me, Rick had frozen into a solid lump. The young executive swung round in his chair and looked out of the window. Below us, Camden market was a pattern of tarpaulin-roofed stalls and bustling shoppers. Above the traffic noise, traders calls rang out. It was all on offer here: bargain clothes, hats, jewellery, records. Everyone was knocking prices down, making offers, doing a deal. The executive's gaze followed a bloke carrying a double bass above his head, as he threaded through the crowds, the huge, unmistakably-shaped case, balanced perfectly. Behind him a punk girl with a violin ran to keep up.

The chair swivelled back to us and sighed. 'Alright. I'll put it to our team. We're half owned by UAA now, so they also have to sign off major contracts. What label would you put it out on?'

'Our own label again – Mix Up.'

'And you really think you could make this work?' He shook his head in disbelief.

'We'll make it work.'

He rolled his eyes. 'I must be fucking mad. You better come back tomorrow when I've had my head examined.'

I stood up. 'Right. When?'

'Afternoon.'

'Look, bring your whole team to see us tonight,' I said. 'We've got another gig at The Triangle.'

He nodded. 'OK, you're on.'

'Rick?' I squeezed his shoulder, and he stood, as if woken from a trance. 'Thanks for your time. See you all tonight.' I propelled Rick downstairs and along the road. When we were out of sight of that window, I shoved him through the door of a pub, fully prepared for a bollocking.

'I'm sorry mate. You know I'd never make you lose any of the weird and wacky bits of your business – the whole beautiful plumbing-recording-transport empire you've so uniquely built up. It'll all stay intact, I promise.'

I turned to the waiting barman. 'Two lagers please and two double whiskies.' Rick was still staring at me. Shit, I'd really overstepped the mark. But something had grabbed at me and I'd run off at the mouth. Suddenly, it had seemed so unfair to hand over everything without a fight, after all our hard work. It was ours; it was *mine!*

I pushed a pint at Rick and he grasped it, pouring half of it down his gullet, and wiped a hand across his mouth.

'You take the fuckin' biscuit Tom. He's going to consider it.' A wide smile swept across his face. 'The best deal in music history – an' he's actually going to consider it!'

26

TOM

The second night, we took The Triangle by storm. There was quite a gathering of mods this time, who shouted their approval of Eddy the minute he appeared in his sharp suit. But the sight of Ragged Moths' executives, drinking halves of lager at the back bar, really pushed Vinnie's button, and in his fury, he slammed into Wasteland too early, meaning we all had to jump in behind him. I noticed Raymond was the first in – his confident chords disguising Vinnie's lone ejaculation – and I smiled. Raymond was a quick learner.

I'd also started inserting a couple of short solos of my own, which even Vinnie had to admit worked. I didn't go for his style – the melodic line rising to a screaming wail – instead I'd experimented with strange angular chord changes, runs of notes with pecking little disharmonies. 'It's oddball, but I like it,' Charlie had said, and Devon nodded. So I kept them in.

And now, even after Vinnie's ropey start, we kicked ass. After weeks of exhaustion, our ability to play live was infallible. And in that big, low-ceilinged, sweaty venue, our elated fans all pounded up and down in helpless reaction to the ska beat, cheerfully singing Eddy's words of misery back to him – hundreds of beaming faces incanting the bleak lyrics, with total recognition on every level.

I looked at the back of the venue, and saw the puppy-faced record guy and his colleague nodding. Rick stood on his tiptoes, and stuck both of his thumbs up to me. The monumental importance of this moment suddenly hit me. We were playing at London's most famous nobodies-to-somebodies launch pad, and a key independent record company were considering us. *This could really be it!* The potential shimmered in front of me. It was all possible – getting out of Coventry for good, becoming something, making it. I stepped forward to give my short solo burst and the audience cheered, so laughing like a loon, I finished in a Hendrix-style chord crash, holding my guitar over my head.

Vinnie mouthed 'Wanker!' at me, but then we were both back at the mic, backing up the chorus – singing, along with four hundred other voices.

And then everything went into fast forward. The audience surged onto the stage to dance and we had to do three encores before we extricated ourselves from the chaos. In the dressing room, I stripped off my drenched shirt and grabbed a T-shirt.

Charlie grabbed my guitar and pushed me out. 'Go, speak to the big boys Tom – I'll sort this lot.' The three executives were handing round spirits now. I shook hands with them and introduce them to each of the band. The PA was belting out classic mod and reggae numbers, and it was difficult to hear what was being said.

'I think they might buy it!' Rick shouted in my ear.

'What, the whole deal?' I said.

'I showed them the Mix Up logos and they like them,' he yelled. 'Told them we commissioned a graphics studio.'

I laughed. Len, Eddy and I designed our record logo in The Cobblers, drawing on peeled beer mats, and lining them up along the table – until old Frank brought over a telephone pad and urged us to use that instead. The image was two lines on a grey background, one black and one white, doodling around each other before making two rude boys profiles in pork pie hats. It had been a quick job one afternoon, when our first records were being pressed and the company rang to request our label design. As for 'Original Mix', that came from a packet of tandoori spices I bought in an Indian shop. After a year arguing over hundreds of names, scrawled in a bulging book, it was the first suggestion that didn't end up in a huge argument – which was as good as it ever got.

'We need a proper contract,' I hollered into Rick's hair-curtained ear, as someone handed him another Jimmy Beam. 'Can't let our guard down, even with an independent. They'll fleece us if they can.'

'Could get used to this though,' he said raising his glass. And when the next shots came our way, there was a sense of entitlement in his short, troll-like shoulders.

Further down the bar, Len and Devon were talking with great animation to two Moths, no doubt reasoning with them, Jamaican–style, on why they should back us. And at the end of the bar I spotted Vinnie teaching Raymond how to down shots in one, having somehow managed to obtain an actual J.B. bottle in front of him. I noticed Eddy buying his own pint, his face a mask of suspicion and cynicism, as puppy-face himself leant against the bar, trying to engage him in conversation. Good luck in charming Eddy, I thought.

People crowded in, with congratulations – thumping me on the back. Charlie started boring anyone who would listen, to muso-crap about his new bass. And a group of lads were enthralled.

'Looks like you did it, Tom!' Fozz appeared at my side, blinking through his glasses and nodding rapidly.

'Nothing signed yet,' I said.

'You desperate ol' bastard – let's go celebrate!' He flicked his eyes sideways indicating the door to the Gents. 'Got hold of some great new stuff. Time you relaxed.'

After jumping around on stage for two hours, then downing a couple of beers and three shots of whiskey, I now felt my stomach growl. 'Dunno Fozz, I'm bloody starvin'.'

He peered at me, intensely. 'This'll cure all that. You'll see.'

His earnest face made me laugh, but he was right. The world was sparkling with potential and ripe for new experiences. 'You're a mad fucker, Fozz. But you got us this far. Come on then. Party time!'

♪♫

'Tom, Tom, wake up man. Jesus! First you can't get him to shut up and sleep, and now he's fucking comatose.' Someone was hauling my shoulder back and forth. I opened my eyes to see assorted denim-clad thighs clustered at my head. Painful fibres were shooting across the top of my skull and burning through my brain like electric currents. My mouth tasted like battery acid.

'Raymond's been hurt,' said Charlie. 'We gotta go see him.'

As I rolled my legs out of the duvet, the bile rose in my stomach. My head weighed far too much for my neck.

'We could stick him under a cold shower,' I heard Vinnie suggest helpfully.

'Let me through!' I shoved at several chests and lunged at the toilet bowl. A stream of acrid poison issued out of my throat, but as soon as I felt the relief, my stomach spasmed again and another came out, then another, and another. When my innards had finally finished their dance of death, I knelt back and rested my cheek on the bathroom wall. The cold was like an angel's blessing. I opened my eyes. Vinnie was at the door lighting a fag.

'C'mon man, this is serious. Raymond's been mashed.' Devon shoved past Vinnie and hauled me on to my feet. His broad, anxious face was straight opposite mine.

'What happened?' Now I wasn't dying myself, I could give Raymond due concern.

'Woah!' Devon jerked back. 'You need to deal with that nastiness first.' He handed me a toothbrush and paste.

'Oi! Not *that* one!' Charlie snatched it away and shoved another at me.

'Get cleaned up Tom,' said Devon. 'Raymond got jumped last night by some beefheads and they put him in hospital. Len's over there now.'

'Fuck, where…?' I said through a froth of toothpaste. I couldn't remember anything much after telling puppy-face he was the best mate in the world, and believing it.

'He went off with Cheryl's mate, after you all decided to go to the other nightclub.' There was an alarming void in my memory, but this wasn't the time to worry about it. I spit out and wiped my mouth.

'How bad is he?'

'We don't know. Eddy got a message through that bloke Adam.'

'Who?'

'Ragged Moth man.' Devon was looking at me strangely. 'You hit your head or something last night Tom?'

Raymond was propped up on pillows, wearing a green gown. His face was puffed up on one side, one eye was closed and he had purple bruises on his face and arms. He tried to sit up, but Len waved him down with a commanding hand.

'Am thorry.'

'Jesus, Raymond. It's not your fault. What happened?' I said.

'I wath with Linda,' he said, wincing as he moved his jaw. 'Two skinths came out from a doorway. They kept athking what she wath doing with a coon. We tried to keep goin', but they jumped me from behind.'

'Them bastards!' Devon's voice was deep hiss. Beside me, I heard Len breathing heavily.

'Linda ran to fetcht two copperths from nearby. But she said they slowed down when they saw the thituathon.'

'Shit!'

'Thoth skinheadths got plenty more kickth in, before they were pulled off me.' He put a hand up to his aching cheek.

We surveyed the bruises. Each one mapped where a steel toe cap had smashed against his tender flesh, crushing the tissues until blood seeped under the skin, spreading like purple juice. I felt nauseous.

'They didn't get my handth.' He grinned faintly, only one side of his mouth responding, and wiggled his fingers. Then he grimaced. 'But my faith and armth are thore.'

'What the doctor say, Raymond?' asked Devon.

'He wanth to check therth no internal bleeding. But I told him, I had one arm over my sthomach, and anyway they were aiming for my ballth.'

'Awww!' We chorused, and each of us cradled a hand round his own crotch.

'I tried to be a hethog.'

'A what?' I said gently.

'Hethog.' Raymond, nodded with insistence.

I looked at Len, but he shrugged.

'Hethogg, hethogg.' Raymond was becoming agitated. I wondered if he had some sort of concussion.

'Describe it mebbee?' said Devon.

Raymond rolled his eyes. 'Heth-ogg!' he said. 'Cometh in the garden, drinkth milk, rollth into a thpikey thing.'

'HEDGEHOG!' we all shouted.

At the same time a young red-haired nurse entered the room. She slapped a jug of water down on the bed-end table, and shot us an eagle-sharp look. 'You're not to excite him. He's had enough trouble.' She moved out, her clip-clap heels and crisp uniform leaving a stern warning no words could muster.

Devon leant forward to Raymond. 'Did the police catch them bastards?'

'Didn't try. Let them run off.'

'Char! They're worse than animals!' I'd never seen Devon this angry.

'Before the ambulanth came, I tried to give a dethcripthon, but they weren't interethted. Said I wath drunk.'

'Just as well,' I said. 'Probably numbed the pain,'

Raymond pulled himself up, his dark eyes pricked with anxiety. 'The doctorth coming back at three, with thtronger painkillers. I can thtill play tonight.'

'There's no gig tonight,' said Len. 'You can't play now, anyways.'

Raymond grabbed his wrist. 'Don't thend me back to Coventry, Len!'

'Char!' Len sucked his teeth in derision. 'Where we get another keyboard player like you, rude boy?'

Raymond gave a lob-sided smile and sunk back into the pillows.

'We've got some free days,' said Devon.

'Plenty time to heal up,' I added.

The door opened a bit, and Eddy's head poked round the edge. He entered, with Charlie and Vinnie behind. Charlie held a balloon with *Congratulations! It's a boy!* printed on it.

'Jesus, I hope the other guy looks worse.' He held the balloon out. Raymond nodded his thanks. 'The hospital shop didn't have *Shit! You've been beaten up by neo-Nazis!*' Charlie added.

'Should get 'em in – might be a good earner,' muttered Eddy.

'What's this, a party?' The young nurse was frowning at the door, a bedpan in one hand.

'Fuck! What's that thing?' said Len.

'Only three visitors at a time,' she said, holding the door ajar. So we trooped out into the corridor. Devon was shaking his head and Len was silent, lips pursed tight. I tried not to imagine how shit-scared Raymond must have been and to concentrate on breathing through my mouth, blocking out the combined smell of chemicals and cabbage, which threatened to make me gag again.

After a couple of minutes Vinnie came out, looking grey. He'd been kind of phobic about hospitals since his mum was killed in a car accident when we were kids. 'Need a fag.' He strode off without looking back.

Outside, the four of us sat on a low wall, watching ambulances pull up. On the other side of the path, a young black guy hobbled out on crutches, his leg heavily stiff under a cast, one leg of his jeans roughly cut away, as if in a hurry. He took out cigarettes and nodded to Len and Devon.

'Yer gotta hope his injury was from football,' I said.

'Still a prize fuck off though,' said Vinnie.

'And what would you know about it?' said Len, his voice a growl.

'I'm just sayin'. ' Vinnie looked at Len with surprise.

'Well don't say!' Len was on his feet, yanking Vinnie up by the collar of his leather jacket. 'Jus' where the fuck were you last night?'

'What?' Vinnie bristled, ready for a fight.

'Raymond would have looked out for hisself, if he hadn't been so pissed up.'

'C'mon man,' said Devon. 'We all got some blame there. Me and Charlie left the second club aroun' the same time as Raymond and his girl, but we didn't walk with them either.'

Len looked at him in question, and Devon shrugged. 'Two's company and four's enough for poker – but they weren't interested in cards, if you know what I'm sayin', man.'

Len's hands fell down uselessly at his sides, the sudden despair incongruous with his jaunty dog check jacket and pork pie hat. 'Last thing me aunty said was take good care of Raymond an' mek sure he don't get into trouble.' He sighed heavily.

Len's aunt was an intimidating woman, with God and Righteousness on her side, and she brokered no blurred lines. We all considered this.

Devon sucked his teeth, and shrugged. 'Char! It's not so bad.' He gave a wry grin. 'So he's took up drinkin', and been mashed by skinheads.'

'An' he fell for a white girl,' said Vinnie.

'Plus now he's turned into a 'hethog',' I added.

'Arh man, she gonna box me ears to Jamaica!' said Len. But as we chuckled, his smile slowly re-emerged.

At that point the others came out. 'Doctor says he'll be out tomorrow if he can piss in a glass pot!' yelled Charlie.

'From how far back?' I called.

'Shame Trevor's took the van away,' said Devon.

'Me and Len will fetch him in a taxi,' said Charlie as they reached us.

'You're just hoping to see that red haired nurse again,' said Eddy.

Charlie raised his eyebrows at me. 'I like them stern. An' you could see everythin' under that uniform when she bent over. Oh man!' He put a hand to his heart and pretended to swoon. 'I know nurses don't get paid much, but those panties were well skimpy.'

I shook my head. 'You sad little perv.'

'What we doing now?' said Len.

'Drink,' said Vinnie.

'No!' I said. 'We're seeing the record people in two hours.'

'Plenty of time then,' he replied, striding for the nearest pub.

'Don't look at me,' said Eddy. 'He's your problem.'

'Since when?' I snapped.

'Since long time.' Devon raised himself from the wall. And Len patted me on the back in consolation.

♫♪

27

TOM

A few hours later at the Ragged Moth office, we perched on chairs and on sofas, in unruly combinations. My whole body was still toxic, and thoughts waded slowly through the cold, heavy porridge filling my tender head.

Puppy-face, whose name was indeed Adam, introduced the first idea. 'Okaaay!' He lit a cigarette and swivelled in his chair, surveying us for a bit. My eyes followed the fat gold signet ring on his middle finger, and I dimly registered that I hadn't seen him in the same suit twice. Today's ensemble was a pale grey with a pink shirt, which I supposed must be a Camden thing.

'We'd like to get you on board,' he said.

'On what, the good ship fairy cake?' muttered Vinnie.

'Shut the fuck up,' I said wearily.

Len put a restraining hand on his shoulder. 'C'mon Vinnie, let the man say his thing.'

Adam outlined the deal, punctuating particular points by poking the air with his cigarette.

'Hang on. What's that bit about writers and royalties?' Vinnie sat up.

'The credited songwriters receive an extra publishing percentage.'

'Like fuck they do!'

'It's standard practice.'

'We work as a team here – equal splits,' said Vinnie, arms folded.

'Oh yeah? Which lyrics did you write then?' said Eddy.

'That's irrelevant.' Vinnie's mouth was resolute. 'We take equal shares, don't we Tom?' Several heads shot round, at the sound of Vinnie calling me anything as civil as Tom.

Len sat forward. 'When you say lyrics – does the toastin' count?'

Adam thought for a moment. 'Lyrics would be any words that are part of the song, and can be written down – so yes.'

Len sat back with a grin. 'Never thought of myself as a songwriter.'

'Hang on a minute,' said Eddy. 'You wrote this much.' He put up his forefinger and thumb as if holding a short stick of air. 'And I wrote this much.' His palms encompassed a vast space.

'True. But my bit gets repeated over and over,' said Len, nodding.

'It don't fuckin' matter, 'COS WE'RE ALL GETTING THE SAME!' Vinnie jumped to his feet.

Then everyone was shouting at once, even Rick, until my head throbbed like my skull was being bored by a pile-driver. I looked at Adam, whose eyes flicked from person to person, and his mouth tightened.

'Be quiet!' he bawled. Everyone shut up.

'Now please sit down. Clearly there are fine details to sort out, but the main thing is you're going to be under our wing now.'

'That your ragged wing?'

'SHUT UP VINNIE!' everyone yelled in unison.

It felt good to agree on something.

'Let's leave it for now. We'll talk again tomorrow.' Adam got on his feet, to round up the proceedings. 'Tom and Rick, I want to map out some extra gigs, so, if you can stay around for a moment…'
As everyone left, Eddy hung back.

'It's okay Eddy, I can sort this out with these guys,' said Adam. A look which I dimly recognised passed between them, but my head was in too much physical anguish to examine it.

I leaned back and surveyed the acidic and fluorescent coloured posters on the walls. Mainly punk groups, with spiky hair, bad teeth and ripped clothes, gobbing phlegm at their fans.

'These walls must have heard a lotta rows,' I said.

'Actually your outfit pretty much takes the prize,' said Adam. 'Listen, I'll be honest. This band would rise quicker if you lost some ballast.'

'Ballast?' I gave Rick a warning glance.

'You've got three guitars and you could lose one,' Adam said conversationally. He picked up a gold packet and tapped out a cigarette. 'Help yourself.'

I craved nicotine so much my fingers itched. 'No thanks.' My voice was cold. 'You making some conditions here?'

'Just suggestions.' He inhaled and leant back. 'Course, with extra capacity, you could also consider having real horns instead of using synth sounds.'

'What, and lose our keyboard player too!'

'No, Tom. I'm just saying. Before you take the next steps, you'd be advised to review the line up.'

'Oh, are you? This is the same bloody line up that's played countless dire towns and gone down a storm. But I forgot! You didn't bother to come and see those! Anyway, the kids love Len's toasting, it's a vital part of the ska sound.'

'You know I'm not talking about Len.'

'Same goes for Vinnie – he's part of the mix too.'

Adam took another long drag. 'Well, it's up to you. What d'you think Rick?'

Rick's face was stoney. 'Tom decides what he wants on stage. That's his job.'

I could have hugged him.

Adam stubbed out his fag. 'Alright then. Let's talk about the immediate future. We need to get that EP re-recorded, plus a single of Wasteland, and set some more London gigs.'

As we walked from the office and a light summer breeze wafted up the stairs, and I realized I'd left my jacket behind. I pushed his door open, and saw Adam was gesticulating at someone on the street below. 'Forgot this,' I grabbed my leather and made to go.

Adam spun round. 'Wait up Tom.' I hesitated. 'Listen, your loyalty is touching – but I mean it when I say this is the right time to review the band.' I stared at him with barely-disguised loathing. 'I like you Tom,' he said. 'But this is a tough–ass business. You'll need to harden up.'

'That it?'

'Not all. You should consider dispensing with the services of Mr. Double Denim now too.'

'What? Rick?' But I wasn't sufficiently shocked, and Adam spotted my split second's hesitation. 'Fuck off,' I added.

He grinned. 'Original Mix could be really big Tom – but then, you know that. Lose all dead weights.'

I departed, shaking my head and, without looking back, I pivoted my right elbow to give him the benefit of my middle finger. His laughter followed me down the stairs.

A familiar figure stood below and I gunned my sights up at the window, where Adam's silhouette quickly disappeared. 'Alright Ed. Whatcha still doing here?' I said.

He shrugged. 'Just looking round the market. Listen Tom, we've got to sort out the royalties, man. You and me wrote most of the songs... an' give Len his due too, of course.'

'Christ Eddy, I've got the daddy of all hangovers. Can't this wait?'

'I suppose.' His eyes narrowed. 'What you gonna do now?'

'Either sleep, or start again.'

As if I'd said the magic words, Fozz was at my side with a little shy smile and some birdie head nods. 'Charlie and Rick said you'd be here. Word is, you've gotta come and take your medicine, like a man.'

'Where are they?'

'Pub at the end of the market,' he said. 'An' Charlie said it was important to tell you – Rick's buyin'.'

Fozz couldn't possibly understand the unique significance of this. We sprinted down the road, leaving him standing on the pavement, bemused.

♫

28

TOM

Once Raymond was out of hospital, Adam booked us into Ragged Moth's studio, so we could re-record Wasteland to professional standards. The premises were grotty, but the equipment was pretty impressive, and we spent most of the first day trying things out, so the engineer – now my co-producer – could recreate our sound.

Afterwards, the others all disappeared to the West End, and I went to a gig in Soho with Fozz, at his suggestion.

'Look, I know jazz is for old gits. Moth eaten cardigans, food in their beards. But you've gotta hear this band,' he said.

In a pub nearby we had a couple of lines each, to soften the culture shock, and the horror of paying so much to get into 'London's number one jazz venue'.

'Is that cos there's only one?' I said, wondering why I'd let him talk me into this.

Then we sat at the back of the venue, nursing overpriced beer and surrounded by thickly perfumed, starched-haired old dames and beet-faced whiskery gents, who clearly thought that red socks with brogues were the sign of a free heart. The band walked on stage, nodded politely at the audience and smiled at a few people they knew. Christ, it was going to be worse than a dinner dance. A short black bloke in a suit said it was a privilege to be here, and that this was the launch of their new album. Everyone clapped politely and one person gave a short whistle. I thought: big bloody launch – to fifty old biddies. But maybe this was their entire market.

Then he picked up a clarinet and played the most sublime line of notes I'd ever heard, winding its way up the scale, moving from major to minor in a heartbeat, starting classical, then pure Arabian Nights and on to a new form, then another, getting faster and weaving up and down the register. My heartbeat increased, as I tried to follow the sounds, recognise the inferences, leaning forward as if it would help me keep up. It was music like sex. Not the physical, but the inside feelings, where anger and sadness and joy intermingle, overlap and swirl round. But before he reached a sound climax, he pulled back, took the music down like a kite, and reeled it in. The audience clapped ecstatically – which was just bloody weird, because the band definitely hadn't finished. The drummer started caressing pads with metal brushes, like he was painting is favourite shed, then he beat out a soft rattling rhythm, and the bass player joined the line, picking his notes with unhurried ease – fat throbs, like a plastic drum cascading down a long flight of steps. It was so sparse but so…intelligent. I looked at Fozz. He was leaning back with his eyes shut. As the clarinettist let his notes diminish, the pianist picked up the melody line. His fingers threw out a complex of rhythms and harmonies, as easy as if he'd been threading beads on a string, and the sound grew again. The clarinet guy picked up a tenor sax and they started the process over again, rising and swelling, until I felt giddy. There was something I recognized about it all, a sense of passion and restraint in counterbalance.

Suddenly I wished to god Josie was there with me. She would understand this music. It wasn't incendiary like punk, and it didn't have the driven joy of ska – but it made me think of other possibilities. I thought of the gigs we'd go to when we both moved to London, and smiled.

Afterwards Fozz said, 'Wanna chat with the band? I know the drummer.'

The guys were having their arms pumped off, by old fellas and beaming women. 'Amazing talent!' One bloke boomed with the volume of a grenadier on parade.

'No, yer alright. Let's get some air.' I didn't know what I'd say anyway. I wasn't even sure what the hell we'd just heard.

'Don't say anything to the others about this,' I said to Fozz in warning. 'I don't need any new aggro.'

The next morning I was shoved back into the vile reality of seven big blokes all shacked up together. We were staying in a small, cheap flat Adam had procured, and it was proving very different to bunking up in B&Bs and cheap hotels. There wasn't much extra space, but the real problem was that it seemed less transitory, more like a territory shared. And without Trevor's easygoing cheer, shining a light on everyone's sheer dickheadedness, we were exposed.

'You stood on me hat yer claartarse!' It was ten a.m. and Len stood in the middle of the lounge, on a mess of bedclothes, in his T-shirt and underpants, dark muscled legs quivering with rage.

'Why you fuckin' leave it on the floor then?' Vinnie unzipped his sleeping bag and stood up from the sofa. 'You knew I'd gerrup up for a piss at some point.'

'You should look where you put your big stupid feet! Why I gotta work aroun' yer ol' man's bladder?'

'Who you callin' an ol' man?' Vinnie rounded on him, his pink and white blotchy chest puffed up like a Christmas turkey.

'For Christ's sake, is this the only fuckin' wake up service we get at this hotel?' Eddy entered the room yawning. The sight of Len and Vinnie, jaws sticking out and hands on hips in their skiddies, stopped him dead. He gave are leery grin.

'Ooh, sorry ladies, didn't know I was interruptin' a pillow fight.'

'An' you can fuck right off too!' Vinnie headbutted Eddy in the stomach and suddenly they were rolling round on the floor throwing punches and yelling curses.

'What the hell started that?' Charlie picked his way across the clothes-littered floor, to where I stood at the breakfast bar, stirring my coffee.

'Ask the cat in the hat.' I pointed at Len with my teaspoon. He was sitting on the sofa, trying to prise his felt brim back into shape.

'Eddy's a great fighter,' said Charlie, in appreciation. 'We gonna stop 'em?'

I took a long slurp of coffee and tried to inhale through my nostrils again. Nope. It was gonna take more than mere human strength to unblock my sinuses, though the previous evening had been worth it.

I thought of the clear, haunting beauty of those clarinet notes, and the look on the drummer's face as he answered with patter of beats – creating a sort of musical conversation with the pianist. And now, in the fug of first morning ciggie smoke, Eddy had a Vinnie on his front in a TV-cop grip. Vinnie was threatening to split his head open and piss in his skull.

'Oh, for cryin' out loud!' I heaved Eddy off, while Charlie made a human shield against Vinnie. 'We're here for a few fuckin' weeks, with a record to cut and Raymond just out of hospital. If you're both so desperate to take over his bed, go to National Front HQ, an' tell them they're cunts for kicking a kid in.'

They both glowered, and after a moment I realised everyone was still staring at me.

'Tom mate,' said Charlie, vaguely pointing at his snout. 'Yer nose is bleedin'.'

♪♫

29

JOSIE

When I wheeled my cycle through the parked cars in the industrial unit, Stan came out of the Scheme's door, as if he'd been waiting for me.

'Josie, I need to speak to you before you start work.' The briefcase, usually welded to his hand, was missing. And those shoulders, primed for the next load of trouble, had sagged. His face was ashen.

'Christ, what's happened?' I did a mental flash, listing of all the problems I'd dealt with recently, deciding what was most likely to come back and bite me.

'Not here. Upstairs.'

Stan steered me into the unit and lurked silently while I locked up my bike. By the time we were sitting in his office I was breathing hard from agitation.

'Just hit me with it Stan. Whatever I've done, I'm really very sorry. I'll try to sort it out.'

'No pet, it's not you. It's Michael.'

I hadn't seen Michael since his court Hearing two days before.

'Oh shit. Did he get custody?'

'Yes, but I'm afraid it's much worse.' Stan put a large hand on his forehead and rubbed his head, flattening his hair. Excess water was puddling in the corner of his eyes. A drop formed on one of his lashes and trickled down beside his nose, disappearing into his beard. He fetched a large cloth handkerchief out of a pocket and wiped his cheek automatically. A sliver of cold sliced into my throat as I recoiled in my chair. It was my father in front of me, tears streaming down his face. *'Bad, bad news Josie. It's your brother Ally....'*

Stan reached over to put his hand on mine.

There was a yelp as if from a hurt dog and my chest shook. The tears fell fast and caustic on my cheeks, but it was over in a matter of seconds. I removed my hand from under Stan's and swiped my cheek.

'How?' A voice very like my own asked.

'He hung himself in the court cell, the same night,' Stan said. 'They hadn't transferred him yet.' He shook his head. 'They're meant to take all belts, laces and ties off people, but they were really busy. Perhaps they forgot.'

Or maybe he hid them, I thought.

'Does anyone else know?' I said.

'We've just been informed. We'll tell the lads after lunch when the tutors all come back from site. I need you to occupy a few of your old group this morning, but then you can leave, if you want.' His watery grey eyes met mine. 'Can you hold it together till then?'

I nodded and stood up. Stan handed me a tissue and I scrubbed at my damp face with rough strokes, making for the door. 'What will you say to them?' I asked, my hand on the handle.

Stan shook his head slowly. 'I honestly don't know.'

Downstairs the lads were filing into the unit for the morning's work, in twos and threes.

'It's true! They're movin' a Paki family into the estate,' Darren was saying.

Adolf's chubby face was red, and he scowled at Mark and Darren. 'Youse don't know what you're fuckin' talking about,' he said.

'It's true, Gob said,' Mark intoned, as if he was repeating a bit of the Bible.

Adolf stared down at the floor thinking, his mouth set in a line.

'Come on gentleman. Liver and onions don't casserole themselves.' I started to unlock the kitchen.

'Goin' toilet,' said Darren and loped off.

'I ain't staying up at Wood Green if it's gonna kick off,' hissed Adolf to Mark as they fell in behind me.

'Me and Darren are,' said Mark. 'In case Gob needs backup.'

I pointed at the pegs near the door, and they donned aprons, making automatic double knots at the front, then carried on talking as if I couldn't hear them.

'Well, o' course,' said Adolf giving his knot a tug. 'I'll be there if I'm needed, like. But I only got three more weeks probation.' He'd jutted his chin out. 'Once no probation officer's on my back, I'll be gettin' lively.'

Mark dropped his gaze. 'Yeah well. Maybe it won't 'appen anyway.'

Darren entered and looked in question from Mark to Adolf. Mark shook his head.

'What would you like to make then?' I asked them.

They all stared, as if I'd been beamed down from another planet.

'Cooking,' I reminded them. 'If you don't fancy casseroles, you can choose.'

'Pasties! said Mark and Darren in unison.

'Okay, go find a recipe,' I pointed to the bookshelf. 'And what about you?' I said to Adolf. By deft sentence structure, I'd managed never to use his nickname.

He sniffed and the familiar grin curled up. 'I might just have a go at that French pastry thing you talked about the other week.'

I frowned. 'What thing?'

'You know, that fancy thing you'd never done, 'cos it was too hard.'

I thought back on our sessions, amazed that he'd listened to anything. So much of the day was taken up with minor squabbles, bickering over workspace, and constant patter about gangs, fights, girls, and all others matters related to their real lives on the estate. Through it all, I continued to talk about nutrition and cooking and how to take care of yourself. But I assumed they heard it just as background noise – like the radio in the carpentry workshop. I recalled flicking over the page dismissively.

'Oh crikey, you don't mean éclairs?'

As he nodded, his smile increased. 'That's it. Them cream cakes with chocolate on top.'

'Nobody makes their own choux pastry though,' I said, alarmed.

'You said the French probably did.'

Christ, how did he remember that?

'I meant that only the French would be daft enough to do it. Everyone else buys their éclairs from the bakery, like a sane person.'

'If the fuckin' frogs can make it so can I.' Adolf's boots were planted solidly apart, belly out and chin lifted. Something like a Dunkirk spirit shone in his eyes.

I thought about the news they were going to get after lunch. 'Alright, if you really want to try,' I said finally. 'But the likelihood of it working is zilch. Do you understand?'

Adolf nodded. 'Leave it to me, Miss. Then I've only got myself to blame.'

I nodded slowly in amazement.

Several long hours later, we stared at three dishes of pastries.

'Mine are best,' Mark said, pointing to his pasties. 'Cos I got the frilly bit right along the top edge, like in the picture.'

'Well mine's got extra meat in.' Darren scrutinised his one massive handiwork, out of which brown stuff flowed from several points, like a burst sewer.

'What do you think, Miss?' Adolf pointed to the recipe book propped up behind his éclairs. The resemblance was amazing.

I clapped my hands slowly, in respect. 'I'm completely in awe of your talent with choux pastry.'

He face was wreathed in happiness. 'The first lot was duff,' he said. 'Had to throw it. But you just have to keep tryin', or you won't get no better. Don't yer Miss?'

'You certainly do.' I'd never get used to the random maturity which sometimes shone out of him like a searchlight.

By the afternoon Stan had called all the trainees back to the unit, to tell them about Michael. Despite his offer of escape, I stayed. It seemed cowardly not to be there, and anyway, where would I go? Stan delivered the news quickly and without drama. There was a collective intake of breath and the staccato sounds of, *Shit!* and *Fuck!* fired softly into the air.

'Michael was on a very serious charge,' said Stan. 'Without much chance of leniency, due to the circumstantial evidence. But still...' He wiped his forehead with a large handkerchief, before continuing. 'We want to say most strongly, even if you ever find you're in extreme trouble, please resist harming yourself. There's always someone to help.'

'How comes no one helped Michael then?' said a voice. 'His Brief was fuckin' shite!'

Everyone looked at Stan. Underneath their expressions – some blank, some screwed in contempt – I saw small signs of anticipation, a face tilting, a leaning forward, an open mouth. They were waiting to receive some words of hope, a 'get out of jail alive' card.

Stan shook his head. 'We can't influence the final decision of the courts, and we couldn't speak to him, because they don't allow visitors before transfer to custody. But we would have helped with his Appeal.'

There was a lot of muttering amongst the trainees. Next to me, a stocky black lad, whose name I'd never caught, leaned in between Darren and Mark, who stood in front of him. 'It's fuckin' bollocks,' he hissed in a whisper. 'Everyone knows which big bastard shafted that girl. It was Gob.'

Adolf gave him a sideways glance, and his brow was creased in consternation.

'Shurrup!' spat Darren, with a kangaroo punch of elbow backwards.

The black lad winced, but his face was set. 'I heard Gob said she wanted it, cos she's a slapper,' he finished in whispered venom.

Stan started speaking again. 'The family's solicitor has told me if anyone has information about the case, they should let him know,' he said. At this, the lad's torso sank and his lower lip pouted in distaste. Stan continued, 'It won't bring Michael back, but it could clear his name.'

In the silence all eyes studied the floor. Stan gave a nervous cough. 'And if anyone wants to talk about their own pending court case, my door is always open.' He gave everyone a sad, crumpled smile and his beard ruffled. Then he looked at Barry and shook his head.

'This is a terrible, terrible thing,' he concluded with a huge sigh.

Barry straightened his shoulders. 'But you all need to carry on and finish the programme,' he said. 'Give yourself the best possible chance, and we'll vouch in court that you're turning things round.' He looked at all the lads with meaning. 'Now – knock off early today, but we'll see you as usual tomorrow.'

The inert group stirred into movement, but there was none of the usual competitive bounding to get out of the door.

Adolf was last to leave. We were the only two still there, and he was wore such a dismayed look that I gave him a small wan smile. 'Well done on your éclairs,' I said. 'Enjoy the rest of your placement.'

'It's not fair, Miss!' he blurted out. The gingerbread man grin had turned upside down, and his eyes were full of desperation. 'Michael never hurt no one.'

30

TOM

We grabbed a quick lunch and ran back to the studio. Once Wasteland was in the bag, we were going to re-record our whole EP in earnest. I tapped the glass to alert the engineer I was there. Shoving the last bite of ham roll into his mouth, he tossed a newspaper aside and swung his legs down as I opened his door.

'Ready to go again?' he said, mouth full of food.

By the sixth take, and a thousand arguments later, it was nearly four o'clock. We crammed into the sound booth and listened to the latest result.

'You're still in early with that riff in the second verse Vinnie,' I said. 'But maybe we can live with it.' I rubbed my temples with thumb and small finger, attempting to stop the throbbing in my head.

'You could always record separately,' the technician suggested again quietly.

'NO!' we all chorused at him.

For once we were in perfect time.

'Only saying.' He rolled his chair back and took out his fags. 'You're doing it the hard way. Lotta bands drop notes in for hours, till they've got it all together. And that's after they've put their sounds down separate, like. Recording like this, someone's bound to be out.'

'Only the git who had three pints in a forty minute lunchtime,' said Eddy.

'I never had three pints,' Raymond appealed to Len.

'Not you, Ray,' said Charlie. 'He means Vinnie Volume, fastest drinker in the Midlands.' He didn't usually have an issue with Vinnie, but now he sounded peeved.

'Oi, wanker!' said Vinnie. 'Drink never effects my playin'.'

'Listen to the tape, man.' Len poked a long finger at the 24 track machine, where the tape still silently rolled round two big discs.

'Gerroff my back. Trouble is, the whole sound is crap in this place!'

'Hey! Howsitt goin' lads – enjoying the studio?' Adam appeared at the door, wearing a pale yellow jumper and an orange scarf.

'Jesus. It's daffy fuckin' duck,' muttered Vinnie, as we filed out of the booth and into the studio.

'It certainly got a lot of everythin', said Devon, waving his hand at the vast mixing console. 'We're just workin' out whether there's aspects we don't need.'

'Oh? Not liking the sound?' Adam looked to Eddy, then me. Eddy turned away, quite rudely.

I leaned forward. 'Thing is, we're used to producing a raw, live sound. This is almost too smooth. I guess that's what makes the errors stand out.'

'They're not my soddin' errors.'

'Vinnie, put a fuckin' sock in it!' I turned to Adam. 'Here – have a listen.'

Much as I distrusted his motives, we had to use his experience. And as Wasteland replayed, he chewed his lip thoughtfully.

'How did you get the original sound on your EP – you know, that echoey thing?'

I thought back to the many long evenings tweaking and mixing, with Petulant Pete. 'Dunno. We hoofed it round quite a bit.'

Adam's brow creased. 'Hoofed?'

'We sent a feed to the outside loo, let it swirl round a bit, picked it up with another mic we'd put in there.'

'You mean that effect of singing in a bathroom, *is* you all singing in a bathroom?' Adam grinned at Eddy.

'Not me,' he said, stony-faced. 'Just the backin' vocals.'

'We did the same with the snare drum,' Devon reminded me. 'We sent it down to the kitchen.'

'Kitchen?' Adam asked Devon.

'Yeah man. It picked up a lickle bit of reverb,' Devon looked innocently at Adam, then his mouth twitched at the corners, as he turned on his richest Jamaican accent, '…an' den some rice an' peas.'

Everyone chortled.

'Very funny.' Adam waited for us to stop laughing. Then he addressed the sound guy, 'Listen to the original with Tom. See which effects need recreating. No point in getting a fuller sound and losing the vibe along the way.' The techie nodded. 'And Tom, we need to talk again about making a video.'

'Wow!' 'Bonza!' The band grinned at each other like kids.

'I've been considering your idea.' I took a deep breath, and faced him. 'We don't want that studio set up, with loads of tossers doing bad acting.'

'Oh?' Adam looked disappointed, as if he'd already alerted his tailor. 'Where then?'

'Coventry of course!'

There was an approving cheer from the lads, and Adam was outnumbered.

♫

Ragged Moth hadn't exactly signed us yet, and the issue of who got what money wasn't settled. Adam had agreed to studio time with that skilled engineer, and distribution of a better recording of our EP – alongside a single of Wasteland – both put out on our own label. Plus he was paying for the video shoot. All with the sole option for Ragged Moth to sign us, if we got into the charts.

'That's all the commitment you're prepared to make?' I asked Adam, as I sat down with Eddy to negotiate again, before we all went home for a swift weekend off.

His face slid into a wry grin. 'You're the one who started playing hardball, Tom. And it's a bloody good deal for starters.'

'Fuck off.' He was an infuriating dickhead and he knew it.

'Though you could also have a small cash advance,' said Adam, his voice casual. 'Most bands do. Tide you over and for buying essentials.'

184

He was trying to get us in hock to Ragged Moth before they'd even signed us. I was itching to thump him.

'No.' My voice was decisive. Beside me I heard a sigh, and Eddy's body sagged. I twisted round, catching his eyes rolling back to position, as if they'd exchanged a look. But when I turned back, Adam's expression wore the same smug benevolence.

Outside I pushed Eddy through the doors of the nearest pub.

'Sit.' I pointed to a table and went to the bar.

When we'd both had a slurp of beer, I spoke. 'We'll be okay, Rick's paying some in.'

Eddy's tilted his head and surveyed me. Our friendship had grown out of music, when we'd both split from the a punk band called Epik – realising they weren't ever going to be – and over several years we'd developed an unspoken respect for each other's part in the mix. Until we'd met Adam, I'd trusted Eddy implicitly. But now he seemed to be siding with the guy. It was unnerving.

'You coulda taken the dosh, it wouldn't have killed us,' his drawl was slow, considered.

'Handouts would put us at a disadvantage,' I said. 'They need to sign us.'

'Jesus, I thought I was paranoid.'

'Yeah, well now it's my turn.'

'You should give Adam more credit, Tom. Perhaps he's genuine.'

I gave Eddy a look of incredulity and pointed the end of my cigarette at him. 'We agreed never to forget the industry's run by talentless crooks and bastards, out for what they can get – even the indies. We need to keep the upper hand.'

But Eddy just gave an exasperated tut, and stalked to the bar – leaving me wondering whether I'd ever really know what was going on in his mind.

♪

31

JOSIE

I cycled to work, full of happiness about the weekend I'd just spent with Tom and thinking of what now lay ahead, because I was starting with a new group. I'd met them during Friday sports sessions, but of course they didn't speak to me – yet. Their allegiance was with Barry, currently off work sick, having strained his back. We'd missed Barry's handover, and the benefit of his stocky reassurance, but it would all be fine – I could handle it.

As I locked my bike in the disused art room, with a usual sigh of regret, and noticed a few new faces, milling about in the Area. I smiled and said a general hello, but nobody replied. There was some kind of secretive business going down, which was obviously more important. So I walked towards the kitchen, smiled at my four, and gestured to the kitchen door. They swapped reluctant glances.

'Come in, I don't bite,' I joked. But their faces remained sullen.

They had donned aprons, washed hands, been given the basics of food hygiene and scrawled names on their log books, before I realised that nobody had said much yet. It seemed this would be a hard bunch to crack.

Deciding they wouldn't be up to an individual interpretation of the full English breakfast, I handed round recipe books. 'You're making shepherd's pie today,' I said. 'These recipes vary slightly, so you'll taste them at the end to see which you prefer, and why.'

Mention of free eating always received a massive reaction.

But nothing.

I tried to make eye contact, without success. 'Okay, let's get on.'

An hour later, I wished there was a kitchen radio. The lads whispered between themselves a bit, but the silence was almost total, and without any come back, my chattering voice sounded empty and parrot-like. Even the tasting went down poorly. When asked which recipe they preferred they all shrugged. The tallest lad finally pointed at one plate.

'Oh? And why?'

'Not many carrots,' he said. 'Don't like 'em.' Then he looked away.

So much for conversation.

I let them go off for their break early. Usually my lads crowed to the others, about what a fantastic dinner they'd made. But they shuffled out in silence, changing to normal speech in the Area, before the big door banged shut. What a weird bunch.

I wandered upstairs to hand Maureen various dockets and receipts, which she processed with her stoney-faced efficiency. This only took a few minutes and I still had an hour to kill.

Back in the kitchen, I spotted the Christmas cake that Michael had made. I unwrapped a piece of the greaseproof paper, and inhaled the aroma of spiced fruits. He'd got the mixture just right. I thought of how he'd tested it, that day Gob came in, carefully poking a skewer into the middle. When he'd pulled out gooey cake mix, his face creased with indecision. He'd wrapped extra paper round the cake to stop the outside burning, then we'd both crouched to look through the oven glass, as if it was a hot aquarium, deciding what temperature was required.

'Another twenty minutes, at gas mark 4?' he'd said. I'd nodded.

'My mum will be made up,' he'd told me when the others had gone out. And for the first time, I'd thought he held some hope for the future.

How wrong I'd been.

The afternoon was even more turgid. My trainees showed no interest in cooking, and enervated by an hour out of the unit, they messed around and chatted amongst themselves, as if I didn't exist. I found two lads huddled in the anteroom, sniggering over a deck of nude playing cards.

'Look, if you're not going to finish those scones, you may as well get off home,' I said in exasperation. They grabbed their jackets and scarpered. The other two turned round with expectant eyes.

'Finish your washing up first please,' I said.

They dumped all the bowls in the sink, gave them a cursory wipe and were gone. The oven pinged, and the scones I removed filled the air with sweet, bready aromas. Normally this would be the time for melting butter, jam and greedy appreciation. I just didn't understand.

I was by the door, squeezing the mop out, when Barry's group returned with another tutor. They were laughing loudly and crudely at something, but they spotted me and their laughter stopped, as if they'd been switched off. They filed past the kitchen in silence, heads turned away from my direction.

Upstairs, in desperation, I spoke to Maureen. 'Is there something I don't know?' I asked. 'Everyone's being very odd today.'

She carefully hung a peppermint green cardigan across the back of her typing chair, and plucked her coat from the stand behind. Her lips pursed in sour disapproval. 'They're very upset about their letters.'

'What letters?' I asked.

'They're all to be interviewed by the Police, because Michael's case is being re-investigated. The police think some of the trainees are withholding evidence.' She stared at me. 'Surely you know – it was your accusation.'

I gawped at her. 'What do you mean, MY accusation? It wasn't like that at all! I just told Stan I heard the lads say they know who really did it.'

She pouted again. 'Well Stan phoned the Chief Inspector and said it was your tip off.' She pursed her lips and considered. 'I knew no good would come from Stan's 'open door' policy. Those twins were up here, handing in time sheets around then. I expect they overheard and told the others.'

The black lad whose name I didn't yet know wandered upstairs with a timesheet. When he saw me, he stopped dead. 'Didn't know there was anyone else snitchin' round up 'ere,' he said to Maureen. 'Got this paper for yer.'

He thrust the document at her and stomped back down the stairs.

As I stood there in shocked silence, Maureen pulled on her coat and shrugged. 'Well you can't expect any sense from this type of boy,' she said, plucking up an ugly handbag and walking to the door. 'But perhaps they'll forgive you, in time.'

I sat down on one of the hard chairs, breathing fast, angry breaths, furious about the unfairness of it all. I'd grassed them up – so the fuckers had sent me to Coventry – *in Coventry!*

Even if the lads relented, I wasn't prepared to apologise to anyone. I thought of how heartbroken Michael's mum must be. She deserved to know that someone else had believed in him.

I walked briskly down to the kitchen, where I fastened an apron tightly round my middle, opened the cupboard and took out icing sugar and a block of almond paste.

At six thirty, I knocked on Stan's door.

'Josie – good grief,' he said. 'Why are you still here?'

I placed a large biscuit tin on the desk in front of him. 'Michael made this for his mum.' I opened the lid, revealing a white iced cake, decorated with green holly leaves and glossy red berries. 'If she tapes the lid to make it airtight, it'll keep fine 'til Christmas.'

Stan removed his spectacles to peer into the tin. 'How marvellous.' He gave a deep painful sigh.

'And this,' I pulled an envelope from my back pocket. 'It's my resignation – one month's written notice.'

Stan's eyes widened. 'Surely not?'

'All I did was speak out Stan. But the trainees have all sent me to Coventry,' I said. 'I'm sorry, but there's no way I can function as a tutor here any more.'

'Ah. I see.' Stan's beard rippled as he chewed at the bottom of his mouth. 'What a terrible shame. Is there nothing I can do?' he asked kindly.

I hesitated. 'There is something.'

His beard ruffled expectantly. 'Yes?'

'Please don't make me work my notice,' I said.

At the bottom of the stairs I bumped into Adolf.

'Oh, hello there.'

He was awkward. 'I ain't really supposed to talk to you, Miss. Cos of you bein' a grass.' He concentrated on his shoes.

I shrugged. 'There's nobody here to know,' I said. 'How's your placement with the plumber?'

He grinned. 'It's alright. We're packing stuff in boxes. An' Rick buys takeaways sometimes. Curry and rice, stuff like that. But it's okay.'

There was a pause. And suddenly I wanted to explain. 'Michael's family need to know he didn't commit an awful crime like that,' I said.

He chewed his lip.

'I didn't mean to cause anyone trouble,' I continued.

'It don't work like that, Miss.' His eyes were full of pity. Not for the joyless task of speaking out, but because I clearly didn't understand. 'You're just not meant to grass,' he said.

I sighed. But I'd always felt that somewhere underneath the dreadful skinhead persona, was a decent lad. I decided to give it one last try.

'Look, life's not that simple.' I stared into his face, ignoring the jacket with fascist logos. 'One day you may be faced with a really big decision between right and wrong.'

I hesitated, checking he was listening.

'When that time comes Alan, I hope you're brave enough to ignore everyone, and take whatever action you know in your heart is right.'

32

TOM

Back in Coventry I bounded up the stairs to the studio and pushed open the office door. 'Alright, yer hairy bastard!'

Rick was hunched over a desk, where he sat amongst the usual detritus – overflowing toolboxes, lengths of rubber tubing, the inside drum from a washing machine. I spotted a pencil stub in his hand and the tatty blue cash book. He'd been working on our accounts.

In a corner, beside a tower of clumsily stacked boxes of EPs, sat on crates were two shaven-headed lads in green jackets, half mast jeans and high laced DM's, sliding records into thin paper sleeves. One of them had crude logos scrawled on his jacket. I was shocked to this type of skinhead in our territory.

'Tom!' Rick jumped up, clapping me on the back with one beefy hand, while clearing a seat of junk with the other.

'Oi! You twos.' Both lads were both ogling at me, the fat one grinning expectantly. 'Bugger off for dinner now. An' take at least an hour, we've stuff to discuss.' They trooped out in obedience, clearly comfortable with this sort of easy discipline. I waited til I heard the bottom door slam shut.

'Blooody hell Rick, you've got hardcore skinheads handling our discs!'

He frowned. 'I told yer ages ago. They're from a youth training scheme – it's all free work.'

'That's hardly the point. The fat one's penned fuckin' swastikas on his jacket!'

Rick's forehead creased. 'Yeah, bit unfortunate that.' His face lit up. 'But he's a real worker, despite the daft coat and the name.'

'What name?'

'Weeeell...to be honest, his mates call him Adolf.'

'Jeesus Christ, Rick! They're exactly the stupid gits we're tryin' not to be associated with!'

Rick flapped his hands about in defence. 'They're only packin' records, man.'

'You dopey twat. If we give them work, we're supporting' their fascist ideals.'

'Don't worry so much Tom, they're as good as gold. Sit down man and tell me what's happenin'.'

'I don't like it one bit Rick.'

He shrugged.'They'll be gone soon. Finished and back on the dole. Kaput.'

'Jeesuz! What a fuckin' country.' I rubbed my forehead.

'Need an aspirin?' asked Rick.

'Not strong enough.' I eyed the pile of boxes in the corner.

'Still shiftin' those old EPs then?'

'Movin' faster than a vegetarian's bowels, mate. Those adverts in Pump City sent it ballistic. I've had calls from small record shops all over the country.'

'Who'd have known.' I started to shake my head, but as my brain bounce painfully inside my skull, thought better of it. I'd been on a bit of a bender with Fozz to celebrate finishing the new EP so it was hardly surprising.

'How you doin' Tom? You look like shit.'

'Thanks a million.'

'Just sayin'. What's the deal with Ragged Moth?'

'As I said on the blower – all promises and no put-out. It's like being married again.'

Rick chortled. 'It's good to see yer. Where's the others?'

'Gone to get cleaned up and laid – not necessarily in that order.'

Not me though, as Josie had gone away to visit her parents. She'd just had time to tell me when I caught her leaving for the station. But this meant I could concentrate on making the video. I stretched over to the blue book. 'How's the figures? Fozz had to bung me a loan.'

'Dealt with, mate. He rang me and we sorted it.'

'That mean we're skint then?' I spun the ledger round and scanned the numbers. 'Christ almighty! Looks like we're doing alright....is this for real?'

Rick's long shaggy hair shook like a spaniel's ears as he nodded. 'An' that's after van repairs.'

I groaned. 'You're not seriously keeping that tub going?

'Nothin' wrong with it. Just needed a tinker and a bit of TLC.'

'Rick, the fuckin' engine exploded!'

'I'll get a brew on.'

When conversations became tricky, our manager was master of the neat swerve.

Rick returned with two Coventry FC mugs and spooned four sugars into his, slopping tea as he stirred. He rummaged noisily in the desk drawer then, with a cry of joy, he pulled out a sizeable spliff and sat back to light it.

'Tell me what's happenin' Tom. It's ages since we had a real pow-wow.'

I thrust a hand at him. 'Oi, pass the peace pipe if you want news from outside the village, Chief Hairygit.'

The dryness of the grass hit my tonsils and I struggled not to cough. God knows how long it had been in that drawer. Rick waited, arms folded on the table, while I exhaled, feeling my shoulders relax, like a rope being unknotted.

'Moth are going to release the new EP and we're shootin' a video,' I said.

Rick waggled a paw in the air, as if erasing my statement from an invisible blackboard. 'I know all that. What's the Big Plan?'

'Same as before.'

I eyed the spliff he was sucking on, with a craving I'd started to recognise. 'Get in the charts. Hit the big time. Blow Coventry once and for all.'

Rick nodded sagely and passed the joint. 'What about the girl?'

'What bloody girl?' Smoke jagged in my throat and I started to cough for real.

'Charlie says there's a mystery woman.'

'Fuckin' Charlie and his big mouth,' I spluttered. 'What's he said?'

'Overheard him speakin' with Trevor at The Triangle. He said the lads were getting angsty about the Moth contract – wonderin' if you've still got yer eyes on the ball.'

I was shaken by this thought. But my instinct to keep Josie a secret had been right after all. 'Look, forget Charlie's sex-starved imagination. Original Mix is still heading for the top. Now tell me about this Rock Against Racism that Jackson's hosting – where's it going to be?'

'That big park under the ringroad. They're callin' it The Freedom Park Gig.'

'Jeesus!' The only freedom offered by that sad stretch of grass and bare flowerbeds was fresh air and wooden benches – a gift taken up wholesale by the city's community of drunks and tramps. But at last we had chance to make a big, public anti-racism statement.

'Who's playing?'

'Local bands, and some guys Jackson's mates have brought in from West Africa.'

'That's great but, bloody hell Rick. Outdoors and in winos haven. When is it?'

'This Saturday. You can use some studio gear and share the rest with Jackson's band. They're on before you.'

'As long as we don't get his dub reggae sound too.'

'Don't worry. Pete's gonna be there to turn up the treble.'
He'd thought of everything, except…'How's it being promoted? Haven't seen any posters in town.'

Rick shrugged. 'Yeah well, the police were a bit jittery about a gig outside. Few hold ups with permissions. Nothing we can't handle.'

I frowned. It seemed unlikely this gig would actually take place, but Rick and Jackson could sort that out, I had other things to worry about.

'Who's filming you lot?' Rick asked.

'Brian, that DJ from Birmingham. He's started making band videos. Reckons it could be the next really big thing.'

Rick nodded. 'Could be, I 'spose.'

'He says he'll use three cameras, and we're going for an exposé of urban decay, shots of empty streets, closed factories, everything that shows how the recession's biting – then I'm toyin' with the idea of a mugging. We're drafting the storyboard with Eddy tonight.' I grinned. 'It feels like being back at art college.'

'Top banana.'

'For chrissakes Rick!' I lurched over to grab his wrist. 'Ever say 'top banana' again, and you're fuckin' fired!'

Rick shook his arm free and smirked. 'Like you'd ever fire me,' he said.

♫

33

TOM

The riff I could almost taste was evading me, despite experimenting with Eddy's new lyrics for half an hour. Rick was out on some business to do with licences, the band were having a little down time, plus Josie still wasn't back from her folks. So I'd seized the chance to bag the studio for myself, playing a little drums, some bass and guitar to loosen up a tune, and tinkering round on the keys. The damn song was on the tip of my fingers, I knew it. I stood up to stretch, and found myself looking into the fat, pink face of the skinhead kid whose mates called him Adolf.

'Fuck me. How long you been standing there?'

He stared at the floor. 'Lookin' for Rick.'

'He's out,' I said. 'Where's yer mate?'

The kid scuffled at the bare carpet with the toe of his boot. 'Dunno. Didn't turn up.'

His hands were jammed into the pockets of the offensive green bomber jacket, with its crayoned logos. With his round face and that belly straining over an outfit of tight denims, white shirt, braces, and DM boots, he looked like a Nazi-loving Buddha.

'Well nodody else is here, so you may as well piss off.'

A pair of hangdog eyes met mine. 'Can't I wait? I won't interrupt or nothin'.'

'Bit late for that sunshine.'

I jangled my pockets, trying to recall if Rick had locked up the cash box, and remembered he had. 'You do anything useful like make tea?'

He grinned. 'I'm good in the kitchen.'

I handed him the keys. 'Two sugars – and check the milk's not off.'

'Alright boss.' He practically leapt to it.

When he returned. I was jamming on the guitar. He placed a mug on the amp and took a few steps back.

'Can I sit and listen?'

'Do what you like,' I said. 'Just don't bother me again.'

I adjusted the strap and changed position, so he was out of my line of vision. Then I concentrated on Eddy's verse again, singing as I played, `

Quick step, night attack
Instant fix, knife in back
He's not human
Just a black
When's it going to stop?

No, it needed something jarring – a different end chord. I turned the drum machine on and tried again. After a few minutes I reached down for my tea and humming softly trying to pin down a tune. Of course. It needed to go up to a minor key for two bars, then the chorus could start on a major. There was a rustle. I turned to glare at the kid, who had spread a newspaper open.

'Sorry,' he said, face all apologetic.

After an hour, I'd nailed it. Once I'd realised it called for an E minor for the verse to hang over and then resolve into a G major, the rest fell into place. I switched on the drum machine and played the whole song, singing the verses from the crumpled paper that Eddy had given me. It was as if the tune had always existed for those lyrics, like there couldn't be any other. Just to check, I went round it all again. When I put my guitar down, there were soft polite hand claps from behind me.

'That's brilliant. I never heard no one make a song before.'

I narrowed my eyes, to try and tell if he was taking the piss, but his face wore a genuine open smile.

'Yeah, well. It's just the start.' I lit a cigarette. 'Needs a rhythm section and another guitar line, then we'll add extra stuff.'

'What like?'

'Percussion, synth, backing vocals, maybe some horns. Depends what the rest of the band suggest.'

He grinned. 'Will it be a record?'

'Maybe.'

I sat down. On the road I'd developed the knack of relocating in my head, to a place where no annoying fuckwit could get access. So I'd easily blocked him out while I was working on the tune. Besides, he was Rick's concern, not mine. But now he bothered me.

'What you think of those lyrics then?'

'What?'

'The words. It's an anti-violence song in case you hadn't noticed.'

'Oh yeah.' He was still smiling. 'They're good. Did you write 'em?'

'No, someone else. Why do you like them?'

'Dunno,' he said. 'It's just a good song like.'

'So it's a nonsense to beat up complete strangers?' I asked.

He shrugged. 'I 'spose.'

'So why do you do it?'

'Me?'

'No, the Dali bloody Llama.' He looked confused. 'Yes, you, soft lad.'

'I don't.'

'You've never attacked someone because they were a 'black' or a 'Paki'?'

He sniffed. 'No need to be racist.'

'I'm not the one who's felt penned fucking swastikas on his jacket!' I said.

The little shit had the cheek to look hurt. 'That don't mean nothing.'

'Course it does! That's the fuckin' insignia of the Nazi animals who murdered SIX MILLION Jews, plus a load of gay people and gypsies – for no reason other than they were different to them. To most people it says a helluva lot!'

'I never beat up anyone,' he said sulkily.

'Yeah, right.'

'S'true. Sometimes we go to town, looking for a bit of trouble. But everyone scarpers.'

Suddenly he stood for all the older more threatening skins that we'd seen at our gigs, swastikas tattooed as deep as their resolves, boots bigger, kicks harder and hatred more engrained. In front of me was a small fat version, ready to follow the stupid pack. It was only a matter of time before their prey didn't move fast enough, then him and his mates would get their first taste of group violence.

'If you go looking for fights, you must think our lyrics are bollocks.' I didn't know why I was goading him. There wasn't much point.

'No! Original Mix are great.'

'But?' I said.

'Well you can't just stop being a skin, can you?' His face wore a bewildered look.

'No, I guess not,' I sneered.' Once you've bought the jacket and the felt pens, there's no going back.'

There was that hurt look again. I wanted to smack him. 'Plenty of lads wear bomber jackets and DMs without upgrading to neo Nazis.' I said. 'It doesn't make you a man.'

Why was I bothering? He stared back at me blankly, bottom lip pouting. The door at the bottom of the stairs banged open, and the familiar huff and puff of Rick's thirty a day lungs rose up the stairs, like a steam train coming into a station.

'You need to wise up and stop being a dickhead.' I rested my guitar in its case. 'And I'll have my Guardian back, thank you.' I held a hand out for the paper, with it's headline announcing, *'Bob Marley dies, aged 36',* sighing again at this tragic day and the loss of talent.

'It's not yours,' he said.

Bloody hell. Now little fucker was pinching my paper!

'Yours is there.' He gesticulated to the top of the piano.

'Oh.' I grabbed the unopened paper, then pointed to the copy he was folding carefully.

'What happened? Newsagent run out of tabloids?' I gave a nasty laugh.

'No,' he said with a hurt tone. 'I always get this one.'

'What?' I checked his face, but there was no hint of a smirk. 'You trying to tell me you choose to be informed by the liberal Press?'

His gaze was steady. 'The Mail's right wing and the Express is left wing ainit? I prefer readin' this, then I can make up my own mind,' he said.

'Fuck off.' Now I knew he was taking the piss.

'Gottit!' Rick blundered in, brandishing a piece of paper aloft like a heavy metal Chamberlain.

We both stared at him.

'Special licence.' He said. 'Legal right to perform outdoors. Saturday's Rock Against Racism gig, man. It's all on!'

♫

34

TOM
1984

I didn't get too friendly with Recknaw. My job was simple. Load, unload, dodging bottles and fists as necessary. The band had names, but I didn't use them. They never asked mine, referring to me as 'Lugger'. I wore my woolly hat pulled down like a tuna trawlerman, and I worked as hard. Sometimes we took away more equipment than we'd arrived with, but we always left with all of theirs. The first night, I stayed to witness the unmusical horror of their gig, and after that I stayed with the van, checking the audience mood ten minutes before the end, to see how fast they needed to get away. Punks weren't daft kids any more, armed to self harm with piercing guns and home tattoo kits. These were blokes in their late thirties, wearing combat trousers with purpose. They had pierced everything they could on their own faces, and now they were looking to rearrange someone else's. I'd found out the hard way, lunging to rescue a front stage mic before a meaty hand could grab it from the stand. I kept my grip on the mic but was in danger of loosing teeth, when Six Verses spotted the altercation, ran across the stage and launched himself off, like a hippo trying to fly. He returned grinning widely, trouser leg ripped and bleeding across the eyebrow. 'That was a bit of a laarf,' he quipped, as I wound cables, mouth stuffed full of bog roll to staunch the blood. I lost a tooth, but got an extra fiver for my trouble.

At the end of each gig I had the cash for chips and the extras to get me to the next afternoon. It was the only bit of routine in my life. The last few years had passed in a blur and the future was another place, unreal and inconceivable. At night I cured my insomnia with whatever cocktail of super lager and non-prescriptives I could buy. Sleep was often peopled by disappointed faces from the past – Eddy, Devon, Josie, my dad. The nights I had no lugging I got so mashed I often couldn't tell hallucination from reality. Many times I imagined calling my mum and burbling incomprehensible stuff down the phone, and once I dreamt I'd come across Josie in Camden and got on a bus with her. She was wearing a business suit and carrying a plastic bag with a boxed wooden train. I was deliriously happy to see her and I dropped off to sleep with a smile on my face, until I was interrupted by another dream of being hauled away.

'You're not Devon,' I said to the black guy in the knitted Rasta hat, looming over me. 'You stole his hat. Where's he gone?'

'Help me get this big piece o' nonsense off me bus,' a voice said, and several hands lifted and guided me across a graveyard, as though I was weightless. I watched my feet, a million miles below, my worn out DMs scuffing across the grass like I was flying, and I laughed and laughed. That morning I woke in the churchyard behind Hackney bus station, cold and shivering, but buttoned up in my leather coat, on a pillow of newspapers, with a vicar proferring a Styrofoam cup of tea. Non-gig nights often ended like this. Although that time was the only one when I found myself clutching a handful of change as tightly as if it were diamonds.

Twice now I'd woken to blue flashing lights, torches and someone shaking me by the shoulders. It was a rude way to be hauled out of a nice narcotic nirvana. And the walk back from hospital was long and cold the following day.

'You should go to Arlington House,' a helpful porter once said. 'They give you a bed, and help you get back on yer feet.'

'I'm alright,' I said. 'On me feet now aren't I?'

He narrowed his eyes. 'I know you.'

I shook my head. 'Nah mate, I'm not from round 'ere.'

He waggled a finger at me. 'Yeah, yeah, I got it. You played guitar in that band....Original Mix. I use'ta love your music, man. What happened?'

But I was already stumbling off. 'Not me.'

'Wasteland,' he shouted. 'Blaady amazin'. Told it just like it was – still is.'

I couldn't get away fast enough.

202

35

TOM

Shooting the video was a real laugh. The music was being dubbed on later, so we horsed around miming to our own track. I riffed the theme tune from a kids' cowboy series and Vinnie replied with the Mission Impossible anthem.

'He's got enough for a bloody feature film,' I said to Rick later, over a cup of Coventry FC tea. 'Studio footage, along the ringroad, and we even filmed Raymond getting another racist thumping.'

'Where?'

'Mainly in the balls,' I quipped. 'Did it on Anarchy Bridge about 2am.'

'How those two skinhead lads get on with their parts?'

'The big tall lug was surprisingly adept,' I said. 'You'd almost think he'd had practice.'

Rick grinned proudly. 'You're the dog's bollocks accordin' to the short one, Tom. Should hear him go on. Like you're Elvis or somethin'.'

'Did Elvis have a following of neo-fascists?'

Rick nodded slowly. 'Fair point. But he never talks any of that rubbish, so I'm not convinced.' He scratched his forehead. 'Might be like when I was into Electric Rock City, before I heard Purple Viper. Just an embarrassin' stage on the path to enlightenment.'

I sighed. 'Jesus Rick. How the hell did I ever find you?'

'I found you mate, if yer remember.' He chortled. 'Without me you'd never have known how to use a plunger or a wrench. Paradise Plumbing picked you out of the gutter.'

'And I appreciate it all mate.' I swept an expansive wave at the dump that was our home base.

He'd set me thinking though. I'd toyed with 50's R&B, blues, then punk, now ska – each one bringing its own style of dress and mind set.

Perhaps there was hope, even for nasty little skins.

♫

The sun torched down on the park, and in two high-rise blocks overlooking the stage, every balcony was cluttered with people leaning over to see what was happening. From the back of the stage, I counted about five hundred heads, with more people pouring in. A group of local winos waved cans of brutal strength lager in gracious welcome at the gate, and nobody seemed about to jump from Suicide Tower. Perhaps today was auspicious.

After the first set of bands, I stood by the sound desk to watch the speeches. An earnest young man in glasses, introduced some old white bloke in a long collarless African tunic and a little pillbox hat, who explained how long he'd been battling for visas to bring the West African band and their music to the UK. Then an excited black woman in a colourful headscarf and dungarees gushed about how great it was that everyone was performing here free, as a political gesture of solidarity. She held her arms up in triumph, shouting that this was Coventry's first outdoor festival but not the last, and everyone cheered.

It was odd to see this kind of mutual outdoor bonhomie in Coventry – the city which spawned tribes and tribal warfare like a wild frontier – but I was too pleased for cynicism. When the next band walked out on stage, they were met with a huge cheer. And as they started to play, I weaved my way to the grassy area backstage, where Eddy and Devon sat on our gear eating ice creams. Vinnie arrived and jumped up onto the bass amp.

'Rock and roll! Give us a lick.'

Devon yanked his cone away. 'Nuttin' I eat is goin' anywhere near your vile tongue, rude boy.'

I spotted Rick bowling across the rough grass, followed by the fat skinhead, both carrying cardboard boxes. I met him by the rope barrier as he crashed his carton on the grass.

'Watcha! Thought I'd try an' get rid of a few EPs after you've played.'

I frowned. 'Rick, this is a benefit gig man. It doesn't sit right to sell them. How many you got anyway?'

He considered. 'About eighty in a box and there's more in the van – maybe three hundred in all.'

'Look, just give 'em out,' I said. 'And get a donations box from the event people, to stick nearby.' I pointed to the woman in the dungarees, who was talking to two big Rastas.

'Give 'em away? Gratis like?' I might have asked him to drown kittens.

'The new EP's out soon, so's our single,' I said. 'And Christ knows, there's not much in Coventry you get for free, apart from a thumping.'

Rick shook his head with incomprehension.

On stage, Jackson's band started their final number. The deep drop bass vibrated through my rib cage and, as always, the dub reggae sound made me excited and mildly agitated all at once. I hunted round in my jacket pocket, but it was empty.

'Can I give out the records Rick?' The short fat skinhead, whose nickname was Adolf, was eager as punch to help.

I spun round. 'Not in that fuckin' jacket you don't!'

He looked down at the logos felt-penned on his chest. 'I'll take it off.'

'You should fuckin' torch it!' I said, suddenly furious. 'Don't you geddit kid? This is a Rock Against Racism gig, five hundred people enjoying music from across the globe, united against that racist shit.' I jabbed him in the swastika. 'It's mindless, stupid and ignorant. And you've turned that into a crap jacket!'

'I know.'

'What the hell do you know?' He was such a little fuckwit.

'I've outgrown it, but I ain't got nothin' else.'

'Give me the jacket,' I said quietly.

'I don't have no other jacket,' he pleaded.

I rifled in my jeans and pulled out three pound notes. 'Buy yourself a new one.'

Rick rolled his eyes. 'And suddenly we're made of money,' he said.

Vinnie ran over. 'We're on in two minutes!' He stared at the coat in my hands. 'Bloody hell Shepperton, sure that's your size?'

I bundled up the jacket with its orange lining outwards, and handed it to the kid. 'Don't care how you destroy this rag, but if you want to work for us any longer, it better end up beyond wearing.'

I turned to Rick. 'I mean that Rick. No racist shit round my band, and it's *not* negotiable.'

'He's just a lad, Tom. Kids do stupid stuff.'

But I wasn't listening.

I picked up the set list and scrawled, *'I'll do the intro'* by our final song. Then handed it to Eddy. He gave me the thumbs up.

We ran on stage. The homecrowd roared with excitement and started to dance, as we crashed straight in. The mixture of heads bobbing in front looked like someone was shaking a carpet made of pom poms and ping pong balls. We were playing on home turf, all in time, in tune, and of one mind. I grinned at Devon and he mouthed, 'Yeah, man!'

Towards the end of our set, as Eddy extolled the main 'virtues' of Coventry (twenty two pubs on one street and a centrally placed dole office) in his dry introduction to Wasteland, I saw the fat skinhead scuttle to the far side of the stage and plonk down a big metal dustbin, but I didn't give it much thought. We chunked out the first three chords to Wasteland and the crowd surged forward, thrusting punches into the air. If the platform hadn't been so high, they'd have been on there with us for sure.

After the cheers died down Eddy said, 'This is our last song.' There was a collective groan of disappointment from the field. 'And here's Tom Shepperton, to introduce it.' I stepped towards his microphone, and the crowd gave a roar of welcome.

'It's great to be in sunny Coventry! Mixing with our neighbours.' I strained to shout over the whistles and yells, and gestured up to the flats were people were leaning over their balconies waving. Someone screamed down, 'Yo, Original Mix! Go man!'

'An' it's amazing we're all here with no animosity or aggression.' I shielded my eyes against the sun's glare. 'I see casuals, students, trendies, skinheads –.' there was a cheer each time people identified their tribe '– black kids and white.' Then I waved at some lads I recognised, hanging out with apprehension under the archways. 'And our Asian fans of course. And we're all here for one thing – to celebrate being together, with music!' Another huge cheer.

'We don't need to fight! What Original Mix says is –' I played the first five notes of the melody line, priming the band behind me, and I shouted, 'Race Unite!' Their instruments leapt in with perfect timing and the audience screamed in appreciation, hollering the chorus along with Len, creating a beautiful harmonious din. It was a monumental performance. Len teased the crowd, cocking his pork pie hat to them and throwing off guitar riffs as his leather soles slid across the floor, and they loved it. Eddy scowled with disdain but sang as sweetly as the grown up choir boy that I knew him to be. Charlie plucked bass lines, letting them go like drops of molten treacle, and Devon's big arms flew round the drums like swallows in spring. The sweat dripped down my back as Vinnie and I leapt about like loons. I hadn't had so much pure fun playing live for a long time.

Somewhere in the third verse, I spotted the fat skinhead kid on the far corner of the stage, next to Raymond's keyboards, with something under his arm. Raymond gave me a quick shrug and kept on playing. We all leant into our mics for the last chorus, and I saw the fat skinhead holding up his stupid jacket to the crowd. Bloody hell!

It happened too fast to stop. We all sang *'With humanity's might, we'll all unite'* as he pulled a lighter out of his pocket. One minute there was the shocked faces of the audience as he showed them the swastikas, then there was a shot of orange flame, a powerful smell of petrol and a blast of black acrid smoke rose into the air as his jacket burned. The kid dropped it into the metal dustbin where it threw up more foul smoke, until Rick slapped the lid on top. The crowd cheered like crazy, as we finished the line *'Setting the torch of friendship alight!'*, and the lad stuck his two fists in the air and jumped off the stage.

But I had no time to process any of this. The crowd refused to let us leave the stage til we'd done an encore and they would have had a second one, but I ran forward and put my arms round Len and Eddy's shoulders, shouting, 'Thank you everyone! You've been mega. Keep dancin' and give a big Coventry welcome to our friends all the way from West Africa!'

The five guys from the headline act leapt on stage clutching their instruments – a couple of steel strung guitars and three weird stringed things that looked like huge gourds. We slapped palms as our paths crossed, and thanks to the quick work of stage hands, they were plugged in and playing fast riffs before the audience lost their energy. The rhythm was a fantastic mix of beats and half beats, majestic and much more complicated than ska. But ska had some echoes of this music, in the same way that a wild cat is historically related to a lion. The crowd took a few moments to recognise this and to get into the groove, then they were away, dancing, singing and waving their arms. I grabbed my guitar case, pushed through to the sound desk with Eddy, and we stood there transfixed.

After their final number, when the crowds reluctantly started to dissemble, Brian ran up with two other blokes, all hauling big cameras and weighty battery units.

'Tom! That was inspired man! Looked great on camera.'
I'd been so mesmerised by the African band, I'd forgotten everything, including the video. 'Let's go to mine to watch it,' I said to Brian. 'My van's parked in a side street.'
Rick and the lads could pack up the rest of our gear.
'We're getting back to Brum,' said one of the cameramen.
Brian nodded. 'Give us the tapes then,' he said. They opened up their cameras and each popped out a film cassette no bigger than a box of large kitchen matches.

'Wow!' I took one and examined it. 'It's so small. Things have come on since I was at college.'

'Bloody batteries are still like lead though,' said the bloke. He shouldered a bag the size of a small record player with obvious discomfort. 'Here!' He lobbed something like a VHS cassette at me. 'You put the tapes in this, to watch them in your video.'

In my bedsit at the studio, Eddy and I viewed the footage with Brain, deciding how to edit it all.

'Pity you're not releasing Race Unite,' said Brian, as we watched myself and Vinnie cavorting round, like we were running on a wonky treadmill, while Len gave a fisted salute to the guys on the balconies of the flats.

'We can still cut some of this in though,' I said. 'Without the sound, it's pretty much the same tempo. We can use film from both songs and the stuff they shot in the studio.'

'And the sizzling swastikas of course.' Eddy grinned. 'How d'you get him to do it?'

'I keep telling you, I didn't! That was his own idea.'

Eddy shook his head. 'He's not that bright Tom. Showing that fat skinhead beating up Raymond, then remouncing fascism was genius. You must have said something.'

He could be right, but I didn't know what.

'Christ! The look on that copper's face when he saw the kid click open his lighter.' Brian had been filming the audience from behind me. He popped his tape into the video player and pressed fast forward. Sure enough there was a policeman, looking stern and unimpressed, until his mouth suddenly formed a wide 'O' then he clearly said the word,'Fuck!'

'That's what I call a beautiful moment,' I said to Eddy. 'We should definitely use it.'

Eddy's face was thoughtful. 'That wouldn't be secret subversion like the Pink Panther,' he said to me, and Brian's brow creased with puzzlement.

'Yeah, and we'll get a right old bollocking from Ragged Moth.' I raised an eyebrow at him, in questioning challenge.

'True...Adam will go ape,' said Eddy. But I could see from his face that there were more important things at stake.

'We've gotta do it Ed!' I said. And Eddy nodded.

'Let's 'ave a quick shufty at what else we'll use,' said Brian. He rewound the tape, then played it through in fast mode.

There were a lot of people dancing and a few zoom ins. At one point I saw a couple of blonds. 'Whoa! Go back,' I said. There was Josie, dressed in a striped top and tight white trousers, with her arm round her mate Simon, also in white pants. I sat up, grinning.

'You wanna use sailor boy and his girl?' Brian paused the tape.

Eddy gave a hoot. 'Way too attractive. They'll steal our thunder.'

'Oh yeah, which one?' I said, trying not to stare at the screen, where Josie was frozen, carefree and beautiful.

Eddy kicked me. 'Together I mean.'

'Let it roll, normal speed,' I said to Brain, and Josie started moving to the beat, saying something to Simon, her lips brushing his ear to be heard against the music. I wished I'd known she was there. I'd have stayed to find her afterwards. The camera zoomed in on Josie as she waved up at the stage, and then it panned round sideways and I saw Vinnie grinning as he gave one of his windmill-arm chord crashes, ending with a thumbs up sign.

'One of Vinnie's birds,' said Brian, with a wry grin.

'Keep going,' I said quickly. 'Let's choose our key images and work a storyboard round them, before we go out.'

'Take it she's not a key image then.' Brian's finger hovered over the fast forward button.

I shook my head. The picture of Josie's hips moving as she danced, was now burnt into my retinas, but it wasn't for public consumption.

'Where we meeting the others?' asked Eddy.

'The Weasal,' I said. 'Vinnie's choice. Don't ask me why he chose that hell hole.'

♫

36

JOSIE

By the time we arrived at The Weasel the din inside told us it was packed. I recognised a punk skinning up outside, whose Mohican was now dyed a parroty green and yellow. 'Great hair,' I said. He grunted hi, then offered back, 'Nice skirt.'

Simon had insisted we dress up, so I was wearing a pink ballet skirt with DMs and long satin gloves, and he was still sporting his sailor boy garb. We looked like singing puppets from an old Danny Kaye film.

Before we walked in I said, 'I can't believe this is our last night out together.'

'No sentimentals now,' Simon replied. 'Let's make it a night to remember.'

As we squeezed into the crush at the bar Vinnie elbowed his way in behind us. 'Alright kids. How 'bout a pint for a hard working musician.'

And there was Tom, facing away, across the horseshoe shaped bar. My heart raced. He was talking to the dark haired woman with the stylish bob cut. The one I was trying to forget existed. A large bloke pushed past to get served, and Tom reached out a hand to move her aside and let the guy in. I couldn't see her features, just the movement of her glossy hair as she spoke, and the look of concern on Tom's face. And the fact that he didn't seem to have taken his hand away again.

'Where's the drinks then?' Vinnie's hot breath came over my shoulder. 'You not been served yet? Oi! Mate!' He gave a shrill dog whistle which alerted most of the pub, including Tom. Seeing me, he gave a huge smile, releasing his hand and leant across his side of the bar to mouth 'Hi!' The woman gave me a fleeting look, hair swinging like a bead curtain, and when he turned to face her again, she grabbed his chin with crimson painted fingers and kissed him firmly and confidently on the lips. I backed away from the cramped bar, suddenly unable to breathe.

'Who's that woman with Tom Shepperton?' I asked Vinnie. He glanced over, barely registering her. Then he cocked his head to one side and took a long drag from his cigarette, surveying me. 'Why d'ya wanna know?' he said.

'Just wondered.' I tried to sound casual.

Vinnie looked back over at Tom, who had grasped the woman by both arms and was talking urgently to her. He darted a anxious look in my direction. When I turned back to Vinnie he was giving me a crooked grin, as if he's just realised something.

'Her,' he said, pointing with his cigarette. 'That's Yvonne.' He faced me straight and shrugged. 'Me sister, as it goes, as well as being Tom's missus.'

The bile rose in my stomach, like a lump of fat from a dirty bowl. I was surely going to be as sick as a dog.

'Hey, where yer goin'?'

I left Vinnie's voice behind, as I stumbled outside, past the punks and round the corner, into the anonymous darkness of the railway arches.

I was stupid, stupid, to think that anyone as beautiful and talented as Tom wouldn't be taken. Stupid to imagine he'd seen me as anything more than a casual fling. It was obvious now. I was just a bit of fun on the side, while his wife was at home arranging the double quilt on the bed and phoning the in laws. I was dry heaving onto a patch of oil-soaked concrete, gasping for air, my heart pounding as my throat spasmed. A train rumbled overhead and its wheels screeched and keened on the metal track. The screaming receded, but a thumping continued. Big black boots appeared in the oil patch in front of me.

'*Thought* it was you.'

I raised my head. 'You're that bird from the training scheme. The one that got me Suspended.' Gob's skull shone pale in the dark tunnel and there was only nastiness in his eyes. I edged towards the entrance and the safety of the street light.

'Hey, where you goin'?' His hand shot out and his fingers bit into my arm like thick steel wires. 'I got somethin' to ask yer.'

'Need to find my friend.' I pulled away, but he didn't budge. 'Yeah I know 'im.' His voice was a sneer. 'Yer poofdah mate.' He leaned in closer and peered at me. 'Saw you in the pub, lookin' like a couple of fuckin' queers.'

'Please let go.'

He craned in further so I jerked away and my head hit the brick of the tunnel. As I pressed backwards the cold dampness crept into my hair and thin jacket. His breath was a mixture of nicotine and meat pie.

'Who you turnin' away from, bitch?'

'Nobody...I just need to go.'

'You think you're better than me, dontcha?'

'No, I...'

He pulled my arm and his grip on me increased. 'Ow!'

'You make me fuckin' sick. Interferin' with honest people.' He squinted into my eyes. ' I bet you think you're Florence fuckin' Nightingale on that scheme, teachin' them poor bastards what's right an' wrong.'

'It's not like that.'

His top lip curled back and he sniffed in disgust. Without loosening his hand, he stepped back and appraised me from crotch to ears, lingering on my breasts.

I was alone with a psycho in a dark tunnel and nobody knew where I was.

'I coulda fancied you,' he said, in a confiding tone. 'But not since I 'eard you was a grass.'

Oh shit!

He smirked. 'Oh yeah. I've got me ears all over in this city. Can't leave things to be run by fuckin' Pakis and Lefties.'

'Nobody listens to me, honest.'

'Maybe not, but when I hear someone's been out of order, I like to put them straight.'

I tried to wriggle free. Without showing any change in emotion, he put a leg across mine, planting his boot against the wall. His grip was like a vice on my wrist and the top button of his jeans dug into my hip. 'It's important it don't get to spread. See what I mean?'

'I'm not spreading anything.'

Suddenly his other hand shot out and was up my skirt, pressing against my crotch. Excitement flashed across his face.

'Now that's where you're wrong, bitch. You're going to spread these. Think of it as payment for your mistake.' His hand was grabbing at my tights. I thrashed with my free hand, but he pushed me against the brickwork with his muscular torso, pinning my arm back. In his side pocket, I felt a thin, solid object poking into my ribs, that I guessed was a knife, and I heard a rip of material.

TOM

It was a crazy night, even by The Weasel's high standards. While Eddy and Brian enthused about the video, I'd just stared into my pint, thinking of Josie and how I'd neglected her in the past few weeks. I was right behind Vinnie on stage. Surely it was me she was waving at and Vinnie had misunderstood? Seeing her on film made me ache to wrap my hands round her waist, and feel those lips brushing my neck. As soon as we'd wrapped everything up with Brian, I'd try to find her.

The pub was pretty full when Yvonne swung over, all dressed up, dark hair shimmering and wearing some sultry perfume. Cleopatra, but twice as dangerous. I steeled myself.

'It's not too late Tom. We could try again.' She smiled, displaying white teeth, glossy red lips. There were all the familiar stirrings in my jeans, and recall of the teenage boy summoned to behave like an idiot, with teases and the promise of sex. If I responded now she'd probably laugh and stalk out like a cat, imperious and triumphant.

'Sounds like pre-wedding jitters, so I'll pretend you didn't say that.' I lifted my beer in a toast. 'Here's to you and wassisname.'

A whistle pierced over the clatter of voices – like the sound of a navvy directing a crane. Or in this case Vinnie, demanding to get served, probably before his turn. And standing beside him was Josie, clutching her purse and reddening at the sudden attention from everyone. She was in wearing a tight black top with long pink gloves, and a lacy bow – 50s sex kitten gone punk. I gave her a big saucy grin and started to move around the bar. But Yvonne barred my way, spouting some nonsense about how nobody else understood her.

'Tom, you're not even listening! Who are you staring at?'

And suddenly, everything was clear. I'd just tell her about Josie. We'd go public here and now – to Yvonne, the band and anyone else who gave a shit. No more secrets.

'Look Yvonne, I've been seeing someone. She's over there.'

I saw a flash of violet in her eyes and then bam! She grabbed my chin and delivered me a smacker of a kiss, full on the lips.

'You'll always be mine at heart, Tom.' She smiled, and wiped her scarlet-tipped finger across my mouth, removing the glossy smear she'd left.

'You're wrong.' A wonderful calm had taken me over. 'I'm all hers, as it goes. And I'm hoping she'll move to London with me soon. So you and Vinnie can go to hell!'

All I wanted was to do now wrap Josie in my arms and kiss her. But when I looked over, she'd disappeared. Vinnie was twisted round, staring behind him. As he turned back his shifty eyes caught mine.

'Where's Josie?' I mouthed. He studied me for a couple of seconds, and then a broad smirk spread across his face – the same damned smug grin he'd given me for years, each time he got one over. He gave a luxurious shrug. I elbowed my way round Yvonne, through the drinkers and past Josie's friend Simon to reach him.

'Where is she? Where's Josie?' I grabbed Vinnie's collar.

'Charlie thought you'd been knobbin' someone,' he said. 'I never guessed it was her.' Fucking Charlie. He just couldn't keep his big milkman's trap shut.

'Where's she gone?'

He shrugged again. 'You must 'ave it bad mate. Never seen you like this before. She's a good lay then?'

I grabbed his jacket by the front. 'What did you say to her?'

He shrugged me of. 'Steady on mate. She just asked who Yvonne was.'

My heart leapt up to the back of my throat. He'd beaten me again, even though I'd been so careful to keep quiet.

'What did you say?'

'Told her, Yvonne's me sister.'

'And?'

He hesitated.

'I mentioned she was also your missus.'

'Ex-missus, you fucker. Jeesus Christ! What the fuck is wrong with you both?'

I pushed through the bodies and grabbed the blond guy by the shoulder. 'Josie's left the pub. Where would she be?'

Simon looked concerned. 'She wouldn't go without me,' he said. 'Not unless someone's upset her.' He looked at Vinnie, busy chatting up a girl, and frowned. 'She's probably outside getting some air. I'll go an' check.' Something in his tone said he'd be better at managing this, so I waited.

Moments later he threw the door open, pink faced and panting. His blue eyes locked mine, with a mad desperation. 'Tom! Get an ambulance. There's been a stabbing!'

I was leaning over the bar in seconds. 'Phone 999!' I yelled. The barman stared uncomprehending, as the pub emptied with excitement. I hollered a second time. 'My girlfriend's been knifed. What you waitin' for? Get an ambulance, you twat!'

38

JOSIE

'Let go, let go!' I screamed. His hand scrabbled for my knickers, scratching the skin on my thighs and invading my underwear, nasty abrasive fingers, seconds away from poking into me.

Voices in the street. A man called, 'Goin' fer a piss Rick.'

Gob clapped his hand over my mouth hard. But I'd recognised the voice.

Who? Someone from work, one of the kids. Footsteps came near and the sound of someone fumbling with a zip. I bit down on a bony finger.

'Ahhh, yer bitch!' Gob let go with both hands.

'ADOLF, HELP!'

I beat out my fists in every direction, hitting wall, chest, air. Adolf's round face flashed towards me, surprised, caught in the streetlight. 'Hey, leave her alone!'

The silhouette of a long haired bloke stepped into the archway. 'Oi, what's goin' on?'

I felt free space as Gob released his grip and I ran out past the long-haired bloke. From behind I heard Gob's footsteps as he bellowed, 'Adolf! You treacherous little cunt. You're a dead man for what you did today!'

His terrifying tone made me spin round. Gob's hand shot out towards Adolf and there was a flash of metal. Adolf's face was caught in a moment between surprise and shock. He looked down and there was black liquid, spreading like oil across his white shirt. My heart dropped a beat, frozen.

Gob brushed past. 'Saving you for next time, bitch.' He pointed a long wet blade at me then, spotting someone coming our way, he set off in a long-strided run like a greyhound. Adolf crumpled against the tunnel wall, then slid down. The long-haired rocker ran over and bent down to look.

'Bloody hell, he's been stabbed!' The rocker was transfixed.

'Josie duck, what you doin'?' Simon was ambling towards us.

'Simon! Someone's been stabbed – run back quick – get an ambulance!' I shouted. I ran back into the tunnel to Adolf. There was such a lot of blood, warm black wetness everywhere.

'We need something to stop it!' What though? I peeled my jacket off and crammed it against his stomach.

'Gob shanked me, Miss.' His eyes were wide, disbelieving.

'Oh god! We need to stop you bleeding.'

Adolf was breathing hard, chest rising and falling like bellows. 'I wanted to be a good skin, Miss. Kno'wharr I mean?'

I had no idea. 'Of course you did.'

His breathing was very fast now. I pressed in on the cloth and felt a wet warmth coming through. 'Need something else! Gimme your jacket!' I thrust my hand back to the rocker guy.

Reluctantly the rocker passed me his denim. 'If there's any way you can avoid the Purple Viper badge…' I scrunched it down on top of mine, and pushed, trying to staunch the blood which was seeping out everywhere.

There was the sound of several hard, fast footsteps, which became echoey as they pattered into the tunnel.

'We need an ambulance!' I yelled over my shoulder. Simon's plimsolls appeared at my side. 'Bloody hell!' he panted.

Another set of feet came up behind me. 'Fuck!' said Vinnie.

'You do this, Rick?'

'Don't be a dick, man.'

There were others now, legs and feet all crowding in. Lighters clicked open to illuminate the dark. Still the warm wetness seeped through the jackets under my palms.

'Stay awake mate,' said the rocker. 'Don't lose it.'

Adolf's eyelids were flickering, his breaths now shallow. As his body sagged, his head fell to one side awkwardly, like a Guy Fawkes's effigy, with a pallor the same as Ally's face when I'd seen him laid out in the viewing room.

'He won't stop bleeding! I think he's dead!' My voice was thick, hoarse. I could hardly get the words out. My vision was blurring, the blackness of the tunnel pressed in from the sides, a thousand dark demons welled up from inside me and screamed to get out of my body. I was suffocating. I willed myself, don't faint, don't faint. There was a scraping of feet, as people were pushed aside.

'Here take this.' Tom's quiet voice was at my ear, his hand squeezed my shoulder. He handed me his jacket, still warm, soft and leathery smelling, and he knelt behind, curled over and around me, chest against my back. His heart thumped hard, urgent, not in random banging panic, like mine. The darkness cleared and my brain stopped flying. I was back in my body. I balled up the jacket and pressed down hard on the boy's open wound, pushing my full weight down, trying to stem the flow.

Leaning across my shoulders, Tom pressed large firm hands over mine.

Finally sirens screamed outside, with blue flashing, and strong torch beams across the grimy tunnel, lighting up crimson, scarlet everywhere, skirt, jackets, dirty grey floor. Two big blokes ran in, with the rustling trousers of paramedics. Shouting instructions at Tom to take over, press harder, help get him into the ambulance. As I stood, legs wobbling, and walked out of the tunnel, people were everywhere. A police car arrived, doors swung open, black uniforms with silver buttons, demanding answers from a white-faced Simon and the denim clad rocker. My legs were shaking and I was overwhelmed with tiredness. I pushed through the milling, muttering, crowded bodies, passed the flashing vehicles and headed down the road. I was cold, shivering. I walked faster and faster, then I ran, and ran. One single, clear line of thought: that Adolf was trying to help me, and he'd been stabbed to death. It was all my fault.

Hot, sticky tears ran down my cheeks as I ran.

Franki. I needed to be with Franki.

39

TOM

I flopped onto my bed, many hours later, exhausted and
covered in dry blood. Josie was desperate to save the kid, so I wanted
to be able to tell her he'd pulled through. I'd sat in the waiting room,
playing with an unlit cigarette, trying not to think about that burning
jacket and how I might have egged him on. Christ, what would Josie
think, when she found out? I kept replaying the whole scene in my
mind.

'Where's the ambulance?' she'd screamed. Then in a low,
cracked tone, 'I can't make it stop! He's bleeding everywhere.'

As his body slumped, and his eyeballs rolled up, she leant over
him crying, 'Ally, Ally! Wake up, WAKE UP!' And I'd realised he
was one of her YTS kids. Then knelt to thrust my balled up jacket
onto the lad and pressed down too.

'Keep pushing on the wound area, big fella.' A green jacket
was beside me, unzipping a bag.

Josie had stood, her lacy skirt ripped and covered in blood, but
I'd kept my palms on the soaking wodge of clothes in the kid's
middle, while the ambulance man bandaged round the whole lot, like
he was making a huge skinhead mummy. 'What's his name?' he
shouted as he wrapped.

'Adolf!' Rick blurted out from behind me.

'Real name, you twat!' I snapped. The wetness seeped through
the bandage, under my palms, and the pub crowd still hung behind
me, silent and fascinated. But I just wanted to hold Josie, tell her
everything was going to be alright.

'Shit, man. Can't remember,' said Rick.

'He might be called Ally,' I said.

'That's it!' said Rick. 'His name's Alan. Alan…Hitchcock.'

The ambulance man shone a light in the kid's eyes. He groaned and stirred underneath my hands. He was breathing fast, like a badly wounded animal.

The stretcher rolled in, and they ran with it to the ambulance, with me running alongside, still pushing down as though holding in his mortality. 'Get in!' yelled the first bloke, as they bundled him into the ambulance. I hesitated, searching the crowd for Josie.

'Come on! I need you to keep up pressure on his abdomen, while I get a line in!'

I grabbed the handles to pull the doors, still casting a desperate eye round. There was no blond to be seen. The siren started, and I'd heaved the doors shut.

Around five a.m. the had doctor returned. 'Your Mr Hitchcock's made of stout stuff.'

'He's alright?'

'Well he's regained consciousness.'

'Can I see him?'

He hesitated. 'Two minutes.'

The kid looked terrible – pallid and sweaty, limbs hooked up to all sorts of machines. But he gave me a weak goofy grin.

I took a chair. 'You'll be okay now, mate. You're in good hands.' I said. 'What exactly happened?'

The faint smile vanished. 'Gob shanked me, for being a traitor.'

Sunk in pillows, without his uniform, he was just a young, scared kid with a shaven head. His eyes clouded. 'Reckon's next time he'll finish me.'

I sighed. He'd taken my advice and tried to make a stand. Now we had a duty to him.

I stood up and patted his shoulder lightly. 'Don't worry, mate. We'll think of something to keep you safe.'

♪

The sound of an insistent doorbell brought me out of a landscape of muddled dreams.

Rick almost fell through the bedsit door. 'Jesus Tom, you're a sound sleeper. Get dressed and grab your gear. You gotta get to London.'

I rubbed my eyes and glanced at the clock. 'I've had four hours sleep Rick. It's the middle of my bloody night.'

Rick dismissed this thought with a wave. 'No time to loll around. Brian spent all night editing the video and Fozz is on his way down to London with it.'

'Fuckin' hell Rick. Why d'you let the film go? I've not even seen it!'

'Ragged Adam rang late last night – said he wanted it toot sweet today, cos he's doing something with it Monday a.m. Fozz says Brian's a bloody genius, Tom. The live feel is stonkin', especially in the studio.' He mugged a bashful smile. 'Even yours truly makes an appearance.'

'Christ. You not even going to ask how the kid is?'

Rick tutted with disdain. 'Seen 'im fer meself. Some people have been out and about while you've been in bed lazin'' He grimaced. 'He's looked better.'

As I rubbed my tender eyeballs, they felt like they'd been lacerated with hot grit.

'So have you, to be fair.' Rick held up a grocery bag. 'Shall I knock up a bacon sarnie, while you wash?'

I nodded. 'Better make it the Yeti Special – but this time without the free hair. How long I got?'

'Next train's in forty minutes,' said Rick. 'You can eat it in the van. Fozz'll meet you at your place in Camden.'

'Better now?' said Fozz, several hours later, as we emerged from the flat and weaved into Camden's bustling market. I grinned, alive again and ready for anything. 'You wouldn't believe the night I've had, Fozz. Don't know what I'd have done without you and the pixie dust.'

I was still worried about not having seen the video, despite Fozz's reassurance. I should have seen the final edit, and the band should have approved it too. This weekend, things had slipped way a long out of my control.

In the Ragged Moth's office, we all sat stunned as the time code counted to the end of the tape and the screen went black. The tape continued to whirr in the machine. Finally, Adam leant over or the 'off' button. He swivelled back to us and blew out his cheeks.

'Jesus H Christ, Tom!' He shook his head then scanned the room, while he thought. None of us moved. My chest was pounding. The video was beautiful, mad even. Brian had delivered everything we'd talked about, and more. He'd overlaid images, so one minute the band was jamming along in the studio, then a quick cut to a sad faced grocer, putting out dented tins and boxes in baskets, with a sign, 'Everything going cheap.' Then rows of closed shops, boarded up factories, and the camera panned across a wall, to a poster showing a condescending, smiling Margaret Thatcher, raising a handbagged to point a finger. I lost track of where we were in our storyboard. Images of derelict flats, unemployed kids kicking round, the boarded up Bingo hall, skins flicking knives to camera, our park audience packed densely together, dancing as fast and furious as the music. And the footage of us playing live was dispersed with little flames, appearing almost subliminally, each time the camera panned out a bit, until at last there was Alan Hitchcock burning his jacket, grinning like the Cheshire cat, as the crude felt pen swastikas melted and burned under his outstretched arm, and a packed crowd of students and trendies danced like crazy in front. It ended with a final sneer from Eddy as he sang, *'It's just a Wasteland!'* then flicked a V and turned his back on the audience.

Adam ran a hand through his hair. 'You should have talked to me Tom. This isn't what we agreed.'

I didn't answer. The video still played in my head. Brian's film captured our music perfectly. I was thrilled and envious, simultaneously.

He sighed heavily. 'We've been given the 'up and coming' slot on 'Video Force' tomorrow night,' he said. 'Can't tell you how many strings I had to pull at the BBC. And I've got to send it over tonight, or they'll use something else.'

He closed his eyes, and patted fingers rapidly on his knee, while bouncing the other foot in agitation. Perhaps he should have been a drummer. 'Shit. *Shit!*' When he opened his eyes he glared at me. 'You've got no bloody idea, have you? They've got hundreds of tapes to choose from, bands with chart-potential, all dancing on clouds and singing to shiny-haired girls. The chances of them playing this are next to zero.'

He was seriously considering not sending it! His eyes slammed round the room again, hitting on a poster of punk band, Guttersnipe, whose lead singer – according to legend – ate his own puke on stage.

'The Beeb played Guttersnipe's film,' I reminded him.

Fozz nodded his head like a parrot. 'Cos they got to number six in the charts, but nobody dared let them play live.' His punk knowledge was unsurpassable.

'They must like to shake it up a bit sometimes?' I persisted to Adam. 'Give the grey hairs something to complain about in The Telegraph.'

Adam gave me a calculating look. 'Look – the guys at Video Force fancy themselves as mavericks, but they're small fry. The programme's got to be passed by management.'

He was interrupted by a buzzing intercom. Moments later, a bloke in motorbike gear stood at the door, holding his helmet.

'Package for the BBC?' he said.

I was amazed how people worked on a Sunday in London. Adam stared at him, then popped our video out of the machine, and into a padded envelope. As the guy trudged downstairs, he said, 'Fuck you Tom. If this backfires, you'll never be touched by Ragged Moth money again!'

I waited for him to calm down.

'What happens now?' I said finally.

Adam sat back in his chair, mouth still tight with fury. 'The Wasteland singles were distributed Friday. We'll have to see if it charts, when the shops start sending in returns. Meantime, I'll wait for another bollocking from the BBC.'

'When was the last one?' I asked.

'After the Guttersnipe film,' he said grimly. 'Just before the lead singer got arrested.'

There was silence as we all recalled the band's demise.

Eventually Adam spoke. 'You staying down here now?'

With our video and single on their way, the band's future was in the lap of the gods. I thought about Josie, and how I needed to make things right. Once I'd cleared up whatever shit Vinnie had stirred, I'd ask her to move down here with me. We could find a small flat, trawl junk shops for furniture. I'd stop living off chips and Fozz's pick up powder. I hoped to god she'd say yes. Time to admit to Josie that I loved her, then everything would be alright.

'No,' I said. 'There's something important I've gotta go back for.'

♫

40

TOM

Looking through the window, I was stunned to see the house had been cleared. The front room was bare except for a sagging armchair, and an angle poise lamp, lying, neck twisted, the wire trailing across the carpet, as if pulled towards the door by something heavier.

'Josie! Josie!' I hollered through the letterbox. But my voice vaulted back, hollow and wooden, from every corner. Through the flap, I saw the living room sofa, devoid of bright cushions, and the kitchen empty except for a lonely kettle in the stove. Fuck!

Where'd she gone? I stood up and searched for clues. Bags were piled up by the bins, but there was no note stuck to the door. The corner shop was shut of course, and elderly Chinese neighbours peeking round their door at me, shook heads and spoke no English. Shit! Where the hell was she? I hadn't got a single number or address for anyone she knew – her mate Franki, that guy Simon, no-one. A terrible thought crept through me with arctic cold. What if I couldn't find her? No way! It wasn't possible. I'd comb Coventry for places and people she knew – maybe Trevor had some information, or the landlord at the Elm. Someone would know where Josie had gone.

♪

'Tom! Snap to it mate.' Charlie was passing me a beer. 'Wasteland's straight in the charts at number 20 and you've gorra face like a wet weekend in Wolver'ampton.'

'I know, it's great.' I lit a cigarette and crumpled the empty packet.

'What the hell's wrong with you man?' Len wiped his glistening brown brow with a cuff then slapped me on the back. 'This is what we've all been workin' for. Enjoy the feelin'! If we get into the Top Ten, we could be on TV.'

We were back in Camden at the pub on the market. Eddy was picking his way from the bar, followed by a grinning Adam, both carrying trays of drinks, and the whole band was clustered round tables, giddy with excitement. They dumped the trays down, and hands shot out to grab pints. Adam poked a quick glance at Vinnie, then said, 'Now you need to get ready for television. Seriously, you can't be over-rehearsed.'

Eddy rolled his eyes. 'Christ, we know our songs backwards. We need to record our album, don't we Tom?'

I'd enlisted Trevor's help and searched all over Coventry. Every pub and the two clubs. No Josie.

Len was shaking his head. 'Nah man, we should get back into gigging. Do some of the London venues, make some proper money.'

'Len's right,' Vinnie chimed in. 'Now we've gorra name, let's get some cash in.'

I'd even been to the art department, found her old tutor and blagged some story about a silly row and a sick friend she'd want to know about, which was partly true. The Alan kid had pulled through and Rick had promised he could be our roadie when he was better.

Eddy grimaced. 'Fuckin' hell. We've done a billion gigs in the last three months. Let's get some new material together before performing again.'

After the whole rigmarole, the tutor had just given me her old Coventry address and wouldn't even tell me where her parents lived. Was it Yorkshire or Lancashire? She was pretty vague about her family.

I'd finally found the landlord's shop open, he said she'd moved to London – for chrissakes, London! – but he didn't know where. Then he handed me my letter – the one I'd posted to the wrong address, which had '*From Tom, on tour somehere in the UK*, on the back on the envelope – saying a neighbour had left it with him. I read it over, wondering why I hadn't just asked her in person. Too late now. I scribbled Rick's phone number at the bottom and handed it back to him. He promised to make sure she got it when she came for the rest of her stuff.

'I agree with Eddy,' Devon's woolly hat wobbled solemnly as he nodded. 'What d'ya think Charlie?'

'Maybe we can do both?' Charlie's head darted from Len to Devon, like a child trying to please both parents. 'It would be handy to have some cash. It's so bloody expensive down here.'

Fozz appeared, not before time, eyes twinkling behind his black frames. As he pumped my hand in congratulation I felt another shiny little packet in my palm. He sat beside me, head bobbing, while the others were still arguing, and said in a low voice, 'Saw Trev in Birmingham. Told me you had a bit of personal set back. Sorry mate.' I must have looked shocked, because his internal metronome increased. ' No, no. I ain't told anyone. Just guessed you might need a pick up.'

I pocketed the gift. 'Thanks mate. That's a life saver.'

Vinnie was waving his pint about now, eyes bright with potential. 'We could do The Triangle again and maybe The Palais in west London, and what's that other big place?'

'Wembley?' said Raymond.

Everyone laughed. 'Steady, rude boy. We're not famous like The Beatles,' said Devon.

'You could be,' said a voice on my left. It was Adam, leant back against the bench, absorbing the vibe. 'What do you want next Tom?' He gave me a sideways look and raised an eyebrow, reminding me what an annoying prick he was, as if I could have forgotten.

I want to find Josie, I just want Josie back.

'Yeah!' I thumped the table, making everyone's drinks jump. 'Let's do it all! New album, big gigs, telly, whatever. Won't get this chance again, so may as well go for broke!'

There was a huge cheer and Adam was outvoted on the need for a second pint.

♪

41

TOM

At the BBC, Adam chivvied us into a dressing room, where white walls were fitted with long mirrored counters. The light from the glowing mirror bulbs sparkling onto large glass ashtrays, and shone off the cellophane shrouding big baskets – filled with miniature bottles and packets of goodies, as if they were prizes in a strange white fairground.

Adam disappeared, and was replaced by two woman who opened huge makeup boxes, and took out orangey stuff to cover our faces.

'I ain't havin' none of that.' Charlie backed off in horror, like a vampire from a crucifix.

'It's so you don't look like a ghost under the lights,' said the younger girl. 'Viewers can't tell you're wearing makeup, honest.'

She held up a nylon cape like a beauty toreador, and Charlie slid into the chair with a sideways wink at me. 'Be gentle then,' he said. When she caressed him with a big make up brush, he started sneezing, and she giggled.

Nothing could take the shine off my excitement though. *This was IT - Top Of The Pops!* It was really happening and millions of people would see us. Christ, I spent my whole youth watching this programme! My chest pounded and I felt a rising nausea. *For gods sake calm down!*

'Cut it out Tom!' Len snapped over his shoulder, as an impressively-matched dark brown powder was applied to his gleaming forehead. 'You're not goin' into a boxing ring.'

'Sorry,' I muttered and stopped cracking my fingers. 'Didn't realise.'

As the makeup women were leaving, Fozz appeared at the door. He was following us round for his article, still hoping to bag a piece in New Sonic Waves. 'Look natural fellas!' He shot us with a fancy new Olympus, as we joshed round, posing with our instruments, pretending to glug wine from the tiny bottles. Vinnie grinned at me, and we both cracked open a bottle to pour the equivalent of a glass of ruby liquid down our throats. Immediately I wanted more.

'Hey man.' The frown Len gave me creased the rich, dark suede of his made up face. 'Save that business for later.'

I nudged Vinnie. 'Oooo! Get Mister Showbiz!' But Len just sucked his teeth, swivelled his chair away and began plucking his guitar. Fozz raised a secretive eyebrow at me, before slinking out towards the gents. I counted to thirty then followed him. A little pick-up wouldn't hurt.

When we returned, Charlie was bouncing up and down on his heels practically doing star jumps, and Eddy was shaking the imaginary creases out of his jacket. Len was now practising riffs. I was even more energized, so to distract myself from the thought we were about to be on national television, I said, 'Hey, I've never seen you practice before Len.' Adding, 'Thought you had had magic fingers.' My laugh was too high, edgy. Len whirled round and jabbed a finger in my side. 'Don't talk 'bout magic before a big thing like this, Tom.' He hissed. 'You're temptin' bad luck.'

Christ almighty. This gig was turning us all into idiots.

I reminded myself the show was ridiculous. Half the acts were shite and no musician worth his salt took it seriously. Everyone knew the pop charts were rigged by big shots who controlled the record industry, they were no indicator of what was really going on in music. Who watched this anyway? It was for teeny-boppers – mindless kids who bought the records they were told to. We were on after 'Chester the Chunky Chicken' for chrissakes – a man in a feathered suit, warbling a ditty about how his egg rolled away and he was too fat to chase it.

'Look, can everyone stop this stuff!' I shouted. 'It's doing my head in.'

'Hey, don't yell, man,' said Charlie. 'We're just excited, that's all.'

'There's over an hour to wait Tom.' Even Devon's deep voice was not quite as measured as usual. 'Gotta do somethin' to fill in the time.'

A camera shutter sounded *kerr-chunk* at my side. 'Stop that Fozz! For fuck's sake! I'm going to check out what we're about to face.'

'They said to stay in here.' Eddy's voice came from the other end of the room.

I shook my head incredulously as I grabbed my jacket. 'Yeah? And when did we start doing what we were told?'

'I'm comin' with yer!' In a flash Vinnie jumped down from the counter, and was at my side.

In a studio covered with wires, huge tripodded cameras were wheeled around like mounted guns, as people scurried around, marking up the floor with coloured electric tape. Underneath hanging light panels a guy barked into a walkie talkie, 'Okay, try the red. And blue. Now yellow,' then gave the thumbs up to a row of headphoned silhouettes in a gallery. Anyone not busy on set, stood in wait with clipboards, tools or charts.

'Hey Tom, my main man!' Adam peeled away from suit and rested a hand on my back. 'Pretty impressive, huh?'

I moved away from Adam's paw, and leaned in to see the tiny TV monitor on the camera nearest me. The cameraman grabbed the handles, swinging the camera from side to side to focus on the central dias – like a first division player getting his eye in for a penalty.

'That's where you'll be,' Adam pointed to a stage on the right.

Vinnie breathed a soft expletive behind me. 'Fuckin' ace!'

My chest tightened. The space looked very open and empty, despite the drums and keyboards. Without thinking, I said, 'What's the sound like?'

Adam laughed. 'You're miming, remember! What the hell d'ya think the sound in here would be like?'

I nodded. My mouth was dry. Without much else on stage, it was just going to be us, Original Mix – pretending to be Original Mix. How the hell would that work? It was playing live which united us.

232

Back in the dressing room the others stared at me expectantly.

In a Hollywood movie, this would be the moment where the leader gave his big rallying speech – inspirational words to motivate a triumphant performance. But as usual I was making it up as I went along. And I was stumped.

Fozz snapped off some photos. I frowned at him and took a deep breath. 'Look,' I said. 'What are we known for on stage?'

'The music man,' said Devon. 'They're blown away by the live ska sound.'

'Well that's a done deal,' I said. 'We gotta deliver something else.'

Blank faces gawped back at me. I was sinking.

'The kids like the whole OM package,' said a quiet voice.

Everyone turned. On the makeup bench, Fozz softly thumped his feet, satchel strap across his chest, camera swinging round his neck, sporting a brown blazer and a trilby, like a 1940's hack. Behind the big specs, his eyes were watchful and rabbity.

He shrugged. 'Well, it's Eddy's deadpanning, Len strutting round like a prize cockerel, you and Vinnie firing out guitar licks at each other.' He nodded towards Devon, Charlie and Raymond. 'An' the rhythm section emphasising those upbeats out of course. It's the whole beautiful thing – an array of disparate young men, creating disjointed mayhem with an anarchic edge.'

We all stared. Fozz had never spoken for this long at one time without a twitch. He blinked twice and bobbed his head, as if he'd just come back from a trance. 'Yeah,' he said. 'But mostly they like the fact that you dick around. Don't take yourselves too seriously, like.'

Everyone laughed

'We're mimin' to our own bloody record,' said Eddy, thoughtfully. 'Which does leave plenty of room for arsing around.'

'Especially as we're on after a man in a soddin' chicken suit,' I added. Now I considered the implications of this, I was pretty knobbed off. 'How often you get a jump at 'post-punk anarchy' on national telly? Let's face it, this programme's a joke. We should do what we like!'

Eddy gave me a secret grin, Charlie and Vinnie whooped. Even Devon smiled widely.

Len summed up the strategy. 'Arriiiight! Let's show them some real rude boys in action.'

♪

After a load of 'rehearsals' – one for camera angles, one for lights, one for fuck-knows-what – it felt like we were just moving mannequins.

'It's so fuckin' *staged*,' I said to Fozz, as he quickly lined up a little recuperative dose in the Gents cubicle.

'Cool it man,' said Fozz. 'Your power's back when they film for real. Do your thing then.'

I wasn't sure what 'my thing' was, but I felt better for the pick up powder and when we were actually filmed I horsed around, swapping riffs with Vinnie, like we had at the RAR festival. One of the camera operators loved it, zooming in to our guitars and as Vinnie's solo came up, it occurred to me how funny it would be if we both mimed it. As Vinnie sank onto a bended knee I did too – so we were both playing simultaneously on our unplugged instruments, like you might in your bedroom, air guitaring to a record. But when I looked up to give a fiendish grin, the camera was aimed solely at me, clearly focussing on my fingers, then my face, until we went into the last verse and chorus, when the cameraman moved out to film Len toasting. The other two cameras stayed with other members of the band, and it was possible that Vinnie hadn't been filmed much at all.

When we ran off stage, Adam's pink face loomed large, all toothy smiles. 'It was great lads!'

Vinnie stormed into the dressing room, picked up a chair, hurled it at a mirror, taking out several surrounding bulbs and smashing the glass into glittering shards. 'That was fucking bollocks!' He grabbed the chair leg as it bounced, bracing for a second blow, but Eddy jabbed him with a punch to the stomach and Len tried to yank the chair away from him. Winded, Vinnie let go and the chair swung out in momentum, making Len topple back, to smash the overhead light with a chair leg, as he regained his balance. Vinnie turned to me and his face was murderous.

'Why did you do it?' he yelled. 'You stole my fuckin' solo!'

I shrugged. 'Dunno. It seemed like a laugh. We were all miming badly and playing out of time on purpose.' I turned to the others. 'Hey! We said we wouldn't take it seriously. Not my fault that camera closed in on me.'

'It was my fuckin' solo!'

Len was brushing bits out glass out of his hat brim, refusing to meet me in the eyes, and Devon just shook his head.

'There's muckin' round and muckin' round, Tom,' said Charlie, his voice serious.

'Fuckin' hell, it wasn't my fault!' I said, exasperated. 'We agreed to dick around.' I looked at their intractable faces. Eddy spread his hands, with the pitying look he usually reserved for Vinnie.

'Oh, sod off!' I grabbed my guitar case. 'I'm going for a drink.'

I brushed past Adam, bustling in with some blokes in suits. 'Shit! What's all this bloody glass?' he spluttered. 'Tom? Where you going?'

I strode past, not bothering to answer.

Fuck Vinnie, I thought. The cunt! Who gave him the right to be sanctimonious? He'd sell your granny for her gold fillings, nick your last fiver to go out on the piss – even tell your amazing, beautiful girlfriend you were married when you weren't.

Fozz caught up with me, on route to the nearest pub. As I ranted, he was wise enough to say nothing. Inside the bar, he gestured at a blousy old landlady with a wrinkled cleavage. When she put down her tea towel, I walked off and let Fozz order, as the sight of her yellowing toothy smile made me sick to my heart. What had happened to the great feeling of earlier? One minute everything was possible and the next...

I took a long drag of my cigarette and closed my eyes. I had the sensation that somehow things were moving out of my control, sinking. When I opened my eyes Fozzz was drumming his fingers on the table, to the background music.

'Daisy Pointer,' he said, referring to the plaintive yowls swirling out of the juke box.

We listened to a verse: lust, betrayal, shotguns – all the sentimental twaddle of Country songs.

'Not surprised her lover left her,' I said. 'She made a right bollocks of that high D.' I ruminated a bit, becoming increasingly agitated. 'She composed all her own stuff you know – won loads of song writing awards. What the hell was she thinking? Why would you write a note in a place you can't fuckin' reach?'

Fozz grinned. 'Brilliant, Tom!' Bloody hell he was laughing at me!

'When you're not being an inspiration.' He bobbed his head in delight, then took off his glasses to wipe his eyes. 'Man, you can be a total dick!'

Eddy slid into the next seat and said in a conspiratorial voice, 'Don't worry. Adam's smoothed it all over with the management.'

I pulled a disgusted face. If Adam wanted the role of band diplomat, he was welcome to it. 'I'm sure he coped.'

'What happened with you, anyway?' Eddy eyed me sideways. 'I mean, Vinnie's an A1 wanker, but miming his solo?' He shook his head. 'That was pretty low.'

'Just drop it Ed.' I looked to the bar, where Raymond and Vinnie were flirting with two girls, I recognised as Cheryl and Linda. Cheryl was wore a tight black skirt and high shoes, and I noticed what great legs she had. She caught me looking and offered me a big flirtatious grin. I gave a small smile back, though I was still smarting inside.

Adam rocked up and started blathering on about how I had to keep the band together because we were on the point of breaking through to the big time. I told him to piss off as I'd got it all under control, then went for a smoke outside before I decked him.

I'd thought that, I could forgive Vinnie for what he'd done at The Weasel – like I'd done all the other times he'd been an arse to me. I'd just find Josie and clear it all up. Then, when my search failed, I'd decided to go back to my dream, and get on with the business of achieving massive success.

But something special was missing now – like a tune which needs that vital key change, to lift it to the next level. With Josie I felt like a better person – more creative, upbeat, acceptable, as if I'd truly found my song. Now I was out of tempo, discordant. Basically, I couldn't reach my own fucking top note.

42

TOM

After our Top of the Pops appearance, Wasteland shot to number 12 in the charts. Complete strangers stood us pints in the Camden Market Tavern, Adam bought new suits – saying he couldn't bear the sweaty pong of our old ones – and it seemed we finally had our due. But it came with changes.

In his office, Adam introduced us to an attractive horse-faced redhead, who wore a tweedy jacket. 'This is Annabel. She'll be managing your PR.'

Vinnie sat up, erect in every way known to man or beast – in his case a combination.

'Yah. I'll be dealing with the television and media side, actually.' She tossed her hair as she spoke. Posh tottie. Way out of Vinnie's league.

'What media?' Rick was squatting on a low stool, looking small and unimportant in his badge-covered denims.

'Here's the schedule, yar?' She passed out photocopies. 'We've been quite selective. The stations are raaarely falling over themselves.'

Devon pulled his woolly hat down, lips pursed. 'How much they payin'?'

'Yesss!' Charlie punched the air. 'Graham Logan show on Radio 1!'

Logan's graveyard slot had a cult following for his punk, and off beat playlist, and the bands who played live sounded like they were performing from his garage. He was a huge hero.

'Tim's Teatime Telly? The Bonkerz Club? Jesus! Why we doing kid's programmes?' Eddy was not impressed.

'Oi! It'll be a great laugh,' said Vinnie. 'I'll dive in the Bubble Tank with Patsy Trimble any day!' Turning his back to Annabel, he flicked a lewd tongue at Charlie, who grinned back.

'Look, we need to talk about more important stuff – like some major gigs and your album,' said Adam. 'I suggest Tom, Eddy and

Rick stay here, and the rest of you go off to discuss the details with Annabel – to a caff maybe?'

'Or the pub!' said Vinnie, as if he'd hit on a novel idea.

'Oh yaar! I'd love a G and T, actually.'

Annabel couldn't possibly know what she was getting into. Everyone leapt up and filed out, with Charlie hanging onto Vinnie's shoulders, trilling the conga tune.

'Charlie mate, try to keep a grip on things,' I said.

'Not possible.' He grinned. 'This train's got its own momentum.'

Len thumped me on the back as he passed, laughing. 'Wow man! Wait till me cousin's boys see me on kiddies' TV!'

'Oh Christ, let them get hammered,' Adam sighed. 'We need to talk money and management.'

And so Eddy, Rick and I settled in front of his desk, like a row of players waiting for our coach's instructions.

Five minutes later Eddy stood by the window smoking, Rick was sat in stunned silence and I stomped up and down behind him.

'Rick helped me build this band from nothing!' I said.

'I know. And you've done a great job man.' Adam put two thumbs up to Rick.

'He bought the tour van, found us great gigs, and provided hours of studio time.'

Adam's expression was patient, unemotional. He just didn't get it.

'And you want us just to dump him like an old boiler?' I twisted round in appeal to Eddy, but his eyes were catching Adam's, sealing some complicit agreement.

'What the hell NOW?' I rounded on him. 'You and your boyfriend got this all sewn up then?' I was seeing red, so this was sheer, idiotic provocation. But Eddy looked in sharp questioning panic at Adam, who produced tiny, fast shakes of his head. It was enough to confirm what, on some level, I'd already known.

I bent over, palms on my knees, staring at the fag-burnt carpet, trying to think. For a long time I'd suspected Eddy's endless secrecy was because he was gay, and his bitterness came from being too different on a tough council estate, having to hold his own with brawn and punches. For weeks now he'd tried to avoid fights with Vinnie. I'd seen him grit his teeth and walk away, storing his fury and pouring it into lyrics. In fact, it was his history of looking after number one which made him brilliant – and dangerous.

When I straightened up, his stubborn dark eyes stared back at me. I spoke directly to him, ignoring Adam.

'Look Ed, I don't care who you fuck, man. Honestly I don't. But please don't fuck us over!'

We stood outside, as two Goth lads selected from trays of nose-studs on a stall nearby and a market trader cried out, 'Get yer classic punk T-shirts – two for a fiver!'

I faced Rick. 'I'm *so* sorry mate.'

He mugged a half-grin. ''S not a problem Tom. Makes more sense for Moth to take on gigs and recordin' now, an' for me to manage…other stuff.'

'We still need you on our side Rick.' The memory of Eddy's impenetrable face came back to me. 'I want you in Coventry, looking after contracts and money, checking nobody's stuffing us. And you'll still get your cut.'

He patted my arm. 'Yeah, I know mate. Don't worry.' His long hair wagged at each side of his head.

'An' I'll call you before agreeing to more changes – talk it through. Especially now we know Eddy's opinion will be skewed.'

'Gonna say anything to the lads 'bout that?' Rick asked.

I blew out my lips. 'Are you mad? If they knew he was shagging the enemy, they'd go berserk. Besides, he doesn't want anyone to know he's gay and I promised to stay schtum.'

Rick checked his watch, as if he was ever on time for anything. 'Best get to the station.'

'Not coming to the pub?' I could see why he wouldn't.

He chewed his mouth, as if thinking. 'Nah, best not. Stuff to do in Cov. Visitin' that Alan kid in hospital, an' the workshop needs a good tidy. Plus, Trev's mate's gonna buy the van, so I need to get it running right.'

But we both stood still, and watched a couple of lads trying on sunglasses in the shape of Big Ben. There'd always been changes throughout our time working together, but this was a seismic shift in our friendship, and neither of us knew what it meant.

I plucked a packet of fags from my top pocket and proffered him one. He jammed it behind his ear and drew his hair over it. 'Save it for the train.'

Finally I said, 'Give a couple of pumps on the juice as you turn her over, and she's fine.'
Rick nodded, then his face brightened. 'Hey, did I tell yer? Fozz got me free tickets for Purple Viper at Tidmouth Stadium. Front seats.'

'Great. You deserve it Rick.'

Rick nodded. 'He's coming over soon, to settle up for the last lot of EP sales.'

'Oh yeah.' I remembered that Pump City was no longer selling our records. Little links were being snapped off one by one.

I ground my cigarette out with a boot and zipped up my jacket. Rick should piss off now, give me chance to get my head together. I needed to stop feeling like such a heartless bastard for letting him go, and work out how to explain to the others how I'd let Adam walk right over my loyalties.

'Tell Fozz if we get to Number One, he's got our exclusive interview.' This was something like loyalty at least.

Rick waggled his head 'Will do.'

He started walking off, then he turned, frowning. 'Hey Tom! What about that media woman an' her Press list? Won't she mind?'

'Fozz gets that first big interview.' I stuck my middle finger up in the air in defiance. 'And if anyone's got a problem, I don't fuckin' care – actually!'

We both chortled for a moment, then he said, 'See ya Tom.'

'Be good, mate,' I replied. And I watched his hunched be-denimed form trot off, until he was swallowed up in the crowds.

43

TOM

For two weeks we'd shuttled round in taxis to radios stations and newspaper offices, giving garbled interviews, with questions ranging from the inane to the downright bizarre. Adam insisted we took taxis, ever since we'd got lost on the tube and missed half a radio slot. Though Len maintained that was due to our natural disinclination to get off at anywhere called 'White City'.

It was all manic fun, but the joy had started to wear thin.

'You two have got to answer some of the questions.' Facing backwards on the drop down seat in a cab, I wagged a finger at Len and Devon opposite, purposefully excluding Vinnie from the equation.

'It's only fair,' I continued. 'The only ones doing the talking are me and Charlie.'

'In more ways than one,' muttered Vinnie.

I stared. Had Vinnie found out about my arrangement with Fozz? He gazed out of the window, and groaned with pleasure as a girl in tight trousers walked past. I decided not. That was just another pointless quip from the bluster of wisecracks which fluttered round him like litter.

'It's better you both do the talkin',' said Len. 'I freeze up, man.'

Devon nodded. 'You got the gift of the gab Tom.'

'Oh come on Devon!' I threw my hands wide in appeal. 'You're the most articulate of us all.' Devon was given to holding long philosophical conversations with Charlie and Eddy, when we were holed up in hotels and dressing rooms, with nothing to do but smoke and wait.

He shook his head. 'Nah man. This is about bein' quick and giving up little snippets of reasonin'. That's not my style.'

I didn't urge Vinnie to speak up. His off the wall crap was not required, and he couldn't be trusted to mind his language when it was vital we stick to the rules. As one presenter had confided in hushed horror, 'I interviewed Guttersnipe in '77 and it nearly ended my career.' In any case, Vinnie and Len had assumed the roles of band jokers, clowning around, as I struggled to say what our favourite colours were and whether we liked London, trying to interject something meaningful about our music. Thank god for Charlie. He brought his easy, milkman's charm to the proceedings and, as the band's official skinhead, everyone loved to quiz him.

The taxis drew up outside the television studio and we jumped out, clattering guitar and keyboard cases onto the tarmac as, thankfully, we could play live this time. Adam stood outside in Bond street attire, one arm out as he mimed checking his watch, the other planted indignantly into his hip, like some sort of expensive-suited teapot.

'Where the hell have you been?' He grabbed my elbow. 'Please tell me nobody's been drinking.'

'Cool it man,' said Devon from behind. 'We're here now – an' ready to go.'

'Only had a few vodkas.' Vinnie stumbled awkwardly as he descended from the cab. 'Nobody'il tell.' He fell over his guitar and righted himself.

I laughed as he wound Adam up because, for once, sobriety had won out. Adam rounded on Eddy in question, but Eddy closed his eyes and turned away. I couldn't tell if he was disgusted at Vinnie for acting the idiot, or Adam for being an old woman. Probably both.

In the Green Room at Bang On Cue, Oli Denmark and Daisy Chandler, the programme's co-hosts were waiting to greet us. Oli shook my hand. Confident and immaculate, he wore a mod-style suit and thin leather tie. Then the diminutive Daisy came tripping over on high heels, in a 50's style dress with a big bow around dyed blond hair. The guys buzzed round her like excitable hornets, as Oli steered me away to talk about how we'd be interviewed.

'It's not like Top of The Pops,' he said. 'You'll have the best live sound, and we treat it like a real gig. They're proper music fans out there, not teeny boppers, you know.'

'That's great,' I said.

'After your song, you'll come to the Bang on Cue sofa for the interview.'

'What, all of us?'

Oli looked over at the band. Len was entertaining Daisy by rolling his pork pie hat down his arm sideways and catching it – a trick from an old film, which had taken him weeks to master. Daisy clapped her hands and asked him to repeat it. Her bottle blond hair reminded me of Josie's. I suddenly missed that familiar touch, the female scent, the way Josie relaxed into my chest when I put my arms around her and how she wound her legs round mine in bed. I missed her voice. And the sex. Oh yes, I definitely missed the sex.

'The sofa's not really big enough for everyone.' Oli said with a frown. 'I'll select three of you, if that's okay?'

The audience were still applauding our song as Charlie, Len and I leapt off stage and clambered through the bodies – big cameras gliding after us – to join Daisy and Oli on their dais.

'Phew! Welcome, welcome!' From his famous director's chair, Oli's expansive arms ushered us to the couch in front. 'Well, Original Mix! That performance was a real hit at Bang on Cue – so we certainly hope it won't be the last!'

I plunked onto the seat, chest pumping with excitement, and Charlie and Len flopped down beside me. Daisy had arranged herself at the far end of the sofa, all frothy dress and pale stockings.

'So, Tom, you're the band leader. And who else have you brought me?' she purred.

I introduced Charlie and Len, then Oli asked some general questions and, as agreed, Charlie led off. Next to Daisy, Len relaxed, grinning in his hat and dog tooth checked jacket, still shiny with tiny drops of perspiration. I waited for my turn to speak. But, after a bit of Charlie's patter, Daisy interjected with a question.

'Len, can you explain something?' Len's smile froze. His shock at being addressed was palpable. We'd agreed that Charlie and I would do the talking, as usual.

Daisy swivelled sideways, tucked her knees against Len's and widened her doll-like eyes, as if there was nobody else in the room. 'What exactly *is* toasting?' she said.

'Errrrr,' he shot me a look of appeal, and bit his lip, before he turned to her. 'I spose it's a kind o' sermon to the people listenin',' he said.

'Oh, reeeally,' Daisy murmured, nestling her legs further towards him, which meant Len had to shuffle sideways to face her. As the camera crept in she smiled. 'Do say more.'

'Well Original Mix uses toastin' to expand the lyrics, an' blend in with the motivation of the song,' said Len.

Daisy didn't take her eyes off him. 'And where did it come from?'

Len blinked and there was a moment's hesitation, before he took a decisive breath.

'Well, it started from Jamaica in the late 50's, when mento and calyspso developed into ska.' He grinned with bashful pride. 'You see, what happened was radio deejays started a way of jive talkin' over records – like they heard the American deejays doin' – then they used it for amusin' the crowds at yard parties, over dub plates – that's a kind of backing track.' He hesitated. 'You want more?' Daisy nodded.

'Then toastin' became like a competition. Producers all tryin' for the best sound system and the vocals man who'll blow the crowds away – usin' his humour and clever words. He'd boast about himself, or comment on what was goin' on, usin' rhymes and storytelling – like an island poetry. You see, the root to all Jamaican music comes from the need to express yourself, tell it like it is.'

As she leant towards him, the small crescents of Daisy's breasts plumped over the neckline of her dress. She smiled. 'How long have you been toasting, Len? Do you compose all your own material?'

Len grinned. 'Been doin' it since I was about thirteen and, yes ma'am, I write it meself.'

The audience chuckled at his quaint formality, but Daisy persisted. 'And can you write a toast about anything?'

'Well my words are mostly political…'

'Could you toast about me?'

Oh shit. As Len's brow creased I didn't dare breathe. What the fuck would he do? This was way out of Len's zone. His writing was indignant – riddled with pithy phrases which he honed and re-honed on sheets of crumpled paper and by practicing over the mic, until he found his pattern. He wasn't given to spouting on the spot about specific people. The studio went quiet as everyone waited.

Len narrowed his eyes and thought for a second. His foot twitched in imaginary beat, then he took a deep breath,

Miss Daisy, she adventurous man,
She love her music, like a ska fan,
She finds her rhythm in the beat,
You bet she'll dance you off her feet.
Man, you don't know what to do,
Because you know, she's Bang on Cue!'

The audience erupted and Daisy threw her arms round Len to plant a kiss on his cheek. They weren't his most eloquent words, but the fact he'd spoken at all was amazing. I tipped my head to him in homage.

Oli looked to me and continued. 'You've clearly got a multi-talented band Tom, and we all love you here –' his sentiment was punctuated by a couple of cheers and a loud whistle from the audience. 'But some people say the lyrics of Wasteland are excessively gloomy, and they accuse you of painting too depressing a picture.' He raised an eyebrow. 'Shouldn't you be writing something jollier?'

I liked Oli, and was grateful for the chance to have a proper dialogue.

'Yeah well we've been touring for weeks, so we've seen a lot of the new Tory Britain, and these things are true. The skint are getting skinter. Across the UK there are so many dole queues and businesses closing down – it's not a construct of us, or the left wing Press. We're becoming a pretty sick nation.'

Oli's face tightened in consternation. 'Strong words indeed. Do you intend to carry on addressing this in your music?'

I told him about the tatty shops we'd seen in countless high streets, mothers picking through remnants of cloth, unlabelled tins and neon-coloured toiletries. Or the sheepish old man who hovered round Coventry market at closing time, scooping up discarded produce from the floor. The unemployed kids who loafed at bus stops and chip shops, or kicked round on waste ground. Every town and city had its own set of male miscreants – the young ones looked bored and defiant, the older ones unmanned and defeated.

'There are some hellish, poverty stricken places out there.' I said. 'Towns where people scrape by on nothing, because their industries are shutting, and the city centres are in decline – places where crime and neo-Fascist groups are on the increase.'

'You sound pretty angry about it –'

'We all are! There's two and a half million people unemployed – with six thousand people joining the dole queues every day! The youthful optimism of our country's being robbed!'

'And that's what inspires your songs?'

I nodded. 'Like Len says, we try to tell it like it is. We've got no solutions, just music.'

Oli smiled. 'For which we're very grateful. And now Wasteland's in the Top Ten, what are your plans?'

I looked to Charlie, then Len. 'More gigging and the release of our first album – Ska Mix Original.'

Oli rubbed his hands. 'Fantastic! When will that be out?'

'Next few days,' I said.

'Well we all look forward to that,' said Oli. 'And now, to whet our appetites, I believe you're going to play us out with your new single.'

As we wound our way back to the stage, Daisy delivered a perfectly timed piece to camera about the next week's guests. She leant back with self-assurance against Oli, who had an arm draped round her neck – an intimacy which had every bloke in Britain thinking 'lucky bastard' on a weekly basis – and finished exactly as I slung my guitar over my shoulder.

'But now, let's give it up for Original Mix and their new song 'Too Polite to Riot'!'

During our four bar intro of descending chords, Eddy glowered at the big preying mantis of a camera, moving in front. Then, with his sweet-but-deadpan voice accentuating each word, he sang,

> *Pretty, poor provincial town,*
> *You're boarded up*
> *Your trade is down*
> *Encased in fields*
> *The young are sealed*
> *But what you gonna do?*
>
> *Inner city sink estate*
> *Too scared to walk*
> *Back home at late*
> *Attacked for just*
> *Your giro cash*
> *But what you gonna do?*

For the chorus we all leant into our mics, adding our 'ooo's of backing vocals:

> *It's not the British thing*
> *Although we'd like to try it*
> *Despite our tendencies*
> *We're too polite to riot!*

Although his face remained expressionless, Eddy's jaunty sarcasm voiced through the chorus. He used his Midlands twang to pronounce 'troiy-it' to rhyme with 'riot'. Across the room Oli smiled and Daisy was clapping with glee. In front of the stage, the audience were dancing and punching the air.

Our final clashing chord finished to colossal applause.

'That's all from Bang on Cue, and our thanks to Original Mix,' Oli shouted over the excited din. 'We'll see you next week – riot or no riot!'

♪

44

JOSIE

Franki and I had moved into two floors of an old house in Hackney, which had peeling wallpaper, loose floorboards and mice scratching behind the skirting in the small hours. After signing on in a packed dole office, whose thick plastic screens were peppered with an arc of what could only be bullet holes, I'd visited every café and restaurant within walking distance. And finally I'd landed some work at a community arts centre called The Arts Hub – a loose, hippy outfit, where I tended bar and made toasted sandwiches.

It was a lively environment, where people made pots, pounded at African drums, silk-screened T-shirts and posters, and took drama classes. And I worked whenever they wanted me, night and day, increasing the menu to include cakes, salads and homemade soups, until people started coming in just for lunch. It wasn't rocket science and work wouldn't mend a broken heart, but by the evening I was too tired to think and at least I could pay my way.

One rare night off, Franki and I went to our local pub with Hilary and her new boyfriend. The outing was a real tonic, as we guffawed at his anecdotes of disastrous casual jobs. Afterwards, we walked home, arms linked, in companionable and mellow mood. It had been good to get out and have some simple fun, and I was still chuckling. As we crossed the road I mimicked Graham's sad, bewildered voice, '…but when I opened the van door, all the chickens had gone.' We both started cackling with laughter again, clutching our sides. It was great to be in the moment again, happy and alive.

'I'm going to wet myself!' I gasped, and as I bent double on the pavement a cold finger of bile poked up through my sternum. Surely I hadn't drunk that much?

It appeared I had.

'Better now?' Franki led me off the vomit-splashed verge. 'I told you to eat more dinner before we came out drinking.'

But I'd been too nauseated at dinner time. Despite all my efforts, it was proving so hard to re-group, structure a sense of normality. My social life was limited to nights in watching TV with Franki and cooking with Axten, our new friend and neighbour. In fact, I'd had one pretty disastrous afternoon of passion with Axten – which resulted in extreme awkwardness once we'd both sobered up, and an agreement to draw a veil over the whole thing. The pub trip was just another escape from reality, from fretting and mulling on the 'what ifs'. But in reality, I still wasn't my old self.

'Let's watch Bang On Cue,' I mumbled through a half-eaten piece of toast. I poked the telly to 'on', and when the set pinged into life, I punched the lowest button, thinking what a thrill it was to have a new fourth channel.

'Daisy Chandler's frock is fab! Come and see!' I called to Franki, who was popping more slices into the toaster. Then my world stopped all over again.

There was Tom. His face was thinner, but he was still beautiful, alert and long-limbed on the sofa, talking about lyrics, touring and a new album. Daisy Chandler clearly thought so too. As the camera zoomed out showing Tom in profile talking to Oli, her face in the background was a picture of rapt attention. Simon's words crept back, *They're supposed to break your heart duck, it's in the small print.* My heart had been made of fine porcelain when a big truck had driven over it. Now the tyres were reversing, crunching it into smaller pieces.

'Want tea?' Franki entered, brandishing a teapot. She spotted the TV screen, 'Oh, blimey!' She plonked herself beside me.

'Tom looks good,' she said when the band members sprang up to rejoin the others on stage. 'Bit gaunt, but he spoke with amazing energy.' She put a hand on my shoulder to give me a consolatory rub, but I was lost to the screen. When the band started playing I moved from the sofa to kneel in front of the television. The camera settled on Tom for a moment, then swooped down to Vinnie's hands, and after a second, swung across the staff to the young keyboard player. It was the programme's trademark filming style, to appear as if the cameraman was drunk.

'Go back, you idiot!'

I'd tried so hard to forget, but now all I wanted was to see Tom's face, though the ache it caused was physical. The camera panned out wide – to show Eddy Knowles singing, with the band behind. I inched forward, crumbs and dirt on the carpet scratching at my knees. I wished I could stick my hand into the TV and pull Tom right out into the room, so he could wrap me in his arms and bring back all my happiness and hope.

When the credits rolled, I turned off the TV then pulled my legs from under me and leant against the sofa. The screen darkened to a little white dot, diminishing and dimming, until it finally disappeared. We sat in silence.

'That new song's great,' I said. 'I bet Tom wrote it.' I stared at a hole in the knee of my tights, then poked my finger in and ripped the tiny fibres apart, piece by piece, until there was a vast open space of pale flesh.

Franki rose and knelt on the floor in front, placing her arms over my shoulders and her forehead resting against mine, until I gave a heavy sigh and she sat up. I had been trying to face up to a new life, but to do this properly I needed to come clean. With Franki and myself.

'Franki, I've got to tell you something.'

'What?' We'd always told each other everything, but I'd broken our bond.

'Before I was working, Axten came over quite a bit, cos he was between jobs too.'

Franki shrugged. 'I know. You shared recipes and he taught you how to make perfect Caribbean rice.' She gave an appreciative laugh. 'And my dinner was ready on the table every night. So?'

I groaned. 'That's not all we shared…'

Under Franki's puzzlement I could see she was hurt. 'Oh? You never said.'

'It was an embarrassing one-off, when decided to get stoned one afternoon. I'd have told you but I didn't want it to affect the way we're all friends.' I grabbed her hand. 'It was just stupid comfort sex, Franki. I missed Tom so much…'

Franki gave a weak smile and leant over to pat my shoulder. 'Hey, we've all been there. It's no biggy.' She nodded with vigour. 'Really, I mean it Jose.'

I pressed my knees up, hugging my stomach. I still hadn't reached the reason why I admitted to this episode, an idiotic mistake, for which I needed Franki's help more than ever.

I took a deep breath. 'The thing is, I think I might be pregnant.'

45

TOM

I'd gathered the band to meet in the tiny, quiet bar of a backstreet pub in Camden, to discuss the second album. Eddy was off on one of his secret missions, so I left him a note. Behind the bar was a bracketed shelf on which sat a portable TV. And now everyone in the pub was transfixed on it, mouths open, as we watched the News.

'Bloody 'ell, those pigs have got riot shields!' said Vinnie, as the camera panned out across a dark main street.

A reporter struggled to be heard above a din of shouts, bottles smashing and sirens. And at least ten rows of blue-uniformed police tried to push forward along the road, against a hail of missiles being thrown by rioters, now in command of the wide open street – black guys, with angry faces.

'Shit!' said Devon at my side. Everyone turned in astonishment at hearing him curse. He shook his head slowly. 'This is bad, bad news, man. Brixton's been heatin' like a pot for years. Looks like the lid just blew.'

Each of his London friends had their worst 'stop and search' story, even his straight-laced cousin Edward, who worked for the council as a chippy, mending cupboards for pensioners and single mums. He'd once told me how he was frisked, when he'd left a job with his tool bag, and hauled off to the police station for protesting his innocence – while his white co-worker, found in possession of a packet of grass, was sent home with a caution.

On TV, the correspondent dodged a missile before he and his cameraman were shoved aside by the line of police. The screen filled with an image of blurry tarmac and the noise of clanking shields and shouts.

'We're getting out of here!' yelled the reporter as the camera swept back up to his face. *'But we'll bring you more news from Brixton, we've relocated somewhere safer.'*

All evening progress reports flashed up, as more men joined the rioters and the high street turned into a battle zone. People were shouting in apoplexic outrage against the increasing massed ranks of coppers, now wearing helmets and visors, the word 'POLICE' in capitals across their circular riot shields – as if there was any doubt. Men were dragged off by their hair, and set about the head by police batons, as they ran up to to the front line to yell or lob missiles. Brixton was saying 'no more' and emphasising it with bricks and glass. It was horrific, exciting, unbelievable.

Devon returned to the bar, panting.

'They're arh'right,' he said.

Len offered his rum and coke, which Devon downed in one. 'Edward an' his wife took the baby to the aunt in Streatham, so they'll stop there.' He glanced at the TV, where a gameshow host now mugged at the nation in complete normality, as if it wasn't on fire.

'He says this been brewin' all week, ever since that Saint Kitts man died in police custody. They thought somethin' might break, but not so big.' Devon dug in a pocket and clunked a fistful of ten pences onto the bar. 'Here's the change back.'

Vinnie pawed several pounds worth towards himself.

I jabbed Vinnie with sharp elbow in the ribs. 'Keep it, Devon. You'll want the phone later.' Vinnie reluctantly pushed the coins back.

'What about Floyd?' Len said, referring to Devon's other cousin.

Devon shook his head, and pulled a face. 'He's a loose cannon, man. No sayin' what he'll do.'

Eddy arrived and edged in alongside me. 'Shit, Tom. Have you seen the news?' He ordered a pint, then grabbed at my arm, pulling me away from the drinkers in hot debate at the bar. We stood by the window in two-man conspiracy.

'We have to withdraw the single!' he hissed.

I stared at him with incomprehension.

'Too Polite to Riot,' he said, as if I'd forgotten.

'No way!' I drew back to eye him. 'Is this you speaking or Adam?'

'It makes sense Tom. We don't wanna get tied up in this trouble. It's nothing to do with us.'

I thought about the lyrics which I'd written. Of course it was a hard-hitting protest song, but none of us imagined it would ever become a reality. The two events weren't connected.

'It's already gone to the distributors,' I reminded him. 'Anyway, that song's on our debut album – and we're not ditching that!'

46

TOM

We gathered at Moth's premises, where we'd been summoned. The phone was pressed to Adam's ear, as he received news.

'Yes, yes, I understand your position. Thank you.' He replaced the receiver and when he looked up his face had lost its pinkly important hue. 'The BBC's banned Too Polite to Riot.'

'Shit!'

'Facist bastards!'

'No fuckin' way!'

When the hubbub died down I said, 'What does this mean?'

Adam's voice was leaden. 'It won't be played on any BBC station, radio or television – national or regional. And they'll avoid mentioning the song by name, in case the title's seen as contentious. Their lawyers are seeking higher legal advice.'

'What for? It's not like we can afford to sue them,' I said.

Adam snorted down his nostrils and looked at me steadily. 'In case the police decide your lyrics were an incitement to riot, Tom.'

'Bloody hell!'

'What about Wasteland?' said Len.

'That's okay. It's holding at Number 3 today,' said Adam. 'They'll continue to play it.' He slowly viewed the line of us. Eddy, smoking on the window ledge, Charlie, Devon and Raymond, bunched up on hard chairs at the far side, Len and Vinnie, straggling the heaped packing boxes. His eyeballing ended with me, perched on stool by the door, under the Guttersnipe poster. He looked lost for words.

'They can't seriously think we had anything to do with this trouble in Brixton?' My mind was whirring. 'It's just a song I wrote to be ironic. The point was that we don't do riots in Britain.'

'We do now.' Eddy drawled from the other side of the room.

Adam was clicking his pen on and off against the table top. I had never seen him agitated before.

257

'I know – we'll get Fozz to do that exclusive!' I said. 'Talk about how we write our lyrics and why.'

'No! Definitely no interviews Tom!' Adam slammed the pen down. 'Not til we've got some direction from United Associated Artists. They've backed it – so it's their album.'

So that was it. The carapace had fallen. Underneath all the style and maverick independent charm, Ragged Moth's hands were tied and Adam was just another corporate puppet. His usual knowing condescension was infuriating – but this was even worse.

'What? The BBC slams a kibosh on our entire fucking output and you're telling me not to put our point of view over?'

'Yes Tom, that's precisely what I'm saying.'

I glared at him. We weren't exactly the best of friends, but I'd had a grudging respect for his knowledge and experience, believing his strategy paralleled mine. Now, without his arrogant self confidence, I was disorientated. If he wasn't prepared to fight our corner at UAA, how could we trust him at all?

As I sprung up, Adam's voice was on my back. 'Where you going?'

'Outside to think.' I flung open the door and propelled myself downstairs.

I strode out of crowded Camden, fast and furious, past lines of old town houses adorned with window boxes outside, and ethnic rugs inside. This was where the modern media men lived, slumming it on the fringes of the market with its stinky oils, punk T-shirts and endless black Goth gear. Smug bastards! Pretending to be cool and left wing, but kowtowing to an establishment of
Tory-voting old Etonians who made the truly important decisions –
like when to slam the brakes on someone's vision and snatch all their dreams away.

At Regent's Park I thundered on in impotent, almost-blind, rage, until the mown lawns and neat beds of roses triggered a flash of recall to that night making love to Josie in the park. Everything had been perfect then. We were on the brink, just needing a small record company behind us. And Ragged Moth seemed perfect, with their reputation for publishing rebellious edgy bands. I hadn't considered how their association with big players UAA would have affected their independence. Bloody hell! Nothing, just nothing, had gone my way since…since when? Yes, it was that night at The Weasel. Vinnie had lied to Josie, she'd disappeared outside, and that bastard Nazi skinhead had knifed the stupid kid who Rick was now keeping safe in my old bedsit. Then everything had started slipping away.

I slowed, gasping at the air, too angry to think straight, fumbling for my fags.

'Tom?'

I jumped. Fozz stood on the grass, about five foot away in his buff mackintosh and a sort of fedora.

'Jesus! What you doing creepin' round here?

He gestured to the Edwardian houses. 'Stayin' at a mate's flat over there.' He grinned. 'Spotted you stompin' across the grass, looking like you could punch someone.' Fozz tilted his head and sniffed. 'Come on up. Unless you gotta be somewhere?'

My brain was crammed with anger and confusion. Maybe Fozz could shine a light on it all. 'Nowhere important,' I said.

'This guy must be loaded,' I said, after a brief tour of the flat. 'What's he do?'

We were in the top storey of a huge residence, where the living room looked like one of those you see in a colour magazine, with some wanker standing in front of a big marble fireplace, elbow resting on the mantle, beside a pile of strategically placed books – which he'd have selected from the bookcases lining the walls. I walked over to examine the titles.

Fozz shrugged. 'Writes about history, makes documentaries an' stuff. Probably got family loot too.'

I sat on the big squashy sofa. 'How the hell d'you know someone like this?'

Fozz brought his battered old satchel over to a vast glass coffee table, and started to chop out a white line of powder. 'Saw him at a party couple of years ago, tryin' to score. Stopped him handin' a tenner to some little grunt for a couple o' bags of talc.'

'No shit!'

Fozz gave two birdy head dips. 'Ha, ha! Just what I said. We're both into jazz, so he got me into The Tundra Club to say thanks. Now he gets hold of tickets and I obtain…other stuff.' Fozz smirked.

'Jammy bugger,' I said.

'What are you doin' to relax, Tom? What's happenin' with our dark haired Midlands beauty?'

'Who – Cheryl?' I did a line, then sank back on the sofa, considering. The locker-room reception from our stalwart fan base – the free drinks and male bravura – was all very satisfying. But Cheryl's perky smile had its own reward.

'She likes you man.'

I gave a soft snort of laughter. 'Yeah well, Vinnie's got hopes there.'

Fozz's raised an eyebrow. 'She's not interested in Vinnie.'

'Yeah!' I laughed again. 'Funny to see him not instantly bagging a shag for once.' I stood up, suddenly needing to be moving. 'Look, I could really use your advice. These riots have sent everything pear-shaped. Let's go to The Wexford – I'm buying!'

As the young barman stood in a trance, trying to persuade my Guinness to settle by hypnotising it, an ITV announcer on the overhead telly silently mouthed the early evening news. There were images of more rioting in the streets of Brixton, then an image of Original Mix popped up on screen. It was the front of our new album, showing the band in a row, slouched and sullen, in front of a graffiti-peppered wall in Coventry – the one which lead to 'Anarchy Bridge'. It was supposed to be edgy of course, but in the context of the riots, we just looked menacing.

'Hey mate, quick, turn the TV up!' I said.

The bar tender spun to the telly. 'Faackin'ell – that's you!'

As he turned the volume knob, Fozz zoomed to the bar. The newscaster was speaking to camera: *Following the BBC's announcement this morning to ban a song, sales have rocketed. The single, called 'Too Polite to Riot', by new band 'Original Mix', has shot to Number 8 in the pop charts. The BBC stands by its decision to ban the record, saying that playing the song would be inappropriate, in light of the current troubles in Brixton. The group's skinhead following has also given much rise to criticism in the music press and concerns by police. Here is the band's leader talking to Radio Hampshire.'*

The screen showed one of Fozz's photos from inside the sleeve – me, laughing and falling backwards off a dressing room stool, as Charlie lobbed an empty can. We looked like, what my dad would call, 'a right pair of hoodlums.'

'Is it true that your fans have been known to chant Seig Heil and give the Nazi salute?'

I recognised the voice. It was some stupid jock in Southampton needling me, too early in the morning, after a big gig and a lot of celebratory lager.

'Look.' That was my own angry retort. *'There's a lot of unemployed kids out there with nothing to do, so who can blame them if they latch on to the strongest influence around. Most of Original Mix's skinhead fans aren't neo fascists or racists – and we can't control the ones that are.'*

I'd realised that this wasn't true, so I'd gone on to correct myself, emphasising that we were a racially mixed band, our songs had an anti racist message, and the Nazi chanting had been stopped immediately. But this last section was all cut off. It was a disaster.

The camera cut back to the reporter, now deploying the expression of a disappointed headmaster explaining how the few had spoiled it for everyone else.

'Ragged Moth, the independent label who distribute Original Mix's records said today that they have taken legal advice and are considering their position. And now to the weather…'

I turned in desperation to Fozz. 'Shit! Shit, shit, shit, shit, SHIT!'

'Can I quote you on that?' he said.

The bar man pushed our pints across with his fingertips, as if they were tainted. 'You really let skinheads chant Seig Heil at your gigs?' He eyed me with obvious doubt.

'It happened once and we turfed them out!' I barked back. 'Fuckin' hell Fozz, what are we goin' to do? Once something's been on telly it's bloody well carved in stone.'

♪

I found a wall phone by the Gents loo – and spent several minutes thumbing coins into the slot, and cursing as they slid right through and reappeared in the hatch at the bottom. Eventually persistence paid off, and I dialled Adam's office.

'Don't come back here Tom!' His voice was full of alarm. 'There's a swarm of Press outside. I had to send the band away, to stop them giving ad hoc interviews.'

'Where are the hell are they now?' I said.

'Shunted them off in cabs to a friend's place in Hertfordshire.' He sighed. 'Tell me where you are. Christ it's such a mess!'

Twenty minutes later he bustled in looking red-faced and panicky, loosening his shirt collar. He waved away the notion of a pint, downed a double whiskey, ordered another and pointed to a far table in a booth. We sat opposite each other, with Fozz at the side, like a referee.

'It's really heavy in Brixton.' He gestured over to the television. 'They've burnt out cars and shops, and there are lots of casualties on both sides. The police are asking for reinforcements.'

'Let me do an interview,' I leant forward. 'How could we have known they'd be riots?'

Adam shook his head. 'Absolutely not. UAA says all Original Mix members are to stay out of public view until the civil disorder's all under control.'

I thumped the table. 'And do what in the meantime? We've got an instant hit and you want us to cower away, just because the song's been called 'contentious'.'

Adam pursed his lips. 'Now they're using the word 'inflammatory'.'

'All the more reason to clear the air.' I spread my arms. 'Make a big statement.'

'And say what Tom?' Adam gripped his tumbler, his face white with fury. 'That you were just playing around? You poked the hornet's nest by mistake? Whatever the hell you say will be turned against you.'

'We didn't start any of this bad feeling – we just named it, and we've got a right to speak out about being censored!' I too, was quivering with anger. 'And fucking hell Adam! What gave you the right to send my band off without asking me?'

'I'd have sent you too, knobhead, if you hadn't gone AWOL!' Adam stood. 'Just grow up, Tom. People are getting hurt – it doesn't need your comments to fan the flames. Here!' He threw a set of keys at me. 'The studio's free for a few days. Lay really low and make some music. I'm going back to field Press calls.' He straightened his jacket, with a rough brush down at the front. At the pub door he hesitated. In a level voice he said, 'Stay out of the limelight, call me tomorrow – and Tom?'

'What!' I snapped.

'Don't do anything stupid.'

I didn't trust myself to reply.

'What now?' said Fozz. The pub was starting to fill with after-work drinkers. 'You can stay at the flat if you like?' He bobbed his head. 'Seb's away til the end of next month.'

I wasn't listening. 'Adam's a cunt!' I said. 'We've got every right to tell it like it is.'

'Come on Tom.' He picked up his fedora and handed it to me. 'Look, you better put this on.'

I snorted at the ridiculousness of this idea, until I saw two blokes nearby nudging each other. 'Oh, alright,' I grabbed the hat and wedged it on my head. 'For fuck's sake, let's get outta here!'

On the pavement I hesitated, jangling Adam's keys in my pocket. 'Think I'll go to the studio or a mess round after all. Might help me think.'

Fozz nodded. 'Stop by later. You know where I am.'

But I was already walking off, brain full of chaotic thoughts. My heart sank at the thought of our best song, and possibly our album being consigned to the bin. I had to get things back on track – and quick! We were so close to hitting the big time, so very *close*!

47

TOM

I rattled through chord changes and guitar riffs, and programmed the drum machine. But it all sounded soulless and flat. My head filled with images of furious black guys, in desperate pitched battle with the police because they couldn't take any more. And the knowledge that I'd unwittingly got us mixed up in it. Managing the band was a nightmare, but music was our saviour. Now even that had become messy, with Adam threatening to pull the album – our real work of art – and piss on my dreams.

I thought about those times when I'd escape to Josie's place, wrap her in my arms and make sense of things in a different way, before Vinnie had put an end to all that.

'Cunt, cunt, cunt!' I lit my last fag and lobbed the packet at the wall, where it ricocheted into the litter bin. A phone began ringing in the control room. I fumbled to find the right key, finally bursting in and yanking up the receiver.

'Yes?' I was surprised at my eagerness for human contact.

'Hey Shepperton, you should see this place – it's amazing!' Vinnie voice was like an excited kid's.

'Oh really?' I didn't hide my sarcasm.

'There's a full-sized pool table, an' a steam room thing – with its own swimming bath!'

'So glad you're having fun,' I said.

There was a loud belch at his end of the line. 'An' he said to help ourselves to food and drink, so we're….hey fuck off, I'm talkin'…'

I heard raised voices and scuffling, then Eddy came on the phone. 'What's goin' on, Tom?'

'Your boyfriend's runnin' scared, that's what!' My mouth was running on unfiltered anger. 'How the hell could you all scarper Eddy?'

'Look, a crowd of journalists followed us to the flat – pesterin' Len and Devon to give statements about the riots in Brixton. Did you know Devon's cousin Floyd's been arrested?'

'Jesus!'

'And they cornered Raymond when he went out for some milk.'

'Oh bugger!' I hadn't considered that sort of possibility.

'Let me speak to Len,' I said. Eddy went off the line, and I finally heard more pattering steps and a grumbling Jamaican voice, which heralded Len's arrival.

'Tom, you interrupted me game o' pool. I was nailin' Vinnie to the floor man. Always knew I was the superior player. Just needed a proper table, not that lumpy thing at The Cobblers.'

'Christ Len, what are you on about?'

He sniffed. 'Jus' makin' use of the facilities. Nothing else to do, man.'

'I need you here Len. Not wankin' around at Little Lord Fontelroy's. What happened?'

There was the sound of Len's lighter clicking open, and the three strikes it always took to produce a flame, then his deep inhale. 'Them hyenas wouldn't leave us alone, Tom. Then Adam had to pull Vinnie away from moonin' outta the window.' Len took another drag of his cigarette. 'He kinda flipped man. I never saw him so excitable.'

'What, Vinnie?'

'No, Adam. He pushed Vinnie against the wall an' told him he was a…lemme see…' Len stopped to think. 'Yeah that's it – an ignorant prick who didn't realise what sorta shit we were in. He said a load of other stuff too. He was out-and-out rantin'.'

This didn't make sense. 'Because of the BBC ban?'

'Nah, man. Cos we owe the main company a pile o' money, an' Adam's in deep too, cos he backed us.'

'Jesus!' I sat down on the chair beside the sound desk. 'But why send you so far out of the way?'

Len sucked in through his teeth. 'Who knows? Protect the nation from facin' Vinnie's backside over their cornflakes?'

Despite my anger, I smiled. Then I said, 'I hear Floyd's in trouble. How's Devon taking it?'

Len gave his juiciest tut. 'Floyd's a pure fool, runnin' with the wrong crew an' involvin' himself in riotin'. Devon's been tryin' to find a lawyer. But they've banged him up good.'

'Oh Christ! Tell Dev to call Rick – he may have some contacts.' I was too impotent in this situation to offer any real help. 'Don't sound so bad up there though?' I said, after a pause.

Len chuckled. 'Never saw nothin' like it. The bathroom's big as my aunty's flat. We're jus' makin' ourselves at home, like the man instructed.'

'Look Len,' I said. 'Get everyone back here soon, will you? Now the album's been stalled by UAA, and Too Polite's banned by the bloody BBC, we need to get a second album together.'

♪

On the way home to the squalid dump the band shared, I bought a woolly hat for a disguise. It was pretty stupid. Eddy's was the only face people knew well. And really, was it such a problem being recognised? But when I turned into our street, I spotted three guys with huge lens cameras, cradling the plastic cups and thermos flasks, chatting, as if they had all the time in the world. I dodged back behind the wall before they saw me. I wasn't facing those determined hacks alone.

'Tom! Come on up!' A sing-song-ey female voice answered Fozz's entry panel before I'd even spoken. Who the hell else knew it would be me? As the buzzer released the door, I frowned.

But at the top of the stairs, my concern fell away.

'Cheryl!' I grinned with relief. She was dressed in tight black jeans, T-shirt and braces. I raised an eyebrow. 'You could be Charlie's younger sister in those.' Her eyelashes flickered with uncertainty. 'I mean, you look great,' I added, patting her shoulder as I entered the flat. 'How come you're in London?'

'Got a try-out at Fredrick Bonache,' she said proudly. Seeing I'd no idea what this meant, she added, 'One of the top hairdressing salons.'

'Oh, cool.' I didn't even know she was a hairdresser. 'Fozz in?'

'How many journos were there?' asked Fozz, when I'd explained my predicament. I
held up three fingers and he shook his head. 'You'll have to stay here.'

'Trouble is, I need my 12 string Les Paul from the flat.'

'I could get it,' said Cheryl shyly. She was stretched out at the other end of a sofa which was so luxurious her small feet didn't even touch my thigh.

'Wow, that would be great.' I leant across to top up her drink, and smiled in appreciation at her beaming face. It seemed an age since I'd last spent time relaxing in female company.

I sipped my drink lazily as Fozz and Cheryl hatched a plan to smuggle my guitar away without arousing attention. She had a small heart-shaped face, with a beauty spot near the hairline above her temple. Behind dark lashes, her eyes were a delicate colour a house paint brochure might call 'watercolour blue'. She fingered her hair as if my gaze was making her self-conscious, slipping it from behind her ear to cover the mole. I gave her a reassuring smile.

'I know – pretend to be a cleaner!' Fozz had a eureka moment. 'Go in with mops and so forth.' He nodded with enthusiasm. 'An come out with the guitar – wrapped in bin bags.'

Cheryl clapped. 'Great idea!' She turned to me. 'What do you think Tom?'

I imagined a young woman in a headscarf walking up the steps to our block, setting down her mops and bucket while she took out door keys. Josie would have jumped at the chance for this sort of adventure and subterfuge. She'd have risen to the act like a blond Mata Hari, acting for the free world. God I missed her.

By midnight they were back, laughing and brandishing my guitar, plus a bag of clothes.

Cheryl passed me the Les Paul. 'Why thanks.' I bowed to her. 'You are the true mistress of espionage.'

She giggled and blushed. 'To be honest there was nobody there, so we both went in. It's not a very nice flat.' She wrinkled her nose, no doubt recalling the concoction of funky male smells and dry rot. 'I thought you'd have a place like this, now you're in the charts.'

'You'd think.' I said. 'But we've not seen any real money yet.' I winced. 'In fact we probably owe a small fortune.'

'How come?'

I shook my head. 'Hey! Let's not worry about that now.'

Fozz appeared from the kitchen, holding a bottle of wine and waggling a packet of white powder, with a questioning look on his face.

'Yes to both.'

I fancied getting a bit drunk, but mainly I wanted to get shit-faced.

♪

Within days, Too Polite to Riot had shot to Number 2 despite – or probably because – of the BBC ban. And UAA procrastinated about withdrawing the album long enough to see which way it was going, then smelled the money. So our first album was also in distribution. Too Polite played constantly in Camden's market stalls and clothes shops, and our photos were still in the papers, as the debate raged about whether we were inciting trouble or just naming the zeitgeist.

I slid over to the studio like a fugitive, avoiding people and main streets, and wrote five songs – two with potential as singles – keeping as a low a profile as a bloke of six four with chestnut hair can. Then I considered shaving it off, but Cheryl persuaded me against it.

'You'll look like you turned skinhead, then the Press will have even more ammunition.'

She was right. About fifteen percent of our audience at gigs were skins, and most of them were alright, following the styles, music, and our anti-violence, anti-racist stance. But we didn't need to look like we were all turning, especially now.

She cocked her head to one side. 'I could give it a good cut if you want though?'

I emerged from the bathroom with wet hair, wearing just jeans, and Cheryl sat me down on the kitchen stool. She walked round the back of me and turned my head from left to right. Her small hands were cool on my neck and when she started to snip, her breasts rubbed softly against my shoulders. I grabbed one of Fozz's mags from the kitchen table, to hide a growing erection, and pretended to flick through it.

'Going to ask about my holidays?' I teased. Cheryl laughed. The bumping of her warm body, combined with her hands rippling through my scalp was excruciating. 'You're done,' she said.

I rose and towelled the itchy fuzz of snippings from my chest. Cheryl looked up at me and stood on tiptoe to brush some stray hair from my shoulder. She smiled, with adoration in her iceberg eyes. She was, after all, sweet, sexy and generous. As I stooped to kiss her, tasting the liquorice of cigarette papers on her mouth and inhaling the berry-scented perfume she wore, I recognised that this was the final admission. I would never find Josie. Not in Coventry, London or anywhere else. She had disappeared from my life and no amount of pure wishing could magic her back.

♬

48

JOSIE

'What do you mean, over the time limit?'

This couldn't be happening. Not when I was finally back on my feet.

I'd just assisted Nancy, the American art teacher, with her chaotic kids' classes during the half term break. Nancy's enthusiasm for her students' work was infectious, and I'd had enormous fun making mad artworks with the kids, happy to be in a creative environment again. Now, with a bit of extra cash in my pocket, my optimism and trust in people had begun sneaking back.

The doctor put down her pen and smiled in kind apology. 'Legally we can offer termination up to 28 weeks – but only so late in exceptional cases. I'll sign off up to eighteen weeks, but I think you're well past that now. A scan will tell us more.'

I gaped at her. I wasn't pregnant by Axten at all. This was Tom's.

'I didn't even know.' The horror spread icy white tendrils up to my brain, reducing everything to slow motion. My voice was distant.

'Are you okay?' She looked concerned. 'I understand this may be a shock.' She ripped a pale green sheet off a pad. 'Here's the referral form. Come and see me after your scan and we can discuss prenatal care.'

I stared at her. What was she talking about? There was no way this could go ahead!

Outside I shivered, though the sun was out. It wasn't possible to have a baby. I was still young, far too poor, and barely taking care of myself. I started walking – up the main road, past shops and cafes, though the churchyard and over the zebra crossing. This couldn't be happening to me. I traipsed through back streets and across the playground, while the sun slipped away and black clouds gathered overhead, my footsteps drumming out a mantra, 'No, no, no, no, no…'

'Josie, you're soaking! Where've you been?' As I trudged in, Franki grabbed a newspaper for me to stand on, dripping, while she fetched a towel.

I wrapped it round my head in a turban, and held out the crumpled green form for her to read.

'Oh, you went.' Franki sat down. 'But they'll do an abortion, right?'

'Sorry Franki, but I'm going to bed.' I said. 'Can't even think about it now.'

The following day at The Arts Hub, I was on my knees scrubbing out the industrial-sized fridge, when there was a tap on the door, and I looked up to see Nancy smiling in at me.

Her class for adults with learning disabilities had just finished for the day, so Nancy's clothes and hair were flecked with paint. Under her apron swelled an unmistakeable hump of pregnant belly.

'Hey, honey!' Her voice was as mellow and sun-kissed as Californian wine. 'You hiding any crackers in here?'

I frowned. 'What do you mean?'

Nancy clicked the door shut and rolled her eyes. 'Morning sickness sure don't restrict itself to mornings. A couple of dry crackers helps, but I forgot to put them in my purse.'

I searched the shelves, opening tubs and tins, until I found some crispbreads. 'These okay?'

She tore open the pack and began nibbling like a hamster, leaning on the food counter and chuckling. 'Being pregnant is the weirdest thing. First I was teary, then totally manic and now – even with this big, fat bowling ball up front – I'm horny as hell. I just want sex, sex, sex. And crackers,' she added. 'My husband thinks I'm a crazy woman. Hey honey, what's wrong?'

Big fat tears were pooling on the stainless steel in front of me. My chest heaved uncontrollably and I could hardly breathe.

When I came off the phone Nancy was pouring tea. She smiled as she pushed a cup at me.

'There. Now your scan's all booked and you've got your doctor follow up. Pregnancy's a beautiful thing honey – and it won't just go away.'

I nodded as I sipped, and Nancy started to tell me about her students' progress. Then suddenly there was a tiny flicker inside my lower abdomen, the tiniest tickling sensation. It wasn't my stomach rumbling, it was something else. 'Oh!'

Nancy looked at me in question.

'I felt a kind of....tickle inside.'

She smiled. 'Well hi there, baby.' She raised a teacup. 'Welcome to the conversation. Where were we?'

'You were talking about your classes.'

Nancy scrunched round on her bar stool, trying to balance her weight. 'Okay. You know I was going to pop this dooby out and come right back to work?'

I nodded.

'Well, my husband's just been offered a great job in Denver for two years.'

'Oh.' I wasn't sure what to say.

'I'll sure miss all my gang. But they like you, and it's his turn to shine at work. Besides,' she patted her stomach. 'I guess I'll have plenty to do. Sooo – whadya think?'

I frowned. 'Dunno. Never been to Denver.'

Nancy laughed. 'I mean, will you take over teaching my programme?'

'What? Me?' The same panic rose as in those first days at the Youth Training Scheme.

'Hey, calm down honey. We'll work together, until the adults get used to you – and you've just experienced the craziness of the kids' clubs already.'

'On my own though?' I tried not to look horrified.

Nancy patted my knee. 'It'll tide you over while you re-think. No need to tell anyone about the baby yet. You're lucky to be so far gone, and not even showing. Trust me, this is a perfect plan.' She climbed off her stool. 'I'll go speak to Herr Director.' She winked. 'We're lucky he's too lazy to recruit anyone himself.'

At the door she sighed and shook her head. 'This centre deserves better than that pompous ass. If we come back to England, I sure hope someone like you is running the place instead.'

I gave a nervous laugh, wondering just how I'd manage all those groups of wild, hyped up children and all the personalities in her adult classes?

At the door, she hesitated. 'Josie honey, are you really sure you can't let the baby's father know?' she said.

I shook my head in certainty. 'I don't even know where he is,' I said.

49

TOM

'Yo, dickhead! We're back!' Vinnie's feet thundered up the studio stairs and he punched my arm with vigour. 'Wayhaaay! New guitar and hair cut. Shit! This mean we're finally in the money?'

I shook my head. 'No such luck. Your esteemed sister has finally sold our marital home.'

Vinnie looked pained. He'd never accepted the fact that Yvonne and I were long divorced.

'Oh. How much d'ya get?' he said sulkily.

I shrugged. 'Just a bit for now. Let her keep most of it, to buy that big place she's set her heart on.'

I didn't explain how Yvonne cried down the phone, gulping for air, like a spoiled child who's just wrecked an expensive toy. 'Tom, he's left me – and I've already put down a deposit. You *have* to loan me the money. You must be loaded now, and this is my *dream house*!'

'For chrissakes, calm down Yvonne.' Much as I hated these scenes, I still felt responsible for her happiness. 'Use the money. But I'll need a cut to tide me through.'

The bubbling sobs ceased like I'd just switched off a kettle, and she'd negotiated hard for a person recently so incoherent with emotion. But I got a small sum in the bank, and some readies – for Rick to bring down with him.

Rick was on a flying visit to buy heavy metal albums, so I'd met him in the upstairs bar at Euston station. 'Keep the dosh quiet from the Moth guys,' he warned. 'There's been rumblings about all your living costs.'

'You're kidding!' I said. We're sleeping in the world's nastiest flat, surviving on the last money you issued, and I turned down Adam's offer of an advance. Hope you brought some more for the lads by the way?'

Rick passed me a padded packet under the table.

'Havin' a bit of a battle with UAA, as it goes. Brought old Toombes in to advise.'

William Toombes was Coventry's most bucolic lawyer. After each final recording, we hand-delivered a duplicate of the master to him. Methodically, he'd seal it in a large dated envelope, scrawl his signature across the flap, and ink it with the big company stamp. Then, with huge gravity, he lodged it in his safe. The procedure was supposed to protect our copyright, but it probably just provided the stodgy old suit with an interesting titbit to liven up another dull evening with his wife.

'Bloody hell Rick! We've got two records in the Top Ten, and an album out. Ragged Moth and UAA must be raking it in by now!'

An announcement called out that the Birmingham train was boarding, so Rick had downed his beer and slapped me on the back. 'Take care mate. Good luck with the new album. And don't fret about money – I'm on the case!'

♪

We worked in the studio for five days, cobbling together stuff to fill the vinyl for our second album. There were some solid new songs – including a few tunes that Raymond revealed he'd written in hospital, and shyly played me one night, asking if they were any good. But we only had eight in total. The deadline we'd given UAA was tight – way too tight. Everyone was knackered and tetchy. And come Friday night, instead of living the rock 'n' roll life, I found myself at the flat, gathering dirty jeans and T-shirts to drop off at the laundrette for a service wash.

'This album's not goin' to be ready man.' Eddy entered the bedroom shaking his head.

'It's gotta be.' My voice was steely with determination. I spotted another T-shirt under the bed and stuffed it into the bin bag. 'Rick told Moth we'd get another album out, quick like. UAA are putting a helluva pressure on us to repay them.'

276

Eddy's lip was curled in a sneer. 'How come Rick's makin' promises for us?'

I dropped the laundry bag and faced him. 'He's still managing our label and finances, as you bloody well know,' I said. 'An' if you don't believe me about UAA, ask yer boyfriend!' I added as a taunt.

With a donkey kick backwards, Eddy slammed the door to the bedroom. 'You promised to keep quiet about that!' he spat at me. He was fighting angry – but so was I.

'Course I will. But if you're still so cosy, you should at least get some facts right.'

'What facts?'

I repeated what Rick told me it had cost UAA, via Ragged Moth, to launch the first album.

'What the fuck on?' said Eddy, not unreasonably.

'Full page ads in the music press…'

'I've seen two.'

'…all the promotional work for getting radio interviews – like the session on Graham Logan.'

'Which we haven't done yet!'

'Yeah, I know, but Annabel says we're on the list,' I said.

'Ha! And you believe that posh air mattress?' said Eddy.

He had a point. Annabel was a party girl, who Adam tolerated because, with her network of Oxbridge media types, she could open doors for those of us much lower down the food chain. She dashed in and out of his office, leaving a trail of expensive perfume and cigarettes with promises to 'Speak to Harry over lunch' or 'Mention it to James, when he takes me to the races'.

After a couple of coked up, loose-tongued conversations, Annabel had admitted to me that all she wanted was a rich husband. So I guessed the job at Ragged Moth was an elaborate ruse for meeting contenders. I didn't even think she was that keen on music. I didn't care one way or another except, Eddy was right, she was as reliable as a cat on heat.

'Look Eddy,' I said. 'If you write a couple more songs, I've got something I worked on when you were away playing country squires.'

He gave me a scowl. 'What's it like?'

'Drums on top, like a marching beat in the intro, then fairly speedy, with a really fast bridge Three verses, and the chorus ends with a call-out slogan for Len.'

Eddy slung his legs on the bed and twisted right round to face me. 'What's the slogan?'

'*Cos I'm the Boss Man.* It's about working for peanuts in crappy conditions.'

'It's about Adam!' Eddy huffed out his cheeks in disbelief.

'It is not!'

'Bollocks, it's not!' We locked eyeballs.

'Look,' I said. 'He might have been the inspiration, but it's about anyone trapped in a shit job an' too scared of being sacked to object.'

'Oh yeah?' Eddy sneered again. 'An' what do you know about that?'

I thought of my dad keeping his head down at work, despite the left-wing politics he spouted at home, and how my mum was first to be made redundant, after she'd complained that the women meat packers were picked on by their male supervisor. I thought of Josie too. There'd been something about the way she'd curled in on herself when I asked how it was going, working with those tough kids. It was that anxious, unhappy look, which gave me confidence that she'd move to London with me. And yet here I was, sharing a stinky flat with the band, and no fucking money.

'We all know about crap jobs and bullies.' I gave him a knowing look. 'And everyone knows about unemployment.'

Eddy sighed. 'Alright. What else we gonna stick on the album though?'

I grimaced. We were at least six songs short.

50

JOSIE

I was going to be late for work – again – as I was becoming a slave to sleep. A grey fug of weariness overtook me by eight o'clock at night, and each morning I had to fight for consciousness. I rummaged amongst my clothes for a clean top. Nothing. Then I spotted it. A white T-shirt of Tom's I'd found under the bed in Coventry and thrown into my rucksack. I held the cloth against my face, breathing in his scent – a mixture of coconut hair wax, shower gel and his own clean masculine smell. I slipped it over my head and hugged myself tight.

In the kitchen, I gathered muesli, fruit and yoghurt, my cravings for apples and nuts having reached an all-time high. But as I grappled for a teaspoon on the drainer, a cup slipped out, eluding my grasp, and smashed on the floor. Oh hell! I bent to scoop up the pieces and felt a sharp jab of pain in my hand. When I straightened I saw big splashes of blood all over my precious T- shirt. 'Shit!' I ripped it off in panic and scrubbed at the marks with hand soap.

When Franki came down, I was sitting in a ball on the floor clutching the wet cloth to my chest and weeping, in self pity and frustration.

'Josie, what's happened?'

'I can't do it Franki.' I pointed past my greying bra, to my belly. 'I'm supposed to be creating a whole person in here – but I'm so fucking sick and tired all the time. Even breakfast ends up like the Battle of the bloody Somme.' Franki looked at my hand, swaddled in tissue, then down to the spots of blood decorating the floor tiles, and grimaced. 'I'm so clumsy. What if I drop the baby? Or if it doesn't like me?' I wailed.

Franki gave a chuckle. 'It'll have every right to hate you, if you drop it. Here, grab hold.' She held out her hand to lever me up, and handed me a sheet of kitchen towel to wipe my eyes. 'It's probably the hormones, doll.'

'You look nice.' I sniffed. She wore a funky black jacket decorated with buckles and zips, set off by a wide cowgirl skirt and Doc Marten boots. My baggy clothes could have been issued by the Sally Army. I was a mess outside, and inside my head teemed with anxieties like tadpoles, too numerous and slippery to grasp.

I sighed. 'How am I going to manage it all, Franki?'

She smiled. 'Look, let's concentrate on one set of things at a time. Teach, eat, sleep, make baby fingernails.' She patted my shoulder. 'The rest will take care of itself.'

By the end of a busy day in the art room, I'd also confided in my newest friend Annette, a support worker for the adults. Despite Franki's all-concealing shirt, she'd seen me rub my belly without thinking, and I just couldn't lie.

'So the father's done a bunk?' The beads at the end of her cornrows clacked with indignant sympathy.

'No! No!' I couldn't bear anyone thinking about Tom that way. We just weren't ever…an item.' She frowned in dubious disbelief, so I said quickly, 'He doesn't know anything about the baby. I'm going it alone.'

'Hey, cut it out!' The big dough-faced man beside her was tugging hard at her elbow.

'Lionel's been raving about pink custard all day.' I winked at him. 'I think he's on a promise.'

Annette rolled her eyes and turned. In his yellow and pink vest, courtesy of his nan's knitting needles, Lionel looked like a slice of Battenberg. 'Come on then, sunshine. I can't deny that kind of basic urge. Let's say goodbye to Josie.'

'Bye Josie. Bye, bye, bye, bye, bye.' Lionel's monotone continued, as he dragged Annette away. She shrugged helplessly, but called back, 'You're not alone, Josie. Remember what I said about Willow Nursery Collective. It's free if you go on the rota, and you can work round your shifts here. Come an' check us out!'

The last of her words were punctuated by the slam of the heavy door as Lionel sighted the van and yanked her through.

As the minibus rumbled off, I wandered back to the art room and started gathering discarded clods of clay, patting them into a big ball. I held the lump to my nose and breathing in the heady must. I loved the silken, smooth texture of the damp mud, its chalky smell, primeval and earthy. Without thinking, I pinched off a piece and moulded it into a small figure, curled in a foetal position – a sleeping baby. There was a fluttering sensation inside me. At the sound of footsteps I rolled the clay back onto the ball and rose.

'Hi there!' It was Nancy.

She inspected the trays of art work. 'This Lionel's?' She pointed to a massive coil pot with a sturdy handle and I nodded. 'That group sure love making mugs,' she said, with a wistful note of regret. 'So honey.' She pulled my hand into hers. 'I came by for my final pay check, and to say goodbye and wish you luck.'

'Good luck to you too,' I said. 'And thanks for everything.'

Nancy patted my hand. 'We gals gotta stick together. Hey! Mine is a girl. Know what flavour yours is yet?'

I wrinkled my nose in contemplation. 'I think it's a girl too.'

'Really?' Nancy was surprised. 'They said that?'

I shook my head. 'I just have a feeling.' It was inconceivable that it would be a boy. Boys brought me nothing but trouble and grief.

As I walked home a white van swept past, its radio blaring out the chorus of Wasteland. I thought of the ruined T-shirt and sighed. Of course I didn't need any keepsakes of Tom, when soon I'd have the ultimate reminder. I slid a hand under my coat and stroked my belly again.

'Your daddy's a big pop star now.' I whispered. 'I wonder what you'll be.'

51

TOM

I was reading about Coventry FC's last humiliating away game, when Vinnie slammed open the door to the bathroom.

'Oi! Gerrout, yer git!' This was the last bloody straw.

'It's Number One!' Vinnie clutched his knees panting. 'It's got to Number One!'

My chest tensed with excitement. 'You kiddin'?' This better not be one of his wind ups.

'Straight up. Eddy says he ran into Adam.' Eddy's ability to hide in full view was truly amazing, but I kept my face blank. 'The Gallop poll's just come in,' Vinnie wheezed.

'Bloody hell, that's mega!' Now my heart was banging wildly.

In the living room Charlie and Len were whooping like cheerleaders and Raymond was banging out some sort of triumphant march on the keys.

'Vinnie punched me on the arm. 'Ska-Mix Original's at Number One!' he said. 'That turd in the Daily Mail said it was bollocks. Well he can fuck right off.'

'What? You mean the *album*?' My brain grappled with the information. 'We're top of the *album* charts?' This was even more incredible. Our very first album had zoomed to the top all on its own, without a number one single heading it up.

♪

In west London, at United Associated Artists' glass-fronted HQ, the vast halogen-lit foyer was crowded. Under an uber-modern steel staircase, a line of tables displayed stacks of our album at one end and gleaming armies of wine glasses massed at the other. Waiters in black aprons stood by and, throughout the marbled floor, smiling executives circled in a general pool of self-satisfaction, pawing at us as if we were best mates.

'I swear if that fat git pats my shoulder again, I'm gonna deck him,' I hissed to Eddy.

'Try and be cool Tom.' Eddy's voice was serious. 'This ain't the moment for your grandstanding.'

'What the fuck does that mean?' I said.

Eddy was staring at Adam who was schmoozing some bigwig, like he was about to polish the feller's boots and be rewarded in diamonds. 'Nothing,' said Eddy. 'Just need to be more careful what we say to the Press.'

I felt sick to my stomach. 'What the hell's happened to you, Eddy? You used to be the first to shout 'bollocks' at hypocrisy. Now you want to kowtow to these greasy fuckers? Who are these people? They've never been to a gig and probably not heard the album. We're just a money-making machine to them.'

'Look, this isn't the time, Tom...'

'Ah, the talented songwriters.' An old bloke wandered over. And, like magic, Adam was by our side in seconds, introducing himself.

'Sir Forsythe-Maddley – Adam Chandler, from Ragged Moth.' He dipped his head like a supplicant. 'May I introduce the band's co-writers Tom Shepperton and Eddy Knowles.'

The old chap beamed benignly, and shook our hands with brief anonymous efficiency.

'I believe your second album is about to be released.' He peered at me over half moon glasses.

'We're just finalising the master,' I said. 'And the sleeve's been designed.' We had decided to go for stupid and call this one, 'Mixin' Me Toasties'. The image showed us in a cafe, cheerfully eating toasted sandwiches and wearing rabbit ears, surveyed by a waitress in a 50's frock and Alice band, frowning, as if the world had turned mad. But the lyrics were hard punching and if you looked closer, the table was littered with UB40 benefit claim books and, out of the side window, a line of sickly rabbits queued at a dole office next door.

'And can we expect a third one soon?' he said. 'Nothing like a good stream of albums to keep the fans whirring.' He gave a short laugh at his rubbish joke, but his eyes were as hard as granite.

'Oh yes – definitely. It'll be on release in the next couple of months,' said Adam.

Eddy turned to me aghast, so I gave him a 'told you' look in return.

'Very good, very good,' The old bloke was already moving off, to be greeted by some other lackeys, keen to kiss his benighted feet.

'Who the hell was that?' I said. Adam was dabbing his forehead with a handkerchief. He puffed out his cheeks. 'Christ, it's hot in here,' he said.

'It is if you've got your head jammed right up somebody's arse,' I said. 'Who the fuck's Sir Foreskin-Medley?'

Adam closed his eyes as if my ignorance was a painful thing. 'Only the President of UAA,' he said.

'Well, he didn't know you from…er…Adam.' I gave a sarcastic laugh.

'What's so funny?' Len appeared, clutching a mini pork pie in one hand and a glass of wine in the other.

'Adam here has promised the big cheese a *third* Original Mix album in, what? Post production takes a few weeks, so that's like – a week?'

Len frowned at us all. 'But we've only just come outta the studio, man. An' we've used up all Raymond's new songs.'

'Oh, it'll be fine.' Adam recovered from his brush with corporate royalty and was back to his high-handed self. 'We'll clear the space and you can work round the clock.'

'Yeah, Len,' I said with great sarcasm, plucking the pie from his mitt and taking a bite. 'Sleep's for babies and old women.'

'Char!' Len shook his head in despair, then he chugged back his drink and pushed through the suits towards the buffet for more sustenance.

'You *can* do it though, can't you?' Adam said to me and Eddy, his eyes working anxiously between us. I popped the rest of the pastry into my mouth and chewed thoughtfully as Eddy glowered.

'Oh yes. Anything to further your glowing career Adam.'

He punched me playfully on the arm. 'Great. I knew you could. Let's announce it.' He bustled off to speak to Annabel who was oozing over some American sporting a day-glow tan and pale blue suit.

'You've gorrah stop him Tom!' said Eddy. 'We've as much chance of getting another album out in weeks as Annabel has of shagging that gay bloke.'

I turned to face him. 'You wouldn't believe me when I said they'd want blood. But I reckon we *can* do it, Ed. If we focus and work together.'

Eddy banged his forehead with a fist. 'Shit, I forgot. Teamwork – the band's trump card!'

I jerked my head towards the stage. 'Can't stop it now, anyway. Yer boyfriend's on a roll.'

Eddy shoved both angry hands in his pockets to locate his fags. He studied me with dark bitterness as he lit up. 'Sometimes, I think you're losing yer judgement, Tom.'

Adam stepped up on the dias, tripped over a loose mic cable, then righted himself and laughed loudly to cover his embarrassment. He pulled Annabel up, then banged on the mic to check for sound, like a complete amateur. Annabel adjusted the satiny dress over her hips, and threw her hair over her shoulder in a way she must have thought was sexy.

'My judgement?' I pointed at the stage. 'Look whose talkin'!'

♬

'Jeesus! It's four o'clock in the friggin' morning , Tom. How do I know if it sounds better?' The black circles under Eddy's eyes looked bubonic.

An hour before, Devon had stated his position in no uncertain terms. 'That's it! I've slept nine hours in three days.' He'd thrown down his drum sticks. 'You getting' no more outta me til I had a proper sleep.'

With that, he'd lifted himself off the stool like a pensioner, laced his hands and stretched so a series of bodily cracks issued from his fingers and chest. Then he took the blanket used as a sound damper, out of the bass drum, and slung it over his shoulder. At the door he issued a warning. 'I'm layin' myself on that couch.' He pointed to a tangle of furniture over in the warehouse where Ragged Moth's studio was based. 'Anybody wake me, an' he's a dead man.'

'I thought version 23 was the one,' said Vinnie from his recumbent place on the studio floor. 'I know! Let's wake up Devon to ask him.'

'What do you think Charlie?' I said.

He looked at me with pleading eyes. 'Come on mate, give us a break. Next time I see sunrise, I want a really bad woman beside me.

I threw my hands up. 'Okay, whatever. Not much point having you round without Devon.'

Charlie clucked his tongue at Raymond. They grabbed sleeping bags and scooted out before I changed my mind.

'Thank god!' Eddy followed them. Len was sitting against a wall with his forehead on his knees. Perhaps he had some ideas. 'Len?'

'What?' his jerked up, in bleary confusion. 'Yeah, I'll do it again. Whah?'

'Forget it,' I said. 'Go back to sleep.' I lobbed a sleeping bag at him and he squirmed into it like a caterpillar. Vinnie was splayed out on his back, mouth open, snores puncturing the air like rounds from a Gatling gun.

The producer re-appeared, returned from his brief foray into Camden's night. He waved a little object in the air. I put a finger to my mouth, stepped over Vinnie, and beckoned him into the control booth.

'You gotta pace yourself on these all-weekers,' he said, when I'd shut the door. He chopped out a couple of quick lines on a bit of black acrylic sheeting, kept under the sound desk – possibly for this purpose.

'We'll have a little break to regroup, then listen again.' He stopped. 'Unless you want to grab a few zeds too?'

I shook my head. 'No time. Two more songs to get down, plus a re-mix of that third one.'

He plopped a few blue capsules in front of the console. 'We better take a couple of these too – so we don't hit a wall,' he said.

We hit a wall several times, metaphorically and literally.

'You gonna change that solo every time?' I said to Vinnie on the fifth day. 'Cos it's messing up the riffs I'm doing. Keep it like the first one will you?'

Vinnie threw the guitar strap off, plonked the instrument up against the bass amp and squared up to me.

'I can't remember the fuckin' first one, you twat! I don't even know my own name, no more,' he barked at me.

'Mr Shit for Brains?' Eddy supplied helpfully from behind.

'Piss off dickhead!' Vinnie lunged round.

'Come on guys,' Charlie implored. 'Be cool!'

But Eddy had stepped back and fallen against Len, stamping on his foot.

'Get off, you idiot!' Len's temper snapped and he shoved Eddy back towards Vinnie with such velocity that they both went crashing down, Vin's guitar falling underneath them – with a crack of wood and a high electronic scream. I grabbed Eddy's flailing arm to haul him to his feet and he howled with pain, clutching his shoulder. Vinnie scrambled up, then we all stared at the floor, mouths agape. The entire fretwork of Vinnie's guitar had snapped clean off and was lying alongside its body.

Vinnie picked it up. The neck dangled in a tangle of wires, like a sad puppet. He'd had that guitar since he was eighteen – bought with cash collected by me, with contributions from his dad, his foreman, and a generous top-up from my parents, who'd heard about this dream guitar far too often. It wasn't that great – a third rate Fender Strat, with a twangy pitch which would have been pretty insufferable in anyone else's hands. But with it Vinnie produced his unmistakeable raw sound – aggressive and punchy, with a touch of plaintiveness.

He scooped up the broken pieces and cradled them in his arms, then, saying nothing, he walked out. The door clicked in place after him.

We all shifted awkwardly.

'What now?' said Len.

Finally I said, 'You better go find something to eat, so I can think.'

I found Vinnie on the steps of the back fire exit, opposite the vast bins which overflowed with refuse, from the restaurants fronting the high street. I sat down beside him and offered a cigarette. He took several drags before speaking.

'You're pushing us too hard. This album's gonna be shit,' he said.

'There's some good stuff.' My voice was defensive. 'We'll use your last solo and re-do the rhythm on this track. There's three more days of recording yet.'

He stroked the cherry red lacquer of his broken guitar. 'What can I play? The spare guitar's shite, Len's is too weird, and yours are all left-handers.'

'Let me see.' He passed me the instrument. The wood was splintered near the keys end of the neck. Even if some miracle worker could repair it, the sound would be shot.

I'd handed it back, felt inside the zip pocket of my jacket for my wedge of money and peeled off several large value notes with my thumb. 'Get yourself up to Archie's Guitars in Highgate.'

He stared at the money, then me. 'Where the hell's that come from?'

'I told you – my cut from the house sale. Yvonne's borrowed most of it. This is for emergencies. That enough?'

Vinnie considered. 'Things are fuckin' expensive in London.'

I peeled off several more notes and handed them over.

Vinnie stood up and pocketed the cash. 'I'll pay yer back,' he said.

'Too right you will. And try not to spend it all.'

He was off. As he passed the skip, he slung his dead guitar on top of the bin bags, barely breaking stride.

'Get a cab!' I called. 'You've got two hours, tops!'

I pulled at the exit door, kicking aside the brick that was holding it open. But before going in, I watched Vinnie approach the end of the far building. He stopped, to look sideways at the skip, from where the cherry red curve of lacquered wood poked. His face crumpled a little, and he winced. Then he wiped a hand across his nose, shook his head, cornered the building and was gone.

♪

The last three days of recording were torturous, but somehow we managed to get the final tracks down. Vinnie had returned with an old Gretsch 6120 – a real beauty which had used up all my money. I was furious, but I didn't let on. It was bad enough that the foul atmosphere was doing everyone in. Moody silences and withholding of ideas, hung in a room heavy with cigarette smoke and resentments.

Vinnie and Len occupied opposite sides of the studio and Eddy sang to the floor, or concentrated on the red recording light over the control room door. We took separate fag breaks, and went outside as Devon refused to be kippered any further, and the rota of brew making had broken down irretrievably.

I pushed on as if none of this was happening, replaying and checking the tape, remixing, doubling up instrumental lines where I thought the sound needed thickening. Then I started to disagree with the producer about what was working and what should be ditched.

'Eddy, Len, Vinnie, take half an hour break,' I said, emerging from the umpteenth mix of track ten. Vinnie grabbed his fags and shot out. Eddy and Len followed at a wary distance.

'Devon, can we try some extra percussion in the chorus?' I said. 'And Ray, you know that piano solo I didn't think would work? Well I do now.'

'Still need me?' Charlie's pallid features looked almost skeletal, as his hand hovered over his Crombie.

'Nah – unless you want to offer an opinion.'

He gaped at me as though I was crazy, then clawed up his coat. 'Ran out of opinions by Wednesday,' he said. 'I'm just concentratin' on not falling asleep while I'm playing.'

The producer went out too. 'Get you anything?' he said casually. I raised an eyebrow and he returned a quick nod.

Devon rose from behind the drum kit and rubbed his hands together. 'How 'bout Raymond makes a little tea first?' he said. We both looked at him in surprise. Devon never drank tea or coffee. He pulled a lemon from his bag and held it out. 'I'll have hot water and half this juice. Take time to let it brew.'

Raymond clattered out with a handful of used mugs. When I turned Devon's face was almost grey with weariness and set like concrete.

'What's goin' on?' he demanded.

I shrugged. 'It's a long haul and everyone's knackered.'

'I'm not talkin' 'bout them. What's happenin' with you?'

'Me?' I was the only person holding it together.

Devon's gaze was unflinching. 'You're all jittery an' agitated.'

'I am not!'

His mouth pursed in anger. 'Tom, I'm not blind or stupid. You take a break with that rat-face guy an' suddenly you don't need no sleep like the rest of us. What shit you got yourself hooked on?'

I shook my head. 'It's not like that, Devon. Just the odd pick up, til we get this thing done and dusted. We're all peaking and troughing at different times. Someone's got to stay on an even keel.'

Devon shook his head. He sighed and put a big hand on my shoulder. 'Give it up Tom. Quit while you're still nice to know.'

52

JOSIE

Franki was panting up the hospital corridor, her big purple hat, darting this way and that, searching for me along the rows of ballooning women, sitting in rows of resigned silence.

'Over here!' I waved. 'Where the hell you been?'

'Buses are diverted all round the houses,' she said. 'Central Hackney's closed – cos there's rioting on Marle Street. Hackney's going to be just like Brixton!' She plonked her capacious bag on the floor. 'Thank god I've been to the market, so we've got provisions. We're not going out til the madness is over.'

'Why the hell am I bringing another person into this shitty world?' I said. 'Everything's crap. No jobs, no affordable housing, London's so unequal Franki, and now people are demolishing it. I wish I'd known I was pregnant before it was too late.'

Franki rubbed my arm. 'Remember – just sleep, eat, make baby fingernails. You can take a philosophy course or join a political party later. Know what they're doing today?'

I shrugged. Tom had been in the morning papers. His startled face had looked up from the floor of the newsagents', a photo replicated in all the tabloids – collar up, head down, peering from under his brow, as though he'd been ambushed.

'Black right to riot says OM' declared one headline. *'Originals mix it up as band leader backs rioters!'*, screamed another. I couldn't imagine Tom saying things in this way. Even when passionate, his arguments were measured and layered.

The paper described how Tom had hit out at everyone: the BBC for banning their single, their semi-independent record company for *'sucking up to corporate f**ckwits, who didn't give a sh*t about music as long as they got their 80% cut'* and their band's A&R man, Adam somebody, for being a *'cowardly tw*t who's obsessed by personal ambition and whose sold out to the big players'*. He was quoted as saying he didn't blame the black community for rioting,

'You can only treat people as second-class citizens and harass the f*ck out of them for so long.'

I had tried to clear Tom from my mind, and avoided reading anything about the music scene. But this was different. Why was Tom saying these things to the Press? I could tell he was in deep trouble.

'Mrs Josephine Honeywell?' A white uniformed nurse was in front of me, clipboard in hand.

I stood up. 'Not Mrs – Miz.' I turned to Franki. 'You coming?'

The nurse gave us both a sharp look and opened the door. 'On the table please and raise your shirt.'

When I'd wriggled into position on the paper liner, the doctor squirted a gel onto my rounded belly. Its coldness sent a shiver over my skin and I felt a corresponding flutter inside. How could I have let this happen? It was all such a mess. Tom should have someone by his side right now. Someone to help fight his corner, protect him. Where was his wife?

'.....and that's her legs there.' The doctor was pointing at the screen. Inside the dark cave of my insides, lay a grey alien, looking like the dead magpie chick Ally and I had once found – huge-headed and formless, sharp elbows of bones, shrouded in baggy skin.

Franki took my hand. 'Have a good look Josie. Oh my god, is that her hand?'

The doctor peered back at the screen. 'Yes, that's one hand. But…' She rolled the metal scanner across my belly again, pressing harder and rotating it at angles. 'Oh, is that?…Sorry, let's hear the heart beat first.' She pushed some buttons, moved the scanner again and there was a rhythmical sloshing – like someone tipping a half-filled hot-water bottle up and down in perfect tempo.

'Is it meant to sound like that?' I said. The doctor nodded, but she appeared to be checking something on the picture. She sat up. 'Ah, I thought so,' she said. 'And how many weeks along do you think you are?'

Now I'd seen it for myself, so there was no point in trying to pretend.

Tom's baby had taken up residence months ago, lying quietly, biding its time, and was now curled up inside me, sucking a fist and expanding cell by cell, counting off the seconds with fat, watery heartbeats. Meanwhile Original Mix songs were played everywhere, and he was being decimated by the Press. His big dream and some sort of nightmare were running simultaneously. I could contact him through the record company, of course. But the last thing either of us needed, was for the tabloids and the unforgiving public to discover Tom had an illegitimate child on the way.

I had no choice. I'd have to do this on my own.

'Thanks, man. I just needed a way in.' Fozz nodded eagerly as I passed him a spliff. His small interview, previewing our third album, 'Not Running Ska-ed', had been printed in New Sonic Waves. Not the big scoop he'd hoped for, but it was something.

'Haven't seen you since that last mashing by the Press. How you all gettin' on anyways?' he said, as he exhaled.

I gestured for the puff back. 'Adam's fuckin' furious, Eddy and Vinnie still won't speak to each other – or me. The others escape the bad vibes by going to buy tour stuff, and Devon's up in Coventry collecting everyone's passports.'

Fozz shook his head in disbelief. 'All over Europe then Japan. Wow! I envy you man. It'll be mega!'

'UAA are bloody desperate to get us out of Britain,' I said. 'Those last two gigs were way out of control. Rick and Adam are knee deep in legal arguments.'

Fozz raised an eyebrow. 'Looked like the stage was collapsing at the end.' He held the joint out to me again.

'I lugged a couple of people up on stage, cos they were getting crushed,' I said to Fozz. 'Len and Eddy were screaming at the bouncers to leave people alone. Vinnie was roaring at the stage manager to put the sound back on. It was fuckin' mayhem.'

'They blamin' you for this too?' He pointed to the paper where the headline screamed, *'Fan stabbed, as skinheads tear National Heritage apart'*.

I pulled a face at the tabloid. 'Christ, what a terrible business. That lad was stabbed in a pub. Didn't even have a ticket for the gig. But of course, it's being attributed to us. So UAA want us gone as quick as possible.'

'Still, you're taking the Midlands ska sound across the world Tom....' Fozz swung his head in wonder. 'And gettin' an insight into the Eastern culture.'

I grinned. 'Yeah. Can't wait to leave all this stupidity and see Japan.'

♫

'Remind me why we're still lugging our own gear?' said Charlie, as he piled another flight case onto the airport trolley. My guitar case appeared on the carousel and I grabbed it before it went on another circuit. Flights had been cancelled and delayed throughout our tight schedule. I was dog-tired and disorientated. 'What time is it?' I said, not even caring.

Charlie looked at his watch. 'Tuesday.' Then he added, 'So this must be Belgium!' In the corner of his eye was a manic look, like a beast who's drunk from the wrong bucket.

I pushed off after Len, who was wavering all over, trying to control a ton of gear balanced on an errant trolley. The first sign in English said, '*Welcome to Munich.*' Christ Almighty, another four countries to go. After the usual searches and suspicions at Security, we found a huddle of fans waiting for us to sign autographs. This time Len and Vinnie did the honours. One of the lads was clutching our newly released third album. He waved it at me, across the barrier. I nudged Devon. 'Bet that LP got here faster than us,' I said.

'That record took lot less time to make than this journey's done too,' he grumbled.

I winced. 'Not Running Ska-ed' had soared into the charts, rising high on the thermals from the other two albums. But musically, in both quality and quantity, with this third one, we'd definitely short-changed the fans.

'Tom! Please to sign this?' I turned to see a young man – flat top hair cut, DMs, rolled up jeans, bomber jacket, all startlingly new-looking – brandishing a copy of Wasteland. As I dug out my marker, he proffered the EP – a strange German pressing that I hadn't seen before.

'I am Gunter.' I struggled with the pen top, while he smiled like a Moonie. 'I love the ska and I make my look like a British fan.' He swept a proud hand across his clobber.

'Bang on,' I said, to confirm he'd done right by his tribe. As the cap popped off my marker, I felt a sudden rush of sentiment for the old days – when we'd just donned our most stylish garb, run on stage and made people dance. It had all got far too complicated.

I wrote *'Gunter mate – stay cool and party!'* on the label.

'Wow that's totally super, thank you!' He walked off to join his mates, clutching the record to his chest. 'See you in the concert!' he called.

At the gig we let Gunter and his mates dance on stage. And when they produced some quality weed in the bar, I discreetly siphoned him off, and introduced the notion of something more upbeat. After a huddled discussion with the bar's chef, we sealed the deal in the cold freezer, with Gunter acting as look out, and me hoping I wasn't about to get robbed and locked in.

'Yar, I sell stuff to all the bands,' the chef said airily, leaning on a side of hanging pork, while I checked out a short line. The chemical hit the top of my sinuses and seeped sweetly up to the top of my skull to give me an exciting cranial hug – a warm reunion with an old friend.

'YouPop, Le Punkster, Fourspring Technique…' He waited for me to be impressed. 'Guttersnipe,' he added.

'Wow, really, Guttersnipe?' I said. 'Amazing band.' They were crap, but I was there to buy coke, not deconstruct the punk era. He watched me as casually as an crocodile, while I peeled off enough Kroner to buy a decent amount.

I slid out of the freezer, ready with excuses of having fallen asleep in the dressing room, to find the band had dissipated.

'Len's found another frauline,' explained Charlie, handing me a beer. 'Devon and Ray have gone to the hotel. Eddy's fucked off as usual.'

'Where's Vinnie?'

'We drew the short straw.' He pointed to a booth, where a familiar pair of DMs stuck out between the red velvet couch and the wooden table.

Great. Nothing finished a night off like hauling Vinnie's belligerent carcass home. But at least we now were travelling overland by coach, and I had enough staying powder nestled in my jacket to hack the European leg of the tour.

♪

'Mr Tom – phone call for you in Stage Manager office.' At every turn, our Japanese hosts were there, polite and eager to please. But the gigs were crazy. Thousands of screaming fans. And so many girls!

'Yo, wass the news? Who's rioting now – that bloody chicken?' I yelled down the crackly line to Adam. 'Where's 'Toast Yourself' at?' Last we'd heard, our newest single had been at No. 5 in the UK charts.

'Never mind that.' His voice was serious. 'Tom, you need to call your mum.'

'No time. We're at some reception thing in ten minutes,' I said. 'Promised to phone her tomorrow – when it's daytime here – so she can tell the neighbours she spoke to Tokyo. Tell her she's got the time difference wrong.'

There was silence at the end of the phone.

'Adam? You still there?' I said.

A heavy sigh. 'Tom, your dad's died.'

'What?' Why would he say a thing like that? I'd said a critical few things about him publically, but he couldn't hate me that much.

'I'm so sorry. I'll get you back soon as I can.'

It was the jet lag, the crap phone line, the combination of stuff I'd taken in Paris. I was hearing things.

'Do you understand me, Tom?' Adam's voice was slow and deep.

'I spoke to him from Amsterdam. He was planting dahlias and fixing the garage roof.' The thoughts came from far away – my brain scrambling for sense.

'Listen Tom, your dad had a heart attack and he died in the ambulance,' Adam said slowly. 'Your mum was with him. It was sudden and he wasn't in pain.'

'He's taking me to the Social Club when we get to Number One.' I needed to keep talking. 'I'm standing drinks for everyone in the bar, and the Coventry Echo's doing an interview. I'll say what a rock solid dad he is…'

'I'm so sorry mate.'

Eddy walked in, jabbing at his watch. I dropped the phone receiver in his hand, pushed at the fire exit door and walked into the night.

In downtown Tokyo neon winked and blinked from all heights – advertising brands of film, tissues, music equipment, Japanese cars. Store windows displayed machines for everything. There were automated coin dispensers offering little parcels of rice, exotic drinks and, what looked like sex toys. It was so different from the desolate, shabby towns we'd toured in England, with their bargain buckets and greasy fish and chip shops. Tokyo was vibrant, rich, energetic, throbbing with potential. A city we were desperate to explore. We had finally made it. Produced three charting albums, four singles in the Top Ten, one of which had gone platinum, and we had fans galore. We'd shown them – the doubters and the yes-men, the tabloids and the stupid thick journos. All those who had wrapped us in blankets of half-stories and lies, then thrown us up and down at will, like some bullied child being given sadistic birthday bumps. We had persevered with our stance, our politics. Our fans still came from all backgrounds – workers and unemployed, black and white, skinheads, students and casuals – all united through music.

It had been a fucking long climb, with lots of bruises and lacerations, but I'd just about reached the top of the tree.

And now, none of it mattered at all.

54

JOSIE

Simon was in London a-visiting. He'd arrived clutching his pay packet, desperate to buy me mummy kitsch. And now, on Marle Street, he practically dragged me into 'Mrs Weston's Baby World' – a shop devoted to pastel colours, for 'mothers-to be' who wanted fluffy nonsense and expanding pants, presumably to match their mental states.

My own brain had gone marshmallow soft, in direct correlation to the swelling of my belly. It was all unreal. Surely nobody else did this? My life was pure shapelessness, ruled by bodily functions in a way it had never been before – constipation, indigestion, being suddenly overtaken by a weariness so overwhelming I felt like I could slip into a coma. The night before, I had watched Simon drink a lovely bottle of red while I sipped apple juice. Then I slept badly, woke up antsy and aching, and now I was being asked to admire this crap.

'Ooh, look at this?' Simon waggled a yellow rat at me. Or maybe it was a lemming.

'Where's the punk section?' I said. 'This whole shop is like being inside a sponge cake.'

My belly gave a jolt and I felt a wetness gushing down my legs.

'Watch it, Josie.' Simon pointed to the floor beneath me. 'You're standing in some sort of spillage.'

I stared aghast at the puddle. My heart was thumping. Why hadn't I listened to anything, or attended all the baby classes? I knew why of course. Franki and I had gone once, and were treated like two inept lesbians, attracting a creepy interest from some of the blokes and the smug preggos keeping a distance, as if it might be catching. I was angry at the need to offer explanations. I hadn't wanted pity or prejudice. I just wanted to be left alone. But right now it seemed a bit more knowledge might be useful.

'I think my waters just broke.'

'What the hell are waters?' Simon gave me a horrified stare. 'Shit! You don't mean….?'

'Can I help you?' A pale, skinny girl slipped from behind a pyramid of glassy-eyed dolls. Her name badge, decorated by a blue rabbit nibbling a flower, said, *'Hello, my name is Bernadette'*.

'We're having a baby!' Simon hopped from one foot to another in excited panic. The girl glanced at my protruding belly and issued a condescending smile.

'It takes some men a while for it to sink in,' she said, as if she was Old Mother Hubbard, not some lank teenager.

'No!' he yelled. 'It's happening now!'

The smile dropped and her face turned to horror. 'You can't be due yet.'

'I'm not,' I said flatly, though the involuntary squeezing sensation inside, suggested this could be irrelevant.

'What do we do?' she said, aghast.

'Ring for an ambulance?' I suggested.

'I can't,' she said.

We both gaped at her.

'The phone's dead. We're waiting for the engineer, and Mrs Weston's out at lunch. I said I'd cope.' She promptly burst into tears.

Simon looked to me. 'Go next door,' I gasped, as I was seized by another cramp, this one rather more insistent. 'Quite quickly!' I shouted at his retreating back.

'Need to lie down,' I said to the sniffling assistant, who pointed to a staff-room-come-office. I waddled in, spotted a short sofa covered in soft toys, and, with the arm not supporting my belly I swept them to the floor.

'Oh careful!' said Bernadette. She rescued a big teddy and grabbed a hand towel from the back of the door. 'Er…could you lie on this? That's real suedette.'

My breaths were coming faster now. I shot her a look and collapsed onto the seat, hauling my legs up. The next cramp took all of my concentration. I was dimly aware of her mumbling something about Mrs Weston, then Simon re-appeared.

'*All* the phones are down!' he gasped. 'There's an engineer's at the box outside, trying to reconnect them.'

A huge inner spasm cut off my ability to think. 'Then do something *else!*'

'Oh Christ! I know – hot water and towels!' Simon said to the girl, as if remembering his times tables. He waggled a finger at a kettle on the window ledge.

Bernadette, still clutching the huge bear, grabbed at the kettle, dropped it, picked it up, dropped it again and ran out, sobbing,'Oh god, oh god!'

Simon grabbed my hand. 'It'll be alright duck,' he said, still panting.

'How?' I spluttered, as another spasm rendered me helpless. 'Need to sit up a bit,' I coughed. Simon gathered a selection of fluffy animals to stuff under my head.

A matronly Caribbean woman bustled in. 'Oh my Lord!' she said, dropping her bags. 'Your waters broke?'

'Yes, and the phones are out!' said Simon.

'Oh My Lord,' said Mrs Weston, this time like it was a real prayer. 'How close are the pains?'

'Close!' I grunted, and she said to Simon, 'Go, tell that engineer man to hurry himself, we got a baby on the way.' Simon scooted out. Bernadette appeared with the kettle and a bale of new towels. Mrs Weston sent her back for plastic sheeting and before I knew it she'd slid it under me with a practised hand. Now I was sweating, choking on short panicky breaths. Everything in my abdomen was shifting.

'It's coming.' I said. 'You gotta stop it!'

Mrs Weston knelt down and felt across my belly with a warm hand.

'No stopping it now child. But you got to get in control. Breathe long, like you're blowing on a hot pattie, like this – phoo, phoo, phoo!' I looked up at her large, serious face and into kind dark eyes. Mrs Weston was in her late fifties. She must have kids and even grandkids. She knew how this was done. Together we got into a rhythm – phoo, phoo, phoo! I braced my feet against the arm of the sofa.

'Aaaarghhhh!' The next pain was monumental.

'Better take off your underpants,' she said. 'It won't need a Marks and Spencer hat.'

Still blowing like a train, I struggled out of my knickers.

Simon ran in.

'He got through! Ambulance on the way!' I splayed my knees high and wide. A whole watermelon was trying to force its way out of me and I'd be split like kindle. Mrs Weston shuffled down onto her knees, groaning slightly with the effort.

'Bernadette!' she barked and I looked up to see the girl still there, standing transfixed, a steaming kettle in one hand and a large teddy in the other.

'Give me that water and fetch a clean bowl.' Mrs Weston gestured an impatient hand for the kettle. Towels were pushed under my bottom. The next pain felt like it was tearing me apart.

'Come, daddy.' Mrs Weston beckoned Simon to her side. 'You keep the breathing going, while I wash me hands.'

Simon hesitated, staring at my legs in horror.

'Come now. Nothin' you haven't seen before.' She shoved him forward, to take her place.

'Simon, what's happening?' I panted.

His eyes were like gobstoppers. 'Oh Jesus! I can see the top of a head!'

There was no going back now.

'AaaaaaRRRRHHHHHH!' I pushed like never before, bearing down with every muscle.

'Not yet!' shouted Mrs Weston, as she sloshed water round in the pail. 'Wait until you get the next contraction. Daddy, you're not doing the blowing – phoo, phoo, phoo! Here now, let me through!'

Bernadette and the bear crowded in too, and we blew in frantic unison, like we were trying to start a campfire.

'Now you push when you get the next…'

AaaaaaaRRRRRRRRRRHHHHHHHHHHHHH!!' Violent pain cursed through me again. I thought I might black out. I flailed for

Simon's hand, and he fell to his knees as I clenched downwards, pushing with all my might. Simon's eyes were level with my thighs. 'Oh Christ, oh Christ! It's nearly here. Keep going Josie! Phoo, phoo, phoo....'

Another excruciating, agonising spasm. 'Oh my god, fuck,fuck,fuck!'

'Bloody HELL!' Simon sounded like he was watching the worst ever horror film.

'Move outta me way now.' Mrs Weston pushed him to one side and positioned herself at the end of the sofa. I squeezed Simon's hand as though it was the only sane thing happening in the room. Warm forearms brushed against the inside of my thighs and Mrs Weston braced her shoulders.

'Now – one last push at the next contraction,' she said.

The spasm came and it was like my whole world depended on it.

And for an eternity there was nothing else – just pushing and hurting and screaming and bearing and shoving and panting and pushing and screaming and yelling and cursing and pushing and pushing and hurting and pushing and swearing and pushing and pushing and then....

'Fuckinjesusshitearsebastards!' I screamed, as a whole part of my innards slithered away.

'Josie, you had a baby. You had a BABY!!' Simon was sobbing, tears streaming down his face. Mrs Weston was patting something with towels. I flopped back, exhausted, utterly done for.

Paramedics rushed in. Smiles. Jokes. 'You didn't wait for us then?' Someone rummaging round inside me. 'Let's just check the afterbirth.' 'Doesn't look premature.' A little choking noise and a tiny pair of high pitched vocal chords. An angry sea gull on helium. A medic asked Simon, 'Would you like to cut the cord?' And finally a small towelled package of red-faced infant was laid on my chest.

'Normal size, all healthy. You have a beautiful baby boy,' the medic confirmed. A stretcher was clicked down to my height and I was lifted onto it, arms wrapped tightly round my prize.

Mrs Weston wiped her face with her sleeve and looked at the ceiling. 'Thank you Lord.'

As I was bundled up in blankets I grabbed her hand. 'Thank *you*, Mrs Weston. I'm so grateful you were there.'

'Amazing luck you were in the baby shop.' The female paramedic turned to Mrs W, and gave a dry laugh. 'I expect you've done this a few times before, eh?'

Mrs Weston shook her head sadly. 'I hoped to. But not in fifteen years of business.' She patted my hand. 'I was never blessed with children,' she said. 'It was a joy to be present for a real birth at last.'

'What? You've never seen a baby born?' Simon was appalled.

'Oh yes dear, many times.' She smiled with confidence. 'Never miss an episode of Emergency Room Five.'

I was rolled out to the ambulance, through a nosy crowd, with Simon beside me and Mrs W and Bernadette behind. As the trolley was being strapped down, Simon clambered in, smiling like a lunatic. 'Berndette and Mrs Weston said this is for you.' He held up the big teddy.

There was a snuffle from the bundle in my own arms.

'I did it. And it's a boy!' I said in wonder, looking down at my little sleeping elf, swaddled in towels, head exposed, like a ready-to-eat kebab. 'Simon, are you okay?'

He sat down heavily on the trolley opposite, as the medic bustled round fixing things. 'Christ! That was some experience, duck.'

'Sorry I crushed your artistic hand.' I spoke to the paramedic. 'Will he be able to create beautiful paintings now?'

She laughed. 'I'd say so.'

'Good. 'Cos he couldn't before.'

Simon punched me softly. 'Oi! You're mighty cheeky for someone who just expelled a whole person from her snatch.'

I was giddy with relief. Nothing good had ever come with medics and ambulances for me. Not from Ally's accident, or on that awful night at The Weasal.

But that had all been blown away, consigned to the past.

Now I had a baby – a baby boy! And all I had to do was keep him safe.

For a lifetime.

55

TOM

So much had happened, I couldn't believe that it was only months since we'd first decamped to London. And the ground was still shifting, as the Press were still divided about us. Accolades like, *'Mix Up label forges brave new Ska era'* ran alongside vitriolic headlines such as, *'Originals Mix Trouble for Oi Generation'* and, *'Shepperton – Original and Outspoken, or just an Oik?'*

Instead of uniting us, this coverage had provoked endless bickering about what should be said, when, and who by. Accusations were made that I was making things worse – especially by Adam, who said there was a limit to the adage that 'there's no such thing as bad publicity'. I told him to fuck himself, and refused to be silenced.

Meanwhile, Toast Yourself trod water at Number 2 in the singles charts, then retreated down the list, as the stolid Amercian disco tune stayed at Number 1 for a record-breaking twelve weeks. When it finally moved aside, our newest single Can't Feel My Face – with lyrics I'd written to a tune Raymond wrote in hospital – rushed straight in at Number One.

To celebrate, several UAA execs took us to a fancy bar in Mayfair for Champagne – the second time I'd had it in my life, the other being my wedding day. We all chinked long glasses and as I said sarcastically, 'Cheers Adam – toast yourself!', I was aware of several camera flashes amongst the congratulations. The next day photos of Charlie and Len appeared – Len in his pork pie hat and checked jacket, Charlie in a new Fred Perry with red braces – looking like two barrow boys who'd made good. Headlines reading, *'Mix on Champers while country burns'* and *'Let them drink fizz'*, referred to the fact that rioting had now broken out in North London and Bristol. Nobody reported that after two glasses of expensive pop in that pretentious bar, we'd left them to it and gone to the pub.

At the next day's Press call, in UAA's HQ, we clustered round two mics on a low stage as the cameras clicked and whirred. 'What do you think is causing the continuing riots Tom?' called a reporter.

Adam grabbed the microphone. 'We'd rather talk about the music,' he said leaning into the mic.

'Thought this was our bloody interview,' muttered Vinnie at my other side.

'Is that the band or the record company talking?' said another. 'What do you say, Tom?'

And they all started firing questions. 'Tom! Tom! When will you be on Top of the Pops?' 'Has the BBC lifted your ban?' 'Is Wasteland still your vision of this nation?'

'Yes, it bloody is!' I stepped forward to the microphone. 'Our country's becoming a divisive mess. And it's not down to immigration, single mums or people on benefits. It's because we've got a cold uncaring government who are decimating the infrastructures put in place by socialism – the NHS, state education, the manufacturing industries – so the fat cats can gorge themselves and the rest of us can go to the dogs! People in Newcastle and Sheffield and Coventry are living on subsidence incomes!'

'So how come you're drinking Champagne?' someone shouted.

'I had one fucking glass!' I shouted back. Adam winced. We had promised not to swear. 'Tasted like liquid sherbet. Rather have a beer.'

The reporter laughed. 'What about you Len?'

Len shrugged. 'I'll drink anything if someone else is buyin'.' Cameras flashed again. 'Me too!' Vinnie agreed. He and Charlie struck idiotic poses then arsed around behind me, making rabbit ears with their fingers. The Press clicked and scribbled. They were enjoying themselves.

'Can't Feel My Face is about a racist incident. How are you dealing with your hardcore skinheads?' said an unsmiling bloke at the side of the stage. 'Is it true the neo-fascist wing in your fan base is growing?'

'Most of our skinhead fans are just into the music and the fashions. There's the odd one or two with racist attitudes. If they're at gigs, we'll get them evicted.'

Charlie stopped goofing around and stepped forward. 'We're a inter-racial band. There are both black and white skinheads coming to our gigs,' he said.

'So you condemn those with fascist tendencies?' the serious faced bloke pursued.

'Of course we fuckin' do!' I was exasperated with this guy. Surely it was as clear as glass? At the back of the throng, I noticed the UAA execs in hot, whispered debate. They didn't look pleased. Adam pointed to another reporter who was waving a hand.

'And you always weed them out, Devon?' The bloke used an intimate voice, as if they were in a one to one conversation .

'Like Charlie said, we get them boys turfed out,' Devon replied, his expression wary. 'They've got no place at our gigs.'

'Should the National Front be banned then, Tom?'

Devon put a warning hand on my shoulder, but I'd had enough of this goading.

'Look,' I stared hard at him. 'The National Front is a toxic thread in our country at the moment, there's no doubt about that. But banning it would just drive the fuckers underground. Anyway, it's just a symptom. The real problem is unemployment and the disenfranchised underclass, which is growing rapidly – as a direct result of crap Tory policies!'

Adam stepped up to the mic. 'Ha,ha. Okay, that's enough politics people. Does anyone have questions about the music? Stan?' He pointed at a journo.

'Vinnie, you wrote a lot of tracks on the first album, less on the second and you only co-wrote one track on this album. Care to comment?' This from Stan, a guy in a rocker's leather jacket, not unlike Vinnie's own.

Vinnie shuffled his feet, then shot me and Eddy a look. 'Not really.'

I said quickly, 'Everyone mucks in, we all contribute to the songs in some way.'

'This album shows a departure in terms of style,' Stan addressed me. 'Some of your strictly ska fans think you've lost direction. What do you say to them?'

I took a deep breath. I was expecting this. 'Ska's our foundation, but we've tried to bring in other influences – blues, reggae, jazz...'

There was a snicker round the room and the band shifted uncomfortably. Cameras clicked again. 'How does 'jazz' go down with the skinheads Charlie?' Someone quipped. 'You gonna start wearin' a tux?' The reporters all laughed. Charlie grinned. 'No way!' He stuck thumbs into his red braces to stretch them out. 'This is my style, whatever others we bring into our music.'

The serious-faced reporter interrupted the levity. 'Devon, how do you feel about your cousin being arrested in Brixton's riots?'

Devon's face was stony. 'I ain't got no comment about that. It's nothing to do with Original Mix.

'Is it true Floyd was already known to the police?'

'For chrissakes!' I said. 'Black men are continually being apprehended for nothing more than walking in a particular area. It's police racism!'

'Tom!' said Devon in a low voice. 'Shut it, man. Enough!'

But I continued, 'When we first came to London, Raymond got attacked by racists. Did the nearby police run to help? No. Took their time, waited till the scumbags ran off. Then they treated Ray like the criminal. With this attitude, what chance has Floyd or anyone else in Brixton got for a fair trial?' Everyone fired questions at once. One of the executives at the back threw his hands up and left the room. Adam rushed to the microphone.

'Tom means, we trust that justice will be dispensed fairly and impartially of course, but we really can't comment further.' He stepped back, grim-faced and muttered, 'For chrissakes, stick to the music Tom!'

'Don't fuckin' silence me!' I hissed.

'But fundamentally, you're saying the police are all racist?' Shouted a now-familiar voice from the front.

'I'd say so!' I called back. 'At least enough of them to make it the norm. They're using their stop and search powers to harass ordinary black people going about their business. No wonder people are angry and take to the str...'

Before I could say more, Adam had snatched the microphone out of the stand. 'That about wraps it up gentlemen – oh 'scuse me, and lady,' he nodded at the single woman reporter in the throng. 'Please help yourselves to drinks, copies of the singles, and their third album 'Mixin' Me Toasties' – which are all behind you. Original Mix will be playing live at the Majestic in Clapham for the next two nights – so pick up your complimentary tickets.' He quickly shooed us all off the dias.

As the journos descended on the bar with relish, I spotted Fozz, standing in the middle of the now-empty floor, grinning at me expectantly, with raised eyebrows.

Adam grabbed the back of my sleeve. 'Not so fast Tom. We've got to talk!'

'Not interested, mate.' I tugged my jacket from his grasp and jumped down to join Fozz. 'I won't be censored. If you and UAA don't like it, you can all fuck off.'

56
TOM

Being stuffed together in confined spaces most of the time, we'd definitely had enough of stewing in taxis. So four of us decided to travel to The Majestic by tube – the rest travelling by van with the gear.

Eddy stomped ahead. He was pissed off with me because one of the papers that morning had credited me as being the band's sole songwriter. I failed to see how this was my fault, so there'd been some choice words on the matter. Well if he wanted to sulk like a child, let him get on with it. Nowadays it seemed like Eddy and myself were forever arguing.

We swung onto the top of the escalator at Camden, several fans yelled, 'Original Mix! Hi! Great music!'

Then Vinnie said, 'Hey, look who's here!'

Cheryl was on the ascending staircase, head down, reading a glossy magazine. I hadn't seen her since our week of passion when the band were up in Hertfordshire, and my heart gave a couple of guilty thumps.

Vinnie shouted 'Oi, Cheryl! Watcha!'

She looked up and waved, then she noticed me behind and her face lit up.

'Hey, Tom! I got the job!' She flapped the brochure – some hair stylists' thing. 'I'm moving to London!' Her joy was infectious.

'Wow, congratulations!' I called. 'We're playing at The Majestic in Clapham tonight,' I added. 'I'll put your name on the door.'

We were all about level.

'Great! An' Tom....' she reddened, and lowered her voice. 'I'm staying with Fozz again, if you want to come over.'

Vinnie's face was half-turned in scowling puzzlement. Cheryl and I both turned to look back at each other as we passed. She gave me a bashful smile, then put a hand up in farewell as she stepped off the top. When I turned back round, Vinnie was facing me full on.

'You fuckin' bastard!' he spat. 'You knew I liked Cheryl!'

'Yeah?' I shrugged. 'Well now you know what it feels like.'

'What you talkin' 'bout?' His face was wreathed in incomprehension.

'You and your big lyin' mouth got rid of Josie.' His face was still creased up in frowns. The fucker didn't even remember! 'You told her I was married, yer git!'

'Not the bloody same!' he yelled.

'No, it wasn't!' I was furious now. 'Cheryl never wanted you, but Josie actually cared for me. We had something special.'

Vinnie sneered. 'Special? Oh yeah? Think you were the only one fucking Josie?'

I stared at him. Surely he was lying? Over his shoulder I saw we were almost at the bottom of the staircase. I pointed. 'Watch it!'

He shoved me hard in the chest. 'Fuck off. You slept with my bird!'

'Vinnie, get off,' I warned, as the escalator ran out.

He pushed me again. 'You friggin' get off!'

The escalator stair reached solid ground, slamming Vinnie's feet to a halt and buckling his knees. He keeled backwards, grabbing my lapel and pulled me with him, so I collapsed in a heap on top with a furious yelp.

'You stupid fucking twat!'

Boots and shoes of passengers were scrabbling and jumping all over us, like panicking bison breaching a riverbank. I scrambled up and hoisted Vinnie to his feet, to find Eddy shaking his head, smirking and lighting up a cigarette. There were caustic comments and tuts from people as they passed.

Len came up behind, frowning with disgust. 'What the hell happened? You two idiots incapable of takin' a movin' staircase?'

Under my watch strap, a pain throbbed in my left hand. 'Oh Christ!' I wiggled my fingers experimentally. No lasting damage. 'For fuck's sake Vinnie. You could have broken my wrist!'

Without looking round he shouted, 'Wish I'd broken yer bloody neck!' and he stormed away into the moving throng.

Outside The Majestic, a sizeable queue snaked round the corner. Walking to the stage door, we slapped palms and exchanged greetings with excited fans, until we passed two severe-faced skins – lean, muscled guys, older than our usual fans, well into their late thirties. There was a clear gap, at either side of them, in the crowded line. I was caught in the iron-hard stare of one of the men, who elbowed his mate and nodded towards me with meaning.

'Don't like the look of those blokes,' I muttered to Len, and took a second glance back. 'They look like National Front.'

I'd been pretty outspoken about the NF so I wasn't keen to meet its members.

Len stared at the fellers and then frowned at me. 'Seem like everyone else,' he said. 'You're imaginin' things, Tom.'

In the comparative quiet of the Stage Door corridor, I found my chest was pounding. I administered a little pick up in the gents, then another for good measure, and decided to approach Adam, despite the fact he was barely talking to me. I found him in the technical gallery, speaking with a long-haired technician, one of Rick's tribe.

'There's security for that, Tom. Don't start causing trouble,' he said, after I'd voiced my concerns.

'Look, I know you're not that happy with me, but something's not right with those guys.'

When he turned, his face was red with fury. 'Not that happy? After all the shit you've been spouting to the papers? Any more contentious bollocks from Original Mix and we're all out!'

I pulled an incredulous face. 'Oh come on! Our single's at Number One and we've delivered another charting album. We're their gravy train.'

'One train, Tom. You're one single train in UAA's busy station. Your journey can be cancelled any time.'

I threw open my arms. 'Are you kiddin'? Have you seen the fan letters Annabel's been opening? Or the queues outside?' I pointed to the filling auditorium below. 'These are kids from all over the UK! We're too big to drop now.'

'You're wrong,' he said. 'There's a recession, in case you hadn't noticed. And even the music industry's in it.'

I backed away laughing, suddenly joyous at the crowds and music and life itself.

'Nah, yer wrong. It's like a wave, Adam.'

And I knew it was. One big, beautiful crashing ska wave. We were destined to unite the kids – rich and poor, black, brown and white. Nothing could stop us now. I decided to have another wee line, just to celebrate my good mood.

Outside the dressing room, Len pressed me to the wall with a hand. 'Where you been, man?'

'Looking for Adam.' I said. 'Stupid bastard was in the gallery.'

Len was puzzled. 'Doin' what?'

I shrugged. 'Dunno. Blowing the lighting tech maybe?'

'Char! Don't give me no images, man.' Len peered into my face. 'You alright Tom?'

'Yeah, why?'

He frowned. 'You seem kinda energised and you're shoutin'.'

I brushed him off. 'Jeez! Stop being so fucking suspicious all the time! Just sick of workin' for idiots. Come on, let's get this gig started!' In the dressing room I found Devon and Charlie swapping rhythms with the drummer and bassist from Detonator, one of the support acts, while Eddy and Ray were brushing down their suits and checking themselves in the mirrors.

'Where's Vinnie?' I said.

'Thought he was with you,' said Devon. I checked my watch. Five minutes before Detonator were on. Plenty of time. 'Not with me. Maybe he's in the bog?'

Charlie looked over. 'Oh yes, that's all we need. Vin with a dodgy arsehole,' he said.

'Vinnie *is* a dodgy arsehole,' said Eddy. 'End of.'

Everyone laughed, and it occurred to me that the band vibe was much more relaxed without Vinnie there.

By the time Detonator were into the last five minutes of their set, my irritation was growing. We'd looked in all the backstage areas, and Adam sent someone to scour the local pubs. No Vinnie.

'Think he's back at the flat?' he asked. 'I don't understand why he wasn't with you on the tube? *This* is why you should take taxis, Tom.' He scowled at me and dragged a hand through his hair. 'Did Vinnie say anything?' I shrugged. Adam turned to the rest of the band. 'Does anyone know what the fuck's going on?'

Len shot me a glance and busied himself tuning his guitar. Eddy looked at his feet. Charlie shook his head, without conviction.

'For chrissakes!' said Adam. 'Devon?'

Devon pursed his lips. 'Some lickle stupidness on the way. Don't worry man. He'll blow in soon.'

'Well, okay.' Adam combed a hand through his hair and paced a bit. 'The girl he's so thick with is here, so perhaps that's a good thing. What do you think?' He looked round in question, but we were all occupied with something or other. He turned to me.

'What's your B plan?'

I stared at him. He couldn't be serious. The idea Vinnie wouldn't be there for the gig was ridiculous. He couldn't be so steamed up about Cheryl he'd miss the chance to play. Vinnie's internal furies transformed into energetic showmanship on stage. It was the only time he looked close to real happiness.

I woke myself out of this stunned reverie. 'Nah, man. Devon's right. He's probably at the back of the hall watching. I'll go to the wings and look again.'

The audience were bobbing up and down in a chaotic way to Detonator's ragged stylings. They sounded better live than they had on the demo tape I'd played Adam. He'd maintained they were they were an inferior version of us, but I insisted they had their own take. Besides, they were from Birmingham and Rick already pressed their single on the Mix Up label, so it was a no-brainer. From the wings I scanned the crowds, shielding my eyes from the spotlights. It was dark but Vinnie would be in his usual spot – ten degrees to the right and six yards from the stage, in the spot he said offered optimum sound quality, and where he'd plant his intractable DMs at any gig. The place was occupied by the two thuggish-looking blokes I'd seen earlier, standing waiting, arms folded. How had they been let in? My neck started to prickle. It was hot as hell on stage. I loosened my collar.

'He's not there!' Adam yelled in my ear. I couldn't take my eyes off the big guy's crossed arms, his fingers curled round each big bicep. He must have been about sixteen stone. I imagined trying to fend him off, after he'd jumped on stage. Feeling his vast hands round my throat, a knife slicing into my side.

'We'll fucking well do it without him then!' I shouted back. Bloody hell. Vinnie was spooking me out deliberately – after I'd defended him and his erratic behaviour, god knows how many times. Where the hell was he when I needed some back up?

Detonator finished their final song and ran off stage whooping and hollering – slapping palms with the roadies, and Original Mix members were starting to line up behind me.

Len handed over my guitar. 'You ready Tom? I'll follow your lead.'

My breathing was going crazy. We'd done hundreds of gigs – some much bigger than this, especially in Germany. But all of a sudden it seemed too difficult. Fuck Vinnie. There was a churning in my guts and I thrust my guitar back at Len.

'Tell Detonator to do another encore!' I shouted, and before anyone could object, I ran back to the dressing room, past a puzzled-looking Raymond and bumping into Devon in the doorway. 'Be right back!' I shouted, hurling myself at the toilet door.

In the cubicle, waves of nausea convulsed up from my stomach and my bowels emptied in a way that only the devil himself could have inflicted. 'Jesus! ' I groaned, groping in frantic, clumsy panic, for the toilet roll. After a few moments spent head in hands, staring at the tiles below, I felt for the small bulge of powder in my inner pocket. Over the dressing room relay I heard Detonator's lead singer introducing the band by name, each member playing a few bars or a drum pattern, to whistles and shouts. Thank god. They were going for a big stadium finish. I had more time to pull myself together.

I sauntered back to the stage, drying my hands on my jeans, buzzed up again and eager to play.

'Where you been?' said Charlie. Len thrust my guitar at me for the second time.

I patted my stomach. 'Dodgy pie earlier.'

Charlie frowned, no doubt remembering that I'd waved away the pie and chips they'd brought in for me. 'Or a bad pint,' I added, before we ran on stage.

It was stupid to let anything spoil the magic of a big live London gig. We were the best band in the UK and about to prove it, yet again. When I walked on stage, the roar of approval hit me like the welcome blast of bar room heat on a cold day. I held a palm up in salute and there were a barrage of whistles and cheers. Eddy looked round, covered his mic with a fist, and shouted, 'You doing the intro?' I nodded. It was all okay. I could swerve between my rhythm part and Vinnie's solos. Raymond and Len would fill in where necessary. It would be like those long recording sessions, where we'd fragmented into separate fag breaks, and all become proficient at covering other people's lines.

Three songs into the set and I was labouring, as it was very different live. I played a couple of Vinnie's short solos, but my new guitar was far too mellow to produce his jagged raw sound which lifted the tune, plus my bashed wrist throbbed. And despite the help from my snowy friend, I was struggling to think fast enough for two parts. Len kept glancing over, deep wrinkles in his dark brow as he listened for the cues he'd become used to. Our timing was going awry. I heard Devon shout, 'Slow down man. You're getting ahead!' The fine, beautiful feeling was slipping away. We were drowning.

As I fumbled into another of Vinnie's signature riffs, the whole audience erupted into simultaneous jeers and cheers.

Vinnie bounced up beside me, plugged in his guitar and peeled off a long series of bluesy twangs, which electrified the stage. The crowd roared as he kicked up a leg, then sank down to his knees to give the finest solo he'd ever produced. We were back on track and the tension on stage dissipated. Raymond lost his startled gazelle appearance, and Len high-fived Vinnie as he yomped past, toasting into his mic,

We all unite when we're in a fix,
Goin' for the best with Original Mix!

The fans went wild.

Adam tried to collar me later in the pub, after Fozz introduced me to the two big blokes –
who turned out to be writers of some anti-fascist skinhead fanzine. 'Gonna tell me what the hell's goin' on with Vinnie?' said Adam.

I'd obtained enough supplies to keep me going for a while. Everything was good again. I slung an arm round his shoulder. 'Cool it Adam. Just a bit of bluster. Musical differences – that sort of shit.'

Adam shrugged me off, with impatience. 'I'm not bloody idiot Tom. That was nearly the worst gig you've ever done, that is until…'

I faced him full on, with an ironic grin. 'Yeah? Go on then, say it.'

He sighed. 'Alright. 'Til Vinnie came on stage.'

I laughed. 'So you admit it – we do need the extra ballast?'
Under his expensive jacket, Adam's shoulder's sank.

'Okay, okay. But try to keep him on a short rein, will you?'

'Keep who on a rein?' asked Fozz, proffering pints.

'Vinnie,' I said flatly. I had run out of new ways to react to Adam, but I held Fozz's pint while he spluttered and coughed, trying to control his laughter. Over his shoulder I watched Cheryl talking to Raymond and Linda. Her cheeks were pink with excitement and, as her dark hair fell over one eye, she flicked it over her ear, then immediately back again as she remembered her small birthmark. I couldn't pretend I didn't want sex with her again. It had been like hearing sweet music, after a long period of silence. Not the playful, gut-filling, joyous anthem of being with Josie. But still…

I brushed through the noisy drinkers to Cheryl's side. It was a packed lounge and Vinnie was over in the bar area, clowning around with Charlie, Len and some of the fans. I slid my hand round her waist and she looked up coyly in appreciation. I downed my pint and ordered two large whiskies. We grinned at each other and threw back the shots.

'Let's go,' I said.

I led her out of the side door into the alleyway which ran alongside the pub. We passed Devon, sharing some philosophy and wisdom weed with a couple of black skinheads, both sharp in stay-pressed suits and Fred Perry shirts. 'See ya later Dev,' I said.

'Hold up Tom,' he said. 'I wanna word.' He looked at Cheryl. 'Sorry, sweetheart, it's a private thing.' She dropped back and Devon kept walking, moving me down the wall. I lit a cigarette, and watched the two skinhead lads flirt with Cheryl, offering her the joint. I tried to decide if I was jealous.

'I want you to listen to me, Tom.'

I could probably have other women if I wanted, I thought. We had more of a female following now we were topping the charts. Vinnie and Len got lucky all the time, and Charlie often seemed to have a girl. It was likely I could also take my pick.

'I don't know where your mind is at right now. You've changed man. You're not like the person I know.'

I laughed. 'Jesus, Devon. How strong's that stuff you're smoking? For six bloody months, we've seen more of each other than most marrieds do in a lifetime. I'd say we know each other far too well.'

His normally soft brown eyes had turned into disapproving stones. 'I'm not the only one who's noticed, Tom.'

A cold hand gripped my heart and squeezed it, making me shiver. So that's what was happening now.

'Oh right!' I stepped back. 'So you've all been discussing me, behind my back. Let me tell you Devon, it's been fuckin' hard keeping this band together and getting the albums finished. While you're all out socialising, who's been left alone, trying to write new stuff and mastering the tapes?'

He nodded. 'I know man. But you need to slow down.'

My laughter had a nasty edge which surprised even me. 'Slow down? You know they want a fourth album soon?'

Devon recoiled. 'You're kiddin'? We already broke time records with the last two. You told them it can't be done right?'

Cheryl was letting the best looking lad light her cigarette. He held her hand inside his, to keep the flame alive.

Devon grasped my arm. 'Tom, you told them 'No'?'

He didn't understand. 'We're on the crest of a wave Devon. It's not possible to slow down. We have to grab it, seize tight and ride it out!' Devon frowned and gave me a look I couldn't decipher.

Cheryl was giggling, pulling away from one of the guys, who was trying to put his arm around her, in mock intimacy – the sort of double bluff Vinnie pulled. I decided enough was enough.

As I moved off, Devon's big hand shot out again and grabbed me by the left wrist. 'Oi!' I winced, as it was still sore.

'You and me gotta spend some time later, man.' Devon shook his head. 'We used to talk about everythin', as a band. Reason it out.' I wasn't listening. He followed my stare and narrowed his eyes. 'An' you take care of that little girl, Tom. She's not tough like those punk girl types.'

I thought of Josie and stared at him.

'What the fuck do you mean?'

'Remember you're a decent man, Tom. You treat her right.'

I shook him off and started walking towards Cheryl. 'Chrissakes, Devon! You're not my fuckin' dad!' I shouted.

As the words fell out I had a flash of my dad in his shirt and knitted V-neck, with his quiet determination and inner pride, and it hit me he'd never be there to give me unsolicited advice again. I stumbled, recovered and Cheryl met me halfway. 'You alright Tom?'

'Come on. Let's go.' I walked down the long passageway by the side of the pub and let her follow. The good feeling had dissolved again. It would take something more to get back on track. Devon was wrong. Cheryl had been happy enough to try a couple of lines at Fozz's. She wasn't so much of an innocent, as he thought.

On the tube I put an arm round Cheryl and she snuggled in. The thought of seeing her body, naked and pale as porcelain, sustained me back to Camden. I started to kiss her as we entered Fozz's adopted building and we fell through the door to the flat, giggling and pawing at each other's clothes, both lunging at the big double bed. All I wanted was raw sex, all night.

'Wait,' I said. 'Let's have a bit of a perk up.'

'Thought you were already perky,' Cheryl said with another giggle. She looked very pretty sitting back against the headboard in nothing but her red knickers. I scrambled off the bed to find my jacket. The feel of the crunchy powder gave me a deep, wired kind of hunger, almost stronger than the potential of sex.

'You got it?' called Cheryl.

I grabbed a hand mirror from the dresser and took a fiver from my jeans, and rejoined her, wearing a big, teasing grin. 'Got absolutely everything I need.'

It was true. At last, despite the set backs, I really did have everything. The band was nearly at the top. I was on the cusp of owning the world.

57

TOM

Another typical day in Ragged Moth's now rancid-smelling studio.

'Oh, just fuck off.'

'You fuck off.'

'You can ALL fuck off!' A deep voice rippled over the usual acrimony. Everyone stared in silent shock at Devon, who was dismounting his drum seat like a battle-weary standard bearer.

'I'm pure sick of this nonsense. I haven't seen me lickle girl for weeks, and me family's in turmoil trying to get Floyd outta prison.' He glared at me. 'Not helped by him being notorious, thanks to you Tom. So I got no mind to hear these stupid quarrels anymore.'

Nobody said anything.

Devon continued, 'Remember when we used to argue about politics and music?' He looked round at Eddy and Charlie, to Len and Vinnie, then me. 'Like that night at The Imperial?'

I gave a weak smile, remembering that monumental night in breath-freezing Newcastle, fuelled by peanuts and huge bottles of flame-orange Tizer from a late night garage, the sole guests in a draughty hotel which reeked of bacon and mildew. We had been so excited, sitting round an open fire planning our future, what we needed to say through our music, how we'd create a new world order. What the hell had happened?

As Devon made for the door, he turned an intractable face to me. 'I'm callin' my wife to tell her I love her. Get some of this toxic atmosphere outta me system.'

I must have looked stunned, because he flapped an impatient hand at me. 'Oh, I'll be back alright. Think I'm lettin' that last track go out with those rackety drums on?'

When the door closed an emptiness opened up in the room.

'Alright,' I said after a moment. 'Half an hour break.' There was the clatter and jangle of instruments being laid aside, until just myself and Charlie were left in the room. His pallid face looked more serious than I'd seen in a long time.

'Tom, you know you're pissing Devon right off.' He stopped and sighed. 'Look, I'm goin' to say it, man. He's right – we used to have a laugh with occasional rows, not vice versa.' He fixed me with reproachful eyes.

'What d'you mean, *I'm* pissing him off?'

Charlie used a plectrum to gouge at a bit of loose plastic on the keyboard beside us. 'You know – stringin' that girl Cheryl along, an' getting' out of it all the time.'

'Hey! We all do that!'

Charlie gave an awkward grimace. 'Yeah, but we're lager and weed boys, not the hard stuff.'

'Is that all?' I smiled. 'Okay, I admit I did a bit of speed to get through the last album.' There'd been other things, but he didn't need to know. 'Don't worry, mate. Devon's just being an old woman.' I thumped him on the arm.

'What happened to that special girl Tom? The one you were goin' to introduce us to sometime?'

I turned to stare out of the greasy side window. Camden market was winding down for the day. Mounds of boxes and rubbish heaped the pavements, and a hopeful-looking down-and-out was combing through the contents, with practised hands. He held up a faded T-shirt with the slogan, 'True Punk Never Dies', then placed the garment back on the heap with a rueful look. I thought of what Vinnie had said about him sleeping with Josie. Surely that was just vengeful bollocks? And anyway, it shouldn't matter now I'd moved onto new pastures. But I still felt a pang of pain and jealousy in my chest. And the old longing to find her welled up inside, like a howl.

'Didn't work out,' I shrugged. 'Doesn't matter anyhow. I'm seeing Cheryl now.'

But for how long after last night's debacle? What the hell had happened – or rather not happened? Perhaps I'd done too much coke or drunk too much. One moment I could have used my cock as a hoopla stand and the next thing I just couldn't respond. My face went hot with shame just remembering.

Charlie pulled a face. 'At least you're getting' some. Belinda's moved back to Birmingham.'

'Who's Belinda?'

'Jesus, Tom! It's like you've got no idea what's goin' on round you. The girl I've been seein'. You met her several times, at the pub and the flat.' I looked blankly, trying to recollect.

'Tall, red hair,' he said with irritation.

'You mean the nurse with the visible panties?' I said. 'Wears a green leather jacket?'

He nodded, softly booting a coiled wire out of the way, till it sat under the speaker stand. 'It's not just shagging anymore. I really like her, if you know what I mean?'

I gazed out of the window again. The tramp filled a ragged plastic bag with dozens of loose bananas, which looked like they'd been in a punch up, on the losing side.

'She thinks cos the band's famous, she can't take me seriously.'

Recognition knifed through me. I should have held Josie close to me, not been so casual and sporadic. I'd wanted to make my mark, prove myself in music and it never occurred to me that she wouldn't be there, waiting. The thought of that empty house made my blood run cold.

'After we've got these few tracks done, we'll have a proper break Charlie. You can go up to Brum and confess your undying love.'

'Really?' He grinned. Gone was the wariness and distrust. Back was my old cheery pal. It was just woman trouble making him talk nonsense, after all.

I slapped him on the back 'Promise, mate.'

♫

When the lads returned from their long weekend off I had some news.

'We're on Bang on Cue again, on Friday.'

'Friday? Then why you pull us all back on Tuesday?' Len shouted. 'I could have used two more days to finish the job.' He'd spent the time decorating his aunty's living room. Flocks of magnolia paint clung stubbornly to his ebony forearms. He picked at them in annoyance.

'You're a big star now, man. Why didn't ya get someone in to do it?' said Charlie.

Len scowled at me. 'Maybe if we'd been paid enough I would. Where the hell's our Royalties, man? We better be makin' some serious damn money soon. I'm cleaned out man. Me whole family's convinced I'm rich.'

'Thought you were seeing Rick to find out,' I said.

Len shook his head. 'Went to his house and the studio twice. No sign of him.'

It was getting harder to justify Rick's dissolving presence, especially as he was still primarily responsible for our financial and legal affairs. I felt inside my jacket and peeled off some notes from the wedge that Yvonne had provided. There wasn't much left. 'I can advance everyone two hundred.'

'Oh man! I need more than that,' said Charlie. 'Spent all weekend in a hotel, treatin' my girl.'

Eddy slunk in. No doubt he'd spent the weekend with Adam. 'Oiright all.' He looked round, noting the absence of Vinnie. 'Saw Jackson in Brum on Saturday. Says hello to everyone.'

'You went up home?' I said, surprised.

Charlie and Devon exchanged a look which was impossible to read.

I wondered if I was getting paranoid again. I'd spoken to Fozz about it and he'd suggested I cool it for a while, let my system clear out. Maybe he was right. For four long days the only stimulant I'd had was beer, and I'd have chewed my arm off for a big fat line or two. But mentally I was feeling more together.

'Okaay, let's get this rehearsal started,' I said. 'It's safe to assume that Mr Vincent Perkins will drag himself in when hangover permits.'

To stay on the level it was imperative to keep busy.

On the sixth day I couldn't bear it any longer, so I went round to see Fozz and renege on my chemical-free holiday. I found him in the flat drinking Chinese green tea, having given up on coke, 'cos it was getting in the way of his writing.

'It's not like I need it man. But I just feel so sluggish, like I've got a kinda fluey cold brewing. An' I can't afford to be sick. We need to get this album down.'

Fozz nodded like some sage old priest, his usual array of tics and twitches strangely absent. 'What we need, my friend, is a longer lasting high.' He reached for his funny pencil case. 'Something to deeply relax. You look – if I may say – like shit.'

I sat down and rubbed my temples, an action which eased my head, but produced a stiff ache in the wrist which Vinnie had fallen on a few weeks ago. 'Gee, thanks Fozz. Your honesty is touching, but I'm not using anything that requires needles.'

He wagged the pinkish brown packet at me. 'Been saving this for us to try sometime.'

I eyed the powder. Right then I'd have dumped a spoonful in my tea like sugar if he'd offered. I was old-man weary. A kind of low panic had been keeping me awake at night and making me spiky by day, occasionally breaking into a full on mania in the long evenings of re-mixing. It was like being in one of those weird dreams which turn into nightmares – where I'd lost something, then forgotten what I'd lost, then remembered, in a panicking rush.

'You reckon it could mellow me out?' I said to Fozz.

He blinked. 'Dunno. They say everyone's different.'

I laid back and let my eyes shut. Behind my eyelids, memories rushed back of that awful day in Coventry with Vinnie and Len, groggy with jet-lag after a 14 hour flight and wearing hastily-bought dark suits. My left shoulder suddenly bearing the whole weight of the coffin, as the official pall bearers slotted themselves in between us, to discreetly take up the load.

I still couldn't bear to think about what was in the casket.

Moments before, I'd automatically embraced mum's soft grieving body and hugged my two sisters – like it was all happening to somebody else. Mary's Canadian burr, and the softness of her palm on my cheek, like when I was a small boy.

'I'm fine,' I'd said to both sisters, gazing at me with their undramatic sadness and navy suits. 'You take care of mum. Really. I'm fine, just fine.'

In church I'd stared at the puddles of colour on the marble alter steps, where the sun streaked through the stained glass. And I'd winced when the organ player lost timing slightly, thinking what a hellish fucking instrument this was, as sound poured into the stone speaker of a whole church and swilled round and round in my head, note after resonant note, until I wanted to scream.

I sat up, blood thudding in my chest, alarmed by all this recall. 'Alright,' I said to Fozz. 'Let's try it. Anything to be able to chill out, just for one night.'

♪

58

TOM

21st December 1981

At last the fourth album was finished and out of my hands. It had taken some bloody grim determination and a bit of table thumping to get it sounding how I wanted, and after several gigantic rows I'd sacked the producer. The second producer was also a cocky bastard, but the final tracks were good and we'd incorporated an eclectic mix of sounds, including references to bebop and Afrobeat. Of course we'd hit a few low patches, and there were the usual struggles before we got there. But it was what we did.

At Bang on Cue, we were treated like heroes and old friends.

'Soooo – how are my absolutely fave musicians?' Daisy paused, framed in the doorway, a perfect combination of fragrance and sex appeal. Len and Vinnie stepped forward in clumsy competition and somehow knocked over a bottle of wine. Daisy stepped over the spillage as if it wasn't there, took a seat, and carefully spread her dress out like a fan. We'd be pleased to know that the whole band was on the sofa this time, she said. They had built an extra piece, making it L-shaped, especially for us – just like this one she was sitting on. There was some business about camera angles – she gave a girlish laugh, 'As usual' – but the floor manager would talk us through all that.

'The important thing is to have fun!' said Daisy. 'Oli will introduce your song, then you all come and sit with me.' She patted the space to the left of her. 'Tom, I'd like you here.' She turned to Len. 'Would you sit on my right, sweetie?' Vinnie shot me an incredulous look, but Len grinned and plopped himself down. 'Charlie can perch on the arm, next to Devon, Vinnie and Raymond.' As she pointed, everyone placed themselves as instructed. Most interviewers muddled us up, but this was how she'd get our names right. Miss Daisy was no dippy blond.

She took us through some questions: album dates, who wrote which songs, our favourite Jamaican artists. She knew a hell of a lot about music. We all answered at once, keen as pups to earn one of her special wide eyed smiles.

Oli appeared at the door. 'Hey guys! Daisy treating you alright?'

'Oh yeah!' 'You bet!'

He was sporting a sideburns, hair in a side parting, and a slim cut sepia brown suit, like a poker player from an old cowboy film.

'Eddy, Tom! You must be SO excited about the new single?'

After dishing out the last of Yvonne's money, I'd spent the morning trying to contact Rick, but he hadn't answered his home or studio phone. He was in for a prize bollocking when he did. Then I'd had no time to catch Adam and find out our current position in the charts.

Across Daisy, I gave Len a quizzical look, but he shrugged.

'You don't know?' Oli couldn't believe it. 'Cos I'm the Boss Man has zoomed straight to the top. You're first and second in the charts, so it looks like you'll have the Christmas Number One!'

Expletives and whoops punctured the air, but I also spotted Charlie and Devon exchanging a knowing glance. I thumped Eddy on the back saying, 'Told you it would be a winner!' but he shrunk away from me. I was puzzled and disappointed. We had another Number One hit, and this time at Christmas! Surely this was *it*?

After camera rehearsals, there was time to kill before the show call. 'You're free to roam, but be back here in an hour,' said one of the clipboard-toting runners.

'I'm going to Channel 4's bar, see who's there,' Vinnie said to Raymond, pointedly ignoring me. Surely he couldn't still be sulking over the thing with Cheryl?

Charlie, Len and Raymond followed, keen to join the star spotting. But Eddy and Devon were lain out, commandeering the L-shaped sofa. Devon had on a copious leather cap, accommodating most of his dreads. He pulled the brim down to cover his eyes. 'I'm beat. Wake me ten minutes before the hour's up,' he said.

Eddy grunted from his paperback, which appeared to be a biography of James Dean.

'Oi! Aren't you two excited?' I said. 'We're about to have a Christmas Number One for godssake! Plus we're headlining at Bang on Cue and our fourth album's being pressed. Not sure it gets any better.'

'You said it.' Eddy's voice was truculent.

'What the fuck's wrong now?' I said. 'Look Ed, I know we've had a bit of a rough patch. But can't you stop griping and just enjoy the moment?'

I wanted Eddy to be as excited as I was. We'd crafted Boss Man out together, with hours of careful trial and error spent creating the backing effects. Despite everything, I still respected his judgement and regarded him as my chief musical ally.

He gave me a long look of pity and disdain.

'Ah, forget it. I'm off to find the others.' I was gutted.

I meant to stay clear-headed for the programme, but Devon and Eddy's reactions had shaken me. How could they not be on top of the world about our latest album? The songs were thoughtful and experimental. Once I'd got rid of that first producer, who just wanted more of the same, we'd been free to try new stuff. It was going to be a trailblazer. Everyone would understand, when the reviews were out.

In my annoyance I took a wrong turn, and came to a dead end. As I turned back, I spotted a small room tucked away, right at the end corner. Its name card holder was empty and the door was ajar. I pushed it open and took a few steps in. A dog-eared sign announced, '*Please respect that this is a NO SMOKING Dressing Room.*' Perhaps this explained its air of loneliness. By way of comment, some joker had stubbed a fag out on the corner of the paper, to leave a blackened hole.

In the absence of cigarette smoke, another powdery smell took up the challenge – a chalky, slightly perfumed scent, suggesting bouffant hair and fat pearls. This corridor was quiet, deserted. So I shut the door behind me.

Since the very beginning I'd always seen the original four of us – myself, Eddy, Devon and Len – in harmonious elation at the climax of our success, laughing in two-fingered triumph. This was what we'd dreamed of – music overpowering mundanity. Not with brain-washing, pop hokum, but by lyrics which spoke in truth, music which re-invigorated kids with hope and joy, in one glorious ' fuck you, let's dance' movement. And we had done it. Our fans included plenty of black and Asian kids now, even girls, and even their mums and dads could see we weren't just a joke. We had a message – about fairness and equality – and we'd stuck to it and won them all over. Why wasn't Eddy exultant? And Devon – why wasn't he celebrating the fact that another song inspired by Jamaican music was in the Top Ten?

Fuck them. I deserved a little pure joy anyway. I switched on a set of mirror lights farthest from the door, and extinguished the overhead light.

I was lining up a short moment of snowy happiness when the door clicked open and I heard a rustle of dress as someone entered and the latch clicked shut. I froze. There was a small female gasp.

Unable to turn round, a million excuses piled into my head.

'Tom! You've found my secret room!'

I whipped round. 'Daisy! Fuck, sorry, sorry, I don't usually do this but…'

She picked her way across the carpet and her tiny turquoise stilettos stood beside me.

'I do,' she said and smiled. The top of her dress rose and fell with each light breath. 'Just a little, to sharpen my wits.' She hesitated, swallowed. 'Don't tell anyone, but you wouldn't believe how nervous I get.'

It was my turn for surprise. 'No! You're so confident.'

She sank onto the other chair and shook her head slowly. 'I've worked so hard to get this far, Tom. You can't imagine what the TV industry is like for a woman. You're either too attractive to be taken seriously, or not pretty enough. They don't care how much you know about art and music. Thank god I've got Oli's support.'

I nodded. 'Right. Are you two…?'

Her laughter was like little bells. 'Oh no. We're the best of friends, but Oli's not really my type.'

With all my might, I resisted the terrible urge to stare down at her breasts. She was the most perfect woman in the world. 'Who would be your type then?'

Daisy held my gaze a moment, the answer suspended on her half-open rosy lips, enigmatic and tantalising, then she glanced at her watch.

'Shall we have some of this, before it gets too late?' She pointed a slender digit.

I extracted one of my last tenners to roll up, and we did a couple of short lines each. As the sparkle in her eyes increased, my libido leapt back into action. Perhaps Cheryl was right? Maybe it had been something to do with her. Daisy had a silvery laugh, and, as she bent to inhale the second line, I found my arms round her small waist. She swivelled round, but didn't object, so I lifted her onto the table. 'You're as light as fairy dust,' I said, which seemed incredibly funny. One minute we were both laughing and the next she was tugging at my belt, while I was rifling through the net of her dress – the net reminding me of something, someone, a fragment of a memory – and she was kissing my neck and saying, 'You are, Tom. You're my type,' and I was hard as a rake again and when my fingers touched not underwear, but her soft, velvety flesh, this sealed the deal. I put my hands on her bottom and scooped her forwards and I knew this was the elation I wanted, this was the high of success, to be with – oh god, inside! – the sexiest, most famous, beautiful woman on television, there wasn't a man alive who wouldn't want to be in my position. Oh yes, I had earned my place in the limelight and I was full of joy as I could ever be. It made complete sense. We were perfect together. Nothing else mattered, nothing, nothing could touch me.

'Josie, Josie,' I heard myself mumble. Shocked, I opened my eyes, as the slender face in front of me crumbled into dismay. I put my hand up to stroke Daisy's cheek in reassurance, but she was already wriggling free.

The door slammed open, and thumped back as it was released.

'What the…Cheryl?' Devon wore a stupefied expression, making sense of the image in front of him.

'Christ, Devon!'

'Jus lookin' for a pillow.' Devon turned, fumbled with the door handle, then left without another word.

I turned back to Daisy. She was adjusting her dress. A small inky rivulet had started to course over one cheek bone from the corner of her eye.

'I'm so sorry.' I didn't know where to start.

'I'd like to get down,' she said.

'What?' I was paralysed with the horror of it all.

She sniffed. 'From the table. You're in my way. I'd like to get down please.'

My trousers and underpants were pooled round my ankles and my cock was limp with shame. I shuffled backwards, heaved everything up and, as she slid off the shiny surface, I put a hand out to touch her arm. 'Daisy, I can explain the mix up.' She shucked me off, in cold rebuff and grabbed a stray shoe to fix back on her foot.

At the mirror she started ripping tissues from a box.

'I really like you.' I stood behind her, helpless, as she scrubbed at her cheeks to erase the black makeup. She fluffed up her hair and produced a lipstick from some pocket in her dress.

'You're so beautiful,' I said, as she delineated her perfect rosebud mouth.

When she turned her face was icy. 'I will go out first, then you.'

'Okay,' I said in a cooperative voice. Perhaps we could get past this, recreate the moment somewhere more appropriate, maybe we'd even look back on the incident with amusement.

'I would be grateful if you and Devon did not feel it necessary to share this with the whole band.' Her tone suggested she thought this unlikely.

'Of course!' I couldn't bear that she thought I was such a complete bastard.

She nodded, but I could see the disbelief in her eyes. At the door she turned. 'Tom?'

'Yes?'

'You have no reason to believe me, but I've never done that before.'

'Me neither.'

It was impossible to say which of us was telling the truth, who was lying to themselves, and who believed what. She grasped the door handle, pulled her shoulders back and stepped out. I heard her stilettos tip-tapping on the lino, then another person saying something in greeting, and Daisy's tinkling laugh, now sounding as sad and empty as wind chimes. Finally her footprints disappeared out of earshot.

Two hours later in the dressing room, we were collecting our stuff to leave after the recording.

'What the hell just happened?' hissed Len.

We had delivered our song with gusto but when we came to the interview it was clear, to me at least, that Daisy had decided to have another line or two. Her flawless peachy skin was slightly mottled and her eyes were too wide, her laughter too edgy. Leaving an uncomfortable gap between us on the seat, she flirted so outrageously with Len that he cowed into the corner of the sofa, so she switched to interviewing Eddy, who gave monosyllabic answers and his defensive body language made her appear like some weird nymphomaniac. I decided to step in and answered her question about musical influences.

'We're pretty eclectic in taste,' I blurted out. 'To be honest, we're into almost anything.'

'Oh really?' she didn't quite meet my eyes. 'But there must be things you really get off on?' Her cheeks flushed pink and she looked down quickly at her clip pad.

'Er, yeah.' My mind was suddenly blank. Christ, how could I bring her light, natural confidence back and what the hell did we listen to? We'd travelled thousands of miles, hung round in dressing rooms, sat in the flat for days – all the time listening to hundreds of cassettes we stowed in an old flight case – music which crossed countries, ages and genres, even some of Raymond's classical stuff. And now I couldn't even recall the name of one song or artist.

Everyone was waiting. I ran a hand through my hair. On couches, in the live audience and across the nation in living rooms and bedsits, people were watching. But I'd lost my mind and Daisy had gone into meltdown. I'd said 'Josie'. Why the fuck had I muttered the name Josie?

'To be honest, there's too much to list,' I cut into the silence. 'When you tour as much as we do, there's always something different playing in the bus.

'What Tom is saying, is that we're musical tarts,' chipped in Charlie, with a grin. 'We pick up all sorts and add it to our collection, don't we Tom?' He laughed, a cheeky Charlie laugh. It didn't mean anything, he was just trying to be helpful.

Daisy looked at me alarmed, paranoid. I willed her to calm down.

'During the album we were listening to some old Cajun and bluegrass – Conway Brothers and Cole Pettijohn,' I said, suddenly remembering the last thing I'd listened to. I gave her an encouraging smile. Come on Daisy, I thought. You rehearsed this stuff with us. 'It's corny but kinda interesting.' She continued to stare at me. 'Let me show you.' I quickly grabbed my acoustic guitar and let a couple of swampy riffs fly out. And this seemed to bring Daisy back to life. Vinnie offered a few more riffs on a second guitar placed beside him, and we jammed along for a couple of bars. The delighted audience clapped in time, then applauded. It was pretty naff, and not what we'd agreed to play, but it got us to the end of our slot. By the time Oli had announced next week's guests, Daisy had recovered herself enough to retrieve her trademark sexy smile.

As arranged, she curled against my chest for the final close up. 'And goodbye from me, I've certainly had an Original Mix tonight!'

Jesus. You had to hand it to her, when she got back on script she kept to her lines. As the applause died down and the red lights of the cameras blinked off, her smile dropped. She sat up as fast as if I'd jabbed her with a pin.

The others were looking at each other and shrugging, puzzled at how our loose, friendly interview structure had gone so far off the rails. Before I could speak to Daisy she had gone.

In the dressing room the atmosphere was just as weird.

'Why she get all spooked at you, man?' insisted Len, rubbing makeup off his face with a towel.

'You say somethin' to her before the show, Tom?' asked Charlie. Devon was packing up his roll of drumsticks silently, he turned his head slightly.

'Course not!' I said crossly.

Vinnie looked over. 'Typical Shepperton,' he said, with a sneer. 'How'd you manage to fuck up an interview with the fittest chick on TV?'

'I didn't fuck up anything!' No way was I going to be lectured by him on the subject of women.

'Oh yeah?' Vinnie's hands were on his hips. 'What happened to the R&B, reggae and ska medley we were goin' to play? Now all our fans think we've turned into soddin' hillbillies!'

'It was just a bit of a laugh for the telly. Nobody takes this shit seriously!' I yelled at him.

He stepped towards me. 'Don't get shirty with me, cos everyone in the country watched
you freak out some bird,' he said.

'Shut your big bloody mouth!' I was furious now. 'It's not my soddin' fault if she can't do her job!'

I didn't mean it. It was a reflex – the sort of stupid, shitty remark that Vinnie inspired.

Everyone was silent. Daisy and Oli stood in the doorway, come to convey their thanks, like the consummate professionals they both were. Daisy turned on her heels and Oli gave me an appalled look then followed her. 'Daisy, babe! Wait, I'm sure there's some misunderstanding...'

Charlie said, 'Jesus, Tom. When did you turn into such an arse?'

'Christ, I didn't mean...' I flopped down to a squat and covered my head with my hands. There was silence in the room.

Eddy stood from his seat. 'I suppose this is as good a time to say as any,' he said in a disinterested drawl. 'I made a decision. I'm leavin' the band.'

'WHAT!' Vinnie, Len and I screamed in unison.

Charlie shook his head in disbelief then raised his eyebrows at Devon, who nodded slowly, as if giving some sort of answer.

'Me too,' said Devon. 'Jackson's asked me an' Charlie to join his new band.'

'But you're in a fuckin' band!' said Vinnie. 'And we're at Number One – in case you've forgotten!'

Devon turned to me. 'I'm sorry man but Dawn's pregnant again, an' besides –' he shot me a grave look. 'I think we ran our course here.'

I stared at him. Everything I ever wanted had finally come to fruition. The band was on top of the world. We had acclaim now, proper recognition for what we were about. And now it had imploded – popped like an inflated paper bag. I looked at Eddy. He pulled a semi-apologetic face and shrugged.

An overwhelming sense of weariness overcame me. I picked up my guitar case and walked towards the door. 'See you back at the flat then.'

I collided with Oli as I left. 'Original Mix just split up,' I said simply.

'No!' Oli's face was aghast. 'But you'll reform somehow?'

'Shouldn't think so.' I shook my head. 'Listen Oli, will you tell Daisy something important from me?'

'Depends mate,' he said warily.

'She's the most talented woman on telly – no question. I was a twat to suggest otherwise.'

Oli gave a weak smile. 'Better if you said it yourself.'

I snorted. 'Think I've done enough damage for one day.'

As I walked off I had another thought. 'Hey Oli?' He turned. 'Tell her I meant the other things I said about her too. She'll know what I mean.'

He nodded. 'Okay. Take care of yourself, Tom.'

'Yeah,' I said. 'I'll try.'

♪

Back at the flat I looked around at the debris of ashtrays, music sheets, unwashed dishes and discarded clothes. Devon was right – we had run our course. I thought of the inevitable rows and recriminations to come. There would be repercussions from Ragged Moth and UUA too. Fuck knows what the financial implications would be. I peeled off my stage suit and pulled on jeans, grabbed a T-shirt which looked like mine, then stuffed some extra clothes and a few toiletries into a holdall. Looking in my wallet I found about fifty quid – enough to pay for an anonymous hotel room for a few nights, and some time to think. I slung the bag over my shoulder and picked up my best six string.

Camden was as buzzing as ever, people spilling out of pub doorways, drinking pints, offering each other smokes, happy to be with friends, living normal lives. Normal little lives. Why the fuck hadn't this been enough?

I scooted past, head down, passing a group of lads on their way to The Wexford, probably to see their favourite band. As their laughter mushroomed, I was consumed with envy and a deep hollow well of yearning.

'Oi! Mind out!'

'Oh, sorry mate. You alright?'

I'd bashed someone's legs with my guitar case. A stringy guy, in shabby trousers was rubbing his shin. He straightened up, glanced at the instrument then studied me for a moment. He didn't recognise me but his eyes narrowed. 'Wanna buy some weed?'

I hesitated. 'That all you got?'

He took a quick look side to side, and beckoned me closer with a jerk of his head. 'What you lookin' for? Got some quality H.'

I stared at him, checking for a possible trap, but there wasn't a jot of recognition in his eyes.

'Only if it's stuff you can smoke,' I said in a flat voice.

'Alright. Take a bit longer, but it can be done.'

As we walked down the side streets to a brick building which looked like a derelict warehouse, he gave a dry laugh. 'Quite hard to find pure smoking gear. Lucky it's me you knocked into.'

He pushed at a door, and as I stepped over a threshold, I kicked a couple of plastic syringes and nearly fell over someone's legs.

'Oh yeah,' I said. 'Today's been bang full of luck.'

♫♪ ♫♪

59

JOSIE

23rd December 1981

'Josie, you gotta come now!' Franki ran into the bedroom.

'Ssh!' I hissed. 'He's finally dropped off.'

I laid down my son as if he might go off like a hair-triggered bomb – which in a way he would.

Franki beckoned frantically from the door. 'Quick, quick! You've got to hear this!'

As I closed the door she yanked my wrist and pulled me down stairs. On TV, the midday newscaster announced that three million people were now unemployed and Margaret Thatcher was the most unpopular post-war Prime Minister.

'Oh god!' I groaned. 'How awful to be out of work at Christmas.'

'Wait. That's not it.'

'And finally, Britain's most controversial pop group, Original Mix, have disbanded – at the point when they have four charting albums, and two records topping the singles pop charts, one of which is set to be this year's Christmas Number One.'

'Oh no!' I clapped both hands over my mouth.

'This morning the band's.A&R man, Adam Chandler issued a statement to the Press.'

A well-groomed man in a soft grey suit with a pink shirt was standing on some steps with huge cameras popping all around him.

'It is with huge regret that I have to announce the members of Original Mix have decided to go their own ways. The band thank all their fans for the amazing support, and hope their message of fighting for equality will live on in their songs. Thank you gentlemen, that is all.' The camera cut back to the studio. Behind the news reader's head, the footage ran silently, showing the hapless promoter trying to fend off an artillery charge of questions.

'Original Mix first shot to fame with their song 'Wasteland' which some commentators said summed up Britain's current

economic and social problems,' the newsman read. The screen cut to show live footage of the group – Eddy Knowles scowling at the camera, and behind him, Tom grinning at Vinnie, as they gunned their guitars at each other in mock 'rock band' poses. *'But their next hit 'Too Polite to Riot' was banned by the BBC, as it heralded the outbreak of civil disturbances in Brixton and other big cities. The group's leader, Tom Shepperton, was heavily criticised for his outspoken views and the fact that, despite their messages of racial harmony, the band attracted a skinhead following.'* This was over footage of Tom pointing an angry finger at some journalist and shouting, as cameras flashed around him.

'Original Mix re-introduced the nation to ska – a musical form which originated in 1960's Jamaica, alongside reggae. The revival gave rise to a series of Britsh ska bands, mainly released on the band's own record label, Mix Up. None of the band members were available for comment. And now to the Sports Desk –'

Franki shoved the 'off' button, to silence the football news, and I sat down heavily.

'Bet it was Vinnie's fault,' she said. 'Tom's got sick of his drinking.'

'There was something wrong with Tom on last night's Bang On Cue,' I said. 'He looked really stressed and unhappy.'

Franki nodded. 'What d'you think he'll do now?'

I wondered if this was a good time to let him know he was a father. Probably not. I tried to imagine him in the matrimonial kitchen being consoled in the arms of his wife, or at their studio ranting about Vinnie and planning a new band line up. Try as I might I couldn't see him in either place.

In fact, I couldn't imagine where he was, or with who. During our love affair, I'd been convinced we understood each other down to the marrow. True soul mates. But that had been like the fantasy of a stupid, gushing teenager. The reality was, I hadn't known him at all.

60

TOM

1984

The squat I lived in was worse than most, with burned out floorboards, constantly changing inhabitants, everything up for grabs. My self-elected quarters were in the basement, and I'd often woken to find someone rifling through my pockets. So I slept in the long leather coat I'd found, arms across my chest to protect any meagre cash. If I felt anything touch me, I'd pummel like a demon first and check who it was later. One night, following a run of Recknaw gigs, I returned to the squat with a two litre bottle of cider, and the determination to get nicely paralytic. I drank half the cider and, as carefully as a wartime petrol siphoner, I emptied a couple of tins of lager into the bottle. Glugging at this, I eased the loose brick away from the wall by my mattress, to check my stash. Still there.

I took a combination of pills, lay back and waited for oblivion. The next thing I was aware of was something scratching at my hands and a sharp pain on my thumb. Instantly, I punched and beat at a big, furry thing. There was a furious 'eek!' as it hit the wall with a sickening thwack. Then silence. I sat up clumsily to check it wasn't still twitching, then sank back into the nether world.

Many hours later I woke to the sound of heavy boots and voices. 'Ere, look at this Gob. It's a fuckin' huge dead rat.'

'I'm not fuckin' dead though,' I shouted, from under an old sleeping bag. It wouldn't be the first time someone had freaked out at my inert form.

The two blokes finished examining the rodent corpse and began skinning up a joint. I'd had this empty basement to myself for a few weeks so I felt quite territorial, but if they had a smoke…

I propped myself up on an elbow, and eyed the two skinheads from under the small peak of my woolly hat.

'What we doin' now Gob?' asked the younger bloke. With his tight jeans, fuzzy scalp and pallid face, he reminded me of Charlie. For a moment I wondered if Charlie might have forgiven me. I remembered the look of shock and disgust when he'd found out how the Royalites were being split, just before the band had imploded. How he'd sat huddled in the sunken arm chair, knees up, dark eyes studying me, like he couldn't trust what I would do next.

'We're goin' to lie low until the Brick Lane march,' said the tall, ugly skinhead. 'Then we'll join the others and let those Paki bastards have it, well an' good.'

I rolled onto my back and pulled the sleeping bag over my face. Bad enough to have my squalid den infiltrated by rats, but Neo-Nazis? Jesus! Then a deep, gnawing in my stomach told me it was time for food or drink – or something which would wipe out the need for either. I sat up and stumbled to my feet.

'Fuckin' hell, you're a bloody giant,' said the young guy, as my head grazed the beams of the floor above. I stooped to prop the mattress against a wall, and roll up my bedding purposefully. Since I'd flogged my guitar that sleeping bag was all I owned.

'Will ya watch my stuff while I go for a piss?' I spoke to the young guy, as he looked most amenable.

'Oiright mate.' He inhaled deeply and handed the spliff back to his mate.

Outside I took a leak in the scrub of the back garden, taking care to avoid heaps of turd which appeared more human than animal. Trains rattled on the track which ran overhead and a big magpie chattered noisily on the wall. This had once been a neat little 1950's home, with a pipe-smoking husband and a wife in a floral pinny. People who ate cottage pie for their tea. Like my parents.

I walked back into the doorless kitchen and through the little hallway. On the stairwell stood a tattooed bloke in camouflage trousers, who went by the name of Spanner. He maintained he was a squaddie on the run, supposed to be serving his second tour of duty in Belfast. But everyone here was full of shit.

343

'You seen those skinheads?' he said.

I jerked a head towards the stairs down to my basement lair.

He cleared his throat noisily and spat over the banister – a juicy gobbet, which landed behind me on what remained of the stained floorboards. 'I got a bone to pick with those two low-lifes,' he said.

I shrugged and went out into the grey morning.

I was getting used to people leaving a huge empty zone around me, even crossing the road sometimes. I was dishevelled, dirty and possibly a bit ripe-smelling. So when a stout, pink-faced punk bounded over he took me by surprise.

'Hey, Lugger! Been lookin' for you!' Six Verses seemed exceptionally pleased with himself. 'We've gorra gig at The Triangle, supporting Depth Charge.'

'What? That American metal band?' I was incredulous.

'Yeah. Mad, innit? Their support act got sent back by Customs, so they want someone pronto – don't care if it's metal as long as it's loud. We need yer as our roadie.'

'Tonight?' I said.

'Tomorrow, six o'clock. An' bring someone else, cos we ain't got long to set up and soundcheck.'

Soundcheck? Since when had Recknaw checked anything pre-gig, apart from their alcohol levels?

As he bounced off, Six Verses turned back. 'Don't be late will yer?' His brow was creased in consternation. 'There's forty quid between you an' yer mate.'

So Reknaw were getting their first big gig. They were tasting excitement, while all I could taste was bitter envy. Of course Recknaw wouldn't make the real big time. They were an old-style punk outfit, roaring out lyrics with vitriol and spittle, when the pop stars I saw on silent screens in TV shop windows, wore flouncy hair, mascara and lacy cuffs. The music scene was now full of wistful men, looking tragic in trench coats and swirling dry ice. Recknaw were out of sync, out of tune and out of sentiment. Besides that, they were crap. But what I envied was the hope welling up inside Six Verses' eyes. That tingling of potential – like it was all in front of them.

After the gig, Recknaw were jubilant. They had been booed, spat on and missiles were thrown. A full beer can was aimed at Piercing's head as he sang. He jumped up and head-butted it back into the crowd. The tin's edge left an angry welt on his forehead.

'They fuckin' loved us!' He thumped me on the back, as we passed. I nodded, keen to finish our get out before I was recognised by the technician, the Fozz had nicknamed, 'Ska-mad Steve'. I yanked my hat down and started shifting gear. 'You bring the drums offstage and I'll pack 'em,' I said to the young skinhead I'd brought along. I removed the cymbals and spun the nut back onto the stand to tighten it up. Even with a no-talent outfit like Recknaw, the idea of losing kit through carelessness annoyed me.

'Filch a couple of their cables!' Six Verses shouted in my ear, over the sound of classic Purple Viper, screaming through the PA. I stole a glance to Ska-mad Steve, as he set up for Depth Charge, and knew that I wouldn't.

Back at the squat I emptied two litres of cider down my throat, and washed down a handful of pills. Then I loosened the brick to extract a small bag of brownish powder and some rolling papers. The young skinhead was still out spending his fifteen quid, but I'd invested some of my cut in some quality smokable and besides, I was dog tired. The idea of sinking into a nice even high was compelling.

Sometime later I was dimly aware of an ache thumping in my side.

'Oi, you! Where's me mate, Boz?'

I slid away from the hard object that was punctuating these words like a boot, and saw an ugly skull right in my face, slitty eyes filled with general hatred. I had no idea what this meant.

'No fuckin' idea.' Sometimes I got a dodgy trip, but I decided it was best to answer back, even if the thing was hallucinatory.

'Word is, 'e went out with you.'

I forced my eyelids apart, despite the throbbing in my head, and attempted sustained visual contact. He was still there, his bony cheekbones illuminated by a white light, which stole through a vent to the street.

'Who the fuck are you?' My voice was slurred and I started to shiver. I was pissed off to be losing the good feeling that had taken me away from all this.

'Gob. An' I've recognised who you are, yer sorry bastard.'

His spittle spattered my cheeks, and I wiped it away with the back of my hand.

'Tom fuckin' Shepperton. Not so fuckin' clever now are yer?'

I struggled to sit up against the wall. He seemed sort of familiar, the Midlands accent, the clothes and he was definitely real. I remembered. Two skins had been down here before.

'Wherra all yer fuckin' nig-nog lovin' ska fans now?' he said.

'Your mate stayed at the Triangle.' I felt behind me for the knife I'd hidden in the gap between the bricks. It wasn't that sharp, but it was all I had.

Gob was squatting on his haunches, one bony knee splayed out to brace himself, looking at me with repulsion, like I was a mangy dog he'd just run down. He poked me in the chest. 'You bad-mouthed the Front, an' you've been on our list for years,' he said. 'We thought you musta left the country, with that other arse bandit.'

He pulled a flick knife out of his back pocket and weighed it in his hand thoughtfully. 'You shoulda done mate. You're beyond embarrassment now.'

My fingers touched cold metal. I gently pushed the steel towards the wall and the knife handle pivoted out silently. I was so high that his skull swirled in front of me, zooming in and out. I tried to concentrate, keeping my eyes on his face.

For ages I'd realised I couldn't go on living like this, but I'd had no idea how to clamber back on top. And now, somewhere inside me, was the cool, satin feeling of inevitability. It was clear. The only way out was obviously down, and I certainly wasn't going out alone.

'What are you fuckin' smiling about, yer cunt?' Gob's face hardened, and his mouth tightened like a cat's arse. The knobbled plastic of the knife was in my left hand. I grasped my knuckles around it. The white light illuminated his cheekbones – he looked skeletal, corpse-like. I started to laugh. So that was it. This *was* another hallucination. He didn't actually exist – none of this was real. There was only one way to get rid of Neo-fascist apparitions. You had to slice them to little pieces.

There was the heavy sound of several boots falling down the stairs.

'You attacked an old lady, yer bastard!' A voice like the squaddie's. The skeleton rose.

'She was a fuckin' Paki!'

The darkness was cluttered with silhouettes. Scuffling. The thumping of fists on muscle.

I was kicked several times, as I tried to stand up, falling again at each blow. Put my hands on the floor to get upright. I felt a hard object under my right palm. Grasped the flick knife. It fell out of my grasp. I stood and waivered, trying to focus in the dark. The room wheeled as I moved my head. Spanner and Gob were throwing punches at each other on the floor. A hand shot out and grabbed the knife from the floor front of me. I still grasped the other one in my left hand. Gob struggled free and leapt up, flicked out the blade, ready to cut the squaddie. I kicked his shin and he reeled. Fell into me. We both went down on the mattress. I plunged my knife into something, heard material rip and then sponginess. A sharp pain on my ear. Fucker had cut me. I rolled away then dug in again, and again, each time I was punched and punched. The room was swimming. I smelled bad breath, mouse droppings and dust, as I heard grunts, kicks, and finally a great sigh from someone.

Before I blacked out.

♫♪

White spot lights, blue lights flashing through the vent. Boots thumping everywhere.

'Jesus Christ!'

Not this again. For god's sake, why couldn't they let me sleep?

'Hey, mate!'

I was being called. Slapped awake. Hauled to my feet.

'Go'way, I'm alright. No fuckin' hospitals!' I shielded my eyes against the powerful glare of torches. Police radios buzzed. Arms dragged up my back. Someone reciting my right to remain silent, as if we were on a cop show. My wrists cuffed together in hard cold metal. Panic.

I looked down as the torchlight passed across me, and my shirt was stained maroon. My ear throbbed.

'Get him away.' The copper kneeling beside me stood up.

'Dead as a dodo,' he said. The skinhead lay on the floor, limbs bent awkwardly, a dark stain surrounding him, especially round the middle, where his Fred Perry had been cut several times.

'Looks like it was some time ago,' said the pig holding my cuffs. 'You want to tell us why you did it?'

I stared at the body, trying to remember anything at all.

'What day is it?'

The copper opposite gave a hollow laugh. 'Sunday,' he said.

'Just found this.' Another copper held up my bag of gear and a bit of resin in a foil wrap. And these –' He opened the tobacco tin I'd kept hidden, and revealed pills rolling round, like sweets. He shone a light in my eyes.

'Looks like you an' yer mate had a disagreement. Some argument over drugs?'

I struggled to remember. A white skull over me, stabbing a soft something, the fact the skinhead had beaten up an Asian grandmother. Though how did I know this? The memories merged with other bad trips.

'Pretty frenzied attack Serg. Look at the state of this mattress. We'll need to bag everything.'

A painful grip on my upper arm and I was shoved towards the stairs. 'Right, let's get this junkie out first. Was anyone else here?' He barked at me. The last thing I remembered clearly was the young skin taking his fifteen notes and waving them at me saying. 'I'm off to Canning Town! See yer tomorra.'

I looked down at the older skinhead. His side was slashed with a long cut, like someone had started gutting a fish, his mouth open and eyeballs fixed, lifeless. His opposite arm was twisted round as if he'd tried to defend himself, push me away, the pallid underside showing a thick, bluey-inked homemade swastika. A memory of holding a weapon flew across my mind like a moth.

'This your's sunshine?' The uniform who'd been snuffling round the basement walls held a knife up.

'Use this Pete,' grunted the other, brandishing a white cloth square from his top pocket. I recognised the kitchen knife and nodded, dumbly.

'An this one too?' he picked up another, long bladed, and studied it. 'Looks like army issue.'

'You'll go down a long time for this,' said the copper gripping my arm.

I shrugged. None of this was real.

On the stairs someone relayed instructions into a walkie talkie. As they led me out I looked back over my shoulder at the crumpled body on the floor. He looked like something discarded, his posture a reminder of old black and white wartime images of pale corpses tossed into vast holes with genocidic dispassion. But still, I felt as much pity for this neo-fascist thug, as he would have done for any of the blacks, Asians or gays him and his mates wanted to extinguish.

The real horror, uncurling like a dark snake in my head, was that it must have been me who killed him.

So what did that make me?

Part 2

1999

61

TOM

September 1999

I lit my last cigarette and rolled the small box across the top of my leg, flattening it with the heel of my hand. I'd been buying tens to cut down, but concern for my own mortality was still intermittent. It would be better if I had someone else to look after, but there was just me. Ah well. I pressed the intercom button to the studio.

'When you're ready lads. Sounding good.' It all sounded crap, but after three days with these musicless fuckwits, I'd lost the will to care.

The youths on the other side of the glass stopped arguing for five seconds, and turned sullen eyes at me – enough time to register that I was still there, sitting behind three huge consoles and flanked by two racked towers of red and green winking digital units. Then they returned to their heated, air-poking shouting match. Thankfully, they'd stopped arguing about the verse which spoke of being 'bang up inda clink', as clearly the worst place they'd ever been incarcerated was their stinky bedrooms. Now the debate was based around whether the third line of the rap was, 'I knife him in da back cos he a big pussy,' or 'I knife him in da bathroom cos he done my pussy.' Three lads, aged about 19, one white and two black, were arguing about the correct narrative rationale for stabbing a man, with casual reference to a female only by her sexual parts. And me? I was waiting patiently to give their backing tape the perfect mix, so they could stomp around stage in heavy chains and baseball caps, rapping this sermon to clubs full of young, gang culture wannabes. I'd heard some decent rap, of course – but this wasn't it. When did I sell out so completely? I dragged on my cigarette, looking ruefully at the flat empty pack, and ruminated on the history of spoken voice in music.

The perfect mental picture of Len seeped into my head, with a deep pain which coursed through me like a shot – tall and proud in his sharp dogtooth jacket and white shirt, pork pie hat pulled over sweat-beaded ebony brow, long lean legs bouncing across the stage. I imagined those vocals, rich and throaty, with his toaster's indignant, fast 'reasoning' – choice words and dry Jamaican humour, delivered with equal measures of wit and fury. Despite his bluster, Len was anti-violence, though Christ knows he'd defended himself if pushed. It was one opinion which had united the band, despite the spats between Eddy and Vinnie. For chrissakes, I'd never seen a stabbing until that big skinhead stuck a knife in Alan, in that dark tunnel behind The Weasal, back when the idiot was still calling himself Adolf. Which was, of course, in fact, the very last I saw Josie. Before the band got big and I pissed everyone off then blew it all away by being a brainless, drug-fuelled dickhead.

I was breathing too fast and my head had started throbbing. Enough self loathing now, enough. I stopped the memory reel. No reason for going back on all that. You can't change the past.

The mixed race lad with the droopy jeans and the bumfluff on his chin seemed to have won the row. He banged one fist on a speaker, hitching his denims up a centimetre with his other. If his pants fell down they'd be four daft pricks hanging out in that studio. I poked the mic button again, 'All sorted then?'

'It's my fuckin' rap bro, it's gotta be jus' right!'

I recalled Six Verses' face wearing the same childish scowl, and stifled a smile.

'Okay, let's record the vocals now,' I said brightly, and pressed 'record', confident that the sudden glow of red light on their side would set them off.

Sure enough, as the backing intro started, they all struck positions.

In the reflection of the glass pane, I noticed the door behind me opening cautiously and a pink head framed by brown dreadlocks emerged, wearing a questioning expression. I beckoned him in. Alan came alongside wearing combat trousers and a purple T-shirt, and bearing the aroma of fresh coffee. I gave a groan of approval.

'Rick sent me to check you're treatin' them right, an' remind you that they're paying good money.' He plonked two mugs down on the small ledge in front of the mixing desk, and sat on a high stool beside me.

'That makes everything hunky-dorey then.' I grimaced at his cup which held a greenish liquid and smelled like brewed grass, then mine up to eye level, admiring the old Coventry FC logo. 'Seems to be an endless supply of these. Where the hell does he get them?'

'Bought a load offa some dodgy geezer in the 80's and never got round to selling 'em on. When we cleared the old Coventry studio we brought four boxes down to London.'

I rolled my eyeballs. 'That's typical of Rick.'

Alan scraped his locks back and shook his head. 'Hey, not fair man. Without Rick neither of us would even be here.'

I swallowed a small involuntary gulp of guilt with my coffee. 'Yeah, yeah, I know.'

'You oughta stop bein' an ungrateful bastard, Tom.' His voice was factual.

He was right. I had everything to be thankful for, since Rick appeared seven years ago on a HMS visit, like some hairy fairy godmother, with big plans and that casual wave, granting me a future I'd not dared to hope for. But I couldn't shake off the stuff that still went on in my head – the loss of years, people, the chance at love.

Behind the glass we slurped our brews and watched the three rappers pace the floor, mouths spewing silent obscenities, faces contorted, each clenching his microphone like a cosh.

'You not even gonna listen?' Alan eyed me with a dubious expression. I tried to remember what he'd looked like as a kid with a shorn head, but it was far too long ago, literally a life sentence. It seemed he'd always had matted ropes of hair, eeling down the back of the Purple Viper T-shirt he wore in perpetual, if somewhat ironic, tribute to Rick. I vaguely recalled braces and a Buddha-like belly, which he said had disappeared when his missus put him on a macrobiotic diet, in the early 90's. Pity he was such a health zealot, or I'd have asked him to pop out for more fags. I lobbed the scrunched up packet across the room, to bounce off the wall and into the bin.

The three rappers came to a triumphant finish. One punched the air and held position for an imaginary camera, the other held his mic like a candle in prayer and the third hung his head like a weight, no doubt bereft of all further solutions, now everyone in the song had been annihilated.

'Great! Shall we hear it?' I pushed playback and sat back nodding into the silence on our side, miming a producer who's finally heard the real thing.

Alan left, tutting, and I swung round to address his retreating back. 'What? Don't take the bloody high ground with me kiddo. Before you lived on green cheese and yurt droppings, you were no fuckin' saint yerself.'

Slowly and with great elegance he gave me the finger. His mouth twisted into an insolent grin and I suddenly got a glimpse of that curious young skinhead – desperate for someone to look up to and a path to follow. How bizarre that it was Rick who'd provided the guiding hand.

'I was sixteen and didn't know no better,' Alan quipped. 'What's your excuse now – bein' an old git of, what, 42?'

I gave a sharp intake of breath and clasped my chest. 'Woah! With fast cuts like that, I coulda used you in prison.'

But as the door shut I wondered if he was right. Maybe I should try to shed my cynicism, find some way to be happier, less bitter, forget the years of incarceration. Because Alan was wrong about my age – I'd just turned 44 and I wasn't getting any younger.

♪

It was fifteen years since I was taken down, but I recalled those first terrifying days, like it was yesterday – especially the panic and fear as my last hit withdrew in slow apology, like a reluctant bride. For days, I'd lain in my own piss on the bare, rough bed, each cell in my body screaming and exploding, too weak to move, too toxic to sleep. Every time blackness slipped over me, I was jolted back to semi-consciousness by white hot-cold pain, as thin piano wire was pulled through my bones, and my gullet rose, writhing upwards.

Fighting spasms in my legs, arms, neck, I lurched sideways and hung over the side of the bed, coughing and choking. Disgorging acid and warm slime, to trickle down my chin. I lay back gasping, stomach bruised, and then my skin was alive, wriggling with a million tiny, needling, ants crawling in and out of every pore. I heard disjointed voices and phrases, 'poor bastard,' 'won't make it,' 'hospital wing'. I screamed and yowled and whimpered, not expecting rescue and too busy retching and shivering to care. There was nobody else in my dark hell. I was dying, and it served me right.

I just hoped it was quick.

Then I'd turned over and my cheek touched a cold pillow. Through bloated eyelids I made out my magnolia-coloured cell was now white. With a brain heavy as cement, I tried to turn over a thought. It didn't smell right for heaven or hell, it smelled of...

'Tomato soup for bed nine?' A chirpy London accent.

'Not yet. I'll see how he's getting on.' A reply.

'Righto.' Chirpy's feet pattered into the distance, accompanied by some squeaky-wheeled
thing. Rustling cloth and footsteps came to my side. A big, dry hand lifted the wrist at the end of my outstretched arm.

'Alright sunshine, back with us? You certainly took a beating, in more ways than one.'

Old fella. Stout, fifties, greying hair, uniform of white cotton pants and tunic. Not a screw. He was frowning at the face of a lapel watch, held between his thumb and forefinger. With a grim smile he placed my hand gently on the blanket.

'You're a lucky sod, coming through clucking like that. Must have guts of iron. Thirsty?'

I'd nodded and my brain sloshed heavily in my skull. My tongue, swollen and crusty against the cave of my mouth, grazed across teeth like slimy gravel. I rolled onto an elbow and tried to push up with a grunt, but my backbone had turned to rubber.

'Take it easy lad. You'll need help.'

He shoved a thick arm under me to yank my body up with ease, plumping pillows with the other hand. When he leaned over, my eyes faced the V of his tunic, which revealed pink skin and greying chest hairs. As he adjusted pillows, I was held in an intimate zone of warm body smells and a piney aftershave. I yanked my head sideways and poking from his short sleeve was a bluey-black tattoo, showing a woman's ankle and high heel shoe.

I lay back, overwhelmed by so much life.

'There you go son.' He was gone, leaving me seized by panic, but he returned, carrying a plastic beaker of water. I tried to take the drink, but my arm muscles shook so violently I dropped my hand back on the sheet where it lay, a weird object – dark red, knotted with veins, fingers curled up and scabbed, nails black with filth. He scraped a chair towards me and held the cup to my mouth. As he tilted, I concentrated on sucking. The cool sweet liquid washed over my foul tongue and gritty teeth. In all those years of heavy drinking, nothing had tasted so good. When I'd taken as much as I could, I let my head flop back on the pillow, glad to be relieved of its weight.

So I'd survived. And for a fleeting second I wondered – what now?

The male nurse watched me with steady eyes. 'You'll be alright lad. Take it step by step, and you'll be putting in an app to phone your bird by the end of next week.'

♫

And here I was fifteen years on – back out and gainfully employed.

When the three rappers left, clutching their demo, Rick opened the sound booth door. His hair was a bit shorter nowadays and his jeans bordered on being fashionable, but he was the same basic model souped up – as always, at least a decade behind.

'Coming to the pub, Tom?'

I considered this idea carefully, as I always did now.

'Alright. Just one – taken in the form of two halves.'

'Righto.' Rick shrugged. He'd never let anything – chemical or emotional – grapple with his essential Rick-ness, and he couldn't ever understand the pull and push involved.

'There's somethin' I want to talk about.' He gave a series of mysterious nods then walked out, rubbing his chin.

I turned off all the power, contemplating what could be up. He probably wanted me to agree to a bit of kit he was thinking of investing in – some shiny digital thing he'd spotted in one of the technical mags. The industry was chucking out new stuff all the time, and Rick was right on it – soaking in the reviews, where big hairy techies gave other hairy techies the benefit of their wisdom. He knew names, numbers, pros and cons, for each gismo. I was more sceptical. A lot of it seemed just another way to separate you from your money. It was amazing that kids could make decent quality demos in their bedrooms now – giving them chance to play round with sound, before they rocked up for a professional studio session. But it was only useful if the actual music was better. Without good songs, who cared?

♪

'No fuckin' way man, I'm not doing it!' Other drinkers turned to stare. It was a quiet Tuesday evening in the Dick Turpin, and inappropriate for yelling matches, but I didn't care.

'It's a decent wedge, Tom. Plus expenses.' Rick tick-tocked his head, as if weighing up the money to hassle ratio. 'Plus the publicity will ramp up sales, for when we re-release all the old stuff throughout the year, of course.'

Of course! There was no, 'of course'. I felt so betrayed, I couldn't think.

'I'm goin' for a piss!' My barstool thumped onto the carpet, as I stumbled over to the gents.

At the urinal, vitriol gushed out of me as fast as I peed. *Original Mix re-union gig?* No fucking way! He'd never get me to face the band again. The shame would do me in.

Rick and I had edged round the whole subject of Original Mix, since he'd found me languishing in Her Majesty's B&B. Of course, he knew what everyone had been up to since we split, but I'd made it plain I didn't want to hear anything about the band again. We could restart our business partnership, on the condition we left the past behind – that's what he agreed to, and how I wanted it kept.

But now he wanted to smash the whole thing up, for some bloody stupid Original Mix twentieth anniversary gig, in the year 2000. I just couldn't understand it.

'Yo, Josie!'

As I approached the gateway to Steve Biko House, a familiar lanky figure in an orange knitted hat careened down from the main door. Huge feet clattered on each stone step and long denim-clad legs tensed for just an instant, as he slapped a palm on the brick side wall. When he propelled himself upwards, my ribcage lifted in parallel suspense, air caught hard in my lungs. Then he sprung down on the other side, as easily as a cougar.

I breathed once again. 'I really wish you wouldn't do that Jamie.'

He frowned in puzzlement. 'Why?'

'Because you might misjudge and knock your teeth out.'

He grinned and kissed the top of my head. 'Nah, that won't happen.'

It was true. His PE teacher had practically pleaded with me not to let him drop Athletics Club for extra music lessons. 'It's not my call,' I'd said, secretly pleased my son was becoming more involved in the arts. 'It's Jamie's decision how he spends his time.'

'Where you off to?' I asked.

'Band rehearsals. Back late.'

'You're still doing the Millennium night gig for us, right?'

'Course! It's why we're practising so hard.'

I smiled. How had I given birth to such a clever, handsome young man?

'You *so* need to cut that out.' Jamie gave a mock frown, and wagged a finger.

'What?'

'The proud mum face. You *cannot* do that at the gig. It's *so* uncool.'

I grinned. 'Want me to leave you some dinner?' He was a capable cook though nowadays this wasn't his priority, so I tried to make him eat well, at least some of the time.

'Nah, we'll get pizza. Why don't you invite Simon?'

'He's back?'

But he was already sprinting away. 'Message on the machine!' He shouted over his shoulder. I watched him swerve round a stout Indian woman carrying multiple shopping bags. She said something and he rotated to reply, still running backwards, then turned full circle and took three long leaps before speeding up to full pelt. I held the gate open and waited.

'That son of yours is a streak of wind.'

'Hi Mrs Rasheed.' I unlocked our communal front door. 'Sorry if Jamie's band disturbed you last Saturday.'

She smiled. 'Oh no, dear. We were at my cousin's son's wedding.'

We entered the hallway where a regiment of buggies and bicycles lined the walls of our housing association block. It was eighteen years since I'd stood there fretting about which to take up first – my baby or the shopping – deciding if abandoning him in the flat was riskier than leaving him in the pram. I remembered the first panicky time, running down five flights to grab the groceries, and the moment of pure, untangled relief when I'd found him still there – lying on the carpet, safely gurgling and blowing bubbles.

'How's Mr R?'

Mrs Rasheed gave a grimace. 'Same, same. He misses his sweeties. The wedding food was beautiful but he had to resist all his favourites. Hard to change at our age.'

I pulled a sympathetic face, as I recalled. 'Ah, yes. He's on his diabetic diet now.'

Mrs Rasheed glanced at their door and leaned in conspiratorially. 'On the good side he's lost so much weight, he can fit into his old suits.' She squeezed my forearm and pulled me in, making a mischievous face. 'It's made him feel like a younger man again, Josie – if you know what I mean.'

She giggled.

'Oo er!' I blushed at this intimate detail, though it was heartening to hear that passion could be rekindled in an old marriage. My own life was resolutely loveless, despite odd flings and a few disastrous set ups by friends. Alone, I'd have attempted more relationships, but with Jamie's trusting little heart involved, there'd been too much at stake. And now I wouldn't know where to begin.

Inside the flat, the message machine winked. I dropped my bags and dialled immediately. 'Simon! You have *got* to take me out. I've had total cabin fever with you and Franki both away.'

'Yes, Greece was beautiful and my tan is fantastic. Thanks for asking.'

'Sorry. Was it lovely? Did you or Brian roger the cabin boy?'

A long sigh came down the phone receiver. 'The cruise was blissful, But alas, the crew were unanimously rugged and hirsuit – and not in a good way.'

'You'll have to tell all. Hey, let's go to the South Bank! I think there's a Humphrey Bogart season.' I shuffled the pile of flyers for gigs, plays and festivals on the sideboard. 'Here it is, BFI. Oh YES!'

'African Queen?' Simon's voice was full of hope. 'Had to buy another panama, because the old one blew overboard.'

'Yes, wear your new hat. Can we sit by the river and watch the skateboarders too?'

'You're incorrigible.'

I chuckled. 'It's good to watch other people's sons chucking themselves round like rubber balls. Then I don't feel so bad about Jamie doing it.'

Simon laughed too. 'Ah, the ruthlessness of parents. How is my godless son?'

'Looks more like you every day.'

'Ha, ha. Now tell me Miss Hepburn.' His voice was serious. 'What are *you* going to wear?'

As I dug out Capri pants and a white blouse, I wondered if I was a clingy parent. Of course, there'd been many wrenches – first day at primary, the anxiety of a school trip to Belgium, an impromptu week with Mr and Mrs Rasheed when I was rushed to hospital with appendicitis. But we had weathered them, and Jamie was still here – aged eighteen, large as life and twice as hungry. And, as years passed, the feeling that someone would surely come and remove him from me had decreased.

Jamie was right. He took physical risks, but I needed to remind myself, these were calculated. So the danger years were surely over?

63

TOM

'Whaddya say then, mate? Will you do it?'

Rick's face was animated, as we sat in the studio kitchen taking a break. I peered over my coffee, studying him, wondering how the years had been so kind – a young-faced Rock van Winkle, wearing the surprised air of waking up to find out its no longer 1977.

After my incandescent fury in the pub, he'd been busy with planning the studio refit and I'd retreated into the job of producing music. It was my way of percolating the monstrous idea of reuniting Original Mix. My current 'project' was a young band who regularly hired the smallest rehearsal room. There were a basic three piece outfit – drums, bass and guitarist/singer – fairly raw and unpolished, and still undecided on a band name. I was fascinated by their teamwork and the easy negotiation which took place in making decisions. And when they jammed around, til something brilliant came out of the mayhem, it made my heart ache for the old days sitting round with Vinnie, Len or Eddy, doing just the same.

Their bassist was a shy black lad called Zinad and drummer was Askim, a cheeky kid from a Turkish family, who had an irreverent sense of humour. They were solid players, still learning and crafting their skills. But the real spark of talent was the singer Jamie, a lanky boy who always wore a bright orange beanie, pulled down on his forehead. I had started to offer last minute recording slots when we had a cancellation, so they could hear themselves from a distance, consider what to keep and what to shelve. And now the pressure was on, as they were rehearsing for a big New Year's Eve gig at their local arts centre. They'd be seeing in the year 2000, and a new Millennium – an event which was being screwed to fever pitch in the media. Predictions ranged from global computer failure – which would cause planes to drop from the skies and nuclear attacks to go off – to a catastrophic and mystical end of the world.

My concerns were far more close to home.

'Look, I'm considering it, Rick.' An icy cold expanded across my chest whenever I contemplated meeting members of Original Mix.

'Great! I'll make some calls.'

I jumped up, slopping coffee across the pine floor we'd so carefully laid.

'No calls Rick! I'll think about it. That's all.'

'Yeah, I know mate.' His expectant face wore its familiar waggy-tail look, like a puppy whose worked out what W.A.L.K. means. Except that in no language did T.H.I.N.K spell 'yes'.

The trouble was, you couldn't fault Rick for maintaining 100% optimism and he usually knew what worked. When he'd moved to London with Alan in tow, they'd started small – just basic rehearsals rooms. While this was bringing in money, he designed a different outfit, having sussed out that 90's musos weren't impressed by the grime and mould of the old places. The new unit was all espresso machines, digital kit, and bottles of macadamia nut hand cream in the bogs – whatever the hell that was. We'd talked through the plans on his prison visits, and he persuaded me things had changed a lot while I was inside.

And he was right. I came out to find it wasn't just fashions, technology and pace of life. Attitudes had altered. Blokes related to each other differently, especially the younger ones – like Jamie's band. When they'd first visited us, to check the facilities and talk through payment options, Alan and I had stood at the door watching them walk off down the road. Jamie was talking in earnest to Zinad, who was worried about costs. He'd rested his hand on Zinad's back and kept it there as they walked along, giving him a few extra pats of encouragement.

'You'd get shafted if you touched a bloke like that inside,' I'd mused out loud.

Alan looked at me with disapproval. 'In what way?'

'Either way – or both. Point is, you wouldn't even fuckin' try it.'

In the silence I pondered, yet again, on just how a former National Front supporting skinhead, known as Adolf, came to show me new studio gear, demonstrate using a magic money machine in the wall, help me open an email account – and was now asking what prison was like.

'Tom?' Alan broke the moment. His tone was apologetic.

'What?' I frowned.

'Look, don't take this the wrong way, but you might think about swearing less, man.'

I stared at him. 'You're kidding?'

'It's just not that cool. It sounds kinda aggressive.'

'Fuck off!'

Alan grinned. 'Up to you man. But some of the bands don't seem to like it.'

I leant over and gave him a sarcastic rub on the back and a pat. 'There, there sunshine. We wouldn't want to offend bloody musicians would we?' I retreated down the corridor chuckling.

But gradually, I realised that he wasn't joking. Bands like Jamie's often spoke about how they 'felt' and punctuated their sessions by asking if each other was okay – and, at first, I'd thought they were just taking the piss. After ten years of endless harsh and violent interactions in prison, it was hard to adjust. But gradually I started to realise that young men nowadays were simply better at communicating than we'd been. Things had indeed changed. You didn't even need a new century to begin.

'How's it going lads?' I popped my head into the small rehearsal room where Jamie's band was playing.

'Hi TJ!' they chorused. To continue flying under the radar, I now went by my first two initials – Thomas James – and even Alan and Rick adopted this, when we were in company.

'Got a name yet? Or a new guitarist?' I asked the lads.

They'd been auditioning for rhythm guitar, to beef up their sound, and I'd just seen the last one leave.

Askim shook his head. 'Proper idiot. Couldn't keep time and didn't know half the chords.'

Jamie was sitting on a chair sucking a carton of drink through a straw. Gurgling sounds emitted from the empty box, so he scrunched it up and aimed for the litter bin, where it landed right on target.

'Shot!' I said.

He smiled. 'Used to play basketball. Gave it up for music.'

'Great that it wasn't wasted though,' I laughed. 'What you going to do for a guitarist?'

Zinad raised his eyebrows at Jamie. 'Go on, ask,' he urged.

'Ask me what?' I stepped into the room.

Jamie rubbed a hand under the knitted hat he'd never removed, whatever the ambient temperature. 'Thing is TJ, you know we've got a major gig on New Year's Eve.'

'You had mentioned it,' I said with a grin. They'd talked of nothing else.

'And we're doing three hour-long sets – our own stuff, plus loads of covers from the 60's onwards.'

'Makes sense.'

'The party's at The Arts Hub, the centre Jamie's mum runs.' Askim interrupted, cutting to the chase. 'And she's asked for a whole 80's ska section, with all the classics – Up Tempo, Detonator, Original Mix.'

'Oh?' I gave a chuffed smile. They wanted me to help them choose songs, and I imagined what a laugh it would be to hear them play the old back catalogue.

'So we need another guitarist,' chimed in Zinad. 'But everyone we've tried is crap.'

'Now we're running out of rehearsal time,' said Jamie. 'And we wondered….'

'Especially as you know that era…' Askim butted in.

Zinad said, 'We understand you'll probably say no, but we thought we'd try anyway…'

'What?' I said, smiling. 'Just ask.'

Jamie took a breath. 'Will you play in our band, just for the night?'

Shit! I hadn't seen that coming. I started to chuckle. 'You're kidding?'

Jamie turned to the other two. 'Told you it's a non-starter. We need to place more ads.'

'No!' They all looked startled. 'I mean, yes! I'd be happy to join your band, for a night.' I shrugged. 'Could be a laugh.'

'Wow!'

'That's great!'

'Aren't you going to a Millennium party?' asked Jamie.

I looked at his eager face. What would he say if I told him Original Mix was the band I'd loved and developed, with the same passion as he had for his?

'I'll blow out my other plans,' I said, though there were none. 'On one condition.'

'What?' they chorused.

'You settle on a bloody name!'

♪

And so we rehearsed. I taught them all the old stuff – and played them the 60's ska originals, so they could give the original songs their own twist, like we had. And we rehearsed other covers of course – rock 'n' roll, R&B, bluebeat, Northern soul, Motown, reggae, punk, funk and disco – along with their own stuff, which wasn't too shabby either.

'You're getting very snug with Jamie's lot,' Rick said, a few weeks later, as we hauled out the mixing desk, to eliminate the dust which was threatening to sneak in and foul up the electrics.

'Nice to play with a band again, that's all,' I said, then sensing another onslaught, I clicked on the Hoover to drown him out.

'You could be playing with the original Originals, Tom – instead of the replicas!' He shouted, over the drone of the cleaner.

'Rick, will you leave it out? I'm just enjoying myself. No other kids would ever ask an old git like me to play. And it's just one night!' I yelled, poking the hose under the desk.

'I'm just saying. It's a small opportunity,' he shouted behind me. 'When you could have a much bigger one!' He was relentless.

I threw the nozzle down and kicked the machine off. 'Right, that's it, I'm going upstairs. Finish this job yerself. I'm sick of your nagging.' I walked to the door. 'Original Mix is ancient history, Rick. Why can't you leave it there?'

After I saw Rick going home to his missus, I came back down from my flat, armed with several bulging A4 pads containing the lyrics to all my own songs. I sat down to consider them.

First there was the early furious stuff, mainly about drugs and street violence, which I'd written in solitary, bribing a screw for a red pen, and scrawling in the margins of my Gideon's bible. The Chaplain had spotted this on his mandatory visit, and was so horrified that he promised to help, if I'd stop defacing God's history book. I kept my word and he did too. So when I'd done my time in the block, he obtained chord sheets. He'd never turned me into a God-botherer, but writing music helped me believe in myself again. And, as I explained when I was released, that was a major sort of miracle.

Then there was the sad stuff, which I'd written in the next few years – love songs, ballads, mainly acoustic numbers. Some of these were awful, soul-searching, self-pitying mantras which I kept just to remind myself of how bad it was, places I'd never go again. I'd also composed a lot of jazz-ska-punk-rock-blues-Latin-bluegrass-indie crossover music, when they let me on the educational scheme and got my hands on a guitar again. The only possible upside of being in prison was that nobody tied you to a musical style, told you it wouldn't work, or that it had all been tried before. Inside, nobody gave a shit – about me or my music. A strange kind of liberation indeed.

Down in the studio, I now played some of the more experimental stuff, just to get my fingers going. There was sometimes a stiffness in them which I could never admit, not even to myself. Then I wellied through the old Original Mix play list, which I'd been getting up to speed – though I hadn't let on to Rick. I ended with a sad series of songs I'd written about Josie, when I'd finally admitted to myself I'd never set eyes on her again. The lyrics were both tender and truthful. They were the words I'd tried to put in that letter which didn't reach her, things I'd never managed to say to her face, and stuff about myself I'd have told her if we'd ever met again. Writing these songs, in the middle years of my incarceration, had made me accept my total losses – the band, Josie, my dad – and admit to my own stupidity. And nowadays, singing the words was strangely comforting, as though it put all that squarely behind me.

After midnight I stopped, as there was a busy day ahead. An upcoming female trio to record, then an evening rehearsal with Jamie's 'band with no name'. The thought made me smile. I was having such a good time with those three youngsters – enjoying their easy humour and keenness to learn. They didn't treat me like an old has-been. I was just the producer-engineering guy from the studios, who plays guitar. And that was fine by me. After the gig I'd miss being part of a band, but I was already hatching plans for producing their first album – an idea which I'd mentioned to them casually the other day.

'I don't know if we're ready,' Jamie had said, face creased in consternation.

'No-one's never ready,' I said. 'Just write a load of songs you like and record them – that's all there is to it.'

He'd looked at me uncertainly. 'I'll see if my mum can lend me the money,' he said.

I imagined some mother in a floral dress with soft permed hair, like my own when I was eighteen. Then I realised she'd be about my age, plus she ran the local arts centre – so she was probably a skint old hippy, who wore layers of shapeless tie-dye, purple tights and smelt of Patchouli oil.

I said, 'We'll use the dead time, so it's free. The thing is to seize every chance while you're full of youthful creativity. You'll learn more with a mixture of recording and live gigs.'

'We really appreciate all this,' said Jamie. The other two nodded with vigour. 'You could help any band. But you chose us and we're totally grateful.'

Definitely raised by a polite, tree-hugging hippy – probably a mumsy version of Alan's New Age girlfriend, Skylark.

'No problem lads. Just keep on striving.'

What I didn't say was nobody else at Paradise Studios had such raw talent as Jamie. His lyrics were mature and eloquent for someone so young, and his playing and singing style were spine-tinglingly good, and getting better. Even Rick was impressed. The band was a solid little unit with great potential. And for the first time in many years, it felt okay to have a powerful surge of ambition rising up inside me.

♪♫

64
TOM

New Year's Eve, 1999

'Jamie, listen mate. I've got a real problem.'

'You're not pulling out?' There was panic in his normally easygoing voice. I swapped the wrench to my other hand, trying to balance the phone under my chin. Not an easy feat when you're lying on your back on a wet floor.

'No, no, but I'm gonna be late. A pipe in my bathroom's sprung a massive leak.'

'Shit! You'll never get a plumber on New Year's Eve!'

I emitted a cynical laugh, and banged my head on the underside of the bath. 'Ow! Shittin' hell! That's alright, I can fix it myself. But I need to be sure it's watertight or it'll flood down into the studio.'

Water was seeping through the joint and down my arm. The floor was soaking and we were supposed to be there for six. Thank god I hadn't changed into my suit.

'Christ, it's still pissing out,' I continued. 'Look, get Alan to swing by for my guitar on the way over. You'll have to soundcheck without me.' I sighed. 'Sorry mate. I'll be there soon as. Promise.'

I rang off and fumbled with the phone, dropping it in the puddle. I was getting angry. Of all the nights for a plumbing crisis. Rick and Isabella were in Barcelona seeing in the new Millenium Spanish-style, and Alan had never mastered the skills, as Rick dropped the plumbing side of his 'Paradise' empire when they left Coventry. Not surprising. It was coming back to me why I didn't want to do this on a regular basis. It got you dirty, furious and knuckle grazed. Though in my life, that could also be said for music.

♪

I arrived at The Arts Hub to find people crowded at the entrance, showing tickets. I pushed gently through, and presented myself to the young woman at the door, grinning idiotically.

'I'm with the band.'

'Really?' She looked doubtful.

'Jamie's band.' I realised I didn't know his surname, so I pointed to the banner over the door. 'I'm playing with The Beat Runners.'

She frowned. 'You're pretty late,' she said. 'They're about to start.'

'All the more reason to let me in.' I held out my hands imploringly.

'It's true.' I turned. One of the girls from the three piece was queuing with her boyfriend.

'Hey, Paulette!'

'Hi TJ,' she smiled. 'Can't wait to hear you play.'

The girl nodded me in and I followed the sound of music and flow of people, past a cloakroom staffed by two young people who appeared to be punks, and through two big swing doors. The hall was a basic 'black box' venue, decked out with swags of glittery cloth, coloured lights, and strings of silver and gold helium balloons tied to stage weights. From the ceiling a small rig boasted a series of coloured lamps, and a vast mirrorball showered the whole room with glittery dots of light. Across the bottom of the stage a big banner announced, *'Welcome to 2000 - Happy New Millenium!!'* At cabaret tables, candles flickered inside coloured jars and food was being served by a fleet of kids, who were dressed like punks too. In fact, as I squeezed down the side of the hall, I saw everyone was in fancy dress. There was everything from flared catsuits, mini skirts, safety-pinned T-shirts and pretend Mohicans, to frilly cuffs, mullet wigs and big puffy skirts. I knew it was a retro night, but I hadn't thought beyond our stage gear and the music.

I nudged past a couple of women in their forties, wearing sequinned conical bras over T-shirts, who were striking lewd poses and taking photos, cackling like loons. Beside them, two teenage girls rolled their eyes, not realising the weird parody of punk they presented, with their spiky hair, black lips and bin liner tops. They pointed at some lad in a silver wig, who waved, and both shrieked with laughter. Everyone was in such high spirits it was infectious.

'Great suit and hat!' the DJ shouted. He was a dapper guy in his fifties, wearing a leather cap, with turned up jeans, braces and a Fred Perry T-shirt. 'Kinda 80's rude boy style. Were d'ya get 'em?' He gave me an appraising look.

'Back of me 80's rude boy wardrobe,' I quipped.

'Me too!' he laughed and we bumped knuckles.

It was shaping up to be a fun night.

At stage front, Alan was crouched by the wedges, taping down leads with gaffer. Seeing me he jabbed a finger to a black curtain at the side. I parted the material, unprepared for the way my senses were dragged back by sudden darkness, the rubbery smell of electric cables with that top note of burnt dust, a light dimmed by blue gel, and the glowing green of the obligatory Fire Exit sign. I took a couple of deep breaths to recover. It was over fifteen years since I'd been backstage.

'Tom! Thank god you made it, man.' Askim's usually cheery face appeared anxious and ghoulish in the coloured lights. 'Jamie's lost the set lists. He's in total melt down.'

I entered the dressing room pulling a sheaf of papers from my jacket.

'Hey, kids! Need these?'

'Thank god!'

Backslaps from Askim and palpable relief from Jamie. 'Dunno what happened. They were in my guitar case,' he said in disbelief.

'Always carry spares.' I raised an eyebrow. 'All part of gigging organisation.'

Alan popped his head in. 'All ready?' He grinned at me. 'You're gonna be so awesome, man.'

I stuck my hat firmly on my head, tipped the brim down over my face and, as the DJ introduced us, I let the lads bounce onto stage to the sound of cheers, foot stomping and whistles. Then I slid in behind them, trying not to feel the pull back across the years.

New gig, new millenium, new me.

Jamie turned round quickly to look at the rest of us. His chest was pumping like a trapped bird's. I gave him an authoritative nod. Three clicks of Askim's drumsticks and we were off, straight into the first of the dance numbers I'd arranged for a guitar band – a northern soul classic. Its fast on-beat rhythms weren't the most thrilling to my mind, but at the fourth chord, there were squeals of delight and recognition. People swarmed onto the dance floor in front of the stage, keen to get this party started. They were laughing and all seemed to know each other – a great atmosphere for seeing in the New Year. The small rush of excitement inside me was almost like hope.

After a few songs Jamie and the lads relaxed, and we started our funk section. Jamie's tense shoulders dropped, making his playing freer and taking the strain out of his voice. Askim added in some fancy flourishes on the high hat and Zinad was thwanging those deep bass strings like it was '75, in a New York club. He was, in fact, sporting an afro, 12 inch yellow flares and a fringed waistcoat – as once he'd been inspired by those old album covers, there'd been no stopping him.

To stop the harsh spotlights burning my eyes, I stepped into the shadow of the speaker stack. And I began to make out the rest of the venue. Kids dashed round in PVC trousers and fluorescent tutus, serving platters of fried chicken, baskets of breads, salads – some wheeling round on roller skates. Anyone not dancing was eating, pouring wine, or picking their way back from the bar, laden with pints of beer. It was weird to see so many people in retro dress. Nostalgia for my youth welled up in me, especially when we played a late 70's power ballad. Jamie's voice soared out, strong and sweet at the highs and manly on the deeper registers. He'd overcome all nerves now, and was enjoying himself, throwing impromptu changes into his carefully-practised guitar solos. I was impressed. To my right, Askim was giving the drums a good workout. He grinned down at me. His parents were on a table with Zinad's, and the anxious expressions I'd seen, when Askim pointed them out from stageside, were gone. Askim's mother was tapping her fingers on the table, and Zinad's dad was leading his mum towards the dance floor.

We finished our first set, to a groan of disappointment. It was nine o'clock and there were two more to go. In the dressing room I called a band pow-wow.

'It's going great!' I said. 'Keep up the momentum.'

'They really like us!' Zinad's eyes shone. The funky outfit seemed to be giving him courage.

'Make sure you two stay solid.' I said to Zinad and Askim. 'It's hard not to speed up, everyone does it.'

Askim nodded.

'Especially in the ska numbers.' My excitement was growing at the thought of playing Original Mix songs again.

We kicked off the second set with some Motown, a couple of crowd pleasers, which showed off Jamie's ability to hit high alto notes. Then we took it right down with some slow reggae and the dance floor cleared a bit, as people seized the opportunity to renew drinks and catch their breaths. It meant the lads could sit in the groove for a while. I checked Zinad's face as he chunked out the bass line. His shyness had fallen away and he smiled at a pretty girl with long, coffee-coloured legs and corkscrew hair, who was dancing near the stage. When he glanced over, to check we were in sync, I raised an eyebrow at him and smirked. He shrugged back, like he didn't understand, but I saw him watching her dance again. It was all ahead for him, for them all – young love, music, discovery. I felt almost paternal.

Out in the hall, tables were being cleared of plates and platters by the teens in punk dress. They seemed well organised for such youngsters. A woman beckoned one pale young lad wearing chains and a ripped black T-shirt printed with, *'Do Not Resusitate'*. She pulled him in to quiz him about something and he responded with a shy admission. As he departed with an armful of crockery, she gave him an encouraging pat on the arm.

When I looked up again, the same lad was by the kitchen doors, standing next to a tall platinum blond. Something fluttered across my heart. I looked to my guitar, concentrating on my fingers as they shifted up and down the frets in automatic movements, reminding myself not to get complacent, keep in the moment.

We finished the second set on a note of hilarity. Jamie and I had composed a reggae arrangement of that god-awful novelty song by Chucky Egg – the bloke who'd made the Top Ten, back in 1981. Everyone over thirty knew the words – which I'd made even more ridiculous by adding a seriously slow reggae beat – so they all joined in. We left the stage to a huge round of applause and cheers. I hadn't felt this good for years. The DJ put on another 80's novelty song to keep up the vibe and grinned over his shoulder at me, with a kind of recognition. I mugged at him, before stepping into the dressing room.

'Mum's sent food,' said Jamie, through a mouthful of drumstick.

'Thank god, I'm starving,' said Zinad.

'You might wanna go easy on the garlicky stuff,' I said, helping myself to some fritter-type things. 'Or you'll be belching down the mic. Wow, these are good. Who made all this?'

'The kids from Street Foods,' said Askim. 'It's a work experience thing.'

I took a bite from a triangular pastry, and crunched on vegetables and something barbecuey. The label on the tray said 'seaweed and smoked tofu'.

'Wow, this is amazing!' I took another.

As I reminded everyone how we'd attack the final set, the DJ entered. 'So guys, I'll give you the nod at five to twelve, and you'll hand over to me for the countdown.' We all nodded. He grinned again. 'Gonna be special,' he said and slipped out.

'He looks very pleased with himself,' I said. 'I 'spose this is his crowd.'

'He's an old fella – it's his era,' said Jamie.

'Oi, steady!' I pretended to cuff his ear. 'There's others here who could be in that class.'

Jamie laughed. 'Just meant he's got the biggest collection of 70's and 80's discs I ever saw. Vinyl too – proper old school.'

'Right!' I stood up. 'Enough creature comforts. Back in the zone.' I picked up my guitar and started plucking out noiseless chords to the track now playing. 'Time to re-focus Jamie. You're doing a fantastic job. Don't let it slip.'

'Can't wait to play the last song,' he said. 'My mum's gonna be made up.'

Fleetingly, I wondered where she was, then I socked him softly on the arm. 'Go on then mother's boy, get your precious arse on stage.'

We started with a couple of old 60's tunes which mod band, Light Up, used to cover in the 80's, and moved into a series of tunes by Detonator. Then we played a ska version of Purple Viper's 'Screaming Blue Sirens' – that I'd written as a personal flight of fancy. When we finally played the opening bar to Wasteland, there was a cheer from the dancefloor. Jamie's voice sang out the words,

They bombed our town
And showed no pity
We sprang back up
Rebuilt the city
Now you took
That industry
Closed the gates
No place for me

*All abandoned – **our town***
*Not a great land – **our town***
*It's a Wasteland – **our town***

Now he'd relaxed, he was really stretching himself. His voice was strong and melodic, with a hint of the plaintive timbre Eddy used to deliver. My stomach clenched in a sort of complicated knot of pain and joy.

Remaining at his mic, Zinad gave a version of Len's deep-voiced toast. It wasn't as raunchy and he went with his own accent, but it was solid and the girl with the corkscrew curls was clearly enthralled. We were without keyboards, so minus synth horns, but Jamie and I had reworked the guitar parts, so between us we covered most of the holes. I stepped up to my mic to sing the refrain, and listened to our collective sound. It was more than okay. For a four piece, it was a fitting tribute to my old mates.

Almost everyone was on the dancefloor now. Even Alan and his girlfriend Skylark were doing some sort of weird trance-style dance, arms swinging madly. The only people not dancing were the waiting staff, who stood at the back with the blond woman dressed in black. One of the youngsters pointed at Jamie and said something, and she nodded vigourously, with a proud smile. When we'd finished Wasteland, I waited for Jamie to introduce the next song. He held a hand up, shielding his eyes against the spotlights.

'This one's for Neville and everyone at Street Foods,' he said, pointing to the kitchen. There was a great cheer and everyone looked backwards, to where a chef was being dragged out, wearing a checked hat and rubbing his hands on a long spattered apron, to thunderous clapping and foot stomping.

'And of course, to my mum!' said Jamie. 'Who's helped create a lot more peace in this area, by keeping the Arts Hub going!' Another huge cheer. The blond woman nodded coyly to acknowledge the attention. So that was Jamie's mum. It was remarkable. She looked just like…

'Josie, this song's especially for you – Can't Feel My Face!'

Caress my skull with donkey kicks
Find new places you can hurt
Punch my guts and boot my spleen
Let my teeth fall in the dirt

Can't feel my face
Can't feel my face
At least I know
My heart's in place

On autopilot, my fingers picked out the beginning riff, head down, heart beating. I stole a look from under the brim of my hat. It couldn't be, yet the resemblance was uncanny. Same willowy figure, same bright eyes, which were totally transfixed on Jamie, pride radiating from her face. No, it must be coincidence – the whole evening reawakening memories, making me see things.

Cos my skins a darker hue
Think I'm inferior and faulty?
See my blood is scarlet too
My mother's tears are also salty

Can't feel my face
Can't feel my face
At least I know
My heart's in place

Everyone was singing along, dancing, all focussed on Jamie, who was giving such a soulful rendition of Eddy's lyrics. As Askim pounded out the last drum and cymbal crash, a hand waved at us from the record decks and the DJ's voice came over the PA, 'Okay folks, we're nearly there, so get your glasses are ready. We're seconds from the new Millenium!' He was fading up a big band number, for a classy start to the new century.

Jamie's mum ran to the stage, brandishing Champagne and five long-stemmed glasses. She beckoned the lads forward and tipped out frothing wine. I stepped back and turned my head, pretending to be putting my guitar down. *Shit!* It really was her. Face pink with excitement, sparkling eyes, clearly Josie, the girl I'd chased round Coventry trying to find, the girl I'd been in love with – now an attractive woman touching forty. The DJ was announcing that the countdown was about to start. Beside me, from behind the curtains Alan appeared. 'Tom! I've gotta tell you something!'

'Fuckin' hell mate, I know!'

'You do?' He was surprised. 'Look, just to warn you, he's gonna say something.'

'Who you talking about?'

'Sorry, gotta get back to Skylark.' And he was gone.

'Ten – nine – eight…' The countdown had started. What did Alan mean?

'Seven – six – five –' Josie was right there, standing ten strides away from me. Askim bounced over and thrust a glass in my hand. I kept my head down, paralysed. Shit. What the hell should I say? 'Hello, remember me?''

'Three – two – one – Happy New Year!!'

There were small explosions and the air was filled with sprinkles of glittery paper. Everyone started kissing and singing Auld Lang's Eyne. I slipped down the side stairs and stood in the dark, panting, still holding the full glass of fizz. This was all unreal. If Josie was Jamie's mum, who was his dad? He'd said his dad died when he was a kid – but didn't he also say he was a musician? *Oh no, it couldn't be!* I sat on the step. The DJ was calling the band back on stage for our last number.

'Hey, come on man!' said Jamie. 'We get to play the first song of the century!'

I threw the drink down me and stumbled up the stairs into place, keeping my face down under my hat, suddenly feeling tall and conspicuous. Josie was at the front, dancing with a dark-haired woman and some of the kids, her hips curling in a figure of eight. Yes, it was definitely her. The DJ faded down the track.

'Got another great surprise folks. We've been listening to the amazing sounds of Original Mix, and guess what? In their midst, The Beat Runners have hidden Original's founder Tom Shepperton!'

He turned and pointed to me with a flourish. 'Say hello Tom. You didn't think you'd keep yourself secret for the whole night?'

Jamie stared at me, mouth open like a gate. There was a surprised 'Woo!' from the audience and people were clapping. All eyes were on me.

There was only one thing to do.

I moved up to my mic, doffed my hat and said, 'Thanks for noticing. It's been a real pleasure playing here tonight.' Jamie stood frozen and gobsmacked, so I added, 'And now we're going to finish with a song Original Mix rarely managed to play live – 'Too Polite to Riot.''

Several excited screams from the audience. I nodded to Jamie, trying to get him back on track, and shot a glance to the others, checking they were ready. Then I moved beside Jamie to sing the opening line, in case he didn't, and I crashed into the first chords. He fudged the first line, but got back in on the second, his focussed face showing he'd put other thoughts aside for now, and he was in full voice by the time we both sang the chorus into the same microphone.

It's not the British thing
Although we'd like to try it
Despite our tendencies
We're too polite to riot!

But in the middle of the dancefloor Josie stood for a moment, as if shellshocked. Her eyes were wide with horror – like all her nightmares had congregated on stage. Then she clapped a hand to her mouth and fled through the crowds.

♫♪

65

TOM

New Year's Day, Year 2000

'Sorry TJ...or should I call you Tom?' Jamie shuffled his stocking feet, on the doorstep to the block where they lived. 'She totally won't speak to you.'

His face was pink with embarrassment and he scratched at a fringe still gunked with gel from the night before. Then he grinned. 'Me, I think it's mega. But mum – Josie – I think she's in some kinda shock.'

Josie. The name made my heart ache with a discordant mix of inner sounds, seeping back painfully through the years, but topped with a high note of thrilling hope. What if I just barged past him and ran up to their flat at the top – the flat where Josie lived? *For Chrissakes, Josie!*

'I 'spose that's understandable,' I said.

Jamie scraped a hand through his russet hair. How come I didn't see it before? Excitement rippled through me again. It was like waking up to see your first expensive guitar propped up against the wall – exotically solid and beautiful. But this was far, far better than that and I was still marvelling at the new reality.

Christ, I had a son! Throughout the previous sleepless night, a fantastic, crazy urge had mushroomed up inside me like hunger. Something – someone! – good had come from the mess of those years after all. Surely now things had to change?

'What do we do?'

Jamie shrugged. 'Dunno. Josie's always dealt with stuff head on – like with the Hub, when she fought off crack-heads and vandals, and argued with the police and Courts for a music licence.' He raised his shoulders again and dropped them heavily. 'I've never seen her hide away from anything before. It's well out of character.'

How could he be so calm and mature, at only eighteen? I paced away for a few steps and then came back.

'Jamie – you really had no idea who your dad was?

'Nope. Not 'til Josie told me everything last night.' He grinned, like he'd just found out he was royalty.

'How come she didn't say before?' My hands were sweaty and I was practically wringing them. This was ridiculous.

Jamie rubbed the back of his neck and scrunched up his mouth, thinking. 'Look, maybe we could get a drink somewhere?' he said.

Even on New Year's day, east London's pubs were doing brisk trade. We found a little table behind a wall and squeezed in. Twelve hours into the year 2000 and nothing cataclysmic had happened to the world. But on a personal level, a big, fat piece of news had fallen out of the air like a huge bombshell: *Josie was living right nearby, with my grown up son!*

As Jamie swilled his pint round, as though mixing his thoughts, I sat back trying to appear relaxed. But my blood raced. I wanted to know everything, no matter how hard it may be to hear. He started to toy with the wet corner of a beer mat, peeling the label away. We'd got on so well for months. I'd been impressed with his playing, his ability to pick stuff up so quickly, his humour and easy attitude. And Jamie had treated me like a much older friend, who he looked to with some kind of appreciation. What on earth did he think of me now?

'I'm so sorry I wasn't there to be a father, mate.' I watched his face like a hawk. 'I never knew I had a kid.' There were other shameful secrets – like the fact I was banged up for years. I wondered when I'd have to tell him that.

'It's alright.' He winced in apology. 'Actually, I didn't miss having a dad.' He shrugged. 'There were always loads of men around – mum's friends, uncle Josh, granddad, Neville, and all the guys working at The Hub. I didn't feel like I missed out.'

'What were you told?'

He took a slug of his beer. 'When I was little, mum said the same thing. She found out my father was married, and moved to London before she realised she was having a baby. So he didn't know he had a son, and he'd never come looking for us.' He shrugged. 'I 'spose that's why I didn't think about it much.'

I breathed slowly. It was important to get this right. 'Did you ever imagine what your father might be like?'

Jamie chewed on his lip and looked sheepish again. 'To be honest, I spent most of my time playing footie, banging drums, and running round the centre with kids like Askim and Zinad. Mum said she'd tell me everything when I was older, so I kinda put it on hold.' His expression was uncomplicated. 'She always made out it was no big deal. It was only later when I heard something….' He laid down the pieces of the beer mat he had shredded. '…I'm not sure if you want to hear this.'

'What?'

'There was a time when uncle Simon – well, he's not my real uncle, he's one of my mum's oldest friends…'

'Yeah, I know him,' I interrupted, fearful he was going to get off the point.

'How?'

I shook my head. 'It's not important. Go on.'

'We first played at a school concert, and afterwards I overheard him tell Josie I was the spitting image of my dad on stage.'

An irrational spurt of envy rushed into my head. That bloke Simon had watched Jamie grow up, seen him as a boy.

'You didn't know I was a musician?'

Jamie shook his head. 'Not 'til my eighteenth birthday last year, when I asked her.'

It wasn't possible to process all this.

'What did she say?'

'She was pretty sure my father was dead, but he'd been a talented musician who had a professional band, way back when.' He grinned. 'She didn't say the band was Original Mix. I love your stuff, man. It's awesome.'

I shifted in my seat. 'Yeah, well. It wasn't such a blessing in the long run.' I leaned in to him. 'And what did she say last night? Did she tell you why she never contacted me, to let me know she was pregnant?'

Jamie face lit up. 'Oh yeah,' he said. Then he blushed, like a school boy who's rushed to answer, then realises it's embarassing. 'She thought someone else was my father.'

A hot knife of jealousy dug into my guts. He meant Vinnie of course.

My last real conversation with Vinnie, had been a couple of nights before our final Bang on Cue appearance. It now flashed through my head – Vinnie bursting into the flat to get something after I'd returned from a bit of a bender, which had become a regular thing, catching me popping a few pills and, in my fumbling panic to hide it, packets of powder falling out of my jacket. His face snarled up in red fury.

'Christ! You've turned into a fuckin' mess Tom! You've got everythin' you ever soddin' wanted – and you're gonna fuck it all up!'

'Bollocks!' I'd been incensed. 'The only person who fucks up my life is you! You're tearing the band apart, you spent all my friggin' money on that guitar, and you fucked up my relationship with Josie – and I'll never forgive you for that!'

'You can't have been that stuck on her,' he said. 'You never even mentioned it.'

'What do you know, yer cunt?' My voice was a slurry yell. 'I had a great thing with Josie and you killed it, with your big stupid gob. I fuckin' loved her!'

He stared at the floor, mouth set tight as a cat's arse, as he absorbed this. Then he pointed at me. 'You don't know nothing.' He paused. Even in my drug and booze induced state, I could still see a thought emerging, a different expression spreading across his face, a calculating kind of look. And his voice was cold and determined.

'Well I was fucking her too,' he said simply. 'For years.'

'You'rra soddin' liar!' I swung at him, but he dodged out of reach.

'No, I'm not.' He turned his face away, and walked to the door. 'She wasn't the love of your life, she was just a two-timing slag. You need to forget her now Tom, and clean yourself up.'

Jamie took a last swig of his pint. 'Another one?' I nodded and watched him unfold from his seat and walk to the bar. He was tall alright, with my broad shoulders and long legs. His eyes were green too, and he had the same unusual bronze-coloured hair I'd had years ago, before strands of white made mine appear sandy. Could he be Vinnie's son though?

When the pints were on the table, I tried to sound casual.

'Who was this other bloke of your mum's then? Do you know?'

Jamie's face went pink again. 'Promise you won't say anything.'

I gave a nod.

'She said it was Zinad's dad, Axten. They had a bit of a fling when she got to London, before his mum came on the scene.'

I tried to process this. 'What, our Zinad – Mr 1970's Afrohead?' My laughter poured out with an odd relief.

Jamie looked serious. 'Please don't tell Zin, Tom. He doesn't know all this embarrassing stuff. Mum was just trying to explain how complicated things got. It's pretty ancient news, after all.'

'Prehistoric.' I grimaced, though twenty years of wondering about Josie wouldn't just go away, or make sense of what Vinnie had said. Maybe nothing ever would.

'Do you think she'll ever speak to me?' I said.

Jamie looked doubtful, and I had a sudden fear that he might withdraw too, in loyalty to Josie. It was vital he understood.

'I wasn't still married Jamie, you got to know that. Someone told her a lie and she ran away. I'd been separated for ages. My ex was planning to re-marry.'

My words felt empty, like some story a distant uncle tells you at a wedding about an old family feud. Jamie was trying to understand, but it was all too far back in history. I tried one last time.

'She must have needed money. How come she never got in touch with me after you were born?'

He was chewing his mouth again, deep in thought. 'I dunno, Tom.' There was something he wasn't saying. His shoulders sank a little as he swished his drink again and sighed. And the air was heavy with the suspicion that we'd both failed each other.

Then he drew himself up and looked at me steadily. 'Look, Tom. I wish I had more details, but you guys should probably clear this up yourselves.'

'You're right, mate.' I smiled, drained my pint and stood. 'Same again with a game o' pool?'

The way forward wasn't grilling Jamie. Neither was it rushing in like a roadie at a catering truck. I'd missed years and years, but maybe, somehow, I could learn about this family of two – for which I was unwittingly responsible.

It depended on whether Josie would talk to me, and whether, this time, I could get close to something precious without ruining it.

♫

66

JOSIE

2nd January 2000

We were at The Hub, tidying up the worst of the New Year's Eve mess. I'd slipped in alone, purely for some space to think. Then Franki turned up on the pretext of assisting Neville, the loving partner come to help her man clean his kitchen. But I knew she was really there to corner me.

'Why not meet Tom and just say how you feel?' she said.

'Because Franki – I don't fuckin' *know* how I feel!'

Her face was aghast. In all our years of friendship, I'd never yelled at her like that. I flopped on a bar stool and sank my head into my arms.

'God, I'm sorry,' I mumbled into the counter. A yeasty smell from the previous night's beer oozed up from the bar towel. I recoiled with disgust. 'Urgh!'

'Don't touch all that, it's still cruddy.' From her tone she was still hurt. We stared at each other, lost for words, until the whooshing sound of the glass washer stopped, and Franki hauled out a steaming tray, which she plonked down on the sink. She held a tumbler up to the light. 'Wow! Nev's new machine is fab. That old one was crap.' She handed me the sparkling glass. 'Look at that!'

'Oh no. I'll miss having smudges of someone else's lipstick with my drink.' I mugged disappointment, then had a thought. 'Should we replace the kitchen dishwasher too?'

She snatched the glass back from me. 'Oh no you don't, missy. We're talking about Tom right now. After all, he's Jamie's dad.'

'Only by sperm,' I said. 'He can't come wriggling his way into our lives now.'

'Why not?' Franki folded her arms. 'None of this is his fault. He didn't know he had a son.'

And there it was again. A deep, guilty pull inside my womb, telling me I was a terrible, dishonest mother, who'd never sat down with her son and explained properly about his own father.

'Franki, don't.' I sighed with despair. 'Jamie's going to hate me.'

She walked round the bar and patted my cheek with the drying cloth in her hand. 'Jamie adores you, and you did what everyone thought was best. It's nobody's fault.'

All the sour smells of the bar reminded me of that awful wino stench of Tom the last time I'd seen him – back in 1984 – wearing a greasy leather coat, so drunk and high, god knows how he'd even recognised me. Pupils like dots, hands and neck the colour of old meat. His coppery hair had been matted with dirt, and he wore a thin greying shirt which offered no defence against the cold. But despite my shock at this desperate state, my main thought was to protect my three year old at home.

For years I'd regretted not helping Tom. As I'd travelled round London, I'd searched into the face of any crack-head who pleaded for cash, and peered at each huddle of vagrants loitering in the parks, searching for him amongst all the raging lost souls – the incoherent, the swearing, the stinking and neglected.

But I never saw Tom again, and as the years went by I began to lose hope.

Then, when Jamie was eight, 'Too Polite To Riot' came over the radio, as it occasionally did – the lyrics now harmless with the passing of time – and Simon had looked up from the kitchen table, where their hotly-contested card game had been suspended for a loo break.

'I wondered what happened to you know who,' he said, peering at me sideways.

I placed Jamie's cards down by the baking board to turn off the radio. Then I crossed my arms protectively around my chest. 'I've thought about that long and hard.'

Simon nodded slowly, his unblinking eyes a clear, sky blue.

'That last time, he was in such a state Simon – penniless, homeless, mashed off his head. I don't know how he could even walk.' I took a deep, painful breath. 'Let's face it, five years ago Tom was a hard core junkie. So by now he must be dead.'

I'd never said this out loud, and as I uttered the words, my heart had broken.

'I think you're right,' Simon said finally.

I bit my lip. 'Tom was the only man I really loved.'

Jamie ran into the room, picked up the cards and narrowed his jade eyes to interrogate me. 'You didn't let *him* see them?' He'd pointed an accusing finger at Simon, who feigned wide-eyed innocence. I shook my head. 'Not a peep.'

'You sure?'

I pretended to be shocked. 'Of course! Mums don't lie.' Then, unable to resist, I'd ruffled his springy hair with my hand.

'Good, 'cos he's a big cheat!' Jamie wriggled back into a chair, rubbing his head automatically. 'Urrgh, mum! You got baking goop on my cards!' He'd laughed, always delighted by mess, enjoying a life full of surprises.

I'd looked down at the bread dough in front of me, which had been splashed by two small tears, and I folded them into the mix. It was over. The waiting, the searching and the hoping against all odds. Tom was long dead. And I'd never see him again.

The trouble was, a decade later here he was, large as life, older, more rugged looking – but healthy and strong. I *had* lied to Jamie, in a way – by not telling him that his father was 80's musician Tom Shepperton. Throughout his teenhood I'd waited for the perfect time to present itself, when I could bear the pain of thinking about what had happened, and frame it in a way Jamie would understand. But that time had just never come.

And now, seeing Tom alive had cracked that old hurt wide apart, and filled me with an awful anger and guilt, and a longing I couldn't even examine. My silence was unreasonable, unworthy and inexplicable. But I couldn't bring myself to speak to him.

67

TOM

'Rick's going over to Fysson's Electrics. Need anything?'
Alan's voice was above me as I crouched on the studio floor behind a
rack of units, staring hard at a mess of cables.

'Yeah. X-Ray vision so I can tell which of these bloody wires
is shorting,' I said. 'If it would just blow instead of making that
crackling noise...'

I shuffled out backwards, on my arse. 'Jesus! It's like
spaghetti junction back there. We'll have to pull out the whole unit
and test each one.'

Two hours later I stood in the main recording room holding a
length of innocuous-looking black wire in my hand.

'Play it again, Sam!' I yelled to the control room. And when
Alan poked the console, I listened keenly at the track for interference.
I'd loaded in one of my recent acoustic numbers, empty and spacious
– ripe for a villainous spark of stray electricity to sully. But no, it was
clean. I gave the thumbs up.

'I like that song.' Alan wandered out of the booth, tying back
his dreadlocks with a bit of coloured cloth which could only have
come from Skylark. 'That what you've been working on, after hours?'

'Actually wrote a lot of it inside.'

Alan looked surprised. I didn't talk about prison, ever. But that
past didn't matter much now. Finding out about Jamie had changed
everything. I woke up bright-eyed and eager to start the day, as if I
had an actual stake in life.

'This is a later song,' I explained. 'The early stuff I wrote in
Seg was just angry.'

'What's Seg?' Alan looked puzzled.

'The segregation unit.' I lowered myself onto a stool and
thought a moment. 'Six months in, I'd started to realise what a
monumental waste I'd made of everything, when some bloke wound
me up the wrong way. And I kinda blew. Had a real melt down.'

Alan's eyes widened. 'You used to hate violence.'

'Still do, mate. I'd never thrown a first punch until prison. And once I'd cleaned up and finished clucking, I decided never to do a single drug again. Then this bloke kept on pushing me to be part of it, wanting to use our cell as a dispensary…anyway, before I knew it four big screws were manhandling me into my own special cell.'

Alan sat down on a speaker and studied me. He was a watchful lad, even in the early days. 'What d'ya mean special?'

I toyed with the damaged wire dangling from my hand and started to twist it into a tight coil, remembering. 'Well it was a normal cell, you know – regulation light custard walls, high windows, solid metal door – but it was spattered with old blood and shit.'

'Ew! Nasty, man!'

I grimaced, recalling the place. 'The shitter in Seg's just a bucket and the bed's a concrete ledge, attached to the wall – so you can't destroy it. Oh yeah – and there's a cardboard seat.'

'Cardboard?'

We both laughed.

'Yeah, you get a stool and table, made from some sturdy cardboard, like it's been supplied by Her Majesty's MFI. You can use it as furniture, or tear it to pieces with your bare hands, without doing yourself any real damage.'

'Which did you do?' Alan raised his eyebrows.

I frowned at the wire in my fist. 'I'd like to say I didn't do the obvious, but I'd be lying.'

I looked up, but Alan wasn't judging, he was just taking it in. So I continued. 'They made me strip off and threw me a boiler suit to wear. I tried to destroy that too, but they're made of something totally unrippable.' I walked over to a peg on the wall, plucked off a roll of gaffer, and taped a piece around the dangerous wire. 'I punched a few people on the way there, so I wasn't exactly treated like a ming vase myself.'

Alan's eyes widened. 'Prison musta been tough, to make you into a fighter Tom.'

I lobbed the wire at a metal bin across the room, where it landed with a satisfying clang.

'Mostly prison's fuckin' boring Alan. You get sick to death of the noise, the smell of sweat, shit, spunk, piss. Everything is colourless, tasteless, tedious – even the fuckin' soap. You know what? They issue these white Windsor soaps, embossed with a posh little crest. What does it smell of? Nothing! Why would they give you scentless soap, just cos you're inside?'

I was starting to rant a bit now, but I couldn't stop myself.

'Don't blokes try to, you know…?' Alan pulled an awkward face.

I shook my head. 'Nah. That's mostly in films. You're more likely to get an unwanted fist in the face than a poke up the arse. But there's no fuckin' privacy anywhere. The bogs have stable doors, so everyone gets to see a tall bloke's facial expressions when he's taking a shit. And if you want a private wank you have to wake up in the middle of the night for it. Then you feel the bunk below jigglin' and you find your cell mate's had the same fuckin' idea!'

'No way!' Alan was trying to keep a straight face.

'It's okay mate, you can laugh. It's the miserable monotony which drives you mad. Being cooped up with the hundreds of barely educated young idiots. No interesting talk, no creativity and no point. That, and the endless time you have to realise what a friggin' waste you've made of your life. There's a big temptation to just get high, kill off the days. And the screws pretend they don't smell it. Suits them fine if half the prison's lying around caned – at least they're not rioting. But I was trying to stay clean and reclaim myself. '

There was silence as we both considered all this. It was the most I'd ever said to anyone about my ten years inside. The recall had made me a bit pissed off, but I realised the heavy knot of pure fury which lived in my sternum had shifted. I felt lighter than I had in years.

Finally I looked at my watch. 'C'mon, let's get some air and pop into the caff. Jamie's lot are coming in at four.'

As we walked down the road, Alan grinned at me. 'It's whacko him being your son..'

I tried not to grin back. 'Yeah, well it's not like I had much to do with it.' I was attempting to be cool, but inside I jumped for joy all over again.

We ordered and settled at a table, with two mugs of steaming tea on the red Formica, plus egg and chips for good measure. I looked round the caff. Two Asian teenagers were debating in incomprehensible street patter, flicking their wrists, fingers clacking like castanets, and laughing themselves silly. On the far side an old man slurped tea and studied the racing pages, pencil poised. Near the door, a young mum ate a sausage sandwich while making eyes at her infant and rocking the buggy with her foot – as Josie might have done when Jamie was little.

What was he was like as a toddler, and a young boy? When did he kick his first ball? Play his earliest guitar? I was eager to hear stories, told from a parent's view. Not the one who was so stupid they got banged up for ten years, of course. The one who raised him to be such a great young man.

'Alan, can I ask you something?'

'Yeahmmm.' He was devouring a chip butty he'd carefully crafted. Just as well Skylark wasn't here.

'You're good with people.'

He raised an eyebrow.

'You know – you're chatty and pretty straightforward. People trust you.'

He shrugged. 'Spose.'

I said in a rush, 'Why won't Josie speak to me?'

Alan ruminated on his sandwich and I waited for the last chewy bulk of it to be washed down with a slug of tea. He gave his pronouncement sniff, the one he reserved for not such great news.

'Tom, how long did it take you to work out how to deal with prison?'

I glanced round, to check nobody was listening. 'Took me ages to accept I was there for the long term,' I said. 'But in the end I settled down, did my time.' I leaned in, suddenly willing to tell all.

'For the last few years I was a bloody Red Band, that's how much a part of the fuckin' institution I was.'

'What's that?'

'You know, a Trustee, with special privileges – like getting on the music scheme, and teaching myself to play again.'

Realisation bloomed on Alan's face, like a sunrise. 'Oh!'

'What? You thought I could pick up a guitar after ten years and play like I used to.'

Alan picked up his tea again. 'To be honest Tom, I thought you probably could.'

I rolled my eyes.

'Anyway,' he said. 'To return to the Josie thing – it's the same – she probably just needs time to adjust.'

'That it?' I said. 'Your sole pearl of psychological wisdom?'

He gave a stoical nod.

'So what do I do?'

'Dunno. When Sky goes off on one, I just hang round the edges till it looks like she's wearing herself down.'

'Then what?'

'Go in for the big hug and say sorry.'

I gave a short laugh. 'Even if it's not your fault?'

Alan shook his head at me in pity. 'Oh man, it's *always* my fault. I offer a genuine apology, she relents and then…' He grinned. 'Well, we make up, like.'

I groaned. 'Oh Christ! Spare me any further details.'

When Jamie, Zinad and Ashkim, arrived at the studio for their first recording, I was all set up.

'Come to the control room, Jamie. I'll show you what mix I've got in mind,' I said.

After we'd chucked a few ideas round I said, 'How's Josie?'

Jamie shook his head slowly, in bewilderment. 'Turbo cleaning. She's starting at the back of the flat and moving forward, like a crazy woman. Throwing out all sorts of stuff.'

I frowned. 'That a good sign?'

'Search me. My job's to haul bags down to the charity shop. Otherwise, I'm staying well clear.'

After the session I handed Jamie their rough cut on CD. 'Look, it sounds okay, but we're not at all finished. This is just so you can work out what's missing. Ask someone who's not heard it yet – maybe your mum?'

Jamie nodded. 'Yeah, she'd be good at that.'

'Great. See you in a few days then.' Like a teenager, I found myself hoping Josie would be impressed with the way I'd mixed their song.

They picked up their gear, and the other two lads bumped knuckles with me in pally goodbyes. They were a good bunch. Nice lads from decent homes. Like I used to be.

I just needed to bide my time, hang round the edges, like Alan said. After all, I was used to waiting. And when the right moment came, I'd try to make some sort of amends.

68

JOSIE

'No problem, changed to 9 a.m. prompt, I'll give him the message.' As I put the phone down I glanced at yesterday's missive on the message pad – *Z says your samosas were mega! At snooker tonite & band rest of week. Jay x.* That meant they were at Tom's studio. But would Jamie come back for dinner or stay late rehearsing?

It was my own fault I didn't know. Jamie understood that Tom's reappearance had thrown me off balance, so he'd started being vague about what he was doing.

I picked up the phone again and called Enquiries. 'Paradise Studios in London, please,' I said. The young man on the other end needed details. 'Sorry, I'm not sure, try Hackney maybe.'

'Is that 54 Fulchurch Road, E8?' he asked. I scribbled down the address. It was only ten minutes away. 'Are there any others?'

'Just one Paradise Studios in London. Do you want the number?'

As the phone rang, I battled with a sensation that I was intruding. I needed to speak to Jamie, and it was my duty as a parent. Why was I always questioning myself now? After three rings an answerphone clicked on and Tom's calm voice suggested I leave a message. I dropped the receiver back and decided to try later.

By six o'clock, and still no answer, I dragged on my coat, succumbing to the inevitable.

Door number 54 appeared residential, but the buzzer was labelled *Paradise Studios*. Heart thumping, I prodded the button.

'Hey,' said a voice. Not deep enough for Tom's, but a bloke, with a slight Midlands twang.

'Erm….is Jamie Honeywell there? It's his mum, Josie. I need to tell him something….' Jamie would be more amused than embarrassed. But still I felt like an idiot. Perhaps I should buy us both mobile phones, like Franki and Neville used.

'Yeah! Yeah! Just push the door!' This person was excited. Probably dead keen to see the musician's mum who tracked him down to the studio. This would become a hilarious story they'd tease him with in the pub.

I entered a white-walled corridor with pine flooring. Not what I was expecting. Black and white framed photos hung along along the walls – a woman sitting at a shiny black grand piano, head bent in concentration, a heavy metal drummer at his drumkit, hand a-blur. Not Press shots. These studies were more intimate, people caught in the moment – two skinny lads with their heads tipped back sharing a laugh, a shy-looking girl handing a guitarist some sheet music, a be-spectacled black man, eyes closed, encased in headphones, conducting with a drumstick. Tom had taken these photos. They weren't labelled or signed. But I knew.

'They're great, aren't they?' The man from the Midlands was beside me. A flushed-faced guy, late thirties, short and sturdy, in combat trousers and a purple T-shirt printed with a snake, his mousy-coloured dreadlocks held back with a piece of khaki netting. He looked like some sort of musical activist, jungle division. I thought maybe I'd seen him before.

'Sorry to disturb you. I need to give Jamie an important message.' Shit! Why hadn't I thought to bring a note? 'They're probably busy, so I'll write it down for you to give him. Have you got a pen?'

The man was staring at me like be couldn't quite believe it, but at the mention of a pen he started. 'No! I mean... he'll want to see you in person.'

I frowned. Scribbled messages were part of our tapestry of communication. 'Really – he won't mind.'

Ignoring this, he walked off, beckoning me to follow. 'Come this way, I'll get you a drink. T...Jamie will definitely want to see you.' He disappeared round the corner, so I had no choice but to follow, admiring the photos as I passed.

'Have a seat,' he opened a door. 'I'll get you a coffee. Black or white?'

'Er, black, please.' I gazed round the room. It was windowless, but light and relaxing, with meditearrean-white walls punctuated by dots of pure colour – a cobalt glass vase, a cheerful patterned rug, a large photo of one pure white cloud in a blue sky. It reminded me of a bedroom I'd once had.

'Great!' The young man grinned like he'd hit the jackpot.

Oh lord. What sort of fool was I making of myself here? He rattled round with cups in the room next door, and I perched on the edge of one of the armchairs, terrified that Tom would walk in. I must leave, before he found me.

'Thing is, Jamie's driving test's been brought forward to 9am tomorrow,' I explained in a rush, when he returned with coffee. 'He'll want to know before they make a big night of it.' It was unnerving how he looked at me – like he knew something I didn't.

I put my palm out. 'Look, he's a grown man – well, nearly. I don't try to control what he get's up to. Once he knows he's got an earlier test, what he does next is up to him.' I becoming getting irritated at the implication that I was being hoodwinked. This man didn't know how things worked in our family.

'That's it really. Please could you just tell him, when you can?' I took a big gulp of my coffee, to show no hard feelings, and stood up to go. 'I'm Josie by the way,'

The man rose, nodding, like he'd reached a decision. 'You don't recognise me, do you?' he said.

So that was it. It wasn't the first time I'd failed to recognise someone. 'Cripes, I'm sorry. I see hundreds of people at the centre where I work. When did we meet?'

'Years ago, in Coventry. You taught me.'

'Coventry? Bloody hell!' An icy finger poked me inside the chest.

'Miss, you swore!' He grinned.

'I don't understand. What did I teach you?'

'Cooking. At the Youth Training Scheme.' He looked sheepish. 'I used to be a skinhead.' His tone was apologetic.

The light of the room was getting dimmer. 'What's your name?'

'Alan, but the kids used to call me Adolf. I'm not proud of that period.'

'But Adolf, Alan he's… he's dead.'

And suddenly his voice seemed far away. I was dropping into a dark tunnel. My legs felt scratched and raw and I was terrified. Wet, hot blood seeped between my fingers, and it was dark, really dark.

'Let me lift her onto the sofa. Jesus, Alan! What the hell were you thinking?'

I was floating in the air, orange light was filtering through the blackness.

'Fetch a glass of water.'

Where was I? I was scared, shivering. The ceiling swam up and down. My head pounded from inside. I tried to sit up.

'Hey, don't panic. It's okay. You fainted.' Tom's voice.

I sank back. If I didn't open my eyes I wouldn't have to speak.

'Here. Drink this.'

Shakily I sat up and took the glass. Tom's green eyes met mine. Eyes like Jamie's. He was squatting by the sofa and stroking my arm. 'I'm *so* sorry Josie. You've had nothing but shocks recently.'

I downed the rest of the water. My head throbbed, I had a general sense of panic, and my pride was in tatters. I was struggling to breath. I just wanted to be back in the safety of my home.

'Please let Jamie know about his test,' I said to Alan, struggling to my feet. I wobbled and Tom steadied me with a hand under my arm.

'Come on, Josie. At least stay til you've recovered. The lads went out for snacks and a quick break. Wait a few minutes and you can speak to him yourself.'

His hand was strong under my elbow. How could he just pop up, so alive and solid, after all these years? And with the dead skinhead lad in tow?

'I'm fine.' I retrieved my arm and wrapped my jacket round me. 'It was the surprise, that's all.' As the blood thumped back into my head, it hurt like hell. I felt stupid and angry. 'After all, I was convinced that boy bled to death in my arms, and I thought you must be dead too. Now you've both sprung back up, larger than life!'

'And twice as ugly.' He smiled.

'It's too bizarre, Tom.'

As I said his name out loud, I felt myself crumbling. 'I need to go.' I brushed past them both as fast as I could without running. At the end of the corridor I pulled at the door, but it wouldn't budge. Tom was behind me.

'Push the button on the wall.'

'Where?' My eyes darted round until I spotted a metal plate and a green button, like at Jamie's old school. I slammed my palm on it and yanked the door open. Then I had a thought and turned.

'Please don't tell Jamie I fainted.' I said. 'He'll only worry.'

'I'm concerned about that too,' said Tom. 'Can I walk you home at least?'

'No thanks, I'm fine on my own.' I pulled the sides of my jacket tight together and walked away, legs shaking.

Nothing good was coming out of these new discoveries. It was turning me idiotic, upsetting my relationship with Jamie, and I'd even asked his new-found father to lie to him.

I wished I'd never set eyes on Tom again.

69

TOM

Several days after Josie's visit, I was in the studio kitchen making a brew and wondering whether I should call her, when Rick bustled in – whistling and carrying a bulging briefcase. It was the one we used to stow the cash in after gigs, the leather now battered and scuffed, its combination lock broken, and the hefty padlock and chain with which I'd secured it to my wrist long gone. I recalled that bolt cutters and a locksmith had been involved, along with a lot of ridicule at my expense for trusting the key to Vinnie.

'Rick! Where the hell you been?' I hadn't seen his troll-like form for days and I was starting to wonder what was going on.

He plonked the briefcase on the table, prodding it with a stubby finger, as if this was an answer.

'In there, my son, are the draft contracts for the return tour of Original Mix!'

'Oh for fuck's sake!' I shouted. 'We agreed that's not going to happen!'

Alan came bouncing in. 'Hey, what's all the yelling?' He spotted Rick and grinned. 'Alright, mate. What's new?'

'Fuckin' gonk-features has been out wheeling and dealin' again – behind my back! So much for partnership!' I said.

Alan shook his head in disappointment. I'd agreed to tone down my language, 'keep the vibe chilled', as he put it. And thanks to all my new interests – playing again, recording the band, Jamie being my son – *my son!* – I'd been Mr Mellowyellow. But Rick's announcement swept all that away.

'You've right royally pissed me off Rick.'

He sighed and wrinkled his nose, considering. 'Okay mate, maybe I should have brought you in sooner.'

'What? Like three minutes before we're due on stage?'

'Tom you're being a bit of a twat, man,' said Alan.

'Chrissakes, Alan! It's not you who's gotta do it.' I turned to Rick. 'How did you even get to the draft contract stage without me?'

The minute I said this I knew. I sat down hard on a chair and thumped my head with a fist. 'You've been using the company?'

Rick smiled sheepishly. 'Technically, we are as one mate.' He took the chair opposite. 'Look, calm down for a minute, think about it.' He held up callused fingers to count off benefits, like he was trying to sell me a second hand car.

'One – we could do with the wedge. Two – the studio's ticking over nicely, but only if we keep upgrading the gear. Three – we've gotta offer better quality masters than you can achieve at home now – or everyone will just record DIY.'

'I know all that – and they're pretty much the same point.'

Rick poked his pinkie in the air to show he hadn't finished. 'And fourth – most importantly, the time's right, mate. I can feel it. Leave it much longer and yer'll be embarrassingly old.'

'Pfuh!' I rolled my eyes. 'I think that boat has sailed.'

'Nah. The kids are already interested in ska again. It's time for a third wave.'

'Actually, it might be fourth,' said Alan helpfully.

Rick flapped an impatient paw at him. 'Whatever. We need the dosh, the band's keen – well, most of them – and the necessary big boys are prepared to bank roll it.'

I narrowed my eyes at him. I didn't doubt Rick's financial acumen for a second. All the years I was in prison, he'd been collating my Royalties and investing them, along with all the cash he'd salvaged from the gigs and anything him and old Toombes had wrestled from the whole Ragged Moth debacle. I'd seen the books – oil-stained pages, peppered with tiny figures, mouse-like but precise, as if a part of his brain was possessed by an accountant with forensic clarity.

And his loyalty as a friend was beyond reproach. After all, it was Rick who traced me to HMS Misery, engaged an ambitious young barrister who re-opened my case, argued the stabbing could only have been done by a right handed man. He even did some of the research himself, becoming something of a lay expert – looked into how the new science of DNA testing could clinch our Appeal, and obtained expert witnesses – and they proved a third person was there.

All this dogged work had allowed me to leave prison with a full pardon. So Rick had given me the ultimate gift – the final knowledge that, even in a selfish, drink-blind, drug-crazed moment, even filled with hatred and at rock bottom, I actually *hadn't* taken another man's life.

'Exactly which band members are keen?' I said slowly.
Rick gave a long whistle. 'Weeeell, let's see.' He ran a hand through his straggly hair. 'Charlie said he'd love to do a tour, as long as it's all in the UK.'
'Well I'm not bloody well touring abroad.'
Shit! Typical Rick tactics. Already I was negotiating terms.
'Raymond's on tour with the Northern Phil in Asia – so I don't think he'll be a goer.' Rick sniffed. 'Besides, he's way out of our league now.'
I gave them both a puzzled frown.
'Ray did the whole music college thing,' said Alan. 'Straight As in classical and jazz piano. Never been out of work.'
I blew out my cheeks in wonder. 'Good for him. Raymond always was a hidden talent. What's Len up to?'
Rick pouted and frowned at me. 'Len wanted to come down so many times, Tom. He was desperate to visit you inside.'
'Yeah, well that wasn't goin' to happen. Anyway – how did he know about that? You swore to keep it secret Rick!'
'I know, but still…' Rick had the good grace to look apologetic, even as he waved off the notion – using both hands this time. 'Anyways, he did an electrical engineer training, got married…'
'What, *Len*!'
'Got divorced. There's two kids – boy and a girl, both went to University. Daughter's a great musician too – keyboard player. Oh an' there's a younger boy – 'cos he married again recently. Works for some company that provides hospital equipment. Did okay for himself. House in Leamington Spa.'

I tipped my head to the ceiling and rocked slightly. 'Oh my God!'

Knowing about the band members' lives meant I had to clear their frozen images from my mind, and wise up to the fact they'd all got old, settled down, compromised, moved to Leamington fucking Spa.

But suddenly it felt right to know, catch up, discover what had become of everyone and their dreams. So in for a penny...

Okay.' I faced Rick again. 'Keep going.'

Rick and Alan exchanged a glance, and Rick said, 'Well, Devon's played with Jackson's bands ever since he left us – Charlie too. They still gig all round the Midlands, and both teach workshops for kids on fairly rough estates. Devon does session work for other bands of course. Oh, an' he's a granddad now.'

'Fucking hell!'

'He says he'd be happy to play a reunion gig – for old times' sake. Sends his regards Tom. Who does that leave?'

'Eddy and Vinnie,' I said.

'Well Eddy can't do it, as he's still in the States.'

'Since when?'

Rick looked surprised. 'Thought you knew all that? Eddy and Adam moved to New York, back in the early eighties. They ran that famous nightclub, Heady Eddy's – you must remember Heady Eddy's?'

'No, Rick. I was somewhat indisposed.'

'Great you're not bitter though.' Alan was leaning aginst the kitchen counter.

'Glad you're enjoying all this.' I aimed a kick at his shin, which he evaded, chuckling. 'So Eddy and Adam are in the States?'

A shadow fell over Rick's face. 'Not Adam. He died of AIDS.'

'Shit!'

'Eddy was devastated. Myself, Charlie an' Len went over for the funeral. It was all we could do to stop him topping himself. But he had some great mates there. Some of them also lost their, yer know, boyfriends or whatever.' Rick squirmed in his chair and sniffed. 'We stayed for two weeks – an' I met every weirdo possible – and heard far, far too much disco music. But I tell yer, hand on heart – Eddy had the sorta mates you'd want around you in a crisis.'

It was all too much to take in.

'Poor sod.' I thought of Adam blustering round the office or studio, in his pink shirts and stylish suits, cheeks flushed and full of energy. 'I know we had our disagreements, but nobody deserves that. How's Eddy now?'

'Yeah, he's fine. Calls me about once a year. Got married a while back.'

'Married?'

'Yeah, to another bloke. Not legally of course – but a big fake ceremony, with matching tuxes and a huge cake.' Rick's face showed a mixture of bafflement and admiration, not being the marrying type himself. 'Invited me over but it was the same time as your Appeal.'

'Phooo!' I exuded a long column of air from my mouth. 'Everyone's been very busy. It's hard to take in.'

We sat in silence for a few moments. Alan looked at Rick in question, and he shrugged.

'You not going to ask about Vinnie?' said Alan.

I rubbed my hands across my forehead and my scalp and then kneaded my fists into each eye. I'd avoided thinking about Vinnie for years.

When Rick had found me in prison, at first I wouldn't see him. Having no visitors had been something of a blessing. Not for me the sadness, self-recriminations and helplessness, as family and friends left Visiting, shocked to see their loved one so totally incarcerated. And I'd stopped listening to other men's stories of the wife's new lover, kids growing up without them, parents who refused to visit. I heard them alright, but just as the white noise of prison, like the night time yelling, or the bells for lock down. I wouldn't let the real meaning of it into my head. To stay sane, you had to impose inner limits – every bit as secure as the prison bars. Mine were to block out all the past, avoid drugs and do my time.

But then a letter from Rick arrived, asking if he could see me. I refused him a Visiting Order. He wrote time and again, giving me bits of news about his scheme to move to London and set up a studio – telling me he wouldn't take no for an answer. I pondered long and hard about what it would be like to get sight of his short hairy form again and, as the idea grew, it started to make me smile. Finally, I thought, why not? So I wrote back – one solitary letter – saying if I sent him a VO, he'd have to swear to keep it top secret, and that I wouldn't speak with him about anything to do with Original Mix.

He promised.

So once a month, he came down on a day return, with the stuff other people's visitors brought – stamps, books, magazines, plus the permitted tenner a month, to spend in the canteen on fags, shaving cream and decent toothpaste. And we kept all our conversation in the present. His plans for moving to London. My endeavours in the education programme – taking classes in creative writing, current affairs and music, which earned me the princely prison wage of four quid a week. By then I wasn't restricted to main movements, as my Red Band privileges allowed me to walk freely through prison, help Clive set up gear for his classes, even bring an acoustic guitar back to my cell and write songs in the evenings. It was good to share these small achievements with someone, and I started to look forward to his visits. Rick was easy to talk to, unjudgemental and he kept it light. Then he wrote to say he'd just run into my mum in Coventry city centre. She was about to move to Canada with Belinda, so they could hook up with my older sister Maureen and become a trio of merry golf-playing widows. It was up to me, of course, but wouldn't I like to see her before she went? He could break the news regarding my whereabouts, if I wanted.

She had aged, of course. Her white hair was thinning, glasses perched on her nose, and she walked with a slight uncertainty. The hand she put out to me was dotted with brown spots and the fingers which clasped mine were cold and shaky. I was glad Rick was waiting to accompany her back home. It was painfully wrong to see her in that place.

'I don't want Yvonne or Vinnie knowing I'm here, mum ,' I said, once she'd relayed all the family news, although Rick must have told her about my desire for secrecy.

'Vinnie's been so worried about you, Tom,' she said. 'They both have. Though Yvonne's tired out with the new baby – her being an older mother.'

I ignored this news. 'Promise me, mum. I don't want him turning up here to gloat.'

'He wouldn't do that.'

'You don't know. There's so much sour blood between us now.'

'He spent ages looking for you when you first went missing.'

'That's what he told you.'

'You grew up together. Practically like brothers.'

'Yeah, an' he tried to steal everything I had.'

My mum shook her head and sighed. Then she put a hand over mine. 'I love you very much Tom, and your dad did too. I've no idea how you ended up here.' She dabbed a hanky under her specs. 'I hate to see you so bitter now, when you were such a happy boy.'

'Don't mum.' I turned my face away until she'd recovered. 'I'll be out in a few years and I'll make you proud again.'

She gave me a brave smile. 'Your dad thought you were the tops. Even when the papers said those awful things about you. Said you had real courage.'

'I was an idiot.' I said. 'A stupid, conceited idiot. I'm glad dad never saw me in here.'

'Me too, love.' Mum shook her head again. 'But he'd have stuck by you, Tom.' She gave a brave smile. 'You're lucky to have a friend like Rick. One day you can both visit us in Canada.'

I patted her hand, knowing they don't give visas to ex-cons, but saying nothing. Everyone needs hope. Before she left she'd said, 'I'll send you letters, Tom. And please write to Vinnie. He'll be so pleased to know you're safe.'

'Doesn't get any safer.' I'd fixed a big smile at her retreating back, knowing she'd look back and touch her fingers to her lips with the secret mum's kiss. Like she used to do at the school gates when me and Vinnie were kids, all those years ago.

'Alright, you better tell me about Vinnie,' I said to Rick. 'But I'll need a drink. Alan, get that whiskey out.'

I lobbed him my keys. The bottle had been an expensive gift from a grateful rock band, when we'd created an urgent demo through two nights straight – with no drugs, just concentration. For several years I had taken strength from knowing the liquor was there, intact, and I had the key. Resistance is a fine, character-building thing, as my dad used to say.

But now it was time to stop resisting. So we settled at the table with our drinks and I looked from Rick to Alan. Then I said, 'Come on then – let's have it. Tell me everything about Vinnie.'

70

JOSIE

I felt like that cartoon cat who gets whacked by a shovel. Stunned. Knocked flat to the wall, with stars and birds haloing round my head.

'Tell me again, Jamie. Slowly, this time.'

His eyes were shining with excitement and wonder. This was evidently the best day of his life, so I mustn't ruin it.

He took several big gulps of air. 'Tom's old band, Original Mix, from the 80's...'

'I know, we've got their CDs,' I said, thinking, *I used to sleep with the band leader, which is how he's your father.*

'They're re-forming for a twentieth anniversary UK tour.'

'UK tour,' I repeated this slowly, preparing for the next bit.

'And he's asked me if I'll be in the band!'

So I had heard right.

'Doing what, love?'

'Taking the lead singer's place – instead of Eddy Knowles.'

Careful. Careful. Don't burst the balloon. 'Wow. That's an amazing offer, Jamie. Let me give you a big musician's mum's hug.'

He put long, broad arms round me and I felt the strength in his arms as we embraced. The little boy had faded away. Here was my big, brave son. My big, brave, trusting son.

'Jamie, where are these gigs?'

'All over! London, Manchester, Sheffield, Coventry. Hey! I'm going to dig out the CDs again. We got them on vinyl too? Are they in the spare room?'

'I think so….'

He was off, bounding up the stairs. I sat down on the sofa, breathing hard, my mind churning through the facts. If I called Franki or Simon, I knew what they'd say: fantastic opportunity, let him have his moment, amazing to be on stage with his dad, in a great band, etc, etc. But inside I boiled with fury at Tom. How dare he swoop in after all these years and take my son away? And why this? Was he so bloody flattered by Jamie's adoration that he'd decided to offer him the moon?

I leapt up and grabbed my coat.

'Jamie, I'm just popping out!' The opening chords of Wasteland boomed from upstairs. I scrawled a message and ran out, before I lost my nerve.

It was impossible to tell from the silent street, whether the place was inhabited. If people were making music inside, it must have incredible sound proofing. I hesitated, chest thumping with anxiety, and the door opened. Three young black women exited, holding guitar cases. They were typical, attractive Hackney girls – cool hairstyles, tight pants, high shoes and trendy jackets. Behind them, standing tall, in a long sleeved T-shirt and jeans, Tom held open the door.

'Bye TJ,' they said.

'Work on those chord changes Paulette, and we'll get it down next time.'

They smiled at him, with clear admiration.

'Oh! I'm *so* sorry!' one of the girls had nearly backed into me. They walked off looking round with curiousity, no doubt thinking I'd got the wrong address.

'*Josie!* Amazing! Come on in.' Tom was beaming.

'I'm here to talk to you about Jamie.' His charm wasn't going to cut it with me. My heart was thumping with anxiety and anger. I needed to calm down and remember my task.

He nodded. 'Oh-kay, we'll go somewhere private. Follow me.' He led me along the L-shaped corridor, through a far door and up some stairs, and we came out into the open living space of a top floor flat, where there were several huge windows, sills crowded with plants, and the winter sun streamed in, bouncing off white walls and illuminating a duck egg blue ceiling. The impression was of light. Lots of light. He smiled and waved at two big yellow sofas facing each other.

'Have a seat. Coffee?'

I shook my head, and took several deep breaths. It was important to stick to my task – not to become angry. Nor to be distracted by the clusters of photos, and small wooden instruments on the bookshelves, and certainly not by Tom's concerned face and his deep seaweed-green eyes, which were viewing me with intensity.

He sat down opposite, a low glass table between us, over which his knees jutted, long thigh muscles visible beneath black denim. He leant forward, elbows on his legs, hands lightly clasped, in readiness for what I was about to say. I hadn't seen him properly for nearly twenty years and now here he was. It was impossible not to stare, take him all in. His hands were sinewy, mature, and there was a long gash along the back of his left one. He caught me looking and spread it out.

'Argument with a big tree branch which didn't want to be pruned.' He gestured at the window. I was surprised at him gardening, however ineptly, and he smiled, as if reading my thoughts. 'Got a secret patch at the back I'm trying to tame. No idea how. I could show you sometime.'

This wasn't how it was meant to go at all.

'Look Tom, I need to know why you've asked Jamie to be in your band.'

His smile dropped. 'Oh. Don't you..? What's.. ? Are you.. worried?' He was taken aback.

I inhaled deeply. 'It sounds like a big tour, major venues, lots of publicity. There must be any number of experienced musicians who'd jump at the chance. So I'd like to hear your rationale for picking Jamie.'

My voice was cold – but I'd been calm and asked. I breathed out with relief.

Tom thought, chewing his lip. Then he sat back and nodded. 'Okay. Fair enough.'

He stared at the ceiling as he spoke, as if sparing himself the awkwardness that hung about us as heavy as unlit gas.

'Until New Year's, I'd no idea Jamie was your son.' He must have sensed me bristle. 'Even less he could be mine,' he added quickly. 'We get a lot of young wannabes in here, as you can imagine. Some of them make it due to bags of charisma and sex appeal – which can disguise a lack of talent – and some will do alright, cos they have a modicum of ability and work really hard. But occasionally, rarely, you meet someone who's just got musical bones – like they're wired for it. They often play by ear and make choices instinctively. Music comes out of them like breath.'

He sat forward and stared at me steadily. 'Jamie's got that. Ask my studio partner Rick – or Alan. We all saw it, right from the start. Stood out like a beacon. I asked him because he can play and sing – and write, if needs be.' He looked down, massaging his fingers, then faced me again. 'I never wanted this tour, but my arm's being twisted right up my back. So I said I'd only do it if there's someone with energy and talent to replace Eddy Knowles. Remind us old codgers what impetuous youth felt like.'

'You're not that old,' I said, without meaning to.

He gave a short laugh, then said softly. 'It's you who's hardly changed, Josie.'

I ignored the flattery, the intimacy of my name, and his acknowledgement of Jamie's talents. None of this could cut through my anger. 'Jamie's really young. He's only just turned eighteen.' My voice was steely.

'Oh god, I'll take such good care of him. Make sure he doesn't go all rock 'n' roll.' Tom's brow creased in consternation as he said this. He wasn't kidding.

'It's not that, for chrissakes!' I felt myself losing control. 'Jamie grew up in east London. He's seen more drugs and alcohol than I ever have – probably tried things I never knew existed. We've been quite open about all that.'

Tom raised his eyebrows. 'Oh.' Then he looked puzzled. 'What then?'

'Look, he's had a lot of stuff happening recently. Discovering his father, and you two… you know, getting on.' Did Tom realise how Jamie worshipped him? I was gripped by fear again. 'But what if it all goes tits up?' I was ranting now. 'What if the press and your old fans start gunning for this new band – hate Jamie for taking Eddy Knowles place? Those are pretty big shoes to fill you know. Have you thought how that would be for Jamie? And such big venues – nothing like

Sunday lunch in the Boar and Bucket!' My voice was becoming shrill, panicky-sounding, the level tone of reason gone.

'We'll look after him Josie. It'll be okay, I promise.'

I so much wanted this to be true, and if he'd said something convincing, I might have bought it. But I saw a look of uncertainty flicker across the seabed of those eyes.

I stood up. 'No, Tom! You can't make that promise. Because you just don't know what'll happen. You're old enough to take another knockback, and you've been through it all before.' As I thought of my little boy being lambasted in the Press like Tom had, I was almost shouting. 'Jamie's mature in lots of ways – but he's also still *really* young. I don't know how he'd respond to that amount of pressure, neither does he – and *you* certainly don't!'

Now it was Tom who looked stunned. I willed him to argue back, produce new facts, show me a hidden safety net. But he just sat there.

'Anyway, the decision's with Jamie, not me.' I picked up my bag. 'I wanted to hear why you chose him, but I'm not an interfering mum. He follows his own dreams and I'll support him all the way.'

Jamie was talented, I knew that. And I believed Tom's explanation, though I didn't think it was the whole truth. But Tom would never understand how it felt hovering by, watching your son's heartbreak – the dead hamster, the lovingly drawn pictures that weren't picked for children's TV, the soccer try-outs missed by a whisker, the careless girl who broke his fifteen-year old heart. He'd never seen Jamie's disappointed tears, the pillow-punching anger and his brave, hopeful resilience as he got up the next day to try again. *He'd never been there!*

Our eyes locked and all we saw in each other was distrust and hurt.

I tried to regain my breath, find the reasoning part of my brain.

'All I'm asking is that you think it through. I don't know how long you're thinking of staying in the picture. Or if you intend to tell the world you're his biological father.' Hearing my hard and unforgiving voice, Tom's face tightened. 'But Jamie's my only child and I don't want to see him monumentally and publically hurt.'

Tom stood too. 'Okay...' He looked shocked. '...well, I guess you've told me what's on your mind. It's a good thing to be clear...'

He followed me out, at a distance. In the downstairs kitchen, a figure in khaki was hunched over a table, reading a paper.

'Hey, Josie!' The bloke looked up, and scraped back his chair. 'Didn't know you were here!'

'Hello, er, Alan.' I paused, uncertain about how to proceed with the conversation. I studied his face, trying to see the kid from twenty years ago.

No. It was too long ago. Surely all those memories and feelings had long faded. They belonged to other people from another era.

It was hard to imagine they ever existed at all.

71

TOM

'Sit down Tom, for chrissakes. You'll wear a hole in yer carpet,' said Rick as I paced about my flat. Never, even throughout the years in prison, had minutes ticked off so slowly.

I checked my watch. 'Maybe they're lost again.'

It was an hour since Charlie had rung from the M1, on a mobile phone.

'Watcha Shepperton!' The cheeky laddish tone hadn't changed at all. 'So we're finally goin' to meet again. Tell me you're bald and fat, you old git!'

'Yeah, but I've grown a long ginger beard to compensate,' I joked, grinning like an idiot. As his voice hurtled through the ages, squeezing time like an accordion, I wondered what he looked like. They'd been suspended within my memory, like bubbles in ice cubes, until Rick had regaled me with details of jobs, families, kids, health scares, and finally convinced me that decades and the business of living had washed old grievances away. Alan had added that by refusing to think about the whole era I was, in fact, hanging onto the past. As he put it, I needed to, 'Have a few drinks, remember the good times and get over yerself, man.' It was the most philosophical we three had ever got. The whiskey had probably helped.

In the past few weeks, I'd tried to assimilate the personal information and remember that for everyone else it was all ancient news. My biggest worry was that we'd all be too ropey to recreate the Original Mix sound. Josie was right, of course. We were old and ugly enough to weather the reviews. After this tour, we'd return to jobs, families, lives – whatever they held. But what about Jamie?

I hadn't lied. I wouldn't have asked him if he wasn't up to it, though that wasn't the whole reason.

I was redundant as a father, having missed the role so entirely. There was no way to ever make up for that. Then I'd had this brainwave – and it was like fate. It made sense musically, and I would offer the experience as a long overdue gift, from the parent he'd never had.

So it had to work. It just had to.

Finally, after an eon, they piled out from a swish-looking people carrier. First was Devon – he'd grown larger all over, including his hat, which was a massive knitted job, holding a hive of dreads that were now sprinkled with grey at the hairline. A ten ton arm slapped my shoulder.

'Tom! Still a skinny, white strip o' nuttin'? You can come off those prison rations now, man.'

There – he'd said it. Everyone laughed with relief.

Charlie next. I shook my head in wonder. 'You don't look much different, Charlie. Still a skinhead, then?'

He shook my hand matily, and rubbed his shorn head. 'No choice now, Tom. Doesn't grow. Shoulda worn it like Rick's, when I had the chance.'

He stood aside and Len strode up. He wore a red baseball cap embroidered with *Heinrich Das, Technical Services,* his face craggier, but still handsome with that dark, defiant dignity.

'You still owe me twenty quid, rude boy! Don't think I forgot!' His mouth spread into a huge smile as he sprung forward and gave me a fierce, fast bear hug, then let go. 'Missed you, man.' He paused. 'We all did.' No-one contradicted him.

It wasn't the torture I'd expected, but it was still torture.

'You better have a decent place here.' He waved a hand at the studio. 'I ain't rehearsin' in no shit-hole.'

We all laughed again.

And finally, there was Vinnie, leaning against the big car, dragging on a cigarette.

'Watcha, Shepperton. Long time, man.' We eyeballed each other for a moment.

I reminded myself the old Vinnie was someone I knew in the past, more than a life sentence ago. I didn't have a clue who he was now.

'Vinnie! Great to see you!' I stepped towards him, extending my hand. His grip was hard and intense, like neither of us could believe each other's existence, and it felt as familiar as grabbing favourite old boots. When we let go I felt a lump rise up in my throat.

'Looking good, mate,' I said, quickly. His face was older and he was a bit stockier, but he still wore jeans, check shirt and a black leather biker's jacket. 'We the only two here who didn't get old then?'

'Fuck off,' said Charlie. 'Thought we'd come 'ere to make music, not be insulted.' He clapped his hands together. 'Shall we get the gear inside then?'

Rick had done all the explaining required, but when Jamie arrived, I found myself grasping his shoulder for the first time. The connection gave me a rush of protective feeling that I couldn't name. He glanced at me and grinned.

'This is Jamie. He's just gonna watch today, while we get the vibe. When's your daughter coming down Len?'

'Day after tomorrow. Wants to play her own keyboard, an' it's bein' repaired.'

'Great. You an' Vinnie have that morning off, so Jamie and Kadeisha can work with the rhythm section first.' I looked round the room to see how my plans were going down. There were slow nods and agreeing expressions. It occurred to me that I might not be the only one worried about how all this would turn out. Worse – they probably all thought I'd be the one to fuck up again.

♪

'Hey Vin, you came in a bit early there, man.' Devon stopped playing to check with Charlie to his left.

'Er, yeah a bit,' Charlie scratched his head apologetically. 'Like a quarter beat… maybe half.'

'Vinnie glanced at me, then said to Devon, 'Sorry mate. Done too many blue grass and rockabilly gigs. We always get faster.' He hesitated. 'Wanna go again from the top, Tom?'

It wasn't like any of us had forgotten the notes. They were hardwired into our fingers. But some of the exact tempos and a whole lot of lyrics were evading us.

'Yeah, okay. No worries, we'll get there.'

What was happening? No Original Mix rehearsal had ever been so politely restrained.

I looked over at Jamie. He was perched on a high stool, one foot thumping, and a hand pattering on his knee, his body half off the seat – like a lifeguard on Beginners' day at the lido.

After a couple of hours, I couldn't bear it any more.

'Okay – tea break,' I announced as Alan appeared.

'My guys have finished next door. Need anything?' he said.

'Yeah. Can you show everyone where to make a brew, then come back?'

Alan gave me a big grin. 'You bet! This way fellas.'

When they returned, we'd set up several vocal mics, including one at the front.

'Change of plan,' I said. 'Enough electrical acoustics. Time for lead vocals and we need someone who knows all the bloody lyrics. Right Jamie – ' I gestured to the front mic. 'You're on!'

He jumped off his stool, face glowing with anticipation. There was a collective tightening of shoulders in the room, and Eddy's absence was palpable.

'Take it easy,' I said quietly, as I adjusted the microphone height. 'We're just running through, so don't give it your all.'

As we started Wasteland, I focussed on my guitar, pretending it was 1979 and Jamie was just another kid singer trying out for the band. His voice wasn't like Eddy's at all. It was more solemn and mature at the deeper levels, full of modern inflections, with a bluesy plaintive sound in the higher registers – which we'd have judged to be a bit wet, back in the days before men had real feelings. But in 2000 it worked.

Behind Jamie, Vinnie turned to me and gave a few thoughtful nods of approval. I looked across at Charlie, in his trademark stance, legs braced, head cocked sideways, one ear up towards the drums. He caught my eye, smiled and dipped his forehead in acknowledgement. Len was filling in on keyboards – simple clumsy chords, but it would do for now. He frowned at the Korg as if it was deliberately testing him, sucking his teeth when he missed a beat, and when it was time for his toasting section, he was clearly relieved. Before he came back in on the keys, he stood listening to Jamie sing a few lines of the verse, head to one side, lips pouted, deciding – an expression so familiar it sent a rush of warm feeling running through me. He looked over, jutted his chin up at the ceiling, and gave a short nod. Jamie was okay by Len.

We relaxed into a groove and sang the next chorus more joyously than before. And I began to hear that united bond, the voice of the terraces which had taken Wasteland to the top of the charts.

Devon said, 'Yeah, man!' and threw in a few extra flourishes on the high hat.

I began to breathe normally again. It was going to be okay. I could craft this outfit into a new Original Mix after all. Everything would be just fine.

72

JOSIE

One by one, I tugged two big boxes across the beams of the attic, through the layers of dust and cobwebs, in which they'd resided since we'd moved here.

'I'm going to hand them down, Jamie. You still there?'

When I peered through the hole, his face mugged up at me from the ladder. 'Okay, then I gotta go.'

I clutched the sides of a carton with *Marathon Bar* printed on the side, and inched it to the edge. 'Careful. The bottom may fall out.'

But he'd already grabbed it in his strong arms and was reversing down the steps. He came back for the second.

'What's actually in these?' he said, as I hastily rubbed myself free of cobwebs, both real and imaginary.

'Honestly don't know. Stuff I'd stored at my old landlord's shop, which Franki collected on the way to some hat show in Birmingham, when you were a baby. Shoved it all in the attic when we moved here, and it's been there since.'

I studied the two grubby boxes.

'It'll be student rubbish. I'll have a quick look, probably chuck it all.'

Jamie grinned. 'Okay. Have fun mums.' He kissed the top of my head, and I squeezed his bicep in appreciation.

When he opened the front door, I shouted, 'Keys!' and heard his returning footsteps and a metallic scrabbling in the bowl on the shelf. I tutted to myself, then a thought occurred so I called down, 'Hey Jamie! Have you spoken to Vinnie at all?'

He appeared at the bottom stair, frowning. 'Course. You couldn't be in a band with someone and not speak to them, could you?'

'I meant, have you said anything about the money and gifts he's sent over the years – and thanked him, from me?'

Jamie shrugged. He'd stopped wearing the orange beanie hat, which had been welded to his head for the past two years, so he looked much more like Tom – and yet not entirely. He had mannerisms which reminded me of my own dad, still pottering round growing prize dahlias, and some facial expressions like mum's, even Ally's.

He wrinkled his nose – that had definitely been an Ally thing.

'It's a bit awkward to be honest, mum. He was just a name on birthday cards and that. But now he's taught me loads of stuff on the guitar, and he messes round, teasing me. It's kinda hard to bring up...'

I sat on the top stair. 'You're right, love. It's not your job. Don't worry, I'll do it.'

I thought back to the last time I bumped into Vinnie, in the mid 80's, when we'd been visiting the wolf cage at Regents Park, our favourite outing. We'd sat on a blanket eating sandwiches, and Vinnie played his acoustic guitar, which fascinated Jamie. Afterwards Jamie ran around chasing pigeons, and Vinnie watched him, before looking steadily into my eyes and saying, 'He's Tom's son, isn't he?' And I'd not been able to lie.

When the door banged shut, I returned to the mystery boxes. All the spring cleaning had been therapeutic, if difficult. I'd purged Jamie's childhood things, allowing myself to keep one small soft vest which still smelled of talc and baby warmth. Then I'd been equally ruthless with my own possessions. It was a wrench to eject stuff which embodied our history, but also liberating. The flat felt clearer and calmer. This was preparation for the ultimate challenge of course, the one which sent a wave of dread through my entire body. I was rehearsing for the moment when I'd let go of Jamie for good, and he went off to live his own life.

I peeled the masking tape sealing the box, which broke into crispy, brittle pieces. Then I opened the lid and removed a black T-shirt, printed with a stripey cartoon figure of Dennis the Menace. A distant memory surfaced like a dark shape, then disappeared. Underneath were a pile of sketchbooks. I flicked through a series of line drawings entitled, *Coventry City Centre* – an old wino lying asleep on a bench surrounded by pigeons, a Rastafarian man in the precinct, playing a pair of tall African drums, two girls chatting with facing buggies, their toddlers' fat hands stretching out, trying to touch each other. Some of the lines were bold and lyrical. Other areas had been drawn, and erased many times, the fainter lines like a series of frustrations and exasperations. I knew they were mine, but I couldn't recall making them.

A large brown envelope was taped to the top of the second box, with *Josi* scrawled in black marker. I pulled this away and undid the carton – two pairs of heavy, scuffed Doc Marten shoes and more sketchbooks. The first one was small, devoted to quick characterisations – dogs, blackbirds, cats – the students' free models. Underneath this was a large yellow book, which I sat cross-legged to open. The first few drawings showed my younger brother Josh asleep, mum washing up, dad turning earth with a big spade. Then there were a couple of drawings of Ally – his lifeless mouth and eyes making it clear they'd been drawn from a photo. I'd given up after the second attempt and just stuck the photo in. I stared at it for an age. Then, with a big sigh, I turned the page.

And there was Tom. Lying along the couch, legs up, a book open on one thigh, a cigarette dangling from his fingers. The memory of drawing him zoomed back – trying to depict the little curve under his chin, which only appeared when his head was bent. In his white T-shirt and black jeans, his legs seemed unfeasibly long and he looked so very young. I traced the line across the muscled upper arm, overtaken by how much love I'd felt for this man, remembering all the emotions I'd tried so hard not to feel when we were together, and then denied forever, once it was all over.

I thought about the Tom I'd seen in Camden, the one he'd been replaced with. Stinky, drug-crazed, incapable of lucid speech. The Tom who couldn't look after himself, let alone a small boy. It was that crack-head I'd had in mind every time I thought about telling Jamie about his father, the one I'd grown to pity and hate in equal measure.

On other pages I found more drawings and some old photos – Tom with chin propped on hand, Tom viewing me across a table, Tom swathed in sheets on the bed, asleep, Tom sitting cross-legged in just his boxers, laughing over a game of strip Scrabble. Somewhere deep inside me a spring of grief burst through the strata of years, boiled up and came out, in great wracking sobs. I wept for my wasted love, for Tom's optimism and energy, for our youth and our lost opportunities. For Jamie and me not being able to experience Tom as a father.

When my tears came to a shuddering halt, I splashed my face in the bathroom, replaced the sketchbooks, and carried the boxes to our spare room. I'd have to show them to Jamie. I owed him at least that. On the landing I stepped on a big brown envelope, the one with *Josi* on the front. I carried it downstairs to open.

I prised open the gummed flap, to shake the contents out onto the table – old mail addressed to '*30 Richmond Road, Coventry'*. I ripped the envelopes open. Two old bank statements, a missive from Artists' Newsletter about renewing membership, and a cauliflower soup recipe cut from a magazine by mum with, '*Your young people might like this, it's very nutritious!'* scrawled on the bottom – an idea so preposterous that, even twenty years on, it made me laugh out loud. Good old mum, she'd always tried to support my work.

The last was a letter, already torn roughly open. It was addressed to me, but at number 13, in an unfamiliar handwriting – a loopy and carelessly calligraphic, as if written in a hurry. This envelope was scribbled with various notes, '*Not at this address, try 17,'* and '*No Honeywells here – could be No. 5?'* and finally a pencilled suggestion, '*Mr Patel, is this one of your tenants?'*

I turned it over. Scrawled on the back was, '*From Tom – on tour somewhere in the UK.'* There was also the words '*Please, please call me'* and a phone number, written in a different pen. I pulled out two pieces of lined paper, torn from a spiral notepad.

Shore View Hotel
(no shores, no view and not much of a hotel)
15th March 1981

Hi Josie,
I bet this comes as a surprise. It does to me too, because letter-writing is not really my thing. But here goes.

It's 8am in a crappy hotel, where the 70's wallpaper is almost as loud as Vinnie and Devon's snoring. In the last weeks we've played some truly fantastic gigs. There's also been times when people didn't know what the hell to make of us. I'll give you the gruesome details in person soon. But I will say now, there are places in this country so impoverished that even if I was paid top dollar I wouldn't live there. Which kind of comes to why I'm writing – because I've got a question to ask. It's a big risk, but I'm going to seize it while I'm feeling brave.

The thing is, I'm pretty much ready to move out of Coventry for good. I never told you before, but years ago I got married to my teenage sweetheart (Vinnie's sister actually – make of that what you will!). Anyway, it was a bad idea and didn't last long. But now my ex is getting re-married and she's selling our house, where she still lives. So this seems like a good time to ship out of Cov and move to London. Maybe buy a little flat or perhaps rent – I don't really know. But here's the risky bit – I wondered if you would come too? I know we've only been together a short time, but it's great being with you and I think we could make living together work. What do you reckon?

By the way, I've thought about this a lot. It's not just a mad impulse, or cos I'm getting sick of touring (though I've come pretty close sometimes). I want to base myself in London now and I'd love it if you were there too – with your exploding wardrobe and all your paints and arty stuff. You could find work teaching, and in the meantime I've got enough for us to live on. I'm asking you to seriously consider this, Josie. Partly because I think we'd make a good team, but mostly because I love you.

There – now I've said it. So I'll have to post this off quick, before I lose my bottle. Think it over and we'll talk about it when I come back, if I haven't just scared you off (hope not.)

See you soon,

Tom x

I sat back stunned and tried to think. At what point could he have written this? I read it three more times.

The letter had clearly gone astray, but why had he never asked me himself? I tried to recall the sequence of happenings before I ran off to London. But it was all far too long ago, overwritten by a thousand other life events. Did this ancient news really change anything anyway?

I went over to the dresser and tucked the letter into my correspondence drawer, noticing the sun on one of Jamie's photos, illuminating a couple of fingerprints. I wiped them away with the hem of my shirt, and smiled at his baby face. And, as I looked at the photo, I realised this *had* changed things. The image I'd carried for so many years, of Tom as Jamie's homeless, drug-addled father, had been replaced with a much earlier version.

I now remembered a man who had been playful, caring and thoughtful. The man who I'd truly loved, and who I now knew, had also loved me.

♪

73

TOM

After Josie's visit to the studio, I kept thinking of that angry passion in her eyes, the fierce protectiveness she'd shown for Jamie, the way that her lip quivered when she was upset. And the fact I'd had an intense urge to wrap my arms around her as she was leaving, and beg her to stay. As the weeks shot by with rehearsals and plans, I quizzed Jamie, hoping for a sign that she'd like to speak with me again. He always shook his head.

But now I had to push the matter.

I braced myself, and after three rings she answered the phone.

'Josie, it's Tom. We need to speak about the tour. Please don't hang up!'

'Hang up?' She sounded offended.

'I mean, I know you're still er…well, it's been hard…you had a real shock…I mean we haven't got off on the best footing.' Shit! I was riffing like a debut sax player on free jazz night.

I tried again. 'The thing is, you were right to be concerned.'

'I was?' She sounded worried.

'Not because it'll go tits up,' I said quickly. 'I just mean your instincts were protective. That's only natural.' I thumped my head with a fist. Now I was giving her permission to be a parent. Christ almighty!

'Look, could we just sit somewhere and talk?' I said. 'I'll give you all the tour details. And Jamie can be there. Or not. Up to you.' I waited.

I listened to a few short breaths at the end of the phone and then, 'Do you eat seafood paella?'

'Er yeah, I s'pose. Don't think I've ever had it.' In my head I added, HMS Catering doesn't get that fancy, as it goes.

'Come over at seven. Jamie's got a driving lesson. We can talk first, and eat when he gets back.'

Now it was my turn to be surprised. 'Didn't he pass his test?'

A big sigh. 'Sadly not. I've paid for another set of lessons.'

I found myself grinning, at the first piece of parental news ever relayed to me. 'Ouch! I guess that's an expensive gig nowadays?'

'It's not the money.' Josie's tone stiffened. 'Jamie's impetuous. I want him learn to drive safely. If it takes longer, it just takes longer.' She hesitated, and I could hear her breathing again. When she spoke, her voice had softened. 'That's why I worry I suppose.'

It was great to hear her voice again, after all these years. I'd forgotten the northern twang, which had become inflected with Londonisms. Now we were connected I wanted to keep her talking, carry on discovering what she was like, but I checked myself.

'Okay, then. Seven it is. Shall I bring anything?'

'Just yourself.'

My chest was banging at the top of the stairs, and it wasn't just the climb. I stood for a moment, centering myself. Keep calm, you're just visiting another young musician's parent for the usual chats – tour dates, accommodation, medical care...

I raised my knuckles, but the door had opened before I could knock. And there she was, wearing tight blue jeans, a red checked shirt and an apron printed with the slogan, *My other cook's a Michelin Chef.* She was still peachy-skinned and big-eyed, the peroxide hair shorter now, more punk-chic, than punk-with-attitude.

'That's a helluva climb if you forget something,' I said, embarrassed to be caught loitering.

'Keeps you fit.' Josie's mouth curled slightly at the corners – shy and a bit forced, but still a smile. 'And you become very organised – at least some of us do,' she added. 'Come on in.'

She padded away in stocking feet, and I followed, passing a big basket of men's shoes under the stairwell. I was somewhat thrown. Was there a partner? I'd never asked Jamie.

'Do I take my shoes off?' I asked. What bloke owned those big trainers and work boots?

'Not unless you want to.' Josie turned and followed my gaze. 'Oh, I see. Jamie's deciding which ones he's chucking.' She chewed her bottom lip. I'd forgotten how she did that. 'We've been having a bit of a clear out, ready for... well, you know, to make more space.' She picked up a stray plimsoll, and tutted at it before lobbing it on the pile. 'Size 12 – Jamie's got elephant's feet.' She glanced down at my big shoes and blushed.

'Anyway, go through to the lounge. Would you like a cuppa, or maybe some cranberry juice?'

'A cold drink would be great,' I said.

The living room was a colourful mixture of old and new. Walls were painted bright green, yellow and orange and hung with little paintings, semi-abstracts of music and cooking. Window boxes outside overflowed with flowers, and at the far end, an impressive art deco dresser was all carved vine leaves and polished wood. To my left, wicker armchairs and a suede couch with stripey cushions. And on the right a dining table sported a cheerful cloth printed with lemons, plus three chairs. The impression was of being somewhere verdant and blooming.

'This is a great flat.' I walked to the dresser and peered at images of Jamie growing up – his progression from pudding-faced tot to guitar-wielding adolescent.

I sensed Josie's warm female presence at my side. 'Thanks. Here's some juice.' Our hands brushed as I took it. She took a quick sideways step and busied herself straightening a fairly horizontal picture.

'Have the comfy seat.'

The big wicker armchair she'd indicated issued a series of baskety creaks as I settled, and Josie sat opposite in a smaller one. There was an awkward silence as we both sipped our drinks.

'I 'spose this is a bit weird for you too,' Josie said. There were no wrinkles around her warm brown eyes, but there was a knowingness I didn't remember, and a kind of vigilance. I realised I was being seriously assessed.

'I guess so,' I said. How much should I reveal? 'To be honest the last eighteen years have been fairly full on, in various ways.' I hesitated again. 'I'd like to tell you sometime.' I winced, imagining this. 'Probably not now though.'

She gave a brief smile. 'Maybe not. We should stick to our agenda.'

I took another mouthful of juice, feeling her eyes still on me. 'Okay. First thing you should know – I work with my business partner Rick, and also Alan, who you know of old.' I raised an eyebrow, but kept going. 'We've been managing young bands for a few years now, including touring. Why don't I tell you how things work, then you can ask me any questions?'

Josie sat up straight. 'Please do.' Her focus expressed the same eagerness for detail as my barrister's, when he'd asked me to relate everything about that last night at the squat.

After I'd finished my spiel I waited. 'So, that's it really. I'll be there the whole time, of course, and Alan's coming too, as our techie and general go-fer.' I gave an apologetic shrug. 'Probably called it something grander to his face.'

Josie gave a small involuntary chuckle and I felt a buzz of pleasure.

'What else would you like to know?'

She took a deep breath and reached to a small table beside her, her expression serious again. 'At work we complete a risk assessment for each youngster we work with.' I took the paper she was holding out. 'You outline what actions are taken to eliminate these risks.' Her tone was brisk – I guessed it was her centre manager voice.

The form was a standard thing, with 'hazards' in one column. I scanned the list – trips, manual handling, fire, electric shock, working at height, pressurized vessels, use of cutting and welding instruments.

'Jamie won't be at danger from any of this stuff,' I said. 'There'll be guys doing all the get-ins and get-outs – it's not like the old days. All he has to do is carry his guitar onto stage. The only risk is that nobody buys tickets.' I looked up, to see her face cloud over.

'Hey, I'm kidding,' I said quickly. 'Most of the gigs have already sold out.'

Josie looked thwarted. She stood up and went to the kitchen, then returned with a carton. 'Top up?'

I nodded. Finding a path through this awkwardness was proving thirsty work. She wandered to the window and stared out, chewing one side of her lip. Then with a little involuntary sigh, she turned round.

'I just want him to be safe and happy,' she stared at the carpet. 'I suppose that makes me the cliché parent.' She looked up, blushing, as the word 'parent' hung in the air. A few moments ticked past. She finally spoke, in a voice so soft, that I almost didn't hear.

'When Jamie was very small, I met you in Camden.'

I blinked at her. Camden? What did she mean? My heart started to bang and I swallowed, trying to control my breath. Josie swivelled on her stocking toes to face me. 'You won't remember. You were pretty out of it, and you followed me onto a bus. I think you were living rough.'

I stared at her, stunned, remembering and yet not. My persona of music producer and tour manager peeled away for a microsecond, as I recalled the sensation of being that angry, homeless, self-pitying smackhead.

The feeling was gone as soon as it came. I was no longer that man. He'd gone to prison, done his time, cleaned up, then been cleared of all charges. All he'd left was the need for apology.

'I'm so sorry, Joise. It must have been bloody awful to see me in that state.'

She bit her lip and I realised she was fighting real upset. Suddenly I remembered a time, a century ago, when I might have put my arms around her, felt her hands loop round my neck, and we'd both have felt more securely grounded. The desire to reach out was almost painful. She walked over, gently removed the document from my knees, scrunched it into a ball and dropped it into a nearby basket.

'Just keep my son safe, Tom.' Her vision ran across my face like a search light. 'Your son,' she added.

I swallowed again. 'I will, Josie. I promise I will.'

The intercom to the flat buzzed loudly and a waspy voice shouted, 'Yo! Burglar Bill's home!'

Josie's face softened, with the smile of someone who can't help but be happy in the presence of another. She'd forgive him anything.

'I better finish dinner,' she said. 'Burglar Bill's always ravenous. Are you?'

I nodded. 'It smells great,' I said. 'Can I give you a hand?'

Jamie entered to find me setting the table, and Josie carrying in a dish of yellow rice, dotted with spindly-nosed pink prawns, and peppers, bright as traffic lights. He looked to me and grinned. I gave him a little shake of my head, before he made any wisecracks.

'Oh-kaay.' Jamie made a zipping motion across his mouth, then wandered out. 'Fancy a bottle of beer Tom?'

'Yeah, great,' I called.

'Oh no you don't!' I jumped guiltily at Josie's voice. But she was facing the kitchen, hand on hip. 'Jamie, we had a deal. And you said you'd do it the moment you got back.'

Passing me a bottle of lager, he sighed heavily. 'Oh, alright.' And when he disappeared there were a series of thumping noises in the hallway. He returned laughing, as we were sitting down. 'Do I get to eat now?'

Josie dug into the yellow rice with a large spoon, and the intense aromas made my tastebuds tingle. She gestured for me to pass my plate.

'You've kept those black boots, to take with you though?' she asked, without looking round.

'Oh no. Forgot.' Jamie bounded out and a couple more thuds heralded a change of mind.

Josie handed me a steaming plate of food and rolled her eyes. 'Sure you're ready to deal with this?' she said. 'If there was an Airhead Olympics, he'd just about clean up.'

Jamie kissed his mother on the top of her head, then settled in his seat.

'But you still love me,' he said.

'Sometimes.' She pursed her lips and poured some wine, but her disapproval wasn't convincing. Jamie mugged at me, then Josie dropped her pretence, and raised her glass.

'Well here's to you two,' she said. 'To a safe and highly successful tour. Have fun and knock 'em dead.' She gave a short laugh. 'Not literally of course.'

Our eyes met briefly as I chinked my beer bottle against her glass.

'To safety and success,' I said.

74

TOM

The massive double decker tour bus cruised up the narrow residential street of the studio, edging past parked cars, and came to a halt with a discreet sigh. A couple of wheely bins were sticking out ahead, so I ran over and hauled them back into the gutter. When I returned, our pile of equipment sat abandoned on the pavement and everyone was inside, exploring like kids – whacking buttons on the music system, playing with the TV, opening the fridge and switching on lights – as if these were all new gadgets. Jamie was the only one taking it in his stride.

'My grandad's got a luxury caravan in North Wales.' He stretched himself across a comfy settee. 'Bit like this, but on blocks.'

He couldn't understand our hilarity of being on tour with a kitchenette, a lounge on each deck, and real, actual beds! Devon got the first choice of bunk as our 'token grandad'. He made a huge pretence of being offended, but took his time trying them out, before plumping for the solo bed at the rear. Kadeisha got the front single as the only female aboard. The rest of us bounced around, wrestling each other off bunks, until we were laughing like idiots.

Then we helped the driver stow our gear in the hold, along with crates of beer and groceries, before Rick waved us off. And finally, as the tomfoolery died down, everyone found their preferred lounging places, with Jamie and I sitting at a table on the lower deck.

As we left London and motored up the M1, he received a call on his new mobile phone.

'Yo mums! We're on our way!'

I pretended to read my music mag.

'Yeah, I sent it,' he continued. 'But they get loads of applications, so I'm not getting my hopes up.' I watched Jamie frown as he listened to Josie's reply. 'I know that, but it's kinda hard to focus on college right now,' he said. More from the other end. 'Okay, I'll think about it.' Another quick interlude. 'Mum? You coming to the first gig?' There was a tinge of pleading in his voice, then a burst of derisive laughter. 'How'd he do that?' He tutted as she answered, then said, 'Franki's back on Thursday. Can't she help out?' A questioning sound. 'Cos Nev told me,' he replied.

When he put the phone on the table I looked over with casual interest. 'Everything okay?'

Jamie frowned. 'Mum has to work this weekend cos Neville the chef's broken his foot so he can't stand on it.' He pulled a face. 'I thought she was coming up to see us play Bidsworth Castle.'

Bidsworth was the biggest outdoor festival in Nottinghamshire. It was our launch gig, the one which would set the tone for the tour, and attract the most reviews. Josie had passes for every gig of course, and she'd promised to make it to at least three. But still.

'Did you want her there?' I said neutrally.

Jamie screwed up his face. 'I 'spose not.' There was a second of uncertainty. 'No…I mean no.' He looked down at the blank screen of his phone. 'It's no biggy, is it?'

I gave a shrug. 'Shouldn't be. May be better with less distractions the first time.'

I looked across to the opposite set of banquettes where Len was talking to Devon and Charlie. Kadeisha sat beside them flicking through a glamour magazine called 'Black Hair and Beauty.' She was a cool, direct, twenty year old, who luckily hadn't inherited Len's antagonism with the keyboard. Her playing had great fluidity and spirit, also evident in her way of walking and talking. However, every now and then she looked less sure of herself, and several times she'd asked Jamie to remind her of tour details – which of course he couldn't remember either, so had to check with me. Kadeisha and Len often used a series of nods and glances to convey their thoughts, and I envied their family semaphore, built up through the years. It was something I'd be unlikely to achieve with Jamie.

I stared down at the advert in my music journal. It was our tour poster. The photographer had spent time adjusting the precise angles of the instruments, to create 'a narrative journey'. Then he'd said, 'Just imagine the tens of thousands of fans you'll be performing to,' and there was a palpable tension, as our smiles froze. This was the image he'd picked, adding a backing of bright yellow, making us look like a queasy, seaside tribute band. I'd considered objecting but there'd been so much else to do – flight cases to buy, new suits, guitar strings, leads, spare pedals. The list seemed endless. And it all took longer with Jamie in tow, because I felt compelled to share my decision making, like I was handing something on. I reckoned that if this experience was my sole parental gift to him, then it ought to be thorough. After all, he had a whole future of playing live, and surely this was my last ever tour?

'Oi Shepperton, budge up!' Vinnie thumped my knee with his own, and I started to shift.

'You can sit here,' said Jamie, sliding out. 'I'm going to watch telly.'

Vinnie sat opposite, then turned to watch Jamie retiring to the lounge area. 'Like father like son.' He jerked a head to the back of the bus.

'Whatcha mean?'

'Gone for a little sofa time with Kadeisha.' Vinne smirked, as he saw the penny drop with me.

'Ah,' I said. 'Well I'm sure she's in good hands, he's a real gent around women.'

'He better be or Len'll kill him.'

There was a couple of beats as we both grinned. *'With his bare hands!'* we chorused in unison, and then guffawed like it was the funniest line ever.

When we'd recovered, Vinnie picked up a newspaper and started turning the pages. 'That boy looks just like you, twenty years ago.'

'Over twenty five years since I was his age.' I pulled a face. 'You haven't changed much though.' I studied him. 'Bit stouter maybe, and far less belligerent.'

Vinnie shrugged. 'Got over that when I stopped drinking so much.' He looked up and for the first time we fully met each other's gaze.

'Glad you cleaned up and lived on mate.'

I looked down at my hands, not knowing what to say.

'To be honest, didn't think we'd clap eyes on each other again,' he added.

I shifted uncomfortably, then quipped, 'Tried my best to avoid it, but they refused to keep me locked up.'

'Thought you'd bought it, when you disappeared without trace,' Vinnie said.

I stopped joking. 'Look mate, Rick told me what you did – forever searching, putting ads in the music mags to trace me, getting him to write and visit.'

'Didn't think you'd wanna speak to me,' he said in a factual tone.

I shook my head. 'Took me ages to say yes to Rick,' I said. 'All too shameful. Besides, I didn't think anyone would want to know, after everything I'd done.'

'My own behaviour wasn't exemplary,' Vinnie said.

'Didn't get yourself banged up for ten years by mistake though.'

We both gazed out of the window.

'D'ya know what my youngest said to Cheryl when she was about ten?'

I waited.

'She wanted daddy to find his oldest friend, then he could have the best birthday ever.'

I swallowed, watching the cars stream past. Sleek, black and silver motors, driven by intense-looking blokes, hogging the fast lane, determined to beat everyone to their destination – singled-minded, focussed, ungiving.

'I'm so sorry mate. I was a selfish bastard.'

Neither of us said anything, and I added, 'With a really serious drug problem.'

Vinnie nodded and for a moment in his eyes I saw the awful pain that I'd caused to him, Rick, my mum, and the band. All of them.

'It don't matter now,' said Vinnie, folding the paper with finality. 'Yesterday's news, ain'it?'

There was something else which needed to be said.

'I heard about you and Cheryl, and I'm made up you made a life together.' In all honesty I couldn't remember her face, but there were lots of people I had difficulty recalling.

Vinnie gave a short laugh. 'Took an arse like you to make her realise I weren't so bad.' He reached in his jacket pocket, and passed me a dog-eared photo. It showed a dark haired woman with two teenagers – and boy and a girl – on a beach, somewhere hot. Vinnie put on reading glasses and prodded a finger at the boy. 'Tyler opened his own salon last year.' He looked at me over his specs, eyes glinting with mirth. 'Mate, I only spawned a family of fuckin' hairdressers!'

Hearing our cackling, Len came over, 'Right then, what's all this funny business 'bout?'

He rested a hand on my shoulder and lowered himself beside me. As he released it, I realised that the sudden physical contact hadn't made me bristle in fight-readiness. Perhaps I'd finally lost those prison heebie jeebies.

The fridge door made a sucking sound, and everyone looked up. Jamie was extracting a couple of cold cans. 'Kadeisha just floored me at Wordworm,' he said happily.

'Chah! Don't play that girl for money!' Len called. 'She don't even let her own dad off.'

Vinnie leant forward to me, with a knowing look.

'And there's another peach which didn't fall far from the tree,' he said.

♫♪

Finally we approached the gates, and our bus nudged through the hoards like a whale among minnows. We knelt on seats, hands pressed on the darkened windows, gawping at all the hip young things.

'Bloodaay Nora, so many people!' said Charlie. He turned to Devon grinning. 'Hope the speakers are overwhelmingly vast, then I can crank up the bass.' Charlie's sound had become thicker and more throbbing over the years, with the odd slap bass groove thrown in for good measure. When he'd heard our old 24 track recordings, he'd denounced the bassline as 'embarrassingly weedy.'

We'd all changed in fact. Voices were deeper, and our playing styles far more competent but somehow less edgy. Jamie and Kadeisha brought a freshness and immediacy which stopped us short of sounding like an ancient pub band.

Devon studied the site plan. 'Where we playing, Tom?'

I peered over his shoulder and jabbed at the map. 'Main one. We're the second to last support.' I moved in so only he could hear. 'They wanted us headlining on second stage, but I decided that was too much for our first gig.' I scrunched up my face. 'Hope it was a good call.'

Devon thought, then nodded. 'Sounds 'bout right. More people an' less pressure.'

'Can't wait to see everyone from the main stage,' said Vinnie. He thumped Jamie on the back. 'Ready for this Junior?'

Jamie face was alight. 'You bet!'

But first there was a whole lot of palaver obtaining onsite parking passes, site maps, schedules, wrist bands, and food vouchers – each doled out like they were gold cards, by bright young things in skimpy T-shirts and wellie boots, with squawking walkie talkies. Vinnie and I thought it was hilarious seeing so many well known musicians queueing up like we were waiting for school dinners, but our two youngsters were greatly impressed to be in such elevated company.

When we finally ambled over the grass in the sunshine, to my surprise, we were intercepted by fans and I found myself signing a CD, a site map and someone's straw hat. I stopped short of putting my autograph on a drunk lad's chest and his inebriated girlfriend's voluminous boobs.

'That's so wrong,' said Vinnie ruefully, as they stumbled off, hanging onto each other for support. I didn't ask which part of the interaction he meant.

As we chatted to people, Jamie joined the banter with enthusiasm, but he stuck close to my elbow and I began to realise what Josie meant. Off stage, he was clearly still so young and, despite his height, standing next to the solid manly physiques of Vinnie and Len, he appeared like a mere boy. His head darted around as he took in everything anyone said, and a little frown creased the corner of his eyes, when he didn't understand.

I grabbed his shoulder. 'Sorry folks, better get ourselves to stage. C'mon Jamie.' I pulled him away from the throng which had gathered.

'Listen, let's not get drawn in.' Jamie gazed back to where Kadeisha and Len were being photographed with fans. 'You need to keep something back for later.'

I turned my head left and right – facing so many excited thousands, he would need everything he had.

None of us were prepared for the vast thunder of approval which rolled up when Original Mix was finally announced. When we'd last heard that sound, this crowd of half-naked young bodies wouldn't have even been born. As we picked up our guitars, I gestured at Vinnie to both move upstage. The space was bigger than I'd envisaged, and Jamie seemed very small and exposed at the front. Len snatched a mic from the stand and hollered out,

'Twenty years ago, we brought you the Mix Up style o' music and dancin'! So we hope you still remember it, cos we got ourselves a new rude girl!' – he waved at Kadeisha and there were cheers – 'and a new rude boy!' He put a long arm across Jamie's shoulder and they grinned at each other, as the crowd whistled and cheered.

Len continued, 'We gonna mix up some rare sounds for you now. Cos we missed you laaang time! Kaowee!' He ended with a bird-like call and at this cue we all crashed into our first chords then Len pattered out the words,

> *'I'm walkin' in me suit, wid a pocket fulla loot, I'm a –'*
> *__' Dance Hall Skaa-man!'__*
> *'Got on me smart press pants, an' I know how to dance, I'm a –'*
>
> *__' Dance Hall Skaa-man!'__*

The crowd might be young but they knew the songs.

When we came to the bridge, where the tune sped up, I caught Vinnie's eye, and we gunned round the chord changes, exchanging mad grins. There had been times when I couldn't remember anything about being in Original Mix, other than the endless griping arguments, stinky hotel rooms, that shitty flat, or the tormented recording sessions.

But now it all came back - the power of the *n'chah, n'chah, n'chah* beat, the total impossibility of not dancing and the fantastic, amazing feeling of being in sync with some of the finest musicians to come out of the Midlands. In front were thousands of happy bobbing bodies, girls in bikini tops sitting on lads' shoulders, people in fancy wigs and sunglasses, even flags bearing the old Mix Up logo and people wearing pork pie hats. We finished our first song to a deluge of delighted cheering and now it was Jamie's turn to pluck his mic from its stand.

My legs tensed. I was ready to take over if he faltered under the pressure. I'd promised to keep him safe and sound, and stopping him being booed by a thousands-strong crowd was definitely in the remit.

'Hello Bidsworth!' he shouted. There were cheers and a few whistles. He waved at the sky. 'You're all so beautiful from up here!' A huge self-congratulatory roar came up. Good Jamie, keep going. I played a little soft rhythm under his intro, a tiny hint at our next song, and I heard a few sparse piano chords answering mine, as Kadeisha joined in.

'Hey, guess what? I'm trying out a new band.' Jamie gestured at us with a wave, then stepped to the edge of the stage, as if speaking in confidence. 'Whaddya think? They any good?'

There was a peel of laughter, with cheers and whistles. It was a different sort of showmanship than Eddy's, but it was good. He let the cheering die down, then with immaculate timing continued.

'You know, Bidsworth is a great place for a festival. But before they built this site it was just,' he paused for a beat, 'a *Wasteland!*'

And he sang the opening lines, cupping his mic with two hands in reverence, like it was a communion goblet, which somehow gave him permission to take Eddy Knowles' place, before swinging his guitar to the front. Then we all sang the chorus, coming in strong, like a huge swell, a backing support like no other. I looked across the sea of bodies to the clear blue sky, suddenly wishing like hell that Eddy was here to perform on this massive stage. *Four guitars! Christ Eddy, this is like flying with sound!*

Vinnie took his solo, pulling out all the old moves. His legs weren't quite as far apart as they used to be, and he winced slightly as he windmilled his arms round, but his face had lit up like it used to when he was twenty three.

'Steady mate, you'll spring a gasket!' I shouted as we stepped towards each other for our joint riff up and down a series of belting arpeggios.

'Fuck off Shepperton!' he shouted back. And it was like the old days, but this time we were both more mature, wiser, and hopefully less likely to do ourselves an injury, or behave like a prize twat.

After our third encore we finally left the stage. Len had his arm slung over Jamie's shoulder and they exited last, waving farewell to an exhausted crowd.

'Fuckin' mega!' Jamie gabbled at me. 'I was *so* nervous to start, but once we were into Wasteland I was totally there!'

I was buzzing with elation and relief. 'Who'd you bribe for that bass sound?' I yelled at Charlie, as we ran down the steps to the grassy backstage area.

He patted the side of his nose with a forefinger, and yelled back, laughing, 'You've got four fuckin' guitars! I'd have been drowned at sea!'

Behind, Devon slapped me on the shoulder. 'You did it man! You put the old sound back together – even better!'

'We did it!' I said. 'Just like the original Originals!'

For a millisecond our eyes met, as we both had the same thought – except no Eddy.

Then Devon nodded slowly. 'Yeah man – this time Millenium style.'

As we clambered down from the wings, we were mobbed by people with backstage passes. 'Friggin' great!' 'Still got it!' 'Totalled 'em mate!'

In amongst the strangers, I spotted Rick with Isabella, and of course Alan and Skylark – looking very much at home in their tree-hugging outfits, with multi-coloured ribbons threaded into their hair. Everyone was talking at once, high on music, electric with possibilities – extended tour, re-releasing albums, new single. Over the heads of fans I waved at Rick, who was nodding his shaggy dog head in animation, as he talked to some roadies. But before I could get to him, we were borne off to a Media Tent. Photos, interviews, introductions. I repeated the same thing over and over – Kadeisha is Len's daughter, yes, amazing pianist, brought up on ska and Original Mix. Eddy Knowles was a tough act to replace, but I heard Jamie at our studio, spotted a gem. New blood. Different vibe. And so on until I was hoarse and mimed 'drink' at Vinnie, pointing at Jamie who was also surrounded by journos with cameras and digi-recorders. Vinnie moved in like a shark, plucking Jamie from the throng and propelling him my way and out towards the VIP tent.

'Phew! Thought you'd never bloody ask,' said Vinnie, as he kept pace.

'Since when did you need to be asked to drink?' I said.

'Since Cheryl made a decent bloke of me.' Vinnie rolled his eyes, and produced a packet of tobacco. He grinned. 'Still, she ain't on tour yet – so let's go party!'

We ligged around in the VIP tent for several hours, popping out to watch the final support act then back to congratulate them and drink some more. I paced myself and kept a keen eye on Jamie. I'd made a promise that I wasn't going to renege on. So as dusk fell I extracted him, and we went to grab some food.

'Mike from The Swallows has got an amazing guitar sound,' he said through a gobful of gourmet burger. 'But he's a bit of an arse.

Offered me a Double Dove. I mean, bloody hell, I haven't done that since I left school.'

I laughed. 'Jesus! Your bike sheds were a lot more serious than ours. What did you tell him?'

Jamie shrugged. 'Said I'd stick to beer.' He turned to face me. 'I'm loving all this Tom. You said it would be manic – but I had no idea!'

I narrowed my eyes, mellowed by drink and a sudden need for honesty. 'Your mum thinks I'm a fuck up whose gonna take you down with me.'

'What? Nah, she doesn't.'

'How'd you know?' I asked.

'Cos she told me about the old times, before I came away. Showed me some photos and explained what you and the band tried to do.'

I took a gulp from my wobbly plastic pint. 'And?'

Jamie grinned, quite pissed. 'She looked fairly smitten man.' He belched. 'Not that we went there.' He pulled a face. 'We're cool with each other, but she's my mum and there's definitely a line.'

I felt a liquidy smile spread across my own face. 'Let's both agree not to fuck up then?'

Jamie held out a hand and we shook, in drunken solidarity.

A flash gun popped somewhere beside us and there was a shout of, 'Yo, Tom!'

I turned. A tall, dark haired bloke was stooping to enter through a side tent flap. I may not have recognised the squarish face, or the jeans-and-flight-jacket attire. But those TV framed spectacles hadn't much changed.

'Fuck me! Fozz!'

He bowled over, throwing the big camera down on a bar table, and wrapped me in a hug. We both jumped back in surprise and then laughed like idiots. 'Didn't mean literally!' I was mad with joy to see him. 'Oh my god, Fozz, it's really you! Fozz – I can't believe it!' I shook my head and we laughed all over again.

'Jamie, this is Fozz.' He'd stood patiently by, waiting.

'I got that much,' he said, grinning.

'Steven Fossett,' Fozz shook Jamie's hand. 'Love how you deliver those lyrics, man. Steel Bantam meets Heaven's Goat – with a touch a Floyd Simms from Zinconia.'

He saw Jamie's face cloud over in concern.

'But unique,' he added. 'Undefinable.' He considered a moment. 'Probably.'

'*You're* Steven Fossett!' I shook my head. 'Been reading your stuff for years – no idea it was you!' He wrote for two national dailies as well as being a stalwart at New Sonic Waves. 'Looks like you did okay for yourself then?'

Fozz smiled. 'I get by. Great to see you, Tom. Heard a way back from Charlie that you were out.'

'Out of what?' said Jamie.

Fuck! This wasn't the way to tell him.

I said quickly, 'Yeah, finally out of the studio and on tour. Took some doing.' I gave Fozz a meaningful look, and in desperation I emphasised my next words, '*Nobody knows.*'

'Ah.' Fozz nodded. 'Appreciate that, man.' He turned to Jamie. 'So how do you know this old reprobate?'

Jamie gave him the 'we met at the studio' yarn, which he seemed to buy wholesale. Perhaps Charlie was better at keeping the most important secrets nowadays.

We chatted about bands, influences, the current scenes – emo, scream, funky, grime, dubstep – where music might go next, where it had been, what complete cocks Hammerhead Napalm were, and who could have imagined that Coventry City would still be in the Premiere League after thirty odd years.

Fozz offered funny vignettes of what life on the road with us was like, and what dickheads we all were.

'Don't do so many all-nighters nowadays.' Fozz blew out his cheeks. 'Though that'll change soon, as we're about to have another baby.'

'Oh?' I was surprised, having decided long ago his lack of women signified he was gay. Maybe he'd just had the same lack of sex drive as I did, back then. After all, we took the same drugs.

'I know,' he said. 'Thought it was all over, then the missus announces we've scored again. Don't suppose you…' He shuffled awkwardly, no doubt remembering my covert request to stay schtum about prison.

'None I ever knew about.' I raised an eyebrow at Jamie. Now aint that the truth, son.

As the tent filled up with musos, the rest of the band emerged, boozy stomachs demanding fried food, stuffed in a bun. Greetings were made, backs slapped. Kadeisha was introduced and was clearly impressed to be meeting such a major journo.

'You staying the whole weekend?' Charlie asked.

Fozz shook his head. 'No mate. Decided to cover an emerging band, lig along for some of their tour. Might even ask if I can travel in the tour bus, for old time sake.' His beady eyes twinkled behind the specs.

'Which band?' said Kadeisha.

Everyone burst out laughing, and she looked hurt. 'I was only asking!' she said crossly.

'No-one's making fun of you sweetheart.' Devon put an arm round her shoulder. 'This bad man used to tour 'long with us. Always trying to get some big Press scoop.'

'Never got it either.' Fozz shook his head. 'Had to look to Detonator for that.'

Kadeisha gave a weak placated smile, but when she and Jamie went to the bar she was speaking with great indignance. Jamie gave her a consolation hug, and they kept their arms linked loosely round each other, until they were served. We needed to remember that they weren't as tough as old boots, like the rest of us.

Eventually, as we fell into the tour bus, not exactly sober, I remembered something.

'Jamie – you called your mum? We both promised!'

'Oh shit!' he grabbed the wall, stumbling to remove boots and jeans. 'Meant to earlier, but I forgot. Do it tomorrow.' He fell onto his bed and a light snoring signified he was out.

I checked my watch. One o'clock. Josie said she was still a night owl, so I texted: *'Jeez, sorry it's got so late. Gig success. J great. Call you tomorrow?'*

In the time it took me to peel off my clothes and flop onto the bunk, the phone beeped with a text reply: *'Can u call now?'*

I grinned. Course I could.

'Hey how you doing?' I said.

A long sigh. 'I'm so cross with Neville for imagining he's still some young gun. He made a dive at cricket and managed to break two toes. I've been stuck in the bloody kitchen, making sure the kids don't burn the place down.' She tutted with impatience. 'But that's not important. How did it go? Where's Jamie?'

I looked at the bunk opposite where Jamie was sprawled. 'Spark out. We drank quite a lot after the gig. It was amazing.'

Josie laughed. 'The drink or the gig?'

So I told her all about it, lying back on the pillows, thrilling to hear her excitement about Jamie at the end of the line. Her laughter was sexy and guttural when I mentioned I'd declined to sign someone's breasts.

'So Jamie's okay?' she said finally. 'Not forgotten anything?'

'Only to call home,' I said. 'Never slips a beat on stage. When are you likely to get to a gig?'

'I'll come next Thursday,' she said. 'If Nev can't find himself cover, he can bloody well hop in and supervise from a chair.'

'That's the Birmingham gig,' I said. 'Should be special.'

There was a pause.

'So he's really okay?'

'Bit pissed, but fine.'

Another pause.

'I better go,' she said. 'Tomorrow's Under Fives Club make gingerbread houses with our Street Foods kids. Teenagers, infants and too much sugar. No doubt end in tears – probably mine.'

I didn't want her to go, but it was late. 'Shall I call you tomorrow night?'

'A quick update would be great,' she said, 'But only if you get chance.'

I lay back against the headrest, listening to the sound of festival revelry from the field and someone in the bus – probably Devon – snoring deeply, like a purring lion.

Oh yes Josie, I'll make my chances and seize them, I thought. This time no fuck ups.

75

JOSIE

In the following days I received a series of excited calls from Jamie.

'You won't believe our audiences!' I thrilled to hear in the joy in his voice. 'They love Original Mix, and everyone's goes mad dancing to ska! Tom says it's totally different this time – but he's totally buzzed too, I can tell.'

'Do you get nervous?' Perhaps this wasn't a good question, but I asked it anyway.

'No, I mean yes, but in a good way. Kind of nervous excitement. But Tom's always there and Vinnie, and of course Len. Oh my god, I'm learning so much from Len, mum. He holds a crowd and has fun with them. They totally love him. Oh guess what? Last night someone had made a banner with my name on it. Mad or what?'

'How's Tom doing?'

'Yeah, great, he'll call you later. Oh guess what else? I met The Giraffes – all of them, including Matt Taylor! We had photos together. And I was interviewed by one of the papers.'

'Which one?'

'Dunno, a Sunday one I think. Rick sorted it. And Steven Fossett's been following us. Steven Fossett! He's one of Tom's old mates, from way back. It's mega!'

Jamie's words fell over each other – a jumble of intoxicating experiences. He'd be playing it cool with the band, but he was desperate to talk and he didn't need to impress me.

'Is there anyone your age there?' Maybe I should take Askim up with me.

'Ash and Zed are coming up tonight, besides Kadeisha's my age – well, bit older but it doesn't make any difference.'

I recognised this tone of voice from past romances, but I knew not to poke a maternal nose in where it wasn't wanted.

'Well it's good you've got someone to relate to,' I said in a neutral voice, then I gave a short laugh. 'And a female to keep you all in line.'

Jamie said, 'There's a ton of drugs knocking round backstage at some gigs. But Kadeisha's not interested and neither am I.'

'Because you're my big mature son?'

'No, cos I don't want to get out of it. Tom said he can't recall a lot of his time from before. But I want to see everything and have memories. I'm keeping a journal.' He paused. 'Also I don't want to make a complete tit of myself, like on my eighteenth.'

I burst out laughing. 'Yes, you made quite an impact then! I agree though – keep it civilised Jamie, cos everyone's *so* proud of you.'

I meant, don't blow it like your father did.

Tom called each night, just to reassure me. But as we spoke, it felt like we were slowly reconnecting. I had the sense that he really wanted Jamie to have a great time – to enjoy being a young musician in ways he hadn't.

Then a couple of nights before the Birmingham gig, he told me how he'd started to rely on a cocktail of drugs, and what a 'complete twat' he'd been back in the 80's, mainly to the band.

'It's hard to believe they don't all still hold it against me,' he said, adding, 'Where are you, by the way. Not still at work?'

I checked my clock. It was almost midnight.

'Already showered and in bed,' I said without thinking, then thumped a palm against my forehead. Too much information, Josie.

There was a silence, then, 'So am I,' said Tom. 'Lying on my bunk in the bus that is. Only place for some quiet. Everyone's in the bar, being courted by a thousand hangers on.'

His voice was deep and gentle. I sunk down in my pillows, phone wedged against my ear.

'How's my errant son?'

'Not erred yet, as it goes. There's someone who's a good influence – as well as me,' he added quickly.

'The wonderful Kadeisha?'

Tom laughed. 'Oh, he's told you.'

'No, I guessed, from the fact that he mentioned her name three times in as many sentences.' I chuckled. 'Not exactly MI5 material, our boy.'

It was a figure of speech, but *'our boy'* zinged across the line like a spark. There was a moment's pause.

'You did a great job with him,' said Tom. 'Can't have been easy being a single parent.'

The time seemed to be right for truths. 'I'm sorry I didn't tell him about you,' I said. 'I thought it was impossible you were still alive, so it seemed the best thing. But you get on so well…' I hestitated, the sudden urge to confess overtaking me. 'I now realise that I really cheated him by not trying to find you.'

There was a much longer pause. 'You couldn't have found me Josie.' Tom's voice was serious. In the half-lit privacy of our bedrooms we were admitting to things too difficult to say face to face.

'I don't understand.'

'Hmmm. Okay, then.' Tom sounded suddenly decisive. 'I've been meaning to tell you this. And it may come out publically, so I want you to hear it from me.'

Then he told me he'd spent his thirties in prison. It was impossible not to be shocked. All the time I'd been struggling in a run-down centre, and establishing Street Foods to keep local youngsters out of trouble, Tom had been alive after all, and incarcerated in prison for a crime he didn't even commit. *Ten years! A whole decade!* All that wasted time.

'You don't even sound that angry,' I said, eventually.

'I'm not now,' he said. 'It saved me from my worst self. I was living rough, drinking and using a lot of heavy drugs. Who knows where it would have ended.' He sighed. 'Ah well, we probably all know.'

I swallowed, thinking of Tom back then, shambling, dirty and desperate, and the guilt rose in my throat. I could have stopped him going to prison.

'Oh god Tom, I'm *so* sorry I didn't do anything.

'What about?' He was surprised.

'When I saw you in Camden. It was such a shock and I wasn't thinking straight. I should have brought you home and helped you clean up.'

'Josie! No way!' Now there was pity and concern in his voice. 'I'd have taken your money and fucked off to score.' He paused. 'Especially when I saw Jamie. That would have totally freaked me out.'

'Really?' I said uncertainly.

'I was in no state to be helped. Please don't ever imagine I was,' he said. 'I wouldn't have let you.'

This changed everything, but I couldn't yet process how.

'How should I tell Jamie about prison?' asked Tom. 'He mustn't find out from some hack.'

I considered. Jamie and I both knew this territory. I needed to explain how Tom was only human, that back then he'd been like Pete or Shakey, or the other kids we hadn't engaged because they were too firmly in the grip of drugs or gangs.

'I'll give him the basic facts, and you can fill in any details.'

I was protecting them – these two men – from hurting each other. Was this what mums did in a double-parent set-up? We weren't exactly a family here. Twenty years on, and I still didn't know much about Tom's life.

'Tom, may I ask you a personal question? You can tell me to mind my own business.'

'Course, anything.'

'You've been out of prison for what, five years?'

'And counting.'

'Do you have a partner or someone special?'

He laughed. 'You mean apart from Rick and Alan?' Then he said, 'Just kidding. I know what you mean and no.' The no was firm but tinged with regret, like some decision had been reached. 'Been too busy building up the studio and working out how to live a normal life. How about you?'

'Er, no.' I was embarrassed at the question being turned on me.

'I've had a few relationships, of course,' I added quickly. 'But nothing that's stuck. Not sure why.'

There was a pregnant pause, broken by Tom's cynical laugh. 'I set the bar too high. Nobody else offered the same boyfriend-turned-junkie experience.'

I didn't laugh with him.

'It wasn't like that when we were together Tom, and you gave me the best gift in the world – my son.'

There was a deep breathing at the other end of the line. 'Wow! I don't know what to say.'

His voice was so serious that I regretted the statement. It was too much. I tried to find words to back peddle.

'Josie?'

'Yes?'

'That's the most amazing thing anyone's ever said to me. Thank you.'

When I hung up the phone, I found my throat dry and the back of my eyes prickled.

My fury at Tom had lain for years, coiled in a dark corner of me, mean and poisonous. The real rage was not knowing what had happened to him, fuelled by my abject guilt at not acting better. But now, released from these feelings, I was left with a huge sadness for all Tom's wasted years.

Jamie was no saint. He could be stubborn, forgetful, and his table manners weren't always impressive. But he was a caring, funny and fairly modest young man, who could look out for himself.

So I decided. It was Tom's time now.

He should enjoy being with his son, without always apologising to me. I'd stop holding back, and being so protective.

I would give Tom my full approval and trust.

76

TOM

'How's it going with you know who?' Alan rested some god-awful health juice on the table and flopped onto the horseshoe-shaped sofa opposite, while the tour bus cruised along, smooth as a hovercraft.

I peered up from my technical mag, and shifted position.

In the front TV area, four grown men – Fozz, Len, Rick and Vinnie – were in hot competition, hunched in front of a gaming console blowing away demons. There was a piercing death cry as someone got a hit, and a collective squawk of triumphant pleasure.

'Who d'ya mean?'

'Josie.' Alan gave a wicked grin. 'You know, operation Bring Her Round.'

I smiled, mainly to myself. 'Not bad actually. We're getting on pretty well.' I put the magazine aside and considered. 'Got past awkward anyway. And she seems more relaxed about Jamie being on tour.' I pointed at the scattered newspapers on the floor. 'All these reviews helped. She can see journos and fans rate him, and nothing bad has happened.'

'What did she expect?' said Alan.

'Dunno.' I shrugged. 'She just wants him safe and sound, I guess.'

He slurped at the dregs of his drink and, after a moment I said, 'What do you remember about Josie?'

'Not much. Only that she made quite good cooks out of us, but we gave her a hard time.' He laughed. 'We were horrid little oiks.'

'Suggesting you're not now?' I dodged the empty plastic beaker that was aimed at my head, and it bounced off the carpeted ceiling. Alan rose to put it in the bin.

When he sat down again he said, 'Josie treated everyone with respect. Was encouraging, like. Said we could do anything we wanted to with our lives. Nobody on our estate ever thought like that.'

I nodded. I recalled her trying to be scrupulously fair. I remembered other things too, like her playfulness and an impetuous, even wild, streak. Didn't we once have sex in a bush?

Alan broke my thoughts. 'Goin' to the kitchen. Want a drink?' He looked at me quizzically. 'You alright Tom? Got a funny smile goin' there.'

I swung my legs down. 'Yeah fine. Go on, I'll have a beer. Just a stubbie.'

I peered out of the smoked glass window, looking for road signs. 'Should be in Birmingham soon.'

I felt excitement bubbling in my sternum. Practically a home gig, and Josie would be there!

Charlie's boots emerged down the steps.

'Hey Tom, come upstairs! Me and Dev are jamming with the youngsters. Got the makings of a crackin' new tune.'

'Yaay!' 'Mashed their arses!' Fozz and Len slapped palms as they annihilated the other team, and Vinnie reset the game for a grudge match. Clearly some things hadn't changed.

I grabbed my 12 string and my beer, to scoot behind Charlie.

'Can't get over this luxury bus.' I chuckled as we walked along the aisle, flanked with its spongey bunks. 'Sleeping in that old van was bloody awful. Woke up once with my head in Vinnie's crotch.'

Charlie stopped in his tracks and turned. 'Christ, I remember that! Eddy said if you wanted to blow Vinnie that bad, you two should share a room.'

'Jeez, I'd forgotten!' I clapped a hand to my forehead. 'Is that the fight when Trev had to pull over on the hard shoulder?'

Charlie's eyes narrowed. 'Could have been. There were so many between Eddy and Vin. Can't even remember why.'

I sighed, feeling a small squeeze in my chest. 'You know what Charlie? Playing Birmingham without Eddy – it doesn't seem right.'

Charlie gave a small nod, and we both looked down at our feet, as the bus whirred on.

Then I clapped a hand on his back. 'Come on then, let's hear these new songs.'

♪♫

The Arcadia in Digbeth was a grand old red brick theatre, which was having its own anniversary, being a century old. The front of house areas had undergone a refurb – the foyer all glass and modern panelling, open and airy – with banners announcing the *'100 years of The Arcadia'*. Large black and white photos of confident, young theatre luvvies looked down with beautiful, knowing smiles. Our bright yellow tour poster was up too – showing us frozen in uneasy poses. I winced to see it.

Backstage, the main venue smelled of mice and dust, except in the dressing room, where garlicky spices wafted through the square-wired windows from the Punjabi Palace restaurant next door. It was so overpowering that most of the band went to avail themselves of the, *'All you can eat lunchtime buffet.'*

Inside the venue, the red seats may have lost their plush, but its balconies had been smartened up in racing green, with raised swags of gold laurels. On stage right a scaffolding rig had been erected – part of the set for a theatre production, celebrating Birmingham's history. It was a bit of an eyesore, but didn't take up too much of the generous-sized stage, so I'd already agreed we'd ignore it.

As the crew set up our gear, I paced about offering tips, until Alan put a hand on my shoulder.

'Why not go and get somethin' to eat? Let me and Rick finish this, with the lads.' He gestured to three big blokes, currently feeding cables out across the stage, with great rubbery thwacks.

I frowned.

'It's what you're paying them for,' he added, not unreasonably.

'I 'spose.' I'd done my stint roadying for Recknaw, back in the Dark Ages. It was time for some other poor fuckers to pull their back muscles and break their toes. But still I hesitated.

'What?' said Alan.

'I dunno.' I watched the lighting technician refocus a spotlight, from inside the hydraulic bucket of a Genie. 'I've got a funny feeling.'

Alan laughed. 'Called hunger mate. Go an' find the others.' He gave me a shove, so I strolled to the stage edge, and jumped down in front of the seats.

'Find me as soon as you're finished,' I called over to Rick. 'I'd like an early soundcheck.'

'Oiright mate. No problemo!' he shouted back.

But there were problems – lots of problems. First there was intermittent sound from Vinnie's guitar amp. Then Devon drowned us all out because his earphones weren't working, and lastly Kadeisha's microphone was dodgy, before her keyboard amp cut out completely. When I stopped everyone playing for the fifth time, and the technician jumped on stage with another mic, Devon sucked his teeth in disapproval.

'Jesus Tom, can't you do something?' said Vinnie in my ear.

Len came over to join the huddle. 'This is no good man,' he glanced over at his daughter, now in a close unhappy huddle with Jamie. 'It's spookin' the kids – they don't need this.'

I strode to mid-stage. 'Okay, everyone take fifteen, while we sort this out.'

Devon stepped from the drum riser, tapped Charlie on the shoulder and they disappeared, probably for a little de-stressing toke. The others went to the bar.

For the next twenty minutes I tried to analyse the issues with the crew, running round the stage with electrical testers, plugging and unplugging power cables and mains distros. It was such an ancient building, and the electrics had clearly been added to as the years went on.

'Fuckin' hell! Where's he gone now?' I said to Rick. The chief LX had disappeared yet again, and time was ticking on.

'Gone to get the mains wiring manual,' said one of the stage hands.

'For fucks' sake!' There was a squeeze in my chest as I thought how important this gig was. I ran a sweaty hand through my hair and jabbed myself in the neck with the screwdriver I was holding. 'Ow!'

Rick winced in sympathy, then a familiar expression came over his face. 'Tom man, this is just winding you up. Go and get a drink, like a proper musician.'

'But I…'

'You're not actually helping, man,' he interrupted. 'An' you'll be a wreck come showtime.'

I looked round the stage. The big guy behind him raised his eyebrows in agreement and the other two showed no signs of dissent from this opinion. With reluctance, I put the screwdriver down.

''Spose I could use with a short break.'

They gave vigorous nods of agreement.

Alan walked to the auditorium door with me.

'Look Tom,' he spoke in hushed tones. 'You're making the main guy really nervous.'

'Me? I'm just trying to help!' I felt the slight twinge of indigestion. Shouldn't have eaten so much.

I shot a glance back to the stage where the Chief LX was spreading out huge wiring diagrams.

'You're a bit of a legend to him, so he's not concentrating properly. Too much pressure.'

I burst out laughing. 'You're kidding?'

Alan didn't smile as he pushed on my back. 'No time now Tom. Let's just say he's got the whole O.M. back catalogue and he's one of your biggest fans.'

'What' happening?' Vinnie and Len were leaning against the bar.

I raised an eyebrow at the pints in front of them.

'Keep yer shirt on. We're only having one,' said Vinnie. 'This gig's gotta to be spot on.'

Len nodded to the hall. 'They sorted that mess yet?'

I puffed out my cheeks in exasperation. 'No, and Alan's sent me packing. Len, tell me something? Do people see me as a legend?'

Vinnie gave a hoot of laughter, and Len clapped me on the back. 'Youngsters call me that sometimes. Know what it means, Tom?'

I stared at him.

'They're too polite to say they thought you were already dead!'

'Oh god, you're right!' We all chuckled with recognition.

The young woman bar manager came over, smiling broadly. 'Drinks are on your rider of course. What can I get you Tom?'

'Just a small brandy,' I said.

She searched the row of optics, then pointed. 'Old Turkey?'

And then she waited with a puzzled frown, until we'd all stopped laughing.

77

JOSIE

'Josie! Over here!'

In the noisy foyer of the grand old Arcadia, with its sparkling lights and smell of fresh paint, I'd felt as conspicuous as a teenager at their first gig, until I caught sight of Alan on a side staircase, his dreadlocked head searching amongst the throng. He spotted me and waved.

'Tom's asked me to introduce you to people,' he said, when I'd pushed past the excited youngsters queuing for drinks and tickets. 'Come upstairs – there's a private bar.' Nodding at an usher, he unclicked a fat red rope from its stanchions to let me through.

We ascended the stairs, and I saw threadbare carpet and faded silk wallpaper, which denoted where they'd run out of redecorating money. A clear case of *fur coat and no knickers* I thought, smiling as I remembered one of Franki's favourite sayings from our poorer days.

Upstairs, the small wood-panelled bar was dimly lit and and packed.

'Hi Josie!' Inside the door Askim was drinking beer from a bottle. We exchanged a light hug. Over the chatting heads I spotted Zinad talking to some tall guy in specs, but no one else I knew.

'Where's Jamie?'

Behind me Alan said, 'Been some technical issues, so they're still finishing sound checks.'

'Good grief!' I looked at my watch. 'That's cutting it fine. I was hoping to see him before the gig.'

Alan puckered his mouth thoughtfully. 'Come with me. Maybe you can say a quick hi.'

He led me through a maze of stairs and corridors until we emerged in the dark, wire-draped wing area.

Out in the lights, the band stood motionless with their instruments. Nobody looked happy. At the stage front Tom was shielding his eyes against the spotlights, and an excited thrill ran through me. He called up to the technical box, 'And the keys need loads more top. Plus more volume on that foldback monitor, too.'

'Uh-oh. Might be a bad time,' said Alan in a hushed voice.

Opposite, a long-haired guy in denims gesticulated, from the other wing. He seemed vaguely familiar. Alan spotted the frantic waving. 'You better wait here.' He disappeared round the rear of the backdrop.

Hearing our whispers, the black girl at keyboards twisted round. She was attractive in a trim suit and trilby, with her silky dark skin, and lovely bow-shaped lips. So this was Jamie's new love.

'Hi,' I mouthed, pointing at Jamie. 'Jamie's mum – Josie.'

She took a couple of paces backwards and whispered over her shoulder, 'Kadeisha. Great to meet you.'

Her intelligent eyes, and friendly, open demeanour suggested she expected you to be a good person. I could see how Jamie wouldn't want to disappoint her.

Keeping an eye on Tom, she hissed, 'Everything's going wrong. Tom's so pissed off. All my friends are coming and we're going to be terrible!' She looked nervous.

I stepped forwards and said in a low voice, 'Don't worry. The worst checks are the best gigs.'

She looked doubtful.

'Honestly.' I patted the top of her arm.

Jamie turned and spotted me. His face lit up. At the same time Alan reappeared.

'Sorry Josie, one of the spare amps has blown. Gotta do some quick rewiring. Better take you back to the bar.'

The drummer was now testing out his mics, playing a fast patter of jangly high hat and bass drum. I could see they didn't need any interruptions, so I made some quick hand signs to Jamie which said:

'I have to go to the front. Have a great gig.'

He nodded, signing back: *'Okay, mum. Later.'*

I returned: *'Have a great gig. I'm so proud.'* At which he pulled a face, then I added, *'And I love you.'* I longed to give him a hug, but that would have to wait.

As we rushed back along corridors Alan said, 'You both do sign language?'

'There's a deaf club at the Hub,' I said. 'All the staff learned a bit of BSL. Comes in handy at noisy gigs.'

Back in the guests' bar, Zinad introduced me to Steve Fossett, the journalist Jamie had talked about.

'So where does Jamie get his talent?' He passed me a glass of wine. 'Are you musical?'

'No, no, it's not from me.' I laughed, as Zinad gave me a knowing look. 'Jamie's abilities are his own. The lads have all been playing since High School – haven't you?'

I addressed Zinad and Askim, who had joined us, eager to tell him about The Beat Runners and their New Year's gig with Tom, omitting the paternity revelation. I studied Steve's face for any signs he'd spotted me sidestep the question. But he gave the sort of wry grin which older people share when youngsters are gushing – half admiring, and half rueful that you've lost that raw enthusiasm. I smiled back, warming to Steve Fossett as he listened without condescension, and suspecting from his sharp, watchful eyes, that he had an interesting history of his own.

By the time the tannoy proclaimed the house open, the gig was half an hour late. Everyone found their seats in heightened excitement, and there was an almost electric buzz in the vast auditorium. I took my place in the front row, with Steve and the two lads. We were just six foot from the stage, and I was filled with nervous anticipation.

As the lights dimmed and the noise died, a man's voice announced on the PA,

'Twenty years on, and back in the Midlands, where they belong!' Everyone cheered and stamped their feet, then he continued, *'Please give a big Arcadia welcome to... 'Original Mix!'*

Most people leapt to their feet, as the band ran out to take up positions. Jamie held out his arms as if embracing the whole audience, and everyone went wild. He was wearing an authentic looking tonic suit I'd never seen before. I wondered if it was one of Tom's. Then, with two quick beats in the air, Jamie directed the band straight in with Wasteland. As he sang, my smile stretched as wide as the Cheshire Cat's. I drank in the sight of my son. He'd only been away two weeks but I'd not properly seen him for a few months. He appeared to have grown older and he held himself straighter and more confidently – more like a young man than an oversized teenager. In that suit, his shoulders seemed broader and, in fact, his whole stance looked more solid.

To his side Vinnie and Tom strummed at their guitars with fast, but mature, vigour. And when Tom stood behind Jamie, they appeared so alike that I glanced around at the audience singing along. Surely everyone must see it?

Len, the black guy in the pork pie hat and the dogtooth check jacket rattled out a refrain,

> *An' high rise crime is getting' worse*
> *Unemployment – like bein' cursed*
> *It's white on black and black on white*
> *We need to respect each others' fight*

I thought of the fights and gangs in the estates near us – these 80's lyrics were still relevant, all these years later. Thank god Jamie and his friends managed to keep out of all that. And here he was now, a full adult, with the gifts of health, education, music and liberal attitudes. He'd got through it safely.

The audience roared its approval as the song came to an end. Len introduced Jamie and Kadeisha with a joke, and then Jamie said everyone should dance. The whole audience surged forward to fill the space in front of the stage, and for the first time in years I found myself in a mosh pit. Laughing helplessly at Zinad and Steve Fossett, I beckoned them into the crowd with me, to dance.

After the second song, Jamie introduced the members of the band.

They each bowed to sonic waves of approval, which built to a tsunami when Jamie said, 'And on rhythm guitar, Original Mix founder – Tom Shepperton!'

Tom played a rapid waterfall of notes and held up a fist. As the roar from the crowd dissipated, a buzzing sound came out of the sound system. Jamie pulled a comical face at Tom, then shrugged. He wasn't going to let some little technical thing phase him. I could explode with pride for the tall, beautiful, talented man on stage who was my son.

The next two songs were fast and furious. I was completely wrapped in the music, feet pounding the floor, punching the air with my hands, singing along and elated to be alive. Tom was plucking his strings in fluid motions, hips throbbing to the beat. He looked up, our eyes met for a second and he gave me a secret smile. And I knew there was something we shared – apart from Jamie. An understanding. My heart stopped dead for a moment, with a memory so familiar and wonderful that it almost hurt. All my life, I'd really only ever wanted Tom.

He was right. We had been far, far too hard to match.

78

TOM

Despite all the problems, the gig was steaming. Kadeisha negotiated that tricky bridge like a dream, and I bowed my head to her in acknowledgement. Her uncle Raymond would be proud. She mouthed 'Yaay!' pulling a cheeky face, and I mugged back at her, chuckling. Jamie was one lucky young man.

I looked for Josie and there she was, dancing at the front, lively-faced, laughing, her blond head bobbing. Fozz shouted something in her ear and, as she looked up at Jamie with eyes full of pride and love, I felt a small squeeze of my heart.

Len had started his toasting section and I was chunking out upbeats when I heard that buzz again from the front of the stage. I frowned in question to Alan and Rick in the side wing, but they both made puzzled faces and shrugged. There it was again. A kind of crackle. It wasn't just feedback, it was – something else. I stopped playing and cupped my right ear with my hand, in the direction of the front of stage, to show them what I meant. Vinnie started his solo and there was a quick squeal from the speaker – and not in any sort of rock'n'roll way. As we leant in together, for the next fast chorus, he shouted, 'I was nowhere near the fuckin' speaker!' before we peeled apart and up to the mics to sing our refrain.

While Jamie introduced the next song, I tried to work out where the intermittent interference could be coming from. As Devon thumped the tomtoms for the intro, I heard the buzz again. He gave me a quizzical frown. Thankfully, the audience hadn't noticed. They were still jumping up and down energetically, every bit as psyched up as they used to be in 1980, united by Eddy's lyrics, railing against unfairness, racism, poverty, unemployment – even though it was a whole new century and everything was surely different now?

Jesus! There was a crackle again. It was only audible in the bare spaces, and luckily there weren't many. I played on, aware that I was waiting for the next one. Jamie moved round the stage, engaging with the audience, as he sang. He ran to the left, crouched down and slapped hands with a few of the lads dancing at the front. I saw him swap a smile with Josie. Then there was that fucking buzzy noise again. Shit! Definitely coming from near Jamie. What was making it? Something live maybe?

Now at my side of the stage, Jamie put his mic into a stand near the scaffolding. The lads and girls dancing on the far right waved their hands in frantic appeal. Holding the mic stand, Jamie swivelled to sing in their direction. The kids went wild and stretched out their hands – begging for palm to palm, contact. Jamie stepped sideways, and as he bent his knees and reached a hand towards the scaffold to grab it, I knew – the scaff was live! He mustn't touch those metal pipes while holding the mic stand! Everything went into slow motion. I heard Josie's voice in my head, *'Just keep my son safe Tom'*, and Jamie shifted his weight from left leg to right. He was going to use the mic stand as a lever and leap onto the scaff. Of course he was. The audience were practically pushing him up there. I yanked off my guitar, threw it down with a screech and lurched forward, and, as Jamie turned to see what the noise was, I shoved him aside, but then tripped on a wire, went off balance, felt a heavy crushing sensation in my chest. I flailed around to stop myself falling, grabbed the mic stand and, without thinking, put the other hand out to grab the pipe beside me.

Then the world went dark.

♪

79

JOSIE

The youngsters were cheering at Jamie. I took an involuntary gulp of air as he braced himself to jump up onto a small tower at the stage side, then overrode my panic. He'd be fine. He did this sort of thing all the time. But suddenly Tom pushed Jamie aside, and also grasped at his chest, sort of crumpling, grabbing at the microphone stand, then the scaffold. Then he spasmed and steam rose from his whole body – to a collective gasp of horror – and a second later he was shot off stage like a rocket. Everyone jumped back in shock as he crashed onto the floor, and lay spread-eagled like a rag doll.

'Tom! Tom!' I was on my knees beside him.

'Get away!' I yelled as bodies pushed me from behind. 'Askim, help me roll him over, quick!' Pushing Tom's head back, I leant over to hear his breathing. Nothing!

'Call an ambulance! Tell them it's electric shock – no pulse!' I screamed at Zinad. 'Move, move!' I whacked at several ankles around me away, then tilted Tom's head further backwards, hoping to god he'd start breathing. Part of my brain was in horror, paralysed, but I wasn't listening to it. I felt with my fingers on his neck and my ear to his mouth, trying to detect any sound or breath. In all the noise and chaos, I concentrated for a few seconds. Still nothing.

I bent down, pinched his nose, put my mouth to his and blew. His chest inflated. Then I measured under his ribs, fumbling for the place that was much easier to find on a practice mannequin. I slung a leg over his lower body and balled my fists together to push in.

'One and two and three and four and five and six and seven and eight…' Fuck! It was hard. No popping plastic balloon to tell you when you'd done it. This was the real solid muscle and flesh of Tom's chest, and the heart I had to keep pumping. 'Twenty one, and twenty two,and twenty three, and twenty four, and twenty five-', My wrists ached as I counted out loud, ignoring the hubbub and shouting above me. I kept my eyes on his face, immobile and unconscious. *Oh god Tom, please don't die!* 'Twenty seven, twenty eight…' I breathed a lungful of air into him again and pumped. Then again, and again, and again, and again…

'Mum, let me do it now!' Jamie's voice was urgent, commanding. I glanced at his earnest face. We'd done this together in First Aid training.

'Okay', I gasped. Taking long, even breaths, I shuffled to the side of Tom's head, bent over to his mouth, took a deep breath in and gave him as much of my air as I could. 'Now!' I shouted. Jamie was ready to go, his strong hands pushing Tom's chest as I continued counting, 'One and two and three and…' there was a sickening crack from Tom's chest and Jamie looked up at me alarmed. 'FOUR and FIVE and SIX!,' I yelled to keep him going , 'Seven and eight and nine…'

A few moments later I got ready to give another long blast of air, glancing at Tom's motionless face then at Jamie's, trying not to see the tears forming in the corner of his eyes as he panted, in compression after compression, knowing we would do this forever if we had to, while there was a possibility, even a tiny hope, of bringing Tom back.

'Twenty nine and thirty…' *Please, please don't die Tom.* I exhaled into his body – mouth to mouth, lips to lips, lungs to lungs, life to life.

We had been working like twin bellows for an enternity. Sweat dripped from Jamie's forehead and hair. Staff had cleared people back from the whole area. Only Vinnie, Alan and Len remained, crouched by our sides, with a manager who was talking to emergency services down a mobile phone, reporting on progress.

'Keep going son. You're doing great,' said Len, as I continued to count him on.

'Want me to take over?' said Vinnie in a thick voice.

'No,' gasped Jamie, as he pushed his fist into Tom's inert chest. 'I'm alright!'

'Twenty five, twenty six, twenty seven, twenty eight…' I counted.

People were running through the auditorium behind me, with the sounds of rustling and unzipping.

'Okay everyone, stand back!' I locked eyes with Jamie, as we rose. My legs were shakey and stiff. Vinnie took my hand and clasped it firmly in both of his.

A paramedic ripped open Tom's shirt and placed two sticky pads on his chest, while the other hooked up something else.

Please, please! I didn't even know who I was begging. A high pitched whirring of a machine, and Tom's torso jerked up slightly and landed back down with a dry thud. But no further movement.

'Going again. All stay back.'

The machine whirred and Tom's chest rose again in automatic but unresponsive reaction.

After the third time the paramedics looked at each other. I spotted a tiny shake of the head.

'You keep up compressions and I'll get him in the van,' said the man.

'*NO!*' I shouted. 'Try again. *Please!*'

They shot each other a quick glance. 'Alright. Once more, then it's off to A and E.'

I held my breath as the machine whirred and Tom's upper body juddered again.

Please, please, please.

'Got something!' said the woman, staring at a small screen. 'Faint, but it's a heartbeat.'

We moved aside as they bustled round, expertly lifting Tom onto the lowered trolley, strapping him on, then raising him, still attached to the defibrillator, the monitor at his side.

'He's not out of the woods yet,' warned one of the medics, as they sped off with the trolley. 'Might arrest on the way.'

I didn't take in much of what happened as we followed them out. Kadeisha crying in Len's arms. Jamie's hand gripped tight in mine. The shocked faces of the drummer and bass player. A lot of concerned faces. A crowded lobby. Some kind of tannoy message. And through all this, me repeating over and over, 'Get us to the hospital! Please get us to the hospital!' until Alan steered us out of the entrance and pushed me, then Jamie, into a taxi where Vinnie was already waiting, door open.

'Let's go,' he said grimly, to the cabbie. 'Birmingham General.'

♫♪....♫♪....♫♪....♫♪....♫♪....♫♪....♫♪....♫♪....♫♪....♫♪....

It was an age before a doctor entered a family room, where the four of us waited. We all rose. 'Please take a seat, Mrs Shepperton,' he said. We plonked back down, and nobody corrected him.

'Did you see what happened?' he said.

'He was electrocuted,' I said. 'It threw him off stage.'

The doctor leant forward, palms on his knees. 'The thing is, if a current goes through the heart there are burn marks at the entrance and exit points, but there's no evidence of that.'

I put a hand to my mouth in horror. The other was gripping Jamie's. A sensation of near hysteria was still ballooning up inside, along with a terrible sinking feeling.

'What does that mean?' said Vinnie. His voice was gruff, choked.

'We think he may have had a heart attack, just seconds before the electric shock. It might not have been the current which caused the arrest.'

'Christ!' said Vinnie.

'Before he touched that tower, he clutched at his chest,' I remembered.

The doctor looked around us. 'This may actually be a better outcome,' he said. 'Electricity through the heart interrupts the heart pattern, and there's usually extensive damage to internal tissues. The outlook wouldn't be good at all.' He paused. 'As it is, his heart's been

471

restarted and it's holding a steady pace. We need to run a lot more tests but for now he's stable.'

I said, 'Can we see him?'

'He's not conscious,' said the doctor. 'But you can look in, just for a minute.' He turned to Alan and Vinnie. 'Sorry, relatives only at this stage.'

'Vinnie and Tom are like brothers!' I said quickly.

Vinnie gave me a grim smile. His face was ashen. 'You two go. I'm no good in hospitals anyway. We'll wait outside.'

Tom was laid out like a corpse, face sunken and impassive, tubes attached to his chest. I dropped Jamie's hand and sunk down by his side. 'Oh my god!'

Jamie stood behind me, his hands on my shoulders. When I looked up, tears were sliding down his face.

'We'll do whatever it takes to make you better, I promise.' I reached out to cradle his hand, which was warm and muscular. He still had a tiny scar from his gardening accident.

I remembered how angry I'd been with him, thinking he wanted to take my son away and subject him to danger, but he'd done what he promised. He'd protected Jamie.

'Sorry, you'll have to leave now,' said a nurse. She started to check the dials, and added in a kind voice, 'We'll be monitoring him all night. You should go and get some rest. The doctors will know more by tomorrow.'

I stood up and put my arm round Jamie. 'Come on love.'

'Just a minute.' He bent down to give Tom's arm a squeeze. 'Get well mate. We love you.'

As he straightened, the nurse handed me a clump of tissues. I handed half to Jamie. Out in the corridor we hugged each other and he sobbed. The whole experience had been so unreal and so visceral. I could still feel my lips clamped onto Tom's, the imprint of his pinched nose on my fingertips, the feel of his chest, hard and ribbed.

Eventually, Jamie broke apart from me and I rummaged in my handbag for more tissues.

'Sit down a minute,' I said, resisting the urge to put my arms round him again. 'Jamie, we're going to have to be *so* brave. It's very possible that Tom won't pull through.'

'I know,' he said in a small voice. And then, 'Mum, he was trying to stop me touching that tower, 'cos it was live.'

'I know love.'

'I was going to jump onto it.' There was self-recriminaton in his tone. 'Fucking idiot! Showing off and being an arse!'

'No!' I grabbed both his hands in mine, and pulled him down onto a seat. 'Look at me Jamie. This is really important. You were entertaining people. That's a gift, you hear me – a special gift. And you did so well keeping up compressions. You saved his life.'

Jamies eyes were so full of tears and guilt I couldn't bear it.

'Listen, I spent all my youth feeling bad about my brother Ally's death – like I could have done something to stop it – or it should have been me that died. And I wasn't even there!' A long sigh came out of the depth of my guts. 'Sometimes bad accidents just happen and it's nobody's fault. We can't always control what happens, we just can't.'

I swallowed, then said, 'Jamie, if Tom dies, it's not your fault.'

He stared at me for a long moment, trying to comprehend – like he'd done when he was small and I'd explained why he couldn't go to Zinad's birthday party with chickenpox, or have the computer game we couldn't afford. I waited. This truth was much bigger, harder and far more important.

'Say it back to me,' I said softly. 'Go on.'

'If Tom dies, it's not my fault,' he said. And I put my arms round his shoulders and rocked him gently until his wracked sobbing subsided.

Finally he stood up and straightened his shoulders. 'I'm okay now mum.' His voice was back to its normal, masculine timbre. He blew fiercely into the tissues and threw them into a bin.

'Okay, let's find Vinnie and Alan.'

As we descended the staircase to the hospital lobby, I glanced out of the plate glass windows, to see a sizeable crowd had gathered. I grabbed Jamie's arm and pointed down.

'Oh god! I think there's Press outside love.' A camera flashed in the dark.

Jamie looked at my stricken face, and put a protective arm on my back. 'Don't worry mum, I'll deal with them. It's me they'll want to talk to.'

'What will you say?' I said.

His concentrated gaze suggested he was thinking. Then he nodded to himself, as if he'd made up his mind.

'I'll be calm and stick to the facts – just like Tom would.'

80

TOM

I was woken by the sound of air hissing – some joker inflating a balloon round my upper arm. Then beeps and the sensation decreased. 'What the fuc…' I tried to sit up, but my body was weighed down by its own inertia. My eyelids slid shut again, just as I clocked there wasn't a red-carpeted ceiling above my bunk anymore. I tried to make sense of it, then decided it didn't matter. Whatever drugs I'd taken it was seriously good shit. But I hadn't done that for years. Had I? It was all confusing. Curiosity took a grip and I hauled my weary eyelids up again.

'Ah, Mr Shepperton. You're finally with us,' said a female voice.

Shit! I struggled to sit up. 'No more hospitals!' I shouted, confused and panicky. How had I got back on the streets?

A couple of firm hands pressed me back onto the mattress.

'You had an accident,' said the nurse. 'Look, here comes your wife. She can explain.'

Wife?

'Tom, you're awake!' A woman came to my side, blond and smelling nice. It was a relief to see someone familiar.

'Josie! You showered,' I burbled stupidly.

She laughed and laughed, and then she started to cry.

I struggled to lift my arm and pat her hand. 'Don't worry, it's okay,' I said, not knowing what. I felt for her fingers. 'Where's your wedding ring?'

'They assumed we're married, so we let them believe it,' she whispered in my ear, and I felt her warm breath on my cheek. I smiled. Josie was here so everything must be alright.

'I'd marry you in a heartbeat,' I whispered back.

She sat up and stared at me, eyes wide, then said, 'Jamie's here too.'

Jamie stepped into view. 'Tom, how you doing? Need anything?'

'Could do with some liquid and a bit of a kip mate.'

'Would you like a drink?' I heard him say.

'Pint of lager would be great,' I mumbled, as I drifted out of consciousness.

♪

Several days later I was sitting up, joking with the nurses, when Josie tapped on the door.

'He's making more sense today,' said one of the nurses. 'Not ordering beer, at least.' She chuckled as she retreated. 'Oh, you think you've heard it all…'

'Hi,' said Josie and her smile was beautiful. 'We've been back lots of times, but you were always out of it. Jamie's just grabbing some lunch in the canteen.'

'Sorry,' I said to Josie, as she sat down. 'According to Nurse Ratchett I've been tripping. God knows what they're giving me and for what.' I waved a hand round the hospital room. 'Not quite what I planned. I was going to take you both out for a post-gig dinner.'

Her face was filled with concern. 'How're you feeling?'

'Tired and ancient, to be honest. Just want to get out of here.'

She smiled. 'It's so good to see you awake, sitting up and…'

'Alive?'

'Yes definitely.' Her face was unbelievably serious.

'Apparently I owe that to you and Jamie.'

Josie looked away, face reddened. 'We were nearest, that's all.'

'That's not the way Charlie and Len told it,' I said. 'Thank you for saving me.'

Josie shook her head dismissively. 'The important thing is that you recover. What does the doctor say?'

I mugged regret. 'Now I've been recharged, they want me up and at it.' I raised an eyebrow. 'No rest for the electrocuted.'

The twitch of a smile appeared on Josie's face, 'They're not even giving you a jump start?'

I shook my head. 'Say I've got to stand on my own three pins.'

We were still making terrible puns when Fozz came in bearing a newspaper and some fruit. He picked up the clip board from the bottom of the bed and pretended to scan it.

'Ah, good news – grapes are allowed in the Electrocuted Ska Legend care plan. And, ta-dah!'
He held out a copy of The Guardian. 'This is from Monday. You're allowed to read it now you're on the mend.' Fozz chuckled as I took the paper. 'Well, it took twenty years, Tom. But you finally came good, you old bastard – I got that big exclusive!'

I opened the paper with eager hands. Fozz's article started with details of the accident, and how Jamie had jumped in with CPR, then a detailed and funny flashback to touring with us in the 80's. He went on to interview Jamie, who revealed that he was actually my son, and the fantastic coincidence of us finding each other through music. Then Fozz reviewed the gig, and finished with a cliffhanger about whether I'd pull through, with a suggestion that the next ska revival depended on this. I raised an eyebrow and offered it back.

'Sterling stuff mate. Doe he make it?'

Fozzz perched on the bed. 'Thankfully. Are they letting you out soon?'

'Next few days if I promise to take my pills and live a good life.'

'Bad luck, mate.' Fozz pulled a pained face. 'Still it could have been worse. Had many visitors?'

'Saw Len and Charlie this moring. They'll only let two in at once.'

'How come?' he said.

I shrugged. 'Maybe they think we'll start playing and Rick'll charge entry.'

Josie rose. 'Someone's desperate to see you. I'd better make way.' She pointed to the door where Jamie grinned through the glass. Much as I wanted to see him, I felt a pang of disappointment at her going.

'Will you come back later?' I said.

She smiled. 'Course. Shall I bring you anything?'

I shook my head slowly and smiled. 'Just yourself.'

I watched Josie leave, hearing her say, 'Don't stay too long love. He looks exhausted.'

Fozz raised a quizzical eyebrow at me, but Jamie was already by my side, bending to give me a half-hug with an arm round my shoulder. He shook his head in disbelief.

'Shit, Tom. It's amazing to see you conscious again. Everyone thought you'd bought it.'

He pointed to the paper. 'You won't believe how many cards and flowers were sent to the Arcadia. Mum took photos, then we carried them all to an old people's home round the corner.'

Fozz laughed. 'Since my piece, Jamie's been interviewed by the world's press. The story's caused a real stir.'

Jamie rolled his eyes. 'They tried to make me out as some sort of hero, when it was Josie who reacted quickly. But she wanted to stay out of the limelight.'

Suddenly I was overwhelmed with tiredness. Everyone had been part of my big drama except me. I couldn't quite get my head round the idea that I'd nearly died, and I certainly couldn't contemplate the idea of facing interviewers.

'Might need a bit of shut-eye now lads,' I said, as a nurse started fitting me up with another armband. But before Jamie left I said, 'Listen, could you stick some clothes in a bag for me? I'm sick of hospital pyjamas. And can you ask Josie to come by tomorrow with Alan? I've got an escape plan, but I'll need their help.'

Then I lay back and let Nurse Ratchett – whose real name was Gloria – do her thing.

81

TOM

I made it round four laps of the entire corridor before breakfast, and six laps after, feeling better at each step. It was just a matter of persuading the doctors I could manage. But when Alan and Josie heard my plan they shared a look which could only be described as alarm for my sanity.

'You can stay in the cabin Skylark uses for yoga retreats, no problem. But it's so out of the way Tom – there's only a lake, miles of fields and a load of ducks.'

I nodded. 'Just what I need. Somewhere peaceful to hide out for a few days, get my strength back.'

'Will they let you out?' he said.

'Not on my own.' I looked at Josie. 'Look, I know it would be a huge favour, but I wondered if you'd come with me?'

Josie pursed her mouth. 'For how long?'

I gave a half shrug. 'If we defer the tour for two more weeks, that would give me ten days R&R, then another few of days to get in a couple of rehearsals.'

Joise shook her head adamantly. 'Absolutely no way!'

'Okay,' I nodded, trying to hide my crushing disappointment. Thinking she might agree to watch over me for a while had been a long shot. It was too much to ask.

'No gigs for six weeks,' she said. 'With at least four weeks recuperation.'

'You're saying *yes?*'

Alan and I stared at her.

She folded her arms, and pursed her lips. 'That's the deal. Take it or leave it.'

I looked at Alan and we both laughed. 'Was she always like this?' I asked.

'Pretty much,' he said.

So I continued with my campaign of eating, rest and exercise – whilst persuading the powers that be to release me. The conflicting mixture of excitement and apprehension reminded me of the last months in prison.

On the last day, the band arrived en masse to say goodbye, and Gloria shook her head with disbelief, but she didn't evict them.

'When you gettin' out?' said Vinnie. From his pallor I could see he was struggling not to run straight for the door himself.

'Get my discharge papers today, right after the doc's seen me.'

'Got everythin' you need?' said Len.

'Josie's swinging by the bus later for my civvies,' I said. 'Can you lob everything in a bag?'

He nodded.

I looked round at their expectant faces. 'Christ! Sorry I got you all into this. Bit of a mess, huh?'

Charlie grinned. 'Hey mate, you gotta find a better way of crowd surfin' that's all.' He hesitated. 'Fits in quite nicely, as it goes. Me and Dev can do Jackson's gigs after all.'

'Oh?' I turned to Devon, who rolled his eyes.

'Yeah well, we made a choice, but now we can do both.' He made a face at Charlie. 'You never gonna win any sensitivity prizes, man.'

'What'll you two do?' I asked Vinnie and Len.

'Back to Cov,' said Vinnie. 'Looks like I'll be decoratin' the new salon after all.' He pulled a mock sour face, but he was clearly pleased to be going home for a while.

'You goin' back to work Len?'

'No way!' He looked insulted. 'I worked years for this much leave. Going to take the wife to London, an' spend some time in your studio.' He looked at Rick. 'See if we can get that gear up to scratch. Maybe build a little sound system...' I could tell they'd been talking.

'You can stay in the flat.' I reached for my jacket, fiddled in the pocket and threw him the keys. 'Water my plants will you?'

He caught them with a jangle. 'Thanks man. 'Spose you want me to sing to them too?'

'Course.' Then I grinned. 'But you know what they're really listening out for is…' I looked round at everyone, ' – our new album.'

Over by the door, Kadeisha and Jamie squeezed hands, swapping excited grins.

'Oh Christ, no!' said Vinnie. He looked at all the others. 'We're not, are we?'

Everyone exchanged glances and shrugged, but nobody refused.

It seemed we were.

'Yeah, yeah, that's about right.' Rick nodded with vigour. 'Must be time for a fourth wave of ska.'

'Actually it might be the fifth,' said Alan.

Josie was waiting with me when the consultant came for a final time. She took a cursory look at my clipboard notes. 'So, Mr Shepperton, you've had a very lucky escape. But all your bloods and obs are fine, the damage to your heart was surprisingly minimal, and the stents we put in should keep it functioning well. Has anyone spoken to you about what to do now?'

'A bit.'

She went through stuff about regular exercise, eating healthily, not smoking and moderation in all things. Then she looked from me to Josie, and gently pushed the door shut.

'You may also be wondering about sex,' she said.

Josie's eyes saucered and her cheeks flushed. She quickly rose. 'I'll give you some privacy.'

The doctor looked perplexed. 'Well, I prefer to talk to couples together.'

'What?' said Josie.

The doctor smiled kindly. 'It saves misunderstandings later, Mrs Shepperton.'

'Ah.' Josie sat down with a plonk.

I tried to keep my face straight.

'Now I don't suggest you go home and swing from the chandeliers,' said the doctor. 'But just to reassure – you can resume your normal sex life, as soon as you feel ready.'

I bit my lip while Josie stared at the floor, every bit as embarrassed as a nun in a brothel.

'Anyway, it's important not to let this incident stand in the way,' the doctor went on. She looked at me sternly. 'The key things are no heavy lifting, and, as you're a musician Mr Shepperton, I'm going to add – absolutely no unprescribed drugs. But brisk exercise – including sex – is very much allowed.' She gave a chuckle. 'Even encouraged.'

I nodded sagely, not trusting myself to speak.

Eventually we shook hands and she wished me well for the tour. As she left, shutting the door behind her, a whoop of laughter burst out of me.

Josie stood up crossly. 'Don't you *dare* tell anyone else about that!' Her cheeks were the colour of apples.

I picked up my jacket and rested a palm on her shoulder. 'Don't be angry, Jose. I think I was saved for that moment. It was beautiful!'

'Hmm!' she snorted. But I noticed she didn't make me move my hand. So as we walked away I slid it round her shoulders, leaning on her slightly, as if I needed her support.

Which of course I did.

♪

'So now you know all about me and prison,' I said. 'I've told Jamie too.'

We were sitting on a bench outside the cabin, after another of Josie's delicious but healthy dinners, and I'd just related the final episode of my time inside. In front of us the lake was alive with sounds – clucks, honks and tweets – as wildfowl scuddered towards the reeds, and the last of the summer's sun dissolved into the horizon.

Josie sighed. 'Thanks for talking him into music college next year, Tom. He'll get such a lot out of it.'

'I was helped by the fact Kadeisha's going too.'

We both chuckled, then Josie shivered. 'Better get a jacket,' she said.

I rose at the same time. 'Here, have mine.'

I slid the leather round her shoulders. And as she looked up at me, I remembered another place in the countryside, a million years ago, when my heart had drummed with joy just to be this close to her.

And I looked at this woman. The only person who had made me feel like a better man, whose face had haunted my most complex and unresolved dreams for the last twenty years.

'I meant what I said in hospital.' I wasn't so out of it that I'd forgotten. 'I'd marry you in heartbeat.'

Josie blinked. 'Why? For Jamie's sake?'

'Hell, no!' I said. 'Missed that by years. Because I love you. Always have.'

A lone tear coursed down her cheek, but I kissed it away. Then our mouths were finding each other, exploring the old and the new, and we were holding each other as tightly as shipwreck survivors.

♪♪♪♫

Epilogue

TOM

'Wow! You look great!' I said, as Josie emerged from the bathroom. We were all suited and booted, ready for the big day. I slipped my arms round her waist.

'That dress is very sexy and criminally tight. Shall I check if you can still get out of it?' I nodded at the tousled bed where we'd taken brisk exercise – like the doctor ordered.

She laughed. 'Later, alligator. Thought I'd make an effort as the beautiful Daisy Miller's compering.'

'Daisy's no match for you, Jose. Never was.' I wrapped my arms around her, and looked down into her warm bright eyes. 'I love you.'

'And I love you right back.'

'You saved my life,' I said in wonder, stroking her cheek with a finger.

We both sighed at the same time, then she laughed. 'That was an act of pure selfishness.' She smiled a golden smile, as I felt the unified thumping in both our chests.

'How's the heart?' she whispered.

'On the mend,' I replied, as her lips met mine and we kissed. 'Very much on the mend.'

Suddenly she broke free, pointing to the clock. 'Come on, we'll be late!'

She bent to retrieve her jacket, and I gave her bottom a pat. 'For luck.'

'Oi!' She whacked me playfully with her bag and we walked out, hand in hand.

♪

On stage Daisy Miller was received with a gigantic cheer. She was, after all, the nation's darling. The TV cameras in front zoomed in on her, and she glowed.

'Not only is this the first time in nearly twenty years since Original Mix played Coventry!' she shouted over the sound, as thousands of people in the park, clapped and cheered. 'But also the band have got a fantastic surprise for you.'

I turned to Jamie and mouthed. 'What surprise?'

'You'll see!'

Before I could grill him further, Daisy said, 'With no further ado, here's Original Mix!' and we ran out to a wall of sound.

'Right then Coventry!' bellowed Len. 'You ready to do some dancin'?'

We ripped into Toast Yourself, and the park was alive with bodies, bouncing, jumping, skanking, dancing – fans, young and old – people who were male, female, gay, straight, disabled, able bodied, brown, black, white, and everything in between.

I was elated to be playing here again, headlining a festival in my home city, made glorious by sunshine, with my best mates, Josie dancing in the wings, and the voice of my talented son soaring above the guitars. Then, I heard another person singing too, deeper and more mature, and the crowd was screaming, going wild. What the…? I turned to see a figure stroll onstage, clutching a mic. Sharp suit, dark hair, deadpan face with a cynical glint of laughter in his eyes.

My fingers continued in automatic motion, as he came alongside, rested his hand on my shoulder, and gave me a quick squeeze.

'Think I'd let you play the home dump without me?' Eddy shouted in my ear.

Len grinned round and chanted,

We all unite when we're in a fix,
Goin' for the best with Original Mix!

As Eddy sauntered to the front and Jamie grinned back at me, I looked out at all the elated fans waving banners, dancing and singing along. I thought of my new little family, and my big musical tribe.

And then I was sure.

I finally knew what it felt like to have made it.

♬ ♫ ♬ ♫ ♬ ♫ ♫

Acknowledgements

Writing this book has been a labour of love, over seven long years. It started out as a homage to music, and to all those fantastic musicians who make us feel alive with their songs and live performances. It was a personal challenge too – to see if I could bring music to mind, just through the written word. But it also came from my conviction that things had slipped backwards since the 80's, when fighting racism was seen as a joint progressive struggle for all good-minded people, regardless of their race. Perhaps we got richer and lazier, or saw our kids at multicultural schools and assumed the job was done. The increasing rise in racism, and support for far right politics, clearly says this is not the case.

So, with all this in mind, I set out to revisit the times when we were young, our passions were raw and naive, and we wanted our art to make a difference.

But this book could not have been finished without support from my amazing friends, who never gave up on the idea of it being a finished novel (even during the times when I almost did).

For your encouragement, continual nagging, editing tips, advice, and total buy-in to my vision, many, many thanks to: Michael, Roger, Lori and James (my writing group pals), plus Mike, Peter, Stefanie, Elizabeth, Nina, Maggie, Astrid, Ingrid and Barbara.

Also huge thanks to friends who gave me invaluable insights into prison life, drug use and abuse, live music and recording studios (from professional stand points, of course!): Carrie, Nick and John.

Thanks to those who offered vital escapes to write in solitary confinement, to battle with 'not having a fuckin' clue where it all goes next' (as Tom might say): to The Arvon Foundation for a bursary for their inspiring, 'Finishing your Novel' course (even though that still took me another 4 years!), to SG for her Isle of White bungalow with its endless sea vista, to Nick for access to his calm bachelor pad in Hackney, and to Kathrin and Ruary for their generous open invitation to occupy a 'writer's room' in their Llandudno home.

I must take a moment to appreciate all those who play the genre of music which inspired this book – ska. There are too many great ska musicians, dead and alive, to start listing. But for these musicians, I have much respect and admiration, as listening to ska always blasts away the blues and gives me great joy.

And finally, enormous thanks to Susan Elderkin and Nicola Perry, who gave me essential professional advice and insight into the craft of writing and structuring a novel, at such key times.
And thanks to you, the reader. If you have read this far, you've made it all worthwhile. Thank you.

Sam Carlyle

Printed in Great Britain
by Amazon